THE MID...
THE MI...

BY
FIONA McARTHUR

FROM SINGLE MUM
TO LADY

BY
JUDY CAMPBELL

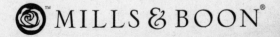

MILLS & BOON

Fairytale endings are in store for two women who
learnt the hard way to rely only
on themselves—and then their very own
Prince Charmings waltz into their lives…!

But money and prestige don't impress fiery midwife
Sophie and single mum Jandy!

Their heroes must prove their love is worth more
than their millions before these women will open their
hearts to love and become…

CINDERELLA BRIDES!

Wishes really do come true in:

THE MIDWIFE AND THE MILLIONAIRE
by Fiona McArthur

and

FROM SINGLE MUM TO LADY
by Judy Campbell

THE MIDWIFE AND THE MILLIONAIRE

BY
FIONA McARTHUR

MILLS & BOON

First published in Great Britain 2010
Harlequin Mills & Boon Limited,
Eton House, 18-24 Paradise Road, Richmond, Surrey TW9 1SR

© Fiona McArthur 2010

ISBN: 978 0 263 87896 7

Harlequin Mills & Boon policy is to use papers that are natural, renewable and recyclable products and made from wood grown in sustainable forests. The logging and manufacturing process conform to the legal environmental regulations of the country of origin.

Printed and bound in Spain
by Litografia Rosés, S.A., Barcelona

A mother to five sons, **Fiona McArthur** is an Australian midwife who loves to write. Mills & Boon® Medical™ Romance gives Fiona the scope to write about all the wonderful aspects of adventure, romance, medicine and midwifery that she feels so passionate about—as well as an excuse to travel! So now that the boys are older, her husband Ian and youngest son Rory are off with Fiona to meet new people, see new places, and have wonderful adventures. Fiona's website is at www.fionamcarthur.com

Recent titles by the same author:

MIDWIFE IN A MILLION
PREGNANT MIDWIFE: FATHER NEEDED
(Lyrebird Lake Maternity)
THE MIDWIFE'S LITTLE MIRACLE
(Lyrebird Lake Maternity)
THE MIDWIFE'S NEW-FOUND FAMILY
(Lyrebird Lake Maternity)
THEIR SPECIAL-CARE BABY

WITH THANKS TO:
Glenn at Heliworks, for his help with helicopters
and moments of unusual interest.
To Fiona, the guide at the Bungle Bungles, who shared
her knowledge and enthusiasm for an amazing place.
And Annie, for being a natural-born teacher
and one of my wonderful Maytone friends.

CHAPTER ONE

ANOTHER squat boab tree dropped its leaves as Sophie Sullivan drove past, a sure sign the wet season was nearly over. She sounded her car horn at the frilled-neck lizard basking in the middle of the dirt track and he reared on hind legs, spread his neck frill and hissed until he seemed much more than he really was.

Typical male.

At least the craggy red mountains that embraced her were true, she thought, as she drove towards the boulder-strewn river—that range was a dear part of home.

Home: far north Western Australia, the Kimberleys and a place blissfully away from the city and men who shed lies like the boab shed leaves.

Even the dusty Gibb River Road looked attractive until she saw the vehicle parked by the Pentecost and the motionless man beside the sluggish water.

More crocodile fodder. She sighed—travellers caused her no end of concern, especially ones who hovered for long periods at the edge of the crocodile-inhabited rivers.

The tourists parked by the river because of the view to the Cockburn Range across the ochre plains. Locals used the designated parking area at the top of the hill, well away from the water.

She pulled up next to the expensive all-terrain vehicle and wound down her window. 'You OK, there?'

The man didn't answer. He must've heard her truck. She was ten feet away from him. Careless *and* rude, she thought and narrowed her eyes. Finally he turned his head and glanced at her dismissively. 'Fine, thanks.'

He was big—Sophie couldn't help but notice—bigger than her brother, Smiley, who topped six-two, and this guy was very nicely muscled so he'd be a mouthful for any croc, but he was too close and too stationary in a dangerous spot. It would be a shame to waste the body, she thought dispassionately, and with the new knowledge from Brand-name Brad she could have done without, it would be a waste of the designer jeans and Rolex watch.

Congratulations were in order for her immunity from the male species. A hard-won but valuable lesson.

Sophie bit back another sigh. How did you tell someone to get back in their vehicle when they blatantly ignored you?

'You've seen the warnings?' She looked at the sign herself, read it under her breath even. 'Crocodiles Inhabit This Area. Keep Away from the Edge. Do Not Enter the Water.' But her reading it didn't make him face her. In fact, no further response to her at all.

Grrr. Spare me from arrogant males. Despite the

flags that waved from the man to say go away, she tried one more time. 'About the crocodiles here?'

'Yes, thanks.' Far less cordial and this time he shifted his feet so he faced her. 'I'm just passing through.'

'You'll pass right through a croc,' she said drily. 'I lost my darling dog in a spot like this once.' And still had nightmares about the tragedy her lack of concentration had caused.

Then he looked directly at her. He wasn't to-die-for handsome, really, but he had those dark, dark lashes and an intense gaze that held her, effortlessly, until he dropped the connection as easily as he'd reeled her in. The trumpet call. *Danger*, and not from crocodiles. Her skin prickled.

'I'm sorry to hear about your pet.' He glanced back at the river before he looked again at her, to assess if she'd be a nuisance by the look of it, and Sophie could feel the warmth of the sun beat in the window, or she hoped that explained the heat.

Best not to become entangled in another look so she concentrated on a small scar on his chin that made him less imposing—more vulnerable, which was a funny thing to think about a stranger, but his mouth… She had a sudden ridiculous urge to see those lips smile.

Sophie searched for the question she'd asked.

He coughed and she looked up in time to see him roll his eyes, obviously used to stunned mullet expressions on passing females, and he didn't bother to hide the sigh. 'If I get attacked by a croc because I had to talk to you I'm going to be extremely unhappy.'

Sophie blinked. What the heck was she doing? So much for immunity! She obviously needed a booster shot against this guy, so leaving was a great idea. 'Right, then. Your funeral.' For the first time in ten years Sophie crunched the gears as she slipped her vehicle into reverse.

Levi Pearson turned back to contemplate the spot where his father had been taken five months ago. Or had he been pushed and the crocodile only secondary to his demise? He'd find out.

That tiny whiff of suspicion, something only he seemed to have sniffed, was the reason he'd flown up here after the wet season and why he'd asked his stubbornly determined sister not to mention their proper connection to Xanadu. That and the fact the other consultant he worked with had recommended a holiday for the tenth time in the past two years.

As soon as he'd confirmed or dismissed the concept of foul play he'd get her the hell out of downtown nowheresville and back to Sydney. The manager here was more than capable of running Xanadu, and Levi didn't need another burden, but he'd discovered a motive he couldn't dismiss.

Lord knew the original owners of the station had enough reason to hate his family if the stories of his father were true.

He took his eye off the bank and risked a glance at the blonde woman's four-wheel-drive vehicle as it ploughed through the river away from him. Nothing else mattered. Hadn't for a long while. Definitely not a pair of concerned blue eyes under two stern

eyebrows. Above a lush little mouth. He frowned.
She'd been an officious little thing but strangely
intriguing.

Still, he'd read the population of the Kimberley
region was about thirty thousand people in an area
slightly bigger than Germany and it was the last place
he'd ever settle. So, he should be safe from bumping
into her again. He didn't need the complication of
fleeting sexual attraction to a cowgirl.

A stealthy splash to the left of where he stood had
his attention firmly back on the water and Levi took a
few steps towards the vehicle he'd borrowed from the
resort. Probably better not to get eaten and give her the
chance to say *I told you so*.

He could feel the twitch of his lips at the thought,
along with surprise at the idea of smiling, something
he hadn't done much of in the past year or two, and
climbed back into his vehicle.

Nearly two hours later Sophie swerved around another
pothole and the old four-wheel drive bounced off the
thousandth corrugation on her way to Jabiru Station
Township. They'd grade the road soon now the rain had
stopped. She gritted her teeth to stop the jarring. Almost
home.

Funnily enough, she wasn't tired. Hadn't been since
the Pentecost. She didn't want to think about the man
at the river any more. It had been one of those moments
in time when you catch another person's eye and, for
a second or two, glances tangle and reverberate, and
then you both look away and the moment passes.

Except the moment seemed to last an eternity and she was still waiting for it to pass.

It had been one of those moments. Just a stranger. With great eyes. And a great body. And a great mouth. Even in the firm line, she remembered, his mouth had hinted at a fullness and dangerous curve that made her wonder how he'd got the scar. She hoped some hot-blooded woman had thrown a plate at him. Her lips twitched but she pulled them back into line. He'd looked like everything she didn't want in a man.

Rude, definitely.

Stupid, obviously. She frowned. He didn't look stupid; actually, he'd looked fearsomely intelligent. So not stupid, maybe reckless. She didn't want that either, did she? No way.

Worst of all, he'd had the trappings of her ex. Stinking, selfishly, blatantly wealthy. Like Dr Brad Gale. The liar. She was finished with doctors and liars and people who thought they could buy you. And serve you a prenuptial at the same time.

She was glad to be home, in a place where people said what they meant and didn't string you along. Where she could be useful to those who needed her, and not as some decorative arm hanging, and definitely not confined to answering only when spoken to.

Sophie did wonder if her poor brother had become used to his bachelor ways while she'd been away. He'd looked surprised when she'd arrived to move back into her own room, even if 'Shortest engagement in history,' was all he'd said.

She drove through the tiny Jabiru Station

Township—mostly pubs and boarded buildings—to their house, a modest timber residence with bull-nosed verandas on all sides and a tiny dry garden. Neat and comfortable, in the same state of disrepair as they'd inherited it from their parents, who'd inherited it from her father's parents after Granddad did that bad thing.

A place where Smiley could save every cent for his dream station, like the one his grandfather had been tricked out of in a card game all those years ago. Against a man who'd lied.

Not that Smiley lusted after Xanadu. He'd his own plans for a different station that accounted for his cattle having to be lodged all over the Kimberley while he saved for the land, but it irked Sophie that her own father and now Smiley had to scrimp so hard to make their way in the place they were born.

'You must've loaded the cattle early, because I didn't see the road train on the way in,' she said as she rounded the veranda, then stopped. He had someone with him.

Her brother's drawl seemed more noticeable, which was saying something, as his normal speech defined the word *leisurely*. 'Sophie.' He looked at her, and then indicated the petite dark-haired woman beside him. 'This is Odette. From Sydney. She's having a baby, and in the area for a week or so, and wanted to meet a midwife in case she had any problems.'

Sophie held out her hand and shook the young woman's perfectly manicured fingers. Nice expensive watch. Brad had bought her one just like it. She'd left it in Perth.

Sophie bit back the thought. He'd made her judge-mental and that wasn't like her—or hadn't been before she'd tripped off to Perth for her midwifery. She needed to get her new prejudice under control. Wealthy tourists kept a lot of people in jobs around here.

'Nice to meet you, Odette. Welcome to Jabiru Station Township. You been waiting long?'

'I flew in an hour ago.' Her coral-coloured lips tilted as she smiled. She had a sweet face, Sophie thought, and well made up, which was interesting as the heat usually melted foundation around here. 'Guess I should have rung first but I thought the clinic was open.'

Sophie looked across the street to the old homestead that'd been turned into the clinic. 'I've been visiting an Aboriginal community. It's "women's health" day. Just takes a few hours to cover the distance around here.'

'So Smiley was explaining.' She looked shyly up at Sophie's brother. Goofily, Smiley actually smiled back, an occurrence that was so rare it had derived his nickname. Sophie felt herself frown. She'd never seen him look like that. Or be much into explaining anything. She'd be lucky to get a dozen words out of him on a normal morning.

'Odette flew herself in a chopper,' he said.

Impressive. 'You're a pilot? Wow.' And very preg-nant, but she didn't say it.

Odette shrugged with a smile. 'I do it for fun. You're a midwife. Wow.'

Sophie had to laugh. 'I do that for fun too. My

friend, Kate, the other midwife, flies her own plane from Jabiru Homestead.'

Odette exuded good nature and Sophie couldn't help liking her. 'So you're having a baby? And want a check-up? Come across to the clinic. Was there something you were worried about?'

Odette turned and smiled at Sophie's brother. 'Thanks, Smiley. I hope I get to see you again.'

He nodded and tipped his hat. The two women crossed the road and Odette looked back. 'Your brother's a handsome man.'

Sophie blinked. She'd never thought about it. He was just...Smiley. 'If he's not in the house he's got an Akubra on so I don't often see his face. I guess I still see skinned knees and freckles.'

'I didn't see any of those.' Odette sounded almost dreamy and Sophie grimaced. City-rich women and Smiley did not mix.

'Is it your husband's helicopter?' Not very subtle.

'I don't have a husband.' Odette was no fool and she met Sophie's eyes without a flicker. 'The father of my baby is dead.'

Bummer, for more reasons than one, Sophie thought. Was she being judgemental again? 'Sorry for being nosy.'

'That's OK. Better to get it out in the open anyway. He wasn't a nice man,' Odette went on. 'And the chopper belongs to the resort where I'm staying.'

'That would be Xanadu, then.' It wasn't a question. Xanadu. Now an ultra-high-end resort a hundred kilometres away, as the chopper flew, that catered for a

Kimberley adventure in five-star luxury. Private suites, fine wine and cuisine, and escorted tours with private sittings in the hot springs and gorges. They'd turned it into a wilderness park with a few token cattle. Not like in Grandfather's day. 'I've never known them to lend the chopper before.'

Odette shrugged. 'I just asked the manager.' She looked across at Sophie. 'I could take you and Smiley up for a fly if you want.'

'Thanks, but maybe another time. Should you be flying when you're pregnant?'

'You sound like my brother.'

Now why did she suddenly think of the man at the river? 'Don't suppose he's a big bloke, scar on his chin, not into smiling.' The one who was 'just passing through.'

'You've met Levi?'

'Levi?' It seemed he was another person who was happy to bend the truth. As opposed to the straightforward people from around here who didn't lie. 'Yep. Guess I have. He was at the Pentecost River crossing.' Sophie didn't say *a little too close to the water* because she didn't want to worry Odette. She shrugged. 'I warned him about the crocodiles.'

Odette pursed her lips for a moment, then visibly pushed away whatever had caused the look. 'He knows about the crocodiles. But thank you. Levi is a good guy, just forgotten how to have fun.'

And too attractive, and Sophie needed to talk about something new because she had the feeling anything else she learnt about him wouldn't help her forget.

'So when's your baby due, Odette?'

'A month.'

Sophie fought to keep her jaw from dropping but she had another look. Surely too small. Maybe Odette had it all tucked away. 'I'd say your brother was right and you shouldn't be flying. Where's your mother?'

'She died when I was a kid.' Oops, Sophie thought. Another foot-in-mouth question.

Luckily Odette didn't seem worried. 'Levi brought me up. Our father ran off with another woman when I was young. That's why Levi's serious. He's been the man of the house for a lot of years.'

Too much information. Not hearing this. 'OK.' Sophie pushed open the door and they went into the small exam room. 'How about I check your blood pressure, feel your tummy and have a listen to your baby's heart rate? If it's OK with you I'll photocopy your antenatal card. Then if you have any worries I can talk you through most of it on the phone.'

Odette grinned. 'This is like booking into a spare hospital.'

Sophie smiled back. 'Except we don't deliver babies here, only the unexpected ones.' She gestured to the chair beside her desk. 'Have a seat.'

Odette settled herself and held out her arm. 'That's OK. We'll probably be back in Sydney in a few days anyway.'

Maybe that justifies as passing through and he didn't technically lie. Though what the heck was he doing bringing someone this pregnant away from home?

Sophie wrapped the cuff around Odette's arm and pumped it up, then let it down. She unhooked the stethoscope from her ears and smiled. 'Blood pressure's perfect. One ten on sixty.' She indicated the footstool beside the examination table. 'If you can climb up there we'll see where this baby of yours is hiding.'

Odette chuckled. 'Everyone says I'm small but I was only five pounds when I was born. The ultrasound said it's a boy.'

Sophie draped a thin sheet over the lower half of Odette's body and Odette lifted her shirt. 'A boy. Wow. Nice tummy.' Sophie was serious. Odette's abdomen curved up in a perfect small hill, brown and smooth, and the baby shifted a body part into a small point as Sophie laughed. 'He's waving.'

Odette slid her hand over the point and the baby subsided as if trained. 'My baby's no sloth. Moves heaps, especially at night.'

'Women tend to feel their babies at night because they're not busy like they are in the daytime. They say the baby already has a rhythm so if he's awake a lot at night you might be in for some sleep deprivation.'

'I don't mind.' Odette smiled dreamily. 'I can't wait.'

I hope you do, Sophie thought, as she measured the mound of Odette's belly and, taking into account the petite mother, the measurements confirmed Odette's estimated due date.

She slid the hand-held Doppler over the area she'd palpated as the baby's shoulder and the sound of the baby's heart rate filled the room. They both listened and their eyes met in mutual acknowledgement of the wonder of childbearing. 'There you go,' Sophie said, as she turned off the Doppler. 'One hundred and forty beats a minute and just as perfect as his mother.'

She helped Odette sit up. 'Everything looks great.'

'Thanks, Sophie. I feel better just talking to you.' Odette climbed down and smoothed her clothes. 'How much do I owe you?'

Sophie shook her head. 'I didn't do anything. Free service. Anyone can walk in and get the same.'

'You and Smiley should come over to Xanadu on the weekend and have dinner with my brother and me. Our treat. As a thank-you for this.' She gestured to the examination couch. 'I could come and get you in the chopper. Or Levi could.'

Lord, no. And she thought they were going in a day or two? It was only Monday. She walked her to the door. 'Thanks, Odette, but the weather's still too un-settled for me to fly—I'm a chicken in the air—and I don't know what Smiley's planned. I've only just moved back from Perth.'

'Sure. I'll ring later in the week.' Odette stopped and turned back with a new idea. 'If you're not keen on fly-ing, you could stay overnight and drive back the next day. In fact, that sounds more fun anyway.'

Sophie felt she was being directed by a small deter-mined whirly wind, like the one that was lifting leaves outside her window and the one inside her chest when she thought of staying anywhere near Odette's brother. 'I'll mention it to Smiley.' Not.

Odette pulled a gold compact from her bag, flicked open the mirror and touched up her lipstick. Not something Sophie did regularly out here in the bush and the thought made her smile to herself.

Odette snapped shut the compact. 'What's your brother's real name?'

Sophie had to think for a moment. 'William.'

Odette nodded as if she liked it. 'I think I'll call him William.'

'It's been a while since anybody has.' Now where was this going? Nowhere, she hoped. 'He may not even remember it.'

'Even more reason to,' Odette said cryptically.

That afternoon, Levi poured his sister a chilled juice and himself a cold beer before he moved to look over the veranda at the gorge below. Then her words sank in. He turned back to her. 'You what?'

'I invited William and Sophie to stay over for a night on the weekend. The midwife and her brother. To have dinner and drive home the next day.'

He'd strangle her. 'Did I mention we didn't want to draw attention until I find out if anyone around here hated our father enough to push him into that river?'

Odette crossed her arms and lent them over her large tummy. 'Hated him more than you?'

Levi shook his head. 'I didn't hate him. I didn't respect him. That's all.'

He fully intended to sign the ownership he'd unexpectedly inherited back over to his sister, another baffling development his estranged father had left for him, when they'd all expected Odette to benefit by the resort automatically.

Odette rolled her eyes. 'Because you've just found out he's had another son to another woman. Humph.' She returned to topic. 'Besides, they wouldn't know anything about Father's accident. Sophie's only just moved back from Perth and William is—' she paused and her mouth curved '—just William. He hasn't a mean bone in his body.'

He flung his hand out towards the view. 'We don't know that. Your new best friends. You've met them, what, once?'

'You've met her too.' Odette sat forward as he frowned.

He'd done his part. He'd avoided meeting anyone. Not likely. 'When?'

'She said she'd met you by the river—' Odette didn't quite poke out her tongue but he knew that look '—this afternoon.' A winning point.

The little honey in the car? The last person he needed to be exposed to, as she seemed lodged like an annoying bindii from the grass in his memory bank. 'Blonde ponytail? Nice, um, features?'

Odette coughed and he couldn't help the curve of his own lips. He really didn't have socialising on his agenda on this trip. He needed to go home; he'd already been away past his expectations, and his theatre list would be a mile long.

His sister would be the death of him. He sighed. Too late now. 'So why can't we fly them in and out? That way they don't have to stay.'

Odette shrugged. 'Sophie doesn't fancy the chopper.'

Chicken, eh? Good. Though she hadn't seemed a shrinking violet. 'Maybe she wouldn't mind so much if the pilot didn't look like she was going to break her waters any moment?'

Odette flapped her hand at him. 'You're too used to your own way. Let me worry about me.'

CHAPTER TWO

Five days later

'I DON'T know how you talked me into this.' Sophie glared at her brother.

Smiley kept his eyes on the road. 'You've been twitchy all week.'

'And you've been moonstruck like a big old cow.'

Smiley turned to look at her briefly but didn't say anything.

It was disappointing. A bit of a spat might have taken her mind off the nerves that were building ridiculously at the thought of meeting the brooding rich man again. She was even avoiding his name in her thoughts. How ridiculous.

Unable to get a rise out of Smiley she turned to watch the scenery flash by. The overhanging escarpment of the Cockburn ranges in the distance ran along the right side of the vehicle and the stumpy gums and dry grass covered the plains to the left before they soared into more ochre-red cliffs that tinged purple as the sun set.

Sophie knew the darkening gorges hid pockets of tangled rainforest and deep cold pools like the dread she could feel at meeting him again.

But the stands of thick and thin trees made her smile. She'd missed the pot bellies of the grey-trunked boabs the most while she'd been in Perth.

'Why don't you like Odette?' Smiley was stewing. Something in his voice warned her not to be flippant.

'Who wouldn't like Odette?' she said carefully. 'She seems lovely. I just don't want you hurt when she flies back to Sydney.'

Smiley frowned at the road ahead and Sophie winced at his displeasure. Now that was something she'd very rarely encountered and she didn't like it. 'I'm sorry, Smiley. I have no right to judge your friends. I think Odette's great. I just can't see her as an outback girl and I can't see you in the city. But it's none of my business.'

'Thank you.' His voice was dry and the two words were a statement. Thanking her for agreeing it was none of her business.

Oops. She really had upset her brother and that was something she'd never consciously do. Since her parents had died she'd become used to bossing Smiley around, giving her opinion, and he'd never seemed to mind.

Obviously she'd crossed the line with Odette. She'd just have to button her lip and trust Smiley's instincts.

It would've been easier if she'd sent him to Xanadu on his own though. She had the feeling her trepidation for Smiley was tied up in the trepidation she held for herself with Odette's mysterious brother.

Smiley turned off the main dirt road onto the red dust of the track through the scrub. They splashed through several watercourses and wound through the ochre-coloured hills until they turned into the Private Property, No Entry sign that hid the homestead.

'Welcoming,' she mumbled, and Smiley glanced at her.

'You've met the brother?'

'Briefly.' She could be just as taciturn. She didn't expand her explanation and Smiley didn't ask again. Then the homestead came into view.

Xanadu Homestead was a long low building, and she'd been too young to remember visiting in her grandparents' day. Apparently now it had been divided up into luxury suites, if what Sophie had heard was right, perched on the edge of the escarpment above the river that flowed beneath it.

The main building faced into the sunset which glowed deep red as it faded. Nice place to holiday if you had the platinum or even a black credit card, but not when you were eight months pregnant. Why would Odette and her brother come here now?

At least the thought gave her something else to concentrate on as they drew up at the house. She wondered what the other guests would think of outsiders being invited to invade their sanctuary. What month was this? April. The resort would only just have opened for the season anyway.

Odette swayed onto the main entrance portico in a muslin caftan that must have cost a bomb, and Sophie wondered how she could still be graceful when she was supposed to be awkward in the last month of pregnancy. Sophie glanced at Smiley and judging by his face he'd just seen the Holy Grail.

Sophie sighed and felt for the handle to climb out of the truck when her door moved away from her grasp.

'Welcome to Xanadu.' Levi held out his hand and Sophie wasn't sure if he wanted to shake hers or help her from the vehicle. Where'd he come from? She'd been hoping to see him from a distance and get her face straight.

She resisted the urge to snap her hand back to her side and forced herself to let him take her fingers. Initially cool, the strength in his fingers surprised her, but not as much as the feeling of insidious connection, a frisson of ridiculous warmth that passed between them and echoed the impact of his eyes. There was something she'd deny with her last breath.

No. She hadn't felt a thing. So why rub her hand surreptitiously behind her back? And why did he look down at her with one enigmatic eyebrow raised as if he'd been surprised as well?

Then Odette was dancing around the car like an elegant puppy as she looked adoringly up at Smiley, and Levi left her to shake Smiley's hand.

'It's so good to see you, William.' Odette flashed a smile at Sophie before she looked back at Smiley and captured his hand. Odette tugged his fingers to make him follow her. 'This is my brother, Levi,' she said dismissively. 'Now, come and see the place.'

'William' looked back at Sophie, who managed a tiny smiling shrug that said she'd be fine.

'My sister can be impetuous,' Levi said grimly.

'My brother can't.' She watched Smiley leap up the stairs after Odette. 'Or I didn't think he could.'

Levi lifted one eyebrow sardonically. 'Welcome to Xanadu. I'll send someone for the bags when we get inside.'

Sophie glanced in the back of the truck. 'Actually, we're used to carrying our own.'

He inclined his head. 'But I'd be offended. Please come in.'

The bags weren't worth standing out here with him so she turned resolutely towards the entrance. He went on. 'The resort's not technically opened for the season and we have the run of the place.'

'Well, that's very nice.' But she couldn't help thinking, How the heck did you do that? They must know the owners extremely well or have unlimited funds. Best not go there. 'When does it open?'

He glanced at the sky. 'Depends on the weather and the state of the roads, though apparently next week, if all continues well.'

She slanted a look across at him. 'I guess you and Odette will be gone by then.'

Another enigmatic brow rose. 'Trying to get rid of us?'

They crossed the gravel drive to the stairs and she paused. 'You did say you were passing through. A week ago,' she said calmly.

'I lied.' Straightfaced, no remorse.

Sophie blinked. She'd known he was dangerous. Like sniffying the briny scent before a storm. Her instincts had been right. He was trouble. She started walking again, faster now, but he kept pace. 'People don't tend to do that up here.' Liar like Brad.

His eyes narrowed as if he sensed some history there. 'Necessity can make liars out of us all.'

She could feel her lip curl. 'So some people say.'

He looked across at her and no doubt he could see her distaste. She hoped so. 'Had a bad experience with a man, have you?'

'I think I'll look for my brother.' She turned away but before she could take a step he caught her hand again and she pulled up short to look back at him with raised eyebrows, actually astounded that he would invade her intimate space.

Maybe he didn't know that people from the bush— used to wide-open spaces and few people—didn't do space invasion well. Smiley tended to wave at people rather than shake their hands. Not like those from the city, who were used to people brushing up against them in elevators and on city streets.

He let go. This time she didn't hide that she rubbed her hand.

'I apologise, Sophie.' To give him his due he looked as confused as she felt. 'We seem to have got off on the wrong foot. Twice.' Those deadly lips of his were as devastating in an almost smile as she'd imagined. Damn him.

'Now why do we rub each other the wrong way, do you think?'

No way was Sophie going there. She looked him up and down. Coolly, she hoped. 'I'm not interested in rubbing anyone at all.'

His almost smile, which she decided was forced anyway, departed and he nodded. 'Let's go in, then.' He gestured with his hand for her to precede him, but he didn't touch her. And she didn't thank him for the courtesy because she could feel his eyes on her back uncomfortably the whole way up the steps. And he was still in her space.

Levi watched her attempt to walk sedately ahead of him; they both knew something had happened. He wanted to come up beside her and put his hand on the small of her back—lay claim, in fact—and he crunched his fingers into his palm to stop from reaching out. She'd invaded his head with the tiny bit he'd seen the other day but in full-blown glory she took his breath away.

Her dress was simple and blue but smoothed the slender line of her back and hips as she swayed in front of him and her legs were bare and brown and long enough to dream about. This was crazy. She smoked, just by walking in front of him.

It felt as if a wire from one of the fences dragged him along in her wake, and there was a tautness he could see in her shoulders that said she wasn't comfortable either.

He didn't know what it was. Apart from totally impractical and heinously inconvenient…but then again the travel agent had quoted the Kimberleys as a destination of adventure. Suddenly he was thinking of a side tour of a different sort.

He ushered her, with great restraint and no contact, through to the veranda where they all shared the sunset, or at least her brother and his sister shared it; he and Sophie separately observed. Maybe not even that because he wasn't looking at hills bathed in purple.

He'd always had a thing about women with long necks and hers flowed like an orchid to her throat. He'd bet her skin felt as soft as a petal. He shifted his scrutiny away from temptation and looked higher. He couldn't see her eyes from where he stood but he knew they were blue. Like her dress. High cheekbones, snubby nose that should have just been snubby but turned out deliciously cute, and those lips. He reefed his eyes away and took a long swallow of his beer. Who was he and what had happened to the normal, sane, overworked man who'd arrived last week?

Shame it wasn't prehistoric times because dragging her off to his cave looked mighty appealing to him at this moment. And no one had appealed for a while. He'd better find something to stay focused on, something apart from how to get her into bed.

'Odette tells me you're a midwife,' he said, and now he could see her eyes. Her pupils were big and dark and he'd read somewhere that was a sign of arousal. He hoped so 'cause he was sure his eyes would be all pupil to his lashes.

She ran her finger around the rim of her glass and even that tiny movement made him swallow. 'And community nurse, and anything else that needs medical attention,' she said.

He almost wished he was sick. 'Sounds diverse. It must be a heavy workload.' He watched her face light up.

'I enjoy it,' she said. 'Love it, in fact. Now it has the added dimension of meeting people like Odette who'd benefit from access to a midwife.'

Passion for her job. Bless her. He used to have that. Now he didn't even want to talk about work. 'Odette said you've just returned from Perth.'

He felt the cold breeze and even her pupils constricted until her eyes were light blue again. She jutted her chin and he regretted the question. Obviously bad choice of conversation and a major setback. Probably a good thing.

'Yes. It's great to be home.' Such a cold voice, so different than when she'd spoken of work.

She put her glass down and turned to his sister. 'The view is wonderful, Odette.' Sophie pretended to be absorbed and tried to fade Levi into the background. She didn't want to think about Perth and the fool she'd made of herself there. Though it served as a reminder not to be foolish here. Just because externally Odette's brother was hard to ignore, internally he'd be the same as Brad. He'd already shown his arrogant, untruthful side. Rich, callous, oblivious to hurting others. And she'd promised she'd never become that vulnerable again.

She just wished he'd stop studying her. She could feel him watching. Could feel the brush of his analytical study as if she were some strange species he hadn't figured out yet and it made her want to think of some witty, slash-cutting thing to make him back off. But of course she couldn't think of something. No doubt tonight in bed it would be there on her tongue.

Well, he could look, but she refused to squirm. He'd be used to city women falling all over him but he'd come to the wrong place for that. Here a woman wanted a man with more to his repertoire than looking good.

'So what do you do, Levi?' Apart from watching me. Not that she was interested.

'I have a business in Sydney.'

City slicker. She'd bet it wasn't a physical job because his hands looked too clean. She wasn't going to comment, even mentally, on his obvious fitness.

He raised his eyebrows. 'You have a very expressive face. By the curl of your lip I'm surprised you think I do anything?'

'Perhaps.' She abandoned the subject. If he didn't want to tell her, then that was fine. The less she knew about him, the better. She turned her shoulder further away from him.

'My sister tells me you don't like helicopters much.'

Politeness meant she had to turn back. No doubt he would see her reluctance and maybe then he'd leave her alone. 'Nothing personal to helicopters, I don't like to fly.'

He shifted his body so she was lined up with him again. 'Shame, then. A pilot's licence would be useful with the distances they have out here.'

Like Kate and her plane. She'd never feel comfortable enough to do that. 'My friend flies. I'll do without.'

He acknowledged her aversion with a flick of his hand. 'It's a different world, immediate, stunning, and even I admit this country is spectacular from the air.'

She felt her hackles rise and she sipped her drink before she answered to damp down her desire to demand he appreciate her home. 'The Kimberleys are spectacular from the ground as well.'

He put his glass down. 'I've offended you again.'

'The bush is not for everyone.' She shrugged, thankfully.

'And you're happy about that?'

It seemed she couldn't cause him offence. 'There are advantages.' Well, at least they were conversing in a fairly normal way, and then a waiter appeared and it was time for dinner.

Levi gestured her ahead of him and Sophie pulled up short at the candlelit veranda; a glass ceiling showcased the glorious starlit sky above a table that glowed with white linen and silver cutlery. 'Amazing room.'

'Very civilised,' Levi agreed, as if he were still surprised by it. Even that offended her, as if they couldn't put on a good show up here in the bush.

She took her seat and, much to Sophie's amazement, dinner proved a delightful affair. They were joined by the resort manager, Steve, a handsome young man—more Odette's age than Levi's—who said and did all the right things and was very anxious to ensure that Odette was safely seated or served, as if she were an invalid. Baby phobia, Sophie guessed, but he left Sophie with a feeling of awkwardness she couldn't explain.

The rapport between Levi and Odette showed genuine affection. Reluctantly Sophie admitted she liked that—family was important—so he had some redeeming features which she didn't really want to see. And Levi devoted himself to being a wonderful host. Then again, her ex, Brad, had been a great host too.

Odette remained animated and 'William' held his own end of the conversation up for a change. Sophie had to shut her mouth when she would normally have answered for her brother until finally she subsided in awe at his previously hidden ability to socialise. He could have come on his own after all. Great!

Until the talk turned to helicopters and the suggestion of a joint expedition the next day. This she couldn't keep silent on. 'I hope you don't expect me to go along. Helicopters fall out of the sky.'

Levi sat back in his chair and smiled at her. 'No, they don't.'

Loosened up by the delightful Margaret River Shiraz, Sophie pointed her finger at him. 'I want to know what happens when the engine stops in a helicopter.'

Her comment came in a lull and stilled the other conversations, and Levi tilted his head at her. 'They glide. Autorotation. Instead of the air being pulled in from the top by the engine, the rotors turn the other way and pull the air in from underneath as you descend. Gives you fairly good forward and downward control. Like a winged aeroplane, just not as far.'

She didn't believe him. 'How far?'

'Enough to get passengers on the ground without hurting them.' He held her gaze, daring her to disbelieve him.

Sounded too simple. 'Then you can take off again?'

He rubbed his chin. 'Maybe not always without hurting the chopper.' He seemed sure of his facts.

Sophie digested that.

'We've two helicopters at Xanadu,' Steve said, 'and never had a problem.' He smiled kindly at her and she almost felt patted like a small dog. Sophie wondered why she had the urge to wipe the smile off his face. Maybe the poor guy had trained himself to be extra accommodating around his VIP guests, but Sophie found his attentions irritating.

She glanced at Levi but she couldn't read anything in his face. He was probably used to people fawning over him.

The conversation moved on and Sophie sat back to observe. She watched mostly Levi, despite her attempts not to be drawn to him. He made no blatant attempt to direct the conversation, he just did. While she didn't like him she had to admit he was smooth. He seemed to know the right thing to bring out the passion in Smiley for the land, and Sophie was surprised by her brother's apparent liking for their host.

Sophie refused to fall for the same thing and she wasn't going to lose. Actually, she wanted to go home or at least get out of this room, away from him.

With the meal cleared away, Sophie drifted towards the end of the veranda where the steps led down to the path around the side of the homestead. The stars winked down at her and the further she moved away from the veranda the brighter the sky lights formed into the constellations and patterns she'd grown up with.

The Southern Cross, the Pot, the Milky Way. A wooden bench under a huge boab looked the perfect place to hide. She sank gratefully down on warm wood in the dimness, and the soft breeze rattled the boab leaves over her head as if to soothe her.

Until Levi strode out onto the veranda with his satellite phone and shattered the magic of the night, along with the calm she'd achieved.

Typical city man. They never stopped. No doubt he couldn't imagine being without a phone at his fingertips, to direct underlings and ensure nobody forgot how important he was, and to order up the next convenience. Or like Brad, to check that his woman was waiting patiently at home, while he dallied somewhere else.

She'd like to see Levi bogged in a bulldust hole with no handy phone. See how resourceful he'd be with nobody but himself to rely on.

Then he saw her, ended the conversation and snapped his phone shut. She leant back into the shadows in a futile move as if he would forget she was there, slightly guilty about her mean thoughts for a man she barely knew, but still bitter by personal experience from the callousness of a man like him.

He paused at the bottom of the steps, and she thought he probably didn't even want to get his shoes dirty out here. Her nose wrinkled.

Levi hesitated at the bottom step, quite sure Sophie didn't want company, and reluctant to force his company on her. 'Coffee is ready if you'd like some.' He glanced at the grass. 'Unless you'd prefer it out here?'

She stood and walked towards him with a swish of her blue dress and he felt the rebuke for ruining her peace. She had attitude all right, he thought, but she carried it well. 'Thank you. Inside will be fine.'

There was no doubt the less she saw of him, the better, and no doubt either that the less he saw of her, the better.

CHAPTER THREE

LEVI stopped as he entered the room for breakfast on the veranda next morning. It seemed he'd interrupted an amusing show.

His sister, with much eye batting and smiles, was trying to convince cowboy William to do the scenic tourist fly in the chopper. Apparently they should fly to the Bungle Bungles, a massive prehistoric range of striped domes at the edge of the Tanami Desert, with a picnic basket, an idea which left a horrified expression on Sophie the orchid's face. Intriguing situation.

He could see a ride in the helicopter was the last thing Sophie wanted to do, make that second last. If he read her expression right when she glanced at him, the last thing she wanted was to stay behind at Xanadu, alone, with him.

Levi could tell. That was amusing too. Sort of. Though he'd never had someone blatantly avoid his company before.

He sat down next to Sophie at breakfast, maybe too deliberately close, so his thigh touched hers when he

turned, and he could actually feel her thrum with awareness. The fresh herby stuff she'd washed her hair with
teased his nose and some psycho inside wanted to sniff
her head. Now that would go over well as a space
invasion.

Even her skin glowed golden in the morning light,
like the honey on the crumpet she nibbled at, and
reminded him he'd spent more than a few hours in bed
last night trying not to remember those lush little hips
and lips. He must be having a crisis.

'Good morning, Sophie.'

'Morning.' Her answer was accompanied by a darting look that came and went as she shrank her shoulders to avoid contact.

He had to bite back a smile. Becoming a habit those
smiles. Very strange. 'Did you sleep well?'

'Fine, thanks.' Another flick of her eyes and he
relented and shifted his chair a few inches away to give
her some space. Her delightful shoulders actually sank
with relief and he wondered why he was playing with
her. He wasn't normally pushy.

'Did you sleep?' It seemed she could talk easier
too.

Now how reluctantly had she asked that? He bit his
lip. 'No, not really. The symphony of the night seemed
especially loud.'

She raised those stern brows of hers. 'Kept awake
by nature? Poor you. Well, it is a wilderness park.' She
tossed her head. 'Sure beats the heck out of traffic
noise.'

Maybe she didn't need sympathy. She could stand

up for herself. So they ate their meal in silence as Odette continued to flirt with William.

Levi rubbed his chin as they all stood to leave because, funnily enough, her lack of enthusiasm for the flight made his skin itch.

'Odette?' he said, and his sister turned back.

'Look after Sophie. Remember, she's not comfortable, so no stunts.'

Odette raised her eyebrows at him and saluted. 'Yes, sir.'

Sophie sent him a semi-grateful look over her shoulder as she dragged her feet to follow the other two to the helipad.

Levi frowned to himself as he went the other way. He needed to concentrate on the paperwork he had to get through before they returned to Sydney, but the ridiculously blue Kimberley sky outside the window invited sacrifice. Odette was too pregnant to be pilot. And Sophie looked unhappy.

Unhappy was too mild a word. Sophie didn't know how she'd agreed to this.

Now Steve, the resort manager, had shooed Odette away from pre-flight checks. 'I can't let a pregnant lady do that,' he said with that tilted smile that prickled right up Sophie's nose. There was something about him that reminded her of someone but she couldn't connect the impression.

She'd never had much to do with the people from Xanadu and apparently he'd been here for a few years and very close to the late owner. She wished he'd mind his own business though.

To make matters worse, just before take-off, Levi appeared and decreed he'd pilot instead of Odette. Suddenly Sophie could have stayed behind. Talk about bad luck.

Everyone was looking out for Odette. Which was a good thing, but Sophie wondered if it was too late to look out for herself. Now the new seating arrangements meant she'd be up front next to Levi. This kept getting better and better. Not.

The front helicopter seat was as bad as she'd imagined. She shrank back into the stiff leather, semi-frozen, not quite believing she'd agreed to this, when Levi reached in from the outside to click her belt into place. His hands pulled the belt firmly across her and snapped it shut. Talk about space invasion. This whole expedition was crazy and way out of her comfort zone. How the heck had she found herself next to him in a doorless chopper with only the seat belt between her and certain death?

And on that note, surely there should have been more seat belts or harnesses or something? One belt didn't seem enough.

Odette and Smiley chatted happily, ensconced in the rear out of sight and out of earshot. Once they got going, she thought bitterly, they'd be safe in their own little world.

Levi climbed in and she squashed herself back against the seat. He pointed to the bulky headphones hooked on the central support in front of her, and indicated she put them on.

'Can you hear me?' His metallic voice made her

jump, and she looked across at him and glared. He nodded and she nodded facetiously back. He frowned, then went on. 'It's automatically switched to receive, so for you to be heard by everyone else just press this button to speak.'

He withdrew his attention from her and glanced in the back. 'You guys all buckled up?'

Odette's voice crackled. 'Roger.'

Levi glanced around the deserted helipad and began the pre-flight sequence. 'All clear,' he said to no one in particular and started the rotors.

The next few minutes Sophie missed as her eyes were tightly shut. The distant noise through the headphones grew louder and she felt the shudder from the flimsy craft right through the backs of her knees, then the first sideways swish of movement through the air and then back the other way.

She opened one eye. It was too hard not to look. They swayed a little from side to side as they edged higher and she could see the downdraught from the rotors beating the bushes below.

Then she could see the river at the bottom of the gorge, the roof of the homestead, the tops of the trees, and it was all a little intriguing, though she still pushed herself deep into her seat. She tried to relax her shoulders but the fear she'd fall out kept her rigid in the chair.

They climbed higher, and despite the lack of doors, she was protected from the wind by the bubble of the front windshield, and actually it didn't feel too bad.

She opened the other eye. There was a Perspex floor

in front of her feet. What sort of sick person designed a helicopter with a see-through floor? If she'd had eyes in the bottom of her soles she'd be able to look through the Perspex to the ground.

Basically she was standing on a thin edge above certain death. Her eyes closed at the vertigo of that thought, then opened again to risk a glance towards Levi as he concentrated on the dials at the front of the cockpit. What was he looking at? Was everything OK? She studied the instrument panel herself for something familiar. Maybe she'd even find a reassuring needle. Shame the guy wasn't more into smiling but at least he was taking the danger of the situation seriously.

Knots—they were doing eighty knots, and that was faster than miles per hour, so fairly fast. Fuel—there were seventy gallons of fuel; tank was full anyway. Guess that meant if they crashed she'd die in a ball of flame.

She looked away. Maybe don't read the dials. They'd climbed higher while she'd been contemplating the manner of their deaths, and she could look down on the escarpment now.

This was pretty amazing. And when she looked back, carefully, towards the homestead and the serpentine river, it made her appreciate how remote the properties were out here.

She'd flown on jets from Perth to Kununurra but they'd been much higher and she'd never really noticed individual stations, though mostly because she'd chosen the aisle seat and not the window.

'We'll fly up and over the waterfall on the property.'

Levi's voice crackled through the headphones. 'Odette likes that and then over to Lake Argyle. We'll pass over a couple of stations William asked to see, then in over the Bungles and back out over the Kimberley diamond mine and home.'

He was telling her this because…? Her stomach sank. She pushed the button to speak. 'Sounds like a long flight. Do we land anywhere?'

His teeth flashed. He couldn't possibly be concentrating enough on his job if he could smile about it, she thought sourly. 'Anywhere you want,' he said.

She resisted saying, *Here*, but not by much, and just nodded and turned away to glance at her watch. They'd be home in a few hours. She hoped.

Actually, the next hour passed fairly quickly. The waterfall looked surreal from above with sparkling drops at the side of the main body of water shimmering on the breeze to the gorge below.

Lake Argyle loomed indigo blue and stretched for ever, apparently seven times the size of Sydney Harbour, so that must be why it seemed to take seven times longer than she expected to cross.

When they flew over the isolation of the two cattle stations, Smiley asked Levi to circle again, so he could point out how they corralled their cattle using the land formations to form a natural bottleneck and arena. These were the stations Smiley had his eye on.

Sophie tried to concentrate on the implications of a station with no contact with the world for at least four months during the wet season, but all she could feel

were the g-forces pulling her towards the open doorway. Her whole body seemed to be straining against
the seat belt as they circled, and she had this horrible
feeling that maybe Levi hadn't fastened her buckle
properly and she'd just pop out of it into spiralling
space.

Now that was a dilemma. She hadn't checked the
belt herself but if she touched it now she might press
the eject button.

Come on. Their aircraft was circling thousands of
feet above the hard earth and Smiley was going on
about the logistical difficulties of cattle to market.

It was no good. 'Can we land soon?' Sophie's voice
cut across Smiley's, squeaky with distress, and she
felt Levi glance at her.

The helicopter levelled out. 'Bungles in fifteen
minutes, you right with that?' Levi's voice was still
tinny, but the strange thing was the lack of humour, just
genuine understanding and concern in his voice and
the reassurance she gained from that. His hand came
across and rested on her upper arm as if to transfer
calmness. From a man she didn't trust it shouldn't
have helped that much. But it did. Like a lifeline.

Funny how she'd never felt that mixture of empathy
and support from Brad's touch and she'd been engaged
to him.

Inexplicably steadied, she nodded, and allowed herself to sag more into the seat and close her eyes. Think
calm thoughts. Take deep breaths. Everything will be
fine.

That was when the engine spluttered, coughed and

died. Her eyes flew open. Slow motion from that moment on.

Suddenly there was no background noise except the wind and the rotors turning without an engine. She watched in horror as Levi kept his hands glued to the controls, correcting the cabin's inclination to yaw. Levi's voice travelled down the tunnel of her frozen mind. 'Have to land fast.' His voice was much louder without the sound of the engine, then she couldn't hear him at all because he'd switched the radio from the cabin to transmit the distress call. But she could watch his lips move, grimly, as he enunciated their position.

Unwilling to stare frozenly out of the Perspex beneath her feet she kept her eyes on Levi.

Glide. Helicopters can glide like planes but not as far. She remembered him saying that. She believed him. But he did lie. Had he lied then too? Surely not about this?

They weren't falling like a stone at the moment, still going forward, but the altimeter was unwinding like a top, much, much faster than it had wound up. Then she remembered that Odette and Smiley were in the back but she couldn't turn her neck to look. They'd all die. Odette's baby too? No. They had to survive. That thought steadied her. She was the midwife. The only medical person. They'd need her. Odette's baby needed her. She'd better survive in one piece.

She stared at Levi, who looked as if his face was hewn from the same stone as the escarpment they hurtled towards as he wrestled with the controls. No panic, just fierce, implacable determination to win. Thank God he'd decided to be the pilot. Even now he inspired confidence.

Then there was no time for thoughts. Just the sickening rush of the ground towards them, and she tucked her chin onto her chest and hugged her knees, so she must have listened to all those hostesses on flights she'd tried to block out. Thank you, hostesses.

They were coming in too fast.

The impact flung her head back as the helicopter slammed into the ground. Someone screamed and she wasn't sure if it was Odette or herself, then they clipped a boulder and the cabin flipped up and tipped sideways and landed once more with a larger crash and, finally, with agonising slowness, tipped back to settle on its base with a rattle of rocks and debris. They'd stopped. Intact.

That first few seconds of cessation of movement was more frightening than the seconds before, where at least she'd known she was alive. She straightened her aching neck to look at Levi. He didn't move; his long lashes were resting on ashen cheeks, and for a horrific moment she thought he was dead. Then she saw the rise and fall of his chest and the relief made the nausea rise in her throat. She reached across for his hand that lay limply pointed at her and felt for his pulse. It was fast but steady and she heaved a sigh of relief.

A soft moan came from behind her and, gingerly, she turned her head. 'Odette? Smiley? You both all right?'

'I think William's unconscious. What about Levi?'

'His pulse is strong but he's out too. We hit some scrub on their side of the aircraft so I think they bore the brunt of it.' She didn't know whether to ask or not. 'Your baby? Everything all right there?'

'I think so.' Odette's voice cracked. 'We need to get out. Get them out. The fuel!'

Sophie's fingers grappled with her belt clasp. The locking mechanism wouldn't open and those ball-of-flame visions returned to add desperation to her frustration. She rattled the catch.

Levi's hand came across and pushed the release and suddenly she was free. 'It's OK. I'll do it.' Why was he whispering?

He was conscious. Thank God. 'You were knocked out.'

'Hmm,' he said, his voice still weak, and rubbed the front of his head. Then he blinked and sat up straighter. 'You OK? Out!' He turned his attention to the back seat but Odette was already on the ground and attempting to rouse Smiley.

Sophie scrambled up from her seat and climbed over the scattered wreckage at the front of the craft to help Odette. Smiley groaned but didn't open his eyes and Sophie lifted his lids to peer into his eyes. His pupils contracted with the light and she heaved a sigh of relief. No time for sympathy. 'Wake up, Smiley. Move!'

Smiley's eyelids fluttered and he groaned. 'What happened?'

Levi was out and beside them now too. He swayed ever so slightly and Sophie watched him with narrowed eyes. 'Later, sport,' Levi said. 'Let's get you out of here, though I think if the tank was going to explode it would have done before now.' He shooed both women with his hand. 'Get away, over by those trees, you two. Now.'

Odette turned and hobbled away but Sophie stood her ground. 'Maybe he shouldn't be moved.'

'No choice.' Levi frowned at Smiley. 'Can you move your fingers and toes?'

'My leg hurts.'

'No tingling?' Smiley shook his head, then grimaced, and tried to pull himself free but recoiled his arm back to his chest with a loud groan.

The hiss of liquid hitting hot metal made them all jump. Levi frowned. 'I'll do the work, just brace your arm.' He heaved Smiley sideways and onto the ground in one huge movement and then dragged him away from the aircraft with Sophie almost glued to his back. The intermittent hiss from behind hastened their steps.

Sophie looked back over her shoulder. 'I'm glad it only just started doing that.'

Levi propped Smiley against a tree. 'I could have lived without it. We'll give it some time to cool down and then see what's happening with the radio, as long as everyone is stable.'

He turned to his sister, who hovered over Smiley. 'What about you, Odette? Your baby?'

'I'm not hurt. He's moving normally. Is William all right?'

'Fine. I'm more worried about you.' He looked at Sophie, who nodded and drew his sister to a fallen tree to sit.

'You need to sit for a while, Odette. We've fallen out

of the sky.' She shook her head. Holy dooley. 'We're alive but it's crazily worse than a car accident and babies don't like being in those. You sure you're not contracting?'

Odette stroked her belly. 'It doesn't hurt.'

'OK. But sit. While I check Smiley.'

'His name is William,' Odette said. 'Smiley sounds like a dummy and he's not that.'

Sophie blinked. Good grief. That's all she needed. 'William,' she said but rolled her eyes as she turned away.

CHAPTER FOUR

LEVI glowered at the wreckage of the aircraft and shook his head as they all gathered their breath. 'An engine should never do that.' His jaw clamped tight and she could see the implacable leader who highly resented mechanical failure.

Well, yes. She wasn't too impressed about it herself but even she knew the unexpected was possible.

Nobody else said anything and Sophie asked the question. 'What happened?'

Levi ignored her and turned to his sister. 'You saw nothing out of order in the pre-flight check, Odette?'

His sister grimaced. 'I only started it—Steve finished it.'

Levi's face stilled. 'It's not your fault.' He spoke very quietly, and Sophie frowned as she tried to gather the thread of undertones and make sense of it, but for some reason the hairs on her arms prickled and stood and she lifted her arms across her chest to rub them.

Levi was muttering. 'I can't believe I didn't do my own pre-flight check as well. You should never do anything last minute when flying. No excuses. First rule of flight.'

He glanced at the sky. 'We're baking in the sun. We need more shade and definitely water. I'll go up the gorge to see if there's a creek or a pool.'

Levi to the rescue? She didn't think so. 'Let me. As soon as I've checked—' she glanced at Odette and corrected herself '—William.'

Levi looked pale; a purple bruise had begun on his temple, and she could see him blaming himself when he'd saved them all. Sophie went on. 'You've been knocked out. You should move to the shade and I'll find the water.' She'd avoided his eyes while she spoke and flicked a glance back to see how he took her suggestion. Not well, judging by the scowl he directed at her.

He straightened, until he loomed over her, but the effect was spoilt when he swayed slightly. 'Who died and elected you captain? I can make my own decisions. Thanks.'

Sophie shrugged. He didn't intimidate her. Grumpy sod. 'It's a small job. As I'm the only medical person and you look like death warmed up, I say you need to rest after your heroics earlier. You're still the captain, just concussed, so that's what you'll do.'

He blinked, didn't quite drop his mouth open, but she knew she'd surprised him. He looked about to say something but didn't and she glanced at Odette and lowered her voice. 'Someone needs to keep an eye on your sister and give me a yell if she complains of any pain too, though I won't be long.'

She looked at her brother. 'But Smiley first.'

Levi hovered while she examined Smiley and it was hard to ignore him. She'd have liked to tell him to sit again but didn't want to push her luck. She doubted anyone had tried to tell him what to do since he was in school. It would do him good. Actually, thinking of him as a scrubby school boy did a lot for her confidence.

She spoke to Smiley. 'How's the head?' She ran her fingers lightly over the swelling under his right eye and then palpated the bulge over his ear. 'You've given it a good whack. Close your eyes for a couple of seconds and then open them.'

He did so and she watched his pupils constrict at the light. They looked equal as much as she could tell.

She checked his ears for discharge but there was none, and it made her think she should do the same for Levi. She looked at him.

'My ears are fine,' he said quickly. 'And I'm sure my pupils are too.'

Sophie shrugged. 'Your choice,' she said, not eager for another clash of wills, and looked back at Smiley.

'So you've dislocated the shoulder again?' A sister's tone.

Smiley grimaced. 'I'd say.'

'We can fix that. We've done it before.' But she really didn't want to think about doing that. 'And the ankle?'

'Pretty sore.' They all looked at it, swollen already, and she ran her hands over it but couldn't feel any blatant deviations of line.

Poor Smiley. 'That's gotta hurt. We'll splint it, get you a walking stick and at least you'll be independent for short walks. You still wear your knife?'

He nodded and patted his hip with his good hand. 'Good,' she said, and looked at him with sympathy for the impending pain. 'You want to do the shoulder now before it swells more?'

Tight-lipped but still brief. 'Quicker the better.'

Sophie looked at Levi. 'Can you help me with this?'

Levi appeared even more dubious. 'You sure you know what you're doing?'

Did he think she did this stuff for fun? 'I've done it for Smiley twice before.' And hated it.

Levi opened his mouth and then closed it again. 'If he's got faith in you, then I'm happy to help. Just tell me what you want me to do.' Deferring to her? Not what he'd said a minute ago but she didn't think it a good time to point that out.

He still looked uncomfortable and she wondered if he was feeling faint again. 'You sure you're OK, Levi?'

'I'm fine.' The terse man was back. He looked at Smiley. 'What about his pain relief.'

She shook her head. 'The sooner I line the bones up again so they'll slide back in, the better. And he's been knocked out anyway. Not a good idea.'

Sophie took a deep breath and hoped everyone couldn't see how sick this made her. She knelt down beside Smiley and cleared the dirt in front of him of rocks and sticks for him to lie down.

She'd need a piece of material to go around Smiley's chest and under his injured armpit that Levi could pull on while she manipulated Smiley's arm. It needed to be strong like clothing. Probably her blouse would be best. Actually, it could be Levi's shirt. She thought about that and decided she didn't want to see his chest. She had a fair idea of the picture that might lodge in her brain.

'We'll use my shirt.' She turned around before anyone could say anything and slipped it off. Businesslike, as if she wasn't really sitting there in front of them all in her lacy bra, and she refused to think about whether she had little rolls of belly as she bent over. This day just kept getting better and better.

She spread her shirt on the ground to roll the material up in a long sausage and slipped it around Smiley's body and under his armpit until the two ends met back on Levi's side.

'Down you go, Smiley. Shuffle forward so you can stretch out on your back.' Smiley eased down with agonised slowness. She looked at Levi. 'Just kneel down facing him on the uninjured side and hold the ends firmly like handles.'

Levi knelt beside Smiley and concentrated on the task as he gathered the ends. He should be doing this, not her, but it didn't seem the right moment to pull rank on her. It had been a lot of years since he'd done any generalist work like dislocations. He'd bet she'd be wild when she found out.

She was directing them like an annoying but perky little conductor in her bra and shorts and he liked her more than when she'd been sexily annoying in her blue dress. Because she was bending towards Smiley her breasts were falling his way. In a gesture of respect he faded out her cleavage, which was no mean feat, and watched her hands.

She surprised him with her calmness and methodical approach to something he could probably have done but not as confidently as she was. Qualifications meant zip against recent experience, he reassured himself.

Sophie nodded. 'Keep both ends together under his good armpit. When I take his other arm you keep the pressure on his chest so he can't follow me.'

Levi could hear his sister mumbling behind him as she agonised over William's impending discomfort. He wished she'd be quiet.

Sophie must have heard her too. 'He'll be fine, Odette. I know we're all still shell-shocked from the crash but he'll be OK.' Sophie looked his way. 'As long as Levi doesn't tickle him, 'cause it hurts to laugh.'

Levi blinked in surprise at her comment and compressed his lips to bite back the smile. Effective stress relief. She was a tough little cookie, though he'd begun to wonder if she really was as tough as she made out, because he could detect a tiny tremor in her hands every now and then. 'Nurses have a dreadful sense of humour, eh, William?'

Smiley had his eyes shut. 'Hmm.'

But the tension had lessened a little and even Odette got the hint to relax. He watched Sophie's face as she concentrated. Something made him want to reach out and touch her arm, just for support, like he had during the flight when he realized she'd started to panic, but he didn't want to interrupt her thoughts. It was almost as if she was rehearsing the steps.

He was right. She was. Sophie knelt down and after a brief stroke of sympathy she took her brother's elbow and gently bent it so that his fingers pointed to the sky they'd just fallen out of. She didn't even want to think about sky-falling. Bend arm at ninety-degree angle from his body, Sophie recited to herself.

'Keep the pressure on now,' she said quietly to Levi, and began to pull, still gently but firmly, on the bent elbow, away from Smiley's body. Then she rotated the arm on the shoulder joint as if Smiley was trying to throw a baseball.

Sweat beaded on Smiley's forehead as she moved it slowly back and forward until the shoulder slid back into place with a click that made everyone wince.

'OK.' Now Sophie felt like crying or heaving or running away but she couldn't do any of those things. 'We need a sling.'

She looked at Smiley and he gave her a small wink. 'Thanks, Sis.'

'Don't do it again. You know I hate it.' She dropped a kiss on his forehead and Levi was there to help her stand. She hadn't even noticed he'd moved, and secretly she was glad of his support because her legs wobbled.

His hand kept hold of hers and he pulled her gently into his chest for a moment in a purely asexual embrace, though his shirt against her nose meant she could only inhale air laced with Levi. His arms rested around her back, firmly but not cloying, just for that moment so she could rest her head on him and close her eyes and regroup. Strangely, the hug wasn't an invasion of space as much as a recoup of resources and exactly what she needed.

She stepped back and his arms fell. 'Thanks. I hate doing that for him.' She flabbergasted herself with the honesty and he looked just as surprised as she did. Normally she wouldn't let anyone know when she felt overwhelmed. She prided herself on self-sufficiency and she would have thought Levi was the last person she'd want to tell about any weakness on her end. It had to be part of the shock.

She watched his hands flick the dirt from her shirt and smooth it, and he even held it out for her to slip her arms in. She felt strangely cosseted but weepy. Not something she was used to at all. And she wasn't even sure she liked the feeling. 'Well done, Sophie,' he said quietly. She couldn't meet his eyes in case he saw the glitter.

She looked at her shirt in his hands. 'Umm. I need to tear a bit off the bottom to make a sling.'

He shook his head. 'Put it on. Mine's bigger. You don't want to get a sunburnt strip around your waist.'

She took it and turned away to collect herself. A hug was OK but sympathy when she was emotional was such a pain. She sniffed unobtrusively. Men were so good at that. Twisting the knife when you were trying to gain control. She heard the rip of his shirt as he made the sling and she kept her eyes averted. She took a couple of deep breaths and turned back to face the group.

To her surprise Levi had achieved a very creditable sling. 'Distinction in a first-aid course, eh?' she said in a poor attempt of a joke. She saw the look from Odette to Levi and Levi's shake of the head but Sophie was too mentally exhausted to go there.

'Something like that.' He looked at Smiley. 'So how's the shoulder now?'

'Good as new.' They all knew it'd still be painful.

Levi gave him a crooked smile. 'I'll bet.' He glanced at Sophie. 'I can do splints and bandages but we'll do that after you check we have a water supply.'

'Yes, Captain.' She couldn't resist. 'Next time we come into land here I'll try to have a look as we approach.'

'Good idea.' He stood. 'There's a couple of water bottles in the chopper. I'll get them and check the radio if it's all cooled down a bit.' He rubbed his chin. 'Though I think I'll come with you, after I discuss something with Odette.'

Sophie sighed. He was determined, then. His funeral. She had to stop saying that. It was obviously a bad omen.

Levi hadn't been keen for her to hang around the wreck so she wandered slowly towards the gully, pleased to have a moment before he joined her.

The chance to walk away from the crash site was welcome and she dawdled along the gorge, watching the ground for signs of animals. She didn't hear him come up beside her and she jumped when he spoke.

'So you think we'll find water?'

She glanced at him. 'Pretty confident.'

'Fine,' he said, but raised his brow sceptically.

She frowned. 'The wet season's not long finished, and rock pools and depressions in the gorge floor should still hold water.' She should know. She'd walked so many gorges in her lifetime apparently preparing for just such an occasion.

Hopefully, the water wouldn't be too old either, but there'd be enough to keep them until help arrived. Which shouldn't be long if the distress call went through.

As they walked, long grey-green grasses poked out at them, and as they brushed past Sophie inhaled the warm air and everything felt brighter and cleaner—and even more precious for nearly being snatched away.

'I can't believe how close we've came to crashing badly.' It was very queer how Levi in command had lessened the horror. That they'd all managed to escape fairly unscathed so far—and that even Odette's baby hadn't been fazed by their rough landing—was a miracle assisted by Levi's determination they would survive.

Levi didn't say anything and she wondered if he'd always been this taciturn. He needed to smell the roses. They were alive!

'See how the cliffs beside us soar into the bluest sky. Don't the walls look like red-brick? It reminds you of millions of years in creation and some of the oldest dated rocks in the world, doesn't it?'

'No, Pollyanna. It reminds me we've had to force land in the middle of nowhere with very little to keep us alive.'

She frowned at him. 'Lighten up. The Aboriginal people survived.' Sophie spread her arms. 'You'll see in the overhangs and caves they'll have left their stories for us on the rock. They've been a part of this land for thousands of years. We'll manage a day or two.'

'Spare me from eternal optimism.'

'And me from a grump.'

She was only a hundred metres from the plane when she found the break in the range she was looking for. They looked back before they turned into a narrow gorge off the main escarpment but Odette and Smiley were still sitting on the boulders they'd left them on.

It was cool in the gully, the sun not yet directly overhead to shine onto the narrow strip of valley floor. 'It would be worthwhile moving the others here to get out of the sun,' she commented. 'Especially if we have to wait long for rescue.'

'I'd been just about to suggest that. You beat me to it.'

She slanted an amused glance at him. 'I'm annoying you, then?'

'Not at all.'

Liar, she thought. Tufts of sharp spinifex scratched at her ankles as she scrambled over boulders that had tumbled down from the walls, and Levi followed her. Within only a few minutes she'd come upon the first pool and she raised her brows at him. See!

'OK,' he said. 'It's water. Looks a bit green.'

'It's just starting to algae, but the middle of the pool will be clear and no doubt cold.' He didn't look convinced. 'It's a good time of the year if you have to crash,' she teased him. 'Those tiny fish don't know their pond'll disappear over the next few months.'

'I guess fish prove the water's clean enough to drink.'

'Yep. In fact, the traditional owners use bunches of sharp spinifex to brush the pools and capture the tiny fish in the barbs. Then they burn it and eat the fish. We might try that later.' She crouched at the edge to fill her bottle, peripherally aware of the snake trail to her left. The smooth indent in the fine gravel was a timely reminder to watch for basking reptiles. She had a feeling he wasn't ready to know that yet.

Levi couldn't believe this woman. She talked as if they were filming for a nature show, not about their survival in one of the most remote places in the world.

She sat back and glanced around as she screwed the lid back on the water bottle, then washed her hands before bathing her face and lower arms. His eyes were drawn to the way she slid the water over the inside of her wrists and then lifted her fingers to allow the trickles to run down her neck and beneath the collar of her blouse.

Hastily he leaned forward and rinsed his own hands. It was cold all right, just what he needed after the heat on the valley floor. Not to mention the other heat.

'So we have water, and a few tiny fish to eat. Our own bush-tucker chef. It could be worse.' He wasn't sure how.

'We're alive.'

He nodded soberly. True. All of them, and that was a miracle. No thanks to the person who'd tampered with the aircraft and the concept still had the power to make him wild enough to want to crush a rock with his bare hands.

She must have noticed his frown because she flicked a tiny drop of water at him. 'Don't suppose you fancy a witchetty grub. Apparently they taste like eggs. I can see a witchetty tree and I could dig the roots up for you.'

He had to smile. Retribution could wait. 'Pass.'

When they returned to the crash site the full extent of their miracle of survival again made itself very plain. Sophie stood for a moment and shook her head and Levi silently agreed. Pieces of the helicopter were strewn from where they first skidded down past the wreck, and the cabin itself looked more like a drink can that had been beaten by a stick than a mode of travel.

The others had moved a few feet back against the canyon wall out of the sun and sat on boulders that had fallen from the cliffs. 'You'd have to be unlucky, but I'm not sure I'd feel real comfortable waiting for another boulder to fall where they're sitting.'

Levi nodded. 'We'll move to the gorge as soon as I empty the aircraft.'

They separated, he to the aircraft and she to Odette.

CHAPTER FIVE

LEVI spread the first-aid kit and the tool box out on the ground to see what was available, and he looked up as Sophie laughed out loud at something Odette had said. At least someone could laugh about the situation they were in. His eyes were drawn to her when she stood and approached his work area.

Her white shirt was dusty and her disarranged hair looked not unlike the spinifex tufting the bottom of the canyon. Actually, she looked pretty fantastic, considering she'd had her worst nightmare confirmed by a crash landing. He'd been mulling over her behaviour since the crash while he worked and he'd come to the conclusion he'd never met a woman like her.

Her composure when she'd reduced her brother's shoulder still impressed him. She'd done a better job than he would have. It was far too long since he'd done any emergency work apart from eyes and he was glad he hadn't had to practise on Smiley.

His lack of disclosure about his medical background had become an elephant he could've done without, but it didn't seem the right moment to correct the impression he'd given. Hopefully, when he did, she'd just laugh it off, though it was unlikely, if the first conversation they'd had at Xanadu was anything to go by. The longer he left it, the bigger the elephant grew, but he really didn't have the capacity to take on a discussion of his work.

Still, she looked pretty pleased with herself and it was a bonus to find something to smile about after what he'd just discovered. 'Odette feels better?' Levi said.

'Yep. And Smiley's fine.'

'That's great.' He paused. 'Do you want the good news or the bad news?'

Her smile died and he regretted that, but he wasn't joking. 'Can I have bad and then good to cheer me up?' she asked reluctantly.

'The bad news is the radio's dead.'

'That's really bad.' Her face fell further. 'And the good news?'

'The good news is the aircraft wouldn't have gone up in flames because the fuel tank was on Empty.'

He watched her think about that until finally she said, 'Then what was the hissing?'

She had a logical mind, he'd give her that. 'The oil dripping on the hot engine.'

A tiny line crinkled between her brows. 'But how could the fuel be on Empty? I saw it at Full on the gauge.'

He had an idea but it wasn't a very nice one. 'Must have sprung a leak.'

The crinkle deepened, and actually she looked cute, but it sure wasn't the time to notice that. 'Do fuel tanks do that?'

Never in his lifetime. He sighed. 'Not usually.'

He watched her shake her head—a lot of that head shaking had been going on around here—and he wished he didn't have to explain the rest. He gave her a minute to mull it over and looked at the minimal supplies they had to survive on. Not much there, which was what he'd had a quick word to Odette about before he'd left with Sophie.

'You say the radio's dead. Why is that dead?'

He appreciated how calmly she'd taken his first news. Hysterics would have really done his head in. 'I'd like to know that too.' He saw the beginnings of comprehension as her eyes widened.

'So what are you saying? Didn't you talk to someone as we were landing? I saw your lips move.'

He remembered that moment. It hadn't been pleasant. 'I wish I could offer more reassurance but I can't. I didn't get a response so I gave the position in case they could hear me, even though I couldn't hear them. I don't know if it worked.'

She made a silent *O* with her mouth. Her face was like a book. No subterfuge. No doubt she'd scorn such a thing. She was so different from any woman he'd met and with such a well of strength that was almost scary. Thank goodness he liked his women sweet and compliant.

By now, Odette and William had left their perch on the boulders to join the others.

'It was a good idea anyway,' Sophie said earnestly, as if sorry he felt bad. She made him smile. That was twice now. Then she said, 'But you've got one of those little GPS tracker things, don't you?'

'ELT. Emergency locator transmitter.' She didn't like what she saw on his face and he watched her transfer her attention to Odette for a more palatable answer.

Odette looked up. 'It seems someone took it out and didn't replace it,' Odette said baldly.

'Someone? Took it out?' Sophie actually squeaked, and suddenly he wanted to put his arm around her, but she backed away as if she knew what he was thinking. How could she know that?

She looked at her brother but all William did was shrug his good shoulder and not comment. Levi admired him for it. There wasn't much to say as the choices were limited. Someone had tried to kill them and nearly succeeded. None of the three of them mentioned the fact the chopper had been tampered with but it simmered there between them, except that Sophie, still focused on the radio not working, didn't get it. No bonus in her knowing.

Sophie sank down on a boulder and, as an afterthought, handed the water bottle again to Odette. She closed her eyes, sighed and visibly relaxed her shoulders. Finally she mumbled, 'Glad I'm not the captain,' opened her eyes and looked straight at him. 'What's the plan? Captain.'

'Now she defers,' he said, but he was inordinately glad of her support. He wasn't quite sure when it was she'd stopped being annoying. 'William says he knows this area from mustering and there's an Aboriginal community a day's walk away if we head north. I'm thinking William and Odette should stay here, and you and I walk out and get help.'

She chewed her lip and glanced around the desolate landscape. 'It's breaking the first rule. Leaving the site. We're not that far from the desert and the sun's a furnace in the sky until five.' She looked at the supplies. 'But there's not a lot to eat out here once we get through the picnic basket.'

'My thoughts exactly.'

She narrowed her eyes. 'If we give them today to send a search party staying put is a good thing.' She looked at his sister and Levi had to keep from shaking his head in disbelief. She seemed so calm about the whole thing. 'How do you feel about that, Odette?' she said. As if it was a mundane cancellation of an appointment.

He watched his sister struggle to match her composure and he wished, fruitlessly, he'd been more firm when she'd been so determined to leave Sydney with him.

Odette brushed the hair off her forehead. 'William can't walk far and I'm not much better. As long as we have water and a bit of food we'll be fine for a day, I guess.'

Sophie nodded and he thanked God again he'd been stranded with sensible people. He wondered if all of the people who lived out here in the back of beyond were like Sophie and William.

Apart from the fact that maybe someone was trying

to kill his sister and him—but that was unproven—the place was growing on him.

'So we leave tomorrow morning early, do you think?' Sophie said.

He almost smiled again. She couldn't help being bossy, though he suspected she'd push herself harder than anyone else. 'Sounds like a plan.'

She nodded and stood. 'What would you like me to do?'

He was right. 'We'll collect wood first for a signal fire, then some for the camp tonight.'

'Sure.' Sophie stopped beside Odette again. 'No pains?' He could almost see the priorities ticking off in her mind.

Odette shook her head but her hand slid protectively over her stomach, as if to ward off the idea. William reached over with his good arm and caught her fingers and held them. Odette squeezed back.

'I'd hate to be the one who's pregnant,' William said.

Levi looked at Sophie. He'd been avoiding that horror. Unfortunately he knew the danger to his sister lay in the sudden deceleration of their landing. Forces that could tear an inelastic placenta off an elastic uterus. He'd seen that in the brief time he'd had in obstetrics, but there was nothing they could do at this moment except watch her.

Sophie crouched down, obviously thinking the same thing because she said, 'So how long since we crashed?'

'I thought it was a forced landing.' Levi pretended to be offended.

'I'm sorry,' she said over her shoulder as she faced Odette. 'How long is it since your incredible brother managed to avert disaster and get us to the ground safely, Odette?' There was humour in the words but none in her voice. She meant every word and he was surprised how they unexpectedly warmed the place that had iced over with the knowledge of foul play.

He'd never thought of himself as needy and he stamped the feeling out.

Odette looked at her watch. 'It feels like minutes but about an hour and a half?'

Sophie crouched and her hand hovered above Odette's uterus. 'May I?' She waited for permission, then rested her hand on the baby bulge. 'I'm thinking the first four hours are the most likely time you'd start contracting if there'd been any problems due to the landing. It's fabulous you haven't gone into labour already. But tell me if you get regular pains.'

Odette shook her head, as if by denying it, it wouldn't happen. 'Don't wish that on me.'

Sophie shook her head vehemently. 'I'm not, believe me. The longer it holds off the less likely your baby has any ill effects from the events.'

Odette chewed her lip as she stroked her belly. 'It's not quite the home birth I'd envisaged.'

Sophie rolled her eyes. 'It's not the day any of us envisaged, except maybe me when we took off.' She smiled ruefully. 'And I apologise if I brought us all bad luck.'

Not the person to blame. 'If it's someone's fault,' Levi said drily, 'it certainly wasn't yours.' He stood. 'I used to be a pretty mean Boy Scout so reckon I could manage a fire in case a plane flies over.'

'Then I'll start collecting wood as soon as we get to the gully.' Sophie looked around. 'So we'll need a campfire and a signal fire?'

Odette wiped her face. 'It's so hot. Hard to imagine we'll need heat.'

'It'll be cold tonight,' Smiley offered and squeezed Odette's hand. Poor Smiley. He'd hate being unable to help. Sophie was glad he was there for Odette. She'd the feeling if he hadn't been Odette would have succumbed to hysterics by now and that wouldn't have been fun. To give her due, she was a city girl and where they'd crashed was as far as she'd get from a city.

Odette scuffed at the dry grass beneath her feet. 'What if we start a bushfire?'

'As long as it blows the other way it's all good,' Smiley said, and spread the map one-handed that Levi had given him from the wreck.

He didn't enlarge so Sophie finished the sentence. 'In the Kimberleys bushfires are a way of life. We try to burn off the whole area every couple of years. Even as far out as here. The Aboriginal people have been burning off for thousands of years. For them it means the scrub stays sparse and they can see the animals they want to hunt. A lot of the trees and shrubs around here don't germinate until they've been through a fire. From our point of view, frequent fires germinate the land and prevent a massive fire that would be impossible to control.'

They packed up their meagre belongings and began

walking towards the gully. Odette gazed around at, what was to her, desolate landscape. 'It's so sparse and different from anywhere I've ever been,' Odette said, as if they'd landed on the moon.

'William and I love it.' Sophie thought of Perth for the first time that day, only the second time since she'd seen Levi. Now that was queer. 'Perth's a pretty place—it has the ocean,' she said, trying to be fair but Brad lived there. 'I wouldn't live anywhere else than here though.' She looked at Levi as she spoke, and remembered that his appreciation of her land was confined to flying over it.

He raised his brows. 'Don't look at me like that. The Kimberleys are growing on me. Though you have great rivers and can't swim in them. And apparently it's the same in the ocean up here.'

'Maybe, but we have rock pools and gorges that are fine. You just have to know where it's safe and where it's not. We're fine here from crocs, but watch the snakes as we walk.'

Levi glanced at his horrified sister and made a strangled sound but Sophie couldn't read anything in his face. Had he just laughed at her?

'I hate snakes.' Odette shuddered.

'If you see one just stop or back off real slowly. They panic too and are just as likely to run the same way as you and you'll think they're chasing you.'

'It won't be really chasing me. OK.' Odette shuddered again.

Levi was watching Sophie and she'd swear he was amused, even though his mouth didn't move. 'So you're a snake lover too?'

Sophie shook her head. 'It's their home too. Someone once told me that a snake has a really short memory, about forty seconds, which always makes me smile when I see one. I imagine them forgetting I'm there.'

After that conversation, when they moved up next to the mouth of the gully, Odette's head swivelled like one of those toy nodding dogs people used to sit on the back window of their cars. She walked with her brother, her hand tightly gripped to his arm.

Smiley leaned heavily on his stick with Sophie on his other side. 'I feel so bloody useless,' he said quietly.

'You're helping Odette which is great. She needs your calm. Will you manage when we go?'

Smiley looked around to ensure the others weren't in earshot. 'As long as she doesn't have the baby.'

Sophie whispered, 'It's just like a calf, Smiley, or a foal.'

He choked back a laugh. 'Great.' They grinned at each other. 'You'll run through a couple of things with me before you leave though?' he said. She nodded. She had to believe Odette wouldn't go into labour in the day they'd be away. It was too frightening a thought. Not that there was anything they could change.

Smiley examined the spot she'd chosen and nodded. 'At least up here I can get my own water.'

'It'll be tricky but you could.'

Levi came up to them with a long branch of dead wood he'd picked up on the way. 'We'll be out of the weather if one of the sudden tropical storms blows up.'

Everyone pitched in and there was a lip of overhang just past the entrance where they'd packed their supplies against the wall.

The afternoon passed as they watched for rescue, without reward, and prepared for the night. Back out in the main canyon they'd erected a signal fire with green leaves on top for smoke as a way to flag down a search plane if one flew over them, but the sky remained blue and clear of aircraft.

Technically they wouldn't be missed at Xanadu until almost nightfall. They'd told Steve they'd be back by late afternoon so they were not technically even missing yet.

Levi began to cut the long grass that Sophie suggested they use for beds for the night along the overhang, while she cleared the ground in front so they could make a fire to keep everyone warm. With the wall behind them the heat would be caught and the flames would keep any animals away.

At four o'clock they sat back and Sophie could see the activity had raised Odette's spirits. 'I'd say we're a clever bunch. We could make it on one of those television survivor shows.'

'Except there's no camera man with a satellite phone.' Odette looked at the depleted picnic basket. 'Who wants to go to the shop for a treat?'

Sophie spread her arms. 'There's plenty to eat around here.'

Levi dropped the last of the sticks for the night fire. 'Spare me from Pollyanna with bush tucker,' Levi said. 'Not witchetty grubs, I hope.'

Sophie refused to be downcast by the lack of enthusiasm. 'Must admit I've never been a fan of the old grub. Though they say ten grubs a day is enough for survival.' Levi didn't look convinced, so Sophie pushed on. 'And I did find a Gubinge tree up one of the gullies. I'll show you where, before dark, in case you want some tomorrow, Odette.' She held up the small greenish-yellow fruit which looked more like a pale pecan nut than a fruit. 'Known also as a Kakadu plum, it's easy to eat.'

Smiley sat quietly amused during her lecture and declined to sample the fruit. She frowned at him for not offering support but forgave him for the discomfort he was still in. No doubt he still felt sick and sore but he wasn't complaining. He never did. Actually, nobody was, so maybe she should revise her opinion a little about some city people.

She directed her attention to Levi and Odette and bit bravely into the skin. The tanginess twisted on her tongue and she fought to keep her face straight as she chewed and swallowed. 'Food for indigenous people for thousands of years and apparently has a hundred times more vitamin C than an orange.' She licked her lips and tried to define the taste. 'The juice crosses between a pear and an apple. There's a zing which I think is from the vitamin C but see what you think.' She tossed one each to Odette and Levi. 'Either way, it's the perfect refreshment if we're right out of grocery shops.'

'Bush tucker.' Levi looked at her from under his brows as if to say, *Are you having us on?* When she nodded encouragingly he bit into the fruit, and then finished it off. 'Not addictive, but not bad.'

Sophie nodded. 'We'll take some with us when we walk out.'

'Awesome.' He rubbed his hands together facetiously. So he did have a sense of humour. Now that was something Brad never had, and why she should think of Brad and Levi in the same minute sent a tiny flicker of fear into her belly which she was determined to ignore.

CHAPTER SIX

JUST before dawn the next morning, when the night birds were settling and the morning budgerigars shared their chatter, Levi and Sophie prepared to leave camp. The gentle breeze lifted the bumps on Sophie's arms and the ground crackled cold and hard beneath her socks. She tucked her chin into her collar as she pulled on her boots.

She glanced across to where Levi wore Smiley's broad Akubra and looked disturbingly like a country man rather than the city slicker she didn't trust. Much more dependable and much more dangerous to her peace of mind.

Sophie could smile at the image of her brother scowling uncomfortably in a baseball cap as he'd handed over his prized possession but not at the image of Levi. What was she doing heading off into the bush with a man she barely knew and didn't even trust?

Then again, there wasn't a lot she could do about it, except be constantly alert for any suspicious behaviour on his part.

Sophie jammed on her own Akubra, and thanked the last fading stars of the night she'd worn sturdy walking shoes, something she needed most places in the Kimberley.

During the night they'd all managed to sleep in snatches after the emotional trauma of the day, and even Odette, apart from the indigestion and backache she normally suffered from, didn't seem any worse for the experiences of the day before.

'Your baby must be one tough little munchkin, Odette,' Sophie said, as she finished her weak tea from the one shared tea bag discovered at the bottom of her bag and boiled over the campfire.

'Tougher than his mother,' Odette said with a wobble in her voice. The young mum's eyes were heavily shadowed and her fingers stroked her belly, as if to re-assure herself and her baby that everything would be fine.

Sophie tamped down her own misgivings. Odette and her baby were the greatest worry. 'I think you're holding up amazingly well.' She tipped out the dregs and rinsed the one cup before she slid her bag over her shoulder. 'We'll be as quick as we can. Your baby needs you to be calm. We've done the hard part and survived the landing. You'll have something to tell the grandchildren about in thirty years.'

'If I have grandchildren.'

Sophie frowned. 'You've water and some food and a safe place.' She paused. 'No matter what happens, don't leave this spot,' Sophie reminded her. 'Sighting of the crash site is still the most probable way for rescue, and lost in the bush is the easiest way to die.'

Odette scrubbed her eyes again and the mascara from yesterday was giving her a sad-and-sorry panda look. 'I'm not going anywhere but I wish I'd never left home.'

Sophie felt the loss of the woman who'd touched up her lipstick at the clinic only a few short days ago. 'I know. It's natural to worry about your baby. You're the one with most to fear. But hey, I'd like to think I'd do as well as you are.'

Odette sniffed. 'You wouldn't cry like I do.'

Sophie hugged her and whispered, 'Didn't you see me yesterday after setting William's shoulder? I was a mess.'

Odette scrubbed her eyes with the back of her hand and peered at Sophie, who nodded. 'Really? I didn't see that.'

'Good,' Sophie said and looked around to make sure none of the men had heard. 'But I felt better afterwards.'

'I'll never be as strong as you but thanks for telling me. It helps to know I'm not the only one who can't help it sometimes.'

'I know. And I'm not that strong. Just on the out-side.' Sophie glanced at her brother, who was probably giving Levi some pointers as well. 'Look,' she said. 'This isn't going to happen, but if you do go into labour, stay cuddled up to William. He'll look after you. Rest and remember you're designed to do it. Be calm and let it happen. Babies only need to be next to their mother. And remember, first babies take a long time and we'll be back. Don't give up on us.'

Odette shook her head and her eyes filled again with tears. 'You shouldn't go. Levi shouldn't leave me.' She clutched at Sophie's arm. 'Don't leave!'

Sophie drew the younger woman into her arms and hugged her. 'You'll be fine. We'll be back as quick as we can, but we need to walk out before it gets too hot.'

Odette started to cry and Sophie chewed her lip and glanced at Levi. She'd made everything worse.

Levi crossed to his sister and drew her into the circle of his arms. 'Shh, honey. One day away. That's all it'll take. You and William have a day on the land, relax and enjoy the scenery.'

Odette hiccoughed, 'Relax?' Her lip quivered as Levi handed her over to William to comfort. 'Please be careful,' Odette said to her brother.

He nodded. 'We'll be back for you in another chopper.'

'He'll fly back for you,' Sophie said drily. 'I'll be cheering from home.'

Odette's lips tugged in an almost smile. 'Chicken.'

'We won't be long.' Levi sighed. Such a dilemma. He hated to leave Odette, and the thought of her going into labour out here without him made him break into a cold sweat. Please God, don't let that happen. He'd spent his life trying to keep her safe and he'd failed dismally.

But he couldn't send Sophie off on her own, even though he suspected she'd be tougher in the outback than him.

He did have faith in William though—not quite sure

how that happened—and they'd be as quick as they could, but there was no use waiting for a rescue that might never happen before they tried to walk out.

They left without looking back and he felt like a deserter as he followed Sophie down a natural trail. Initially he tried to choose the direction but his feet seemed to find the ground more uneven than Sophie did, and eventually he fell in behind her because it was easier going. It felt strange to let another person lead, let alone a woman.

The rocks shifted under his feet as his ankles threatened to twist on the uneven path. It made sense if the whole place was the result of erosion but it made walking fraught for injury.

When he thought about it they'd taken a lot for granted to head off into the hills. He caught up with Sophie and walked beside her. 'I've just had a nasty thought. Actually, we're relying on William's memory of a nomad's camp, from a muster that happened over a year ago?'

She glanced across at him. 'That's what we all decided on.'

He pushed aside a branch that reached across their path. 'What if the camp moved on, which I imagine is likely.'

She raised her eyebrows. 'We can hope the camp moved closer, then, and not further away.'

That was simple, he thought wryly. 'I love the way your mind works.' He bent down and picked up a walking-stick-size branch, tested it and then used it to part the grass in front.

She grinned at him and he found himself grinning back. 'Optimism is the code of the Kimberley.'

Was this woman for real? 'Spare me, Pollyanna. You just made that up.'

'Yep. But you can't change what you can't change.' She glanced around as the first rays of light warned of sunrise. 'More likely a hunter will find us than we'll find them anyway.'

He hadn't thought of that. 'Do they do that? I thought it was all in movies and fiction.'

'The medicine man knows if someone who shouldn't be there is around. I'm just hoping they find us sooner rather than later.'

The growing light allowed them to see the ground in front of them more clearly as the sun crept closer to rising. He'd be interested to see the pace she'd keep up when she could see properly. 'Can we do this? Walk out safely?'

She stopped and looked at him. 'We can be sensible, yes, and cut down the risks, but it's a big land under a bigger sun.' She glanced at the imminent sunrise. 'We should move faster while we can.'

The morning blurred into a fast-paced bushwalk. Sophie pointed out another Gubinge tree and he began to see others now that he recognised them.

She showed him the low-growing, wide-leafed bush tomatoes, which looked more like brown raisins. 'But you have to eat the ripe ones. The green ones are toxic like green potatoes.'

She picked a few and offered him one. When he didn't look inspired she ate one herself and grimaced.

'They're talking about growing these commercially for a savoury spice. They're pretty pungent but you never know when you'll need them.'

He was over bush tucker. It was pretty hard to be the protective male when she held all the cards. A very novel experience for a man who'd always been the one people came to for help. 'Have you ever been to Sydney?' he said.

She didn't even look at him. 'No.'

'Maybe one day I'll show you my favourite restaurant. The chef is one of the top three in Australia.' He'd actually quite like that.

She looked at him as if he'd offered a space shuttle to the moon. 'You think?'

Apparently it wasn't on her wish list. She had to be good for his conceited soul. He laughed and followed her along another ridge that boarded a treeless plain he hoped they didn't have to cross, but she was heading in that direction. Assuming she knew where she was going.

Almost as if she heard his thoughts she paused. 'If we keep the sun on our right shoulder we should be heading north. There's a dry creek bed through the middle of the plain and maybe even a few of the pools will have water in them. We'll conserve what we have and try to make it to the next gorge, and I'm expecting more water by midday. Then we'll rest.'

Unobtrusively he pulled his compass from his pocket and checked what she said. She was right! What did he expect? It was pretty different taking orders from a woman and actually not minding it.

Though he hadn't minded his first-grade teacher either. Miss Tee was a honey and the first woman he'd ever fallen in love with. Probably because she liked to take them outside for games when they got bored with English, but he did remember her long, long legs, like Sophie's. Though he conceded Sophie's legs were even better.

She walked with a loose-limbed gait, sure-footedly in her lace-up leather boots and her knee-length shorts that it seemed women wore here. And despite her determination to appear always in command, she couldn't hide her femininity. Her bottom still jiggled.

He realised how few women he'd seen since he'd been here, and they'd all been wearing those knee-length shorts. Maybe that was why she looked so good. Lack of competition. But he didn't think so. He had a feeling she'd look good on a rue in Paris. He caught her glancing at him and it made him smile more.

'What are you smiling at?'

He straightened his face. 'I've only seen four women since I arrived a week ago. And one of them is my sister.'

She flicked her brows up and down. 'Bet that's different to your usual day.' Was that sarcasm?

She had no idea what his life was like. The hours he worked. The impact of having to tell a patient he couldn't save their sight or the sight of their child—the main reason he'd been unable to get here sooner as he'd tried to clear a backlog of people who needed him desperately. How he'd started to think he'd never be able to make a dent in the need out there. 'Yeah, well, it's hard running a playboy mansion.'

She stopped and faced him. 'You run a playboy mansion?'

That actually hurt. Did she really think him that shallow? Nothing like his surgery full of people with visual nightmares. 'It was a joke.'

She brushed his comment away. 'Good. Don't worry. We get women here. When the tourist season properly starts the Gibb River Road really moves. Campers and off-road vehicles everywhere and the resorts fill up. You'll see plenty of ladies then, if you're still here.' She started walking again and he nearly missed her final comment. 'Which you shouldn't be for someone just passing through.'

She'd brought it up again. Wait till she found out about the other, but he didn't have the energy to go into why he didn't want to talk about work. 'Are you ever going to forgive me for a throwaway comment?'

She looked at him innocently. 'Sure. Nothing to forgive. I just don't trust you.'

Be warned, he told himself. To her, he said, 'Nice.'

She ignored his comment and went back to their original conversation. 'The tourist season is only for a few months from April until the humidity comes back again in October-November. Most people leave then because a person sweats like a horse as soon as they step outside.'

He thought about what she said, wondered about the implications on the health resources from the influx of older travellers for such small amounts of health personnel, but if he commented he might end up embroiled in more lies. Better to leave well enough alone, which was a shame, because he'd begun to value her opinion on a lot of things.

They walked on for an hour without talking and surprisingly it was quite companionable. He couldn't remember the last time he'd been with a woman without feeling he had to make the running or listen to a one-way conversation.

He looked to the scenery ahead and there was more of the same to come. 'So tell me about the camp we're heading to.'

She jolted out of her reverie. 'The family tribe we're looking for is semi-nomadic most of the year. They've returned to the old ways and move with the food, so that means berries available, fattest kangaroos, and they rely on guessing the weather.'

He glanced at the bare plains. 'Do they come into town much?'

'The young men muster when needed and that's how Smiley knows about them. I haven't actually met this family but they'd have met other nurses from other towns. I'd like to see if they want the kids immunised and all's well, so it's a bonus.'

He bit back another laugh. A bonus helicopter crash. So pleased he could accommodate her. He'd never understand her.

They walked until the sun was directly overhead and with relief they entered the foothills of the next range and what little shade that offered.

He was determined he wasn't going to ask for a rest, but he'd used most of his water, except for a little he kept in case she needed it. Not that he imagined she'd ask. But enough unusual things had happened to them over the past twenty-four hours; he wasn't guaranteeing they wouldn't have more excitement.

'There looks to be a subtropical pocket ahead, that's promising,' she said, and he could hear the note of weariness in her voice. Strangely, his own tiredness seemed to melt away and he quickened his step. 'Let me lead for a while—I can see where you mean—and you might catch a little shade from my back.'

'I'm fine.'

'I know. You're amazing. Let me do this bit until we stop. Give me your pack.' When she hesitated, he added, 'For goodness sake, let me feel a little useful.'

'Fine.' She stopped and he overtook her, glancing at her face as he passed. Her cheeks were pink with the heat, and she didn't meet his eyes, but she looked tired, then he was past and she fell into step behind him.

Within half an hour they'd moved from the grass of the plains to the spiral Pandanas of the semi-rainforest, and not much further on they found larger boulders and finally a small pool of algoid water.

The creek bed sloped up the gully and Sophie pointed to the narrowing gorge higher up. 'If we climb a little we'll find cleaner water, and it's probably worth the effort. We'll stay here for a couple of hours until the sun is well behind our backs.'

They both needed to rest, which would be hard with the idea of Odette still back at the wreck site, but Sophie was as aware of that as he.

'No problem,' Levi said. 'You said you'd find water. This place is amazing.' He looked around at the narrow strip of tropical foliage which seemed so out of place in the arid areas they'd just trekked through. There was a definite line where wet met dry and the rest of the gorge stretched away from them back to the plain of red dirt and spinifex.

He heaved himself up and around a few larger boulders and the subtle sound of running water gurgled more loudly.

'The flow must have disappeared into an underground creek because there's no flow further down,' she said.

He looked back and all he could see, water wise, was the green pool. She was a cluey little thing.

One last steep-sided boulder, room-size, stood between them and a ring of promising palm trees, but it was too high to step up onto. He wedged himself between the gorge wall and the boulder and crab walked up the gap, and he was quietly pleased he'd mastered the indoor rock climbing he enjoyed in his youth. Crumbly rock grated against his arm as he heaved himself up and it felt good to do something physical apart from walking. When he craned his neck back the sky was decorated with a palm tree on an impossible angle that arched for the sun.

Then he was up. Not easy but worth it. 'This is great,' he called down to her. The rocky pool lay fringed with ferns. Set deep in the gully under the fuzzy roots of an outstretched palm was a big bath-size rock pool catching the water from above.

'The water's clean and deep.'

When he turned to offer his hand, he expected her

to shimmy up with his support, but she hesitated and turned her head to search for an alternative route, which was crazy when he could see her shoulders droop with weariness. Stubborn little thing.

He felt another spurt of impatience with her reluctance to touch him. His hand fell as he considered her refusal. There was a limit to independence. He'd thought they'd got over that in the walk. Some of his pleasure in the spot dissipated but he tried to keep his voice reasonable.

'I don't bite.' He held his hand out again. 'There's a nice pool up here. Why skin your knees when I can help you up?'

She brushed the hair from her face and looked at him, as if measuring the danger, and the skidding of her eyes confirmed it was the idea of contact that had her worried. He didn't get it.

'You're right,' she said. Finally she took his hand, and he was surprised at how much that meant that she'd decided to trust him. It was a beginning but he wasn't sure of what.

He lifted her easily, which helped his ego no end, and he acknowledged to himself he was a sad case, until she was balanced on the rock beside him and could see the pool and the tiny waterfall at one end.

'Nice.' A tired smile. 'Thanks,' and she moved from him to the other side of the pool, well away from his zone.

They both looked at the pool, he from his side and she from hers. Tiny fish flickered at the edge of the water and the gurgle of the water over rocks from the waterfall dominated the sounds of the bush.

He crouched down and rinsed his water bottle before he drank deeply, then refilled the one in his bag as well. She did the same and he looked across the small expanse of water at her bent head. He didn't get why she was so quiet. 'Is there something you're worried about or not telling me?'

She jumped. He saw it. 'What?' Her voice faltered and then strengthened. 'You mean apart from falling out of the sky? Or having to trek in the sun through a desert to get help?' She raised her eyebrows. 'No. Why should I be worried?'

She had a point but the answer was too glib. He guessed her issues weren't for sharing, then. 'Fine.' He should leave her be, stop trying to get her attention. The woman could make him edgy and awkward like a pimply teenager and he didn't like the sensation. He undid his laces and slipped off his boots and socks. Then he pulled his shirt off. When he reached for his shorts she squeaked and he looked across.

Her eyes had widened. 'What are you doing?'

He stopped and looked around for a reason he shouldn't. 'Bathing. I'm hot and bothered and it looks good.' He raised his eyebrows. 'Is there a problem?'

'Only if you take much more off.' She looked away. 'I'm not used to men stripping in front of me.'

No one had ever complained about his body before. He slid his shorts down and stepped out of them. His boxers were black and perfectly discreet. 'I'll keep that in mind,' he said as he balanced precariously on the uneven stones at the edge of the pool. He realised he had his belly sucked in and almost blew it by laughing out loud. She wouldn't be looking anyway.

He'd turned into a peacock but reality was bringing him down. 'These rocks are nasty on bare feet.' In fact, they hurt like hell as he tried to ease into the water without damage to his toes. The rocks shifted and poked him, as if they were intent on unbalancing him.

He'd have to describe the smile she gave him as evil. 'Yes, aren't they?' She sat without making any move to undress.

She had to be as hot as he was. 'You coming in?'

'I'll see if anything bites you first.' Her voice was deadpan and he had no idea if she was serious or not.

Nice. 'What happened to the lady who said I did a good job of landing the chopper?'

Sophie didn't know. All of a sudden she was fighting to keep distance from him and it was getting harder and harder. She wasn't sure when it happened. Just little moments from after the crash when he'd given her that extra bit of support. An embrace, held her shirt.

Or this morning when she knew he'd be as hot as she was, and never complained once so that she had to keep reminding herself that he was from the city and wasn't used to their headlong scramble over the plains and gorges. He probably worked out on some treadmill in a swanky gym for hours like Brad had.

But she thought the big moment had been when he'd suggested she walk behind him to shade her from the sun and offered to carry her bag. The idea was sweet, and thoughtful, useless because the sun had been overhead, but still… Then that was followed by the constant view of sinewy ripples of muscle in his shoulders through his shirt and strong, determined thighs in his jeans as he walked ahead of her. Not fair.

How was a girl supposed to keep her head when he looked so darn strong and confident? She was tired and starting to doubt that she would be able to find the tribe and shouldn't have agreed to leave Odette in case she birthed with just Smiley there.

And just now, when he'd reached down with those big, capable hands, when he was supposed to be city soft and reliant on her, she knew if she let him she'd just sail to the top of the rock with no effort. That was when she'd got scared. When she'd started to realise he was occupying too much of her mind space.

In fact, nearly all of her mind, as she blanked out the horror of the past twenty-four hours and the fear that she'd made some dangerously bad decisions.

That sort of thing would make you think of mortality, with the good things in life she'd like to taste before the end.

But this wasn't the end. This was just a scary interlude and they would get help, and Odette would be fine. Levi and his sister would fly back to Sydney in a few days and everyone in the Kimberleys would forget them. Even Sophie Sullivan. And they would forget her.

Levi's voice broke into her thoughts. 'I said, nothing bit me, are you coming in?'

She wouldn't mind but it was a very small pool. 'It looks cold.'

CHAPTER SEVEN

LEVI floated on his back which gave her too good a view of his chest and shoulders. She swallowed. She'd known it. Levi without his shirt was a bad thing. 'Deliciously cool and I feel one hundred percent better than I did before I got in,' he said lazily.

His hair was plastered to his head and droplets ran down his strong chin and dripped onto his chest, and she couldn't help comparing him to Brad. Poor Brad.

Levi had corded bulk, not just smooth skin, and the ripples and dips of his six-pack made even Smiley look like a kid. Her stomach knotted and she looked away. She'd never seen such a discreetly muscular man in her life and no matter how much she tried to lie to herself she couldn't help but find him powerfully attractive.

If she got in she could float with her face away from him, whereas it would look silly for her to turn her back now, and he'd already seen her bra.

'Turn around, then.' She waited until his water-speckled back teased her again and then hurriedly stripped off her shoes and socks and trousers, and draped her shirt close to the edge where she could get it as soon as she left the water.

She eased herself down on her bottom. She'd been bruised before by the piled rocks getting into pools, and local knowledge suggested sliding in from a low height. The bottom of the pool would only be waist height if she were to stand but deep enough to hide under, and oh so cool and wonderful after the distance they'd walked in the heat this morning.

The water eddied up her legs and thighs with delicious coolness. Her breath sucked in as the water passed her stomach and breasts, and then came the final shiver as she submerged her shoulders until only her nose and eyes were showing. Not much for him to look at.

She surfaced her mouth again, enough to say, 'I'm in,' and then sank back to nose level.

'You sure you can breathe?' His eyes laughed at her and his mouth curved in that killer smile she'd known would be lethal. Now he had to pull that one out of his arsenal. Darn him.

'What happens if I make a wave?' He crossed his hands and threatened to ripple the water and sink her.

She tried to imagine him as a scrubby toddler, as Odette's teasing brother, as anything but the hunk across from her. She pulled her mouth out of the water. 'Some boys never grow up. Once a bully, always a bully. I bet you were the head of the pack at school. One of those boys who tell everyone else what to do.'

They'd floated quite close now—she on her front

using her hands along the bottom in the shallow places
to drift around the pool. The brilliant idea of maintaining distance and turning her back had been forgotten
as she waited, surprisingly intrigued, for him to
answer.

A shadow passed his face. 'Being at the top of the
pile is much more comfortable than being on the bottom. But I'm not a bully.'

She sniffed and paddled some more. 'That's what
all bullies say.'

He shook his head. 'My father bullied my mother,
even into another baby when she wasn't well enough
to have one—Odette—until it killed her, and I swore
I'd never condone it. Apparently my grandfather, a
very rich man who didn't need to be grasping, was not
a nice person either, so maybe he got it from there.'

A tantalising glimpse at the life of Levi the child
was not something she'd expected and it touched a
maternal instinct bone she didn't know she had. And
didn't need. Please don't tell me more. She didn't want
to know. Really she didn't.

A wild budgerigar, bright green and busy, hopped
with his mate and chattered in a tree above their heads
and she gazed up at it, trying to form the sentence to
change the subject. 'Did he make life hard for you?'
Not the words she intended.

'Not me. While I was young and vulnerable I wasn't
there enough to be harmed by my father. I had an older
brother who bore the brunt in holidays. Kyle was one
of life's gentle men who shielded me. He made sure I
knew the difference between good and bad behaviour

and what was right. I'm eternally grateful to him for that.'

'You said "had"?'

He looked through her. 'He died, when I was thirteen. He had macular degeneration, went blind, then stepped out in front of a truck. My father said Kyle knew the truck was coming. I called him a liar.' He fingered the scar on his chin.

Sophie wanted to reach out and comfort him. 'What do *you* say?'

He focused on her face. 'Never. Kyle hated being blind but he loved us too much to think of leaving us alone.'

She could easily imagine how awful it would be for a young boy losing his big brother, after losing his mother.

'I took over the protector role and made sure Odette was never worried by him.' He rubbed the scar again and she wondered if that was how he got it. No wonder he worried about Odette. He'd feel he had to do for her what Kyle had done for him.

'That's a terrible tragedy for your family to go through.'

He shrugged. 'Even the strongest of us are shaped by events in our childhood.' He shook the droplets of water from his hair as if to shake off the past. 'What about you? There's just you and William?'

She sank back further in the water, loosening her neck as she realised she'd tensed her shoulders while he'd shared his past. 'Just Smiley and me. Our parents died four years ago—truck accident—so I guess we were lucky we weren't children. Smiley's easy to live with and we both have work we love.'

'Smiley. Great name.'

A vision of her brother, tall and serious, with just a twinkle in his eye to let her know he found something she'd said amusing, was the one solid thing in her life. The one person she could trust. But she couldn't quiet that voice that said there were facets in Levi that appealed to her, and not just the external ones, and maybe she could learn to trust him too.

He floated to the edge of the pool and rested his back against a flat rock while he considered her. 'So who let you down and broke your heart?'

Just when she thought she might trust him. 'What makes you think my heart's been broken?'

He shrugged. 'OK. So who let you down?'

She never talked about it. Smiley hadn't asked. Her friend, Kate, had a new baby on the way and was immersed in her new husband. Kate didn't need Sophie's baggage. She'd come back from Perth and buried the lot.

Suddenly it was easy to talk. 'Some guy I worked with.' Was he really interested in this? She glanced across at him and then away. Something in his face told her he hadn't asked her lightly. That he genuinely wanted to understand and she guessed it would help explain why she was the way she was.

The picture of Brad in her mind wasn't quite as sharp as it had been. One good thing. 'He was the head of Obstetrics, in my training hospital actually. Born in Australia but his parents were wealthy immigrants.

He never talked about where their money came from. I guess he grew up with different values than I did.'

'In what way?' He asked the question quietly, not demanding. If she didn't want to answer she didn't have to, but maybe she needed to clarify what went wrong in her own mind.

'The way he treated people.' Yep, that was what she'd disliked the most. 'Like they were servants under his feet. He wanted old money joined with his new wealth. I kept telling him I had no money, but he was so impressed that my great-great-grandfather was one of the first settlers in Western Australia. Kept telling people when he introduced me. That I had a history his family didn't have. Had this funny idea that because two generations ago my great-grandfather opened up the Kimberleys it made me almost outback royalty.'

'Princess Sophie,' he teased.

'Yeah, right. Not a lot of call for a crown out here in the heat and the dust.'

He shredded a leaf while he listened. 'So what attracted you to him?'

She looked past Levi into the fronds behind him. 'The usual, I guess. Not that I'd actually fallen for anyone like him before. He was good-looking, quite powerful, and in the beginning he wanted to do the things I really enjoyed.' She shrugged. 'He courted me—the old-fashioned way—and I liked that.' She avoided his eyes. 'I'm not a person who is easy with casual sex.'

She looked up to see him slap his own hand. 'I'd never have guessed.' She'd swear he was laughing at her but it was strangely liberating to say the things she hadn't said out loud before.

She pulled a face. 'And you're a smart alec.'

He held his hands up. 'I'm sorry. Couldn't resist. So what happened?'

She couldn't believe she was talking about this. 'He changed. Oh, he started off doing the things I wanted to do. Walks, sailing, museums, but really he wanted great restaurants, opening-night shows, to be seen. To show me off on his arm. Don't get me wrong, that was nice too, but when I agreed to marry him it was as if he lost respect for me. I became his property.' And he demanded the sex I hadn't felt ready for, but she didn't say that. 'I had to wear the clothes he bought me. Sign the prenuptial agreement. He'd check my jewellery and shoes and handbag and make sure I had it all coordinated. Had to attend the chosen beauty salon once a week, and he began to talk about me giving up my job.'

Levi whistled. 'That's a few rules.'

'Tell me about it.'

Then Levi asked, 'Did you ever love him?' She really didn't know. She'd thought she had, would have sworn it when they became engaged, but she could see now the unease that had grown enormous had always been there from the beginning.

'I must have because I put up with my reservations by thinking he knew better. Then he began to phone me any time day or night on my mobile. Keeping track. Started this campaign of speak when spoken to.'

'That must have been hard.' Levi tried to keep the smile hidden but he could feel his lips twitch.

She frowned and then reluctantly smiled. He guessed she hadn't succeeded. 'My word it was.'

Not a nice man for Sophie. No wonder she jumped half the time. Levi knew those kinds of men. Image was all-important. And the women had to be aware of the rules. Rules that didn't apply to the men.

He asked the hard one. 'And was he faithful?'

'I thought so.' She looked away. 'I was a fool.'

Levi saw the flash of hurt. The fact that she went on said a lot for her strength and honesty and he had a sudden desire to meet and deal with the jerk for her. And comfort Sophie.

'He'd been sleeping with his secretary the whole time. So everyone knew. He'd told more lies than rocks in this pool.' She glanced at the pebble-lined bath they lay in. 'Apparently it'd been going on for years but he'd never offered to marry her.' Sophie shook her head. 'What offended me the most was his girlfriend wasn't good enough to marry—only to sleep with. Creep.'

Maybe Sophie had given him what he deserved anyway. He wouldn't put it past her. 'What did you do?'

'I sold his ring and gave the money to the homeless. I told him and then I came back home. To Smiley. Got on with my life in a place where people say what they mean and don't cheat. And with a chip on my shoulder about wealthy doctors who lie.'

Levi looked away and winced. Well, he was screwed.

She should shut up. What on earth had she told him

all that for and made herself vulnerable again? It had
been a dismal time. Best to change the subject.

'Home was good. My brother never said a thing.
Except "shortest engagement in history." He's so dead-
pan most of the time, you never know what's going on
in his head, though apparently your sister can read him.
I've never seen him as animated as the other night at
Xanadu.'

Levi shrugged but there was a tiny frown between
his eyes. 'Odette likes him a lot.'

'I don't think you could get two people more dissimi-
lar in upbringing.' Her forehead wrinkled despite the
effort not to. So Levi recognised her misgivings and
maybe had a few of his own. Good. It would never work.

Levi shook his head. 'Before she met the father of
her baby I'd agree with you. That's my greatest regret
so far, that I didn't keep her safe from men like him.
Tom was a dangerous and malicious clown and no loss
to his unborn child, I'm afraid. I think your brother is
restoring Odette's faith in chivalrous men.' He grinned.
'And she's pregnant. No harm can be done.'

Chivalrous. Such an old-fashioned word but, in this
context, perfect. The description of Smiley. 'Are you
chivalrous?' It popped out like froth from the waterfall and subtly the mood in the pool changed.

'Sometimes. Before I became tired and jaded.'

She let his words flow over her to think about later.
Suddenly she was thinking about the way his mouth
moved and that curve to his lips that she was finally
seeing more of. He'd been expressionless most of the
time since that first day.

Originally she'd thought him moody but apparently he'd been worry worn. Well, he was pretty focused right now. She could feel the brush of his perusal as he tilted his head and smiled with that devilish curve to his dangerous mouth.

Time to break back to the previous mood, she thought with a little spurt of panic. 'So what made you tired and jaded?'

The smile straightened and disappeared. 'Someone died two years ago. In a way that affected how I thought about my achievements. I've been running on the treadmill since. But I won't bore you with it.'

Boring me might be safer, she thought but she didn't say it. Couldn't make the effort to turn the tide of awareness she'd begun to drift in.

He floated across the pool and closed in on her. His eyes seemed darker and his lips parted as if he might whisper something—or do something else…

'I must admit I feel more alive than I have in a long time,' he said, and she felt the pricks of gooseflesh along her shoulders and arms.

She tried to move away but her body felt so heavy in the water she barely moved. Sound had receded and even the water temperature faded. 'Might be something to do with the fact we nearly died yesterday.' Now her voice sounded breathy and unsure.

'No doubt.' He sank under the water until not just his strong, brown shoulders were under but his chin as well. Just his angular face showed through, shadowed by the overhanging palms that darkened the planes of his cheeks. 'It's good to be alive.' He pursed his lips and blew a leaf across the water towards her. The leaf spun and twisted and bumped against her chin.

It was just a leaf. She could feel her heart thundering under the water. His gaze locked with hers, and it was as if he blew the air over her skin, but that was ridiculous. She was under the water, for goodness sake.

Yet here she was, with tiny flutters of heated awareness in a cold pond of sudden desire. It shouldn't have been erotic. But it was. A stranger, in a strange place, and strange feelings she hadn't experienced before. Enough to kick in her belly and make her aware of the fullness in her breasts and the beat of her heart.

Then his breath rippled across the water to tickle her face. She moistened her lips to say something inane, but before she could form the words he'd drifted closer until their noses touched with a little bump, like two leaves in a deserted pond, and she shivered.

All the time he stared into her eyes, and she could do little but breathe in and out and stare back and wonder at the dozen different blue rings inside his eyes and those dark, dark lashes drawing her closer.

She knew he was going to kiss her. Should be backing away when, in fact, she was drawn towards him by the primitive magnetism she had no control over.

When his mouth finally touched hers it was incredibly slow and gentle, an open-mouthed brush of his lips that impacted like an earth tremor against hers, and her lids drooped as she breathed in. His mouth slid to her cheek and down her neck, darting electrical tremors along her arms and legs that sent waves of mingled breath and kicks of desire back up into her chest. The sensations expanded in seismic rings of awareness and lust, and suddenly it was closer she needed to be, not further away.

Then he returned, took her mouth and enslaved her with a long draught from a well she hadn't known she had that meshed their souls in this primitive place, a day after they'd nearly died. Somehow, with that potent kiss, he touched the part of her that no one, not even Brad, had ever touched…and she was his. That simple and that complicated.

Immersed in sensation, she sighed as his hands slid from her shoulders down past her waist until he cupped both hips and pulled her toward him. Somehow, her fingers became entangled in his thick hair and luxuriated in the springiness as her breasts were squashed against his chest.

Time passed, moment by glorious moment, and she slipped deeper and deeper under his spell until she realised she was clutching at him as he tried to pull back.

She opened her eyes, focused and, horrified, she jolted herself away and would have moved further if he hadn't put his hand out and stilled her.

'It's OK. It's just a kiss. You're so beautiful,' he said, his voice heavy and deep, and she shuddered another breath in as he lifted a strand of hair off her forehead before he pulled back and floated away. And left her bereft.

The blood pounded in her ears and she watched him, like a rabbit in headlights, mesmerized, as he increased the distance between their bodies. Gradually she began to feel the world again and with it the sounds of the birds overhead and the wind in the leaves and the thunder of her heart.

Levi forced himself away. God, she was beautiful. And luscious and so, so ripe for the taking. And he wanted her. There was no doubt about that, but what the hell was he doing? There was no future in this, just heartbreak for Sophie, and maybe even for him.

It was lucky this pool was cold, which would help, but even then he'd have to stay submerged till he had himself under control. He nearly lost himself—both of them. It would only have taken another minute to pass the point of no return, and she was too innocent and trusting to realise.

He guessed he wasn't chivalrous.

He fisted his hands under the water and forced himself to calm. What had he been thinking? Fool. Of course, he hadn't been thinking—he'd been feeling, indulging in a daydream, or more like an erotic fantasy to play nymphs and satyrs in an oasis. A great way to say thank-you to the woman trying to save them all. But she'd looked so kissable with her satin skin and fine-boned shoulders that it made him ache like he hadn't ached for years. If he were honest, he'd wanted to kiss her since the night she'd come to Xanadu. Do more than kiss, and he'd very nearly had his way. She would have hated him. He would have hated himself.

The silence between them was broken only by the noisy budgerigar and his mate. Levi floated with his back to her while she climbed out, carefully, so as not to hurt her feet.

Sophie's hands shook, were stupidly clumsy as she wiped herself over with her shorts, and her lower limbs still wobbled as she redressed damply. Still in a daze from one kiss? A mouth-tingling caress like nothing she'd ever experienced before.

Sleazebag Brad had been practised, smooth and—now she could see—one dimensional, not like Levi, a city marauder of devastating understatement and finesse.

She shivered, not with cold, but with new knowledge of greater danger. Where was the line between attraction and wanting to be lost in a man's arms and the terrible danger of falling in love? She knew how much pain that could cause.

Her damp shirt stuck to her bra and outlined her nipples and she pulled the material out from her body to air it. It would dry all too quickly when they crossed the next plain but it embarrassed her horribly at this moment. She settled herself facing the gorge they'd climbed and breathed slowly and carefully to regain her composure. She could do that.

Still she couldn't look to the pool at Levi. Her lips thrummed as if she'd just eaten a Kakadu plum. When, in fact, she'd tasted something much better.

The water splashed behind her and a muffled curse forced a reluctant smile. He'd stubbed his toe. Good. Take his mind off kissing her.

She dug in her bag and pulled out the chocolate bar. It bent in her hand, soft and squishy, and she looked at it with a sigh. Hot chocolate was good in winter, and even like this when you hadn't had anything to eat since a tart piece of fruit. Something to take her mind off other parts of her body. The paper ripped in her teeth and the first sweet taste oozed onto her tongue.

She sucked the wrapper as she considered their options. Anything not to think of the pool and what passed between them. They'd cross the plain in the afternoon sun and hopefully find the camp before dark. That was the scary part. If they didn't…

CHAPTER EIGHT

BY TWO they were on their way again and nothing was said of the kiss in the pool. The heat bit into Levi's shoulders through his shirt and the grass crunched drily under their feet. The plain stretched ahead of them in a seemingly endless roll with stunted trees and anthills their only shade.

Levi could feel the difference—the awareness between them had increased, the air vibrated and not just with heat from the sun. He'd caused this. Created her distress. He could regret implementing the kiss but not the kiss itself because there was something about that moment that said it had to be. But his stupid lack of control had caused her discomfort. He needed to find some way to lighten the strain between them. 'So what's with the big anthills?'

She jumped when he spoke. He wished she wouldn't do that. Not for the first time wondered whoever that bloke was he'd like to have a go at him.

'Termite mounds. Not anthills.'

He looked again. Termite mounds, then. Everywhere, from small bumps in the dirt to huge towers taller than a man. Even on the cliff faces when he looked.

More interesting than he expected. 'So tell me about termites.'

She stopped and put her hands on her hips. 'What makes you think I know?'

She had a cute pose. 'You know everything.'

'You are so full of—'

'Ah-ah.' He shook his finger at her and cut her off. 'So you don't know?'

She sighed. 'Termites are blind.' She may pretend to be resigned but he saw the lessening of tension in her and it made him feel good about himself. Strange.

She went on and he smiled at the way she loved to explain things. It was one of those little things he'd grown to recognise and like about her. The passion for her world. He didn't see a lot of passion where he'd come from. Just day-in, day-out twelve-hour days. Certainly he hadn't exhibited any for a while, probably not for a couple of years. Well, not that kind anyway.

'Termites are opaque and the workers can live for thirty years.' She gave him a tentative smile. 'The queen can live eighty years.'

Nice smile. 'That'd be right. Poor man doing all the work.' He gestured to the adult-size tower of dirt. 'So what are these made of?'

She rolled her eyes at him. 'Mounds are made with saliva, spinifex, mud and termite poo, and they grow at a rate of about one foot every ten years.' She pointed to a mound that was broken. 'You can tell when they're abandoned because an active mound that's broken is repaired very quickly.'

He whistled and patted a six-foot mound they were passing. 'There're a lot of years here.'

She paused and looked around with that passion shining from her eyes. 'The story of the Kimberleys— lots of years. This whole area is the product of erosion of a giant mountain range, the Leopold, millions of years ago. That's why the ground's so rocky.'

And why not much grew around here, he guessed. 'So no bushrangers right out here in the past?'

'Not so much bushrangers, not enough people to rob, but there's a story about an escapee who killed a policeman and hid the body inside a termite mound.'

The woman was a mine of scary information. 'Don't tell me. The termites repaired the mound and he was never found.'

'You got it.'

She made him smile. Suddenly, most of the time. Even through this disaster. 'So I'd better not annoy you.'

She showed her teeth. 'Or you'll never be found.'

Sophie had sealed what had happened between them at the pool like the termites sealed their mounds, but she still felt embarrassed that she'd let him kiss her. She didn't have the headspace for the questions that had arisen from that kiss. She was focused now on getting home. Desperately.

She was doubly glad of his environmental interest because she could feel the fear build as the day length-ened. She'd been fairly confident this morning, and still sure they would find the camp at lunch, but this afternoon her water bottle emptied and conversation between them dried up like the sweat on their bodies, and she began to worry about their options.

She must have sighed because he looked across at her and touched her shoulder. 'What's wrong?'

She stopped and unconsciously her hand came over the top of his for comfort. 'It's taking longer than I'd hoped.'

He turned her into his chest and moved so she was out of the sun behind his body—a different type of embrace than the last one she didn't want to think about—and she rested her forehead on him for a moment. His voice rumbled in his chest. 'We'll find them, if not today, then tomorrow. If we don't, we know we can make it back to the others.'

Could they? She thought about how far they'd walked. Yes, they could. She could almost feel the strength transferring from him to her. His confidence boosted hers, probably unjustifiably, not that she wanted him to tell her otherwise. She had enough doubts for both of them.

Her stomach growled. 'I don't know about you but I'm getting hungry,' she mumbled into his shirt.

'Where's a drive-through Gubinge tree when you want one?' He kicked the ground. 'There's always the grubs. Ten fat ones a day, did you say?'

She had to laugh. Or she'd cry. But she did feel better. Then he put her away from him and dug in his pocket. He held up his liquid chocolate bar. 'I was saving this one for you.'

She shook her head vehemently. 'I'm not eating your chocolate.'

'Sure you are.' He pointed to the hills up ahead. 'We'll stop there and fight about it.' Then he patted her hair and took her pack from her back and captured her fingers. 'Let's go.' He pulled her fingers gently, and suddenly the strength came back along with her focus, and she walked beside him with their hands swinging together over the red earth.

She didn't know when it happened but suddenly she did trust him. Was happy to allow him to shoulder some of the burden, something so out of character for her she didn't understand how he'd achieved it. Especially after the kiss. Or was it because of the kiss?

They were close to the last foothills when the Aboriginal elder appeared. His wizened skin crinkled in mahogany folds and his grey hair hung long and straggled. Levi saw him standing beside a termite hill before Sophie did.

He carried a spear for hunting and little else.

Levi stopped suddenly when he saw him but Sophie kept going. 'He wants us to follow him.'

Levi glanced across at her. 'Guess you were right again.'

Sophie sighed with relief. Not before time. They were running out of afternoon. She'd done one thing right, then. 'This was a good one to win.'

The elder took them to a side gully and presented them with another fresh pool to drink and cool themselves. He didn't speak and she watched Levi, with hidden amusement, as he attempted to sign their story but the old man just stared at him.

'I doubt he's learnt English for the little use he'd have for it.' She handed him a stick. 'Maybe if you drew a picture in the sand?'

Levi's sand helicopter left a lot to be desired but a broad grin from the elder seemed as though he'd figured where they'd come from. Levi drew four people and then pointed to himself and Sophie, indicating the other two were still at the helicopter.

The old man nodded, seriously, and pointed to the sun and then an arc in the sky to almost sunset, and gestured they follow him, and that they'd be able to get back to the others after that.

Sophie didn't know if it was her imagination, or just the relief, but the walking was less strenuous, more shaded, and yet seemed as though they covered more ground.

An hour before sunset they came to the camp, a collection of half a dozen lean-tos, with several brown-eyed, brown-skinned toddlers scuffling in the dust.

It was unusually quiet and a quorum of women seemed congregated around a lean-to at the end of the camp. The hair on Sophie's arms stood up. Something was wrong. She glanced at Levi, who raised his brows and shrugged. He could sense it too.

The oldest lady pointed to her. Sophie approached them diffidently, used to not catching the elder's eyes. The lady, probably the grandmother, pointed her finger at Sophie. 'You that nurse, sheila, eh?' She gestured into the lean-to with her head.

Weariness swamped her and Sophie forced her head to lift as she glanced back at Levi. It seemed this day had more in store for her. Lord knew what she'd discover and it seemed she would soon find out.

He took a step to follow her. 'Do you want me to come with you?' But the old lady gestured him away.

Sophie sighed. 'Nice thought but it's not going to happen. I'd say it's secret women's business.' Sophie bent and followed the woman inside, and her heart bumped at the thought of the unknown and what might be expected of her.

The air inside the lean-to was stifling; the place seemed full of aunties and the grandmother. The young girl who lay on the dry grass bed looked more like a frightened rabbit than a woman about to give birth.

'Oh, Lord,' Sophie muttered. The sight of one tiny baby's foot resting between the mother's legs was enough to make Sophie feel like a frightened rabbit too. Footling breech, so the baby's legs would come out long before the head. If it all went well.

'As it should,' she said out loud, to bolster her own conviction.

Of course a Caesarean section would be a nice option to have in the wings in case of complications, Sophie wished fruitlessly, but that wasn't going to happen. All she could think of was the mantra from her training—hands off the breech.

Then she saw the little foot move. So the baby was alive and the day improved enormously.

Now wasn't the time to ask why the girl wasn't near a hospital if she was close to birth time. Far too late for that. Sophie knew that sometimes the fear of being away from their families made the young women hide their pregnancies so they weren't sent away. But Sophie also knew the girl would be in trouble with the elders later.

She knelt down and tried for a smile, then tapped her own chest. 'Sophie.'

The older lady pointed to the girl. 'Pearl.'

'Hello, Pearl,' Sophie said, but Pearl's frightened brown eyes skittered to the gaggle of aunties and refused to return. Sophie gestured for permission to feel the mother's abdomen and the grandmother shooed her on to the task as if to say hurry up.

Pearl's baby seemed smaller than term, which could be a good thing, or maybe it was just because it was breech and a lot of the baby was already in the pelvis. Pearl was fine boned with no extra weight, and Sophie would love to have known how long the labour had been going on.

The next contraction arrived and Pearl screwed her face up and whimpered with the pain. Her baby's little foot descended another centimetre into the world.

At this moment there wasn't much Sophie could do except be there for the end. And pray. She couldn't listen to the baby's heartbeats because she didn't have any form of stethoscope. She didn't have gloves, nor could she even wash her hands, but she couldn't leave Pearl alone either.

Levi's support was denied because culturally Pearl's birthing was women's business and men were banned. Though, if she had a problem when the baby arrived, Sophie knew darn well she'd be yelling for Levi.

Just knowing he was there gave immense reassurance. She'd expect Levi's first-aid skills and common sense would help more than anyone else's.

She guessed that even if she'd some way to contact the Royal Flying Doctor Service the plane wouldn't be here before it was all over. So much for her brief respite from responsibility. There was nothing to be done but settle herself slightly more comfortably on the dusty floor and try to ignore the trickle of perspiration that ran down between her shoulder blades. She licked her lips and tasted the dryness of her mouth. A drink would have been good.

Sophie began to pray for a rapid second stage of labour but there was only so much praying she could do. She glanced around for something else positive to focus on and her gaze rested on a brown shawl she could dry the baby with when it was born. That was a positive thought. When it was born.

The aunties all looked at her as if she should do something and she tried to block out the thoughts that didn't help.

Thoughts about drugs, and oxygen, and paediatricians who may as well be on the moon. Hopefully the baby had grown well and wasn't too premature.

If the young mum had had no antenatal care, then she was probably anaemic to start with which increased her chance of bleeding afterwards, and any blood loss would make her dangerously depleted in red blood cells.

But there wasn't a lot Sophie could do about that either. She could rub the mum's tummy to encourage clamping down of the uterus when the placenta was delivered, and she could put the baby to the breast as soon as possible to release the natural hormones that were there to do the same thing.

Women had been birthing for thousands of years in the camps, she reassured herself, well before twentieth-century medicine had decreed they were safer at the hospitals. Trouble was now the elder women had lost their skills as attendants over the past hundred years.

She needed to think of more positives. At least the heat would make it unlikely the baby would get cold, which breech babies tended to do as their bodies waited for the heads to be born.

For some reason she thought of Levi's Pollyanna comment and it steadied her because there was nothing wrong with looking on the bright side of things.

Pearl moaned again and this time the baby's ankle came down almost to the knee and suddenly there was a second foot. 'You're doing great, Pearl.' Sophie plastered a happy face on and nodded her head at the frightened girl and her attendants. The least she could do was be supportive, instead of a harbinger of doom.

If the cervix was not fully opened, then Pearl was going to push against it anyway. If she sat up it would be easier for the baby and put even more pressure on the cervix. Sophie looked at the grandmother and gestured that they help Pearl to squat in a supported position.

Gravity would help bring the baby down and hopefully all would happen quickly before the baby's cord became too squashed by the after-coming head.

With Pearl upright her labour did seem to progress more quickly. First the baby's knees and the thighs appeared with just the change of position and then Pearl pushed until a swollen black scrotum appeared and the women broke into voluble noise and exclamations at the evidence of a new male for the family.

The elder woman gestured to Sophie to grab the baby but Sophie shook her head emphatically.

This was where "hands off the breech" was most important. Sophie knew the natural curves of the mother's pelvis shaped the baby into having his chin tucked into his chest and the arms by his side. If they pulled the baby downwards, his head would tip back into a bigger diameter and his arms might drag behind his head to create a complication that should never have happened.

'No touch,' Sophie said and waved her hands in a negative sign. 'Baby knows.'

Little skinny buttocks followed by hips, back and umbilical cord all came through next, and Sophie resisted the urge to feel the cord and check the heart rate of the baby. She'd bet it was slower than her own thumping heart was, but the less she touched, the less spasm the cord would endure.

There certainly wasn't anything else Sophie could do except prevent people pulling on the baby as he descended. She'd just ensure Pearl's baby came out with his back facing Sophie, so his head could lift from his chin-on-chest position to birth, just like a head-first baby did.

Grandmother clutched her hair and moaned, and

gestured to Sophie at the paleness of the baby, and Sophie could tell she wanted to help make the baby come quicker. 'Soon,' Sophie soothed. 'All over soon.'

Sophie tried another prayer and slipped her wrist between the baby's legs so that when the chest was through and first one shoulder and then the other was born the baby was hanging all out with only the neck and head to come. Sophie's heart was thumping so loud in her ears she didn't doubt the aunties could hear, but she was strangely calm.

She allowed the weight of the baby to hang a little to ensure the head stayed deflexed until the last moment. Sophie's bent legs ached from squatting in almost under Pearl.

Now. Time to deliver the head. She placed one hand on top of the baby's shoulders and back of the neck and the other underneath on the baby's cheeks so when the head birthed it didn't spring out suddenly. The hardest part.

The baby's head had been rushed through the pelvis. To ease a baby slowly out of the constriction of the birth canal was less risky than a head being forced out quickly into sudden expansion.

'Here he comes,' Sophie muttered. She achingly raised herself from her own squat to lift the baby slowly, holding shoulders and cheeks between her hands as the baby made an arc in front of his mother's belly. His head was born with chin, mouth and nose, then eyes and finally the whole baby was out.

Pearl sagged back onto her heels and then onto her back, and Sophie wiped the still-flaccid baby over with the shawl until his little limbs contracted in reflex and he breathed. She pulled Pearl's T-shirt up and lay her son directly skin to skin across her chest.

At the first touch of his mother's skin he gasped and cried—which by this point was exactly what Sophie felt like doing herself. But there was no time for that.

Grandmother tied the twine where Sophie indicated, and the baby was totally separated from his mother by the lethal-looking knife they cut the cord with, and finally she could back away a little as the aunties crowded in.

Her hands shook and she wiped the sweat from her face with her forearm. Cord and placenta followed shortly and a gush of bright blood seeped and began to form a pool. 'Pearl—' Sophie leant in to catch the young woman's eye '—I need to rub your tummy.'

Sophie nudged the grandmother and showed her how rubbing the now-grapefruit-size uterus in Pearl's belly stopped the flow of blood until the uterus was a hard nub beneath their fingers. The grandmother nodded and brought her gnarled hand in over Sophie's. Sophie wondered if one day another woman would be as lucky if the grandmother remembered this part.

Another aunty put Pearl's baby to her mother's breast and Sophie sat back and drew a deep breath. Baby whimpered and then cried again before he latched and began to suck. They didn't need her any more and she had to get out of here before she fainted from the heat.

CHAPTER NINE

IT SEEMED hours since she'd disappeared. Levi paced himself a worn strip under the tree as he watched the opening of the humpy.

Even hand signals with the children as he attempted to take a health stock of those he could see hadn't passed the time. Eventually he'd found an elder who conversed more easily, immunisation status not something he'd normally have pursued, but Sophie wanted to know. And there was only so much washing and drinking in the creek he could do when all the time he slaked his own thirst he knew she'd be parched. At least he'd soaked a cloth and filled her bottles for when she came out.

But he should have told her earlier about his qualifications, or at least discussed where he could help. The longer she'd spent inside with the women, the deeper his guilt. An uncomfortable feeling he could have done without.

Not that he had a lot of experience with obstetrics, except for Odette's pregnancy and one small obstetric rotation that had him back-pedalling away from something with too much emotion attached to it, but he hadn't forgotten how helpful it could be to have another medical person to discuss things with.

His own career path had opted for something he could achieve on his own, something technical he could master and something he'd decided on when his brother went blind, and he'd been very successful. Though the past two years had been hard since Darla's death, where he'd driven himself to work outrageous hours—and he'd almost burnt out, he realised now—which must be why it felt so different to smile around Sophie so often.

Then again, perhaps a near-death helicopter crash could enliven one too.

But that didn't help his guilt about Sophie. Apart from his sister, he'd been accountable to no one since his brother died. He'd disliked his father, but that was moot now. Women had been in and out of his life, but none had left him with doubts about his behaviour like this outback dynamo did.

When Sophie finally unbent herself from the humpy Levi felt the air whoosh out of his lungs as his shoulders dropped with relief. Now he could watch her draw a deep breath and gather herself. He remembered she did that a lot and it said volumes for her stamina and inner strength. Another thing he admired about her.

He'd bet the air outside seemed sweet and cooler, especially as it approached sunset. The sound of a very new baby roaring his lungs out followed her. This woman continued to amaze him.

For the briefest moment he thought he recognised something in her eyes when she looked at him that made the stress of waiting worthwhile—and brought back the guilt tenfold.

For Sophie, the sight of Levi made her want to throw herself into his arms for comfort. But she needed to wash and she needed a drink and she needed not to think about all the things that could have gone wrong that hadn't.

'Sophie?' Levi took her arm and sat her down under a tree. 'Sit.' He handed her a water bottle and she took a long drink with her eyes closed. It felt so good to be outside.

'Another amazing job?'

She opened her eyes, glanced around at the plains surrounding them and sighed. 'Footling breech. We were all lucky.' The exhaustion hit her as she sagged back against the knobbly trunk behind her.

Levi gave her a searching look. 'I'll get your other drink.' He handed her some damp cloths. 'Here's something to wash with until you're up to a walk to the creek.'

He'd torn both sleeves off his shirt and soaked them. Brilliant. Amazing. Just what she needed. When he offered them to her she could have hugged him or, for a brief, mad second, run her hands over the bulge of his upper arms that were very nicely displayed without sleeves. There was something about a man in a shirt without sleeves that called to her, not that she'd noticed that fetish before—no doubt it was especially true when that man supplied what she desperately wanted most.

It must have shown in her face because he gave her a lopsided grin. 'I've been to the shop. Maybe you'd like a Kakadu plum?'

The giggle surprised her. Probably hysteria but the release of emotion actually felt good. A little out of control, but good. He was cosseting again and she wallowed in it for a few indulgent seconds while she wiped her hands and, with a clean corner of the damp material, her face. The coolness against her forehead was worth a hundred facials Sleazebag Brad had insisted she have.

In fact, she was growing to appreciate this man more and more, though she wouldn't fall for him. But it was hard. He made her feel crazily alive and special. A safe harbour to come into. Strong arms when she needed them. But she wasn't in love. Not going there! She was very glad he was here with her though.

'There's hope for you yet.' She looked across at him but he only grimaced and her euphoria dimmed. He didn't look as happy as she felt.

Levi looked away and rubbed his neck and, to Sophie, the afternoon suddenly seemed stifling again. 'I'm glad,' he said, 'because there's something else I have to tell you.'

Lightly spoken but determined, and her stomach sank as she wondered how much bad news a person could take in one day.

'The good news.' She was too weary for bad at this minute. 'Please.'

'From what I gather, our tracker was on his way back when he found us and the Flying Doctor is coming for your girl. We'll be able to use their radio when they land.'

Her shoulders dropped in a heartfelt sigh. Not just good. 'That's great news.' The day would work out. This whole draining adventure would end. She could get home in the not too distant future, shower and have a cup of tea, and maybe she and Levi—and the others of course, she hastened to remind herself—could share that steak she'd kill for. She didn't want to hear the bad news. She glanced around for something to divert him.

Barefoot, dark-eyed children huddled into a little giggling group to one side and darted mischievous glances across to where Sophie and Levi sat. 'Have you been making friends while I've been busy?'

He smiled at the children and pulled a silly face which sent them off into a new fit of giggles. 'So it seems.'

So he was good with kids too. She sucked her breath in and felt the warmth expand in her stomach. He really did have qualities she admired, and of course he was different to that man in her past. She shied away from the comparison, although it did Levi no disservice against Brad. It was far too early to think about the future.

She looked from him to the little brown bodies that had begun to poke and wriggle amongst themselves. These children looked lean, but full of energy. 'I wonder if the kids are up to date with their immunizations?'

'Apparently,' he said a little smugly, and she had to smile. 'I asked. And they look well.'

He'd asked? Why? Because she'd said once she wanted to know? More warm and fuzzies buzzed in her belly and she smiled up at him. 'You've been busy. Anyone I need to look at?'

He hesitated. 'There's an elder here almost blind with cataracts. He'd benefit from surgery.'

Sophie looked around the camp. Lean-tos, red dust, a couple of shady trees and the creek. 'It's hard to encourage elders to leave their home for something they've learnt to live with.'

Levi shook his head. 'He's sightless. The results would be brilliant.'

Sophie nodded. 'I know. But he has to have the money to travel to the doctor.'

'What money?' Levi looked at her. 'The operation is free in public hospitals.'

Sophie shrugged, only giving half her concentration as she began to relax. She watched the children. Sipped more water. Exhaled. The baby was fine. She'd done the right thing. And now the Flying Doctor could take over the care. She could unwind. 'He'd have to leave here, travel, live away from his family. And for these people the thought of an operation is beyond frightening.'

'It's a minor operation.' Levi was like a terrier and his intensity began to intrude on her equilibrium.

Something in the way he persisted made her look away from the children to him. She spoke slowly as the implications sparked a question, and then a creeping disquiet that maybe she'd missed something. Been blind. More blind than an elder with cataracts? And stupid? 'Do you have much experience at diagnosing cataracts?'

His eyes searched hers and she knew. Felt the red dusty world fall away from under her feet. Felt the heat in her cheeks as she flushed with embarrassment and not a little anger.

'I could have,' he said.

Her eyes narrowed as she looked into his face. The same wary expression as the first time she'd met him. The face of a liar. All the boxes slid into place in her mind—the comments, the looks between his sister and himself, his 'first aid.' She tried to keep the hurt out of her voice. 'What sort of business did you say you had?'

'I didn't.' Still he looked at her so she had to break eye contact.

'And…?' She gazed at the children across the camp.

He paused, waited until she met his eyes again. 'I'm an ophthalmologist specialising in microsurgery. I have a very successful practice in Sydney.'

'You're a doctor?' Quietly. 'You said first aid.' Her voice dropped even lower. 'You lied again.'

His voice was low too. 'I didn't lie.'

'You didn't deny.' It hurt; actually, it crushed her that she'd been fooled again. 'Liar by omission.'

'That was the bad news.'

What did he want? A pat on the head? It was bad all right. She'd started to like him. Like him a lot. Please God, not love him. She'd certainly begun to lean on him more than a little. And he was a doctor. A rich doctor. And a liar. Just like Brad. The man who'd stripped her heart, and taken a part of her that had been precious and new and untarnished, and stamped on it.

And she'd ordered Levi around because she'd been the only medical person. Did he understand how hard it had been to wear that responsibility, and now he tells her he's better qualified? Even if he was a surgeon he'd started as a generalist.

He could have put Smiley's shoulder in. The weight of unshed tears made her face feel heavy. Like a big rock tied to her cheeks, pulling her whole face down. She blinked her stupid stinging eyes and gritted her teeth. No way was she wasting water on this creep.

'I'm struggling to think of a reason you wouldn't make this all easier on me. Was this some kind of test to see how much I'd take before I broke?'

He shook his head and reached his hand out. She looked at his fingers as if they were covered in slime. He must have seen it because his hand dropped. 'Look. Sophie. I think you're amazing.' He dragged his hand through his hair. 'You didn't need my help.'

Holy cow. How dare he? She so didn't want to do this now. Or ever. She climbed wearily to her feet and with her eyes fixed past his shoulder she took off down the hill to the creek to gather herself, almost tripping in her haste to get away from him.

The water splashed cold against her fingers and she plunged her hands and forearms in to shock herself out of the stifling blanket of cotton wool she felt smothered in. She'd been so close, had almost fallen in love with exactly the type of man who could crush her—again—

and in just a few short days. Didn't she learn from her mistakes?

She washed her face, washed the trickles that weren't creek water and then washed it again. Damn him.

Slowly composure returned, or at least her hands stopped shaking and her tears dried. Her head ached with a dense weariness that seemed to wrap around her bones, and she forced tired feet to carry her back to the camp. But she walked straight past him to the humpy to check the mother and baby.

By the time she emerged she had control again and an impenetrable barrier around her higher than the escarpment they'd nearly flown into. The sound of an aeroplane droned in the distance, and Sophie searched for the sight of it over the hills like she needed it to breathe.

Anything instead of looking at Levi.

The sooner that plane landed, the better. She wasn't even worried about flying out of here.

She had to think of Odette, still out in the scrub, unaware that help was coming, and the possibility of her labour. Once she was safe Sophie could release all responsibility. And she would. Posthaste.

When they made town he could worry about the disaster of the helicopter and she and Smiley could go home. With just a little luck she'd never see him again and she could forget what a fool she'd almost been.

Finally the noise of the plane dominated the sky and the shadow crossed the ground in front of them as the pilot circled to land on the area the men had cleared. Bring it on, Sophie said under her breath.

When the twin-engine aircraft landed, surprisingly smoothly on the rocky soil, the plane held three people—the doctor, Jock McDonald, a Scottish larrikin who raised his eyebrows at the sight of Levi and Sophie; the nurse, who strode purposefully towards them; and the pilot, who waved but stayed to shut the engine down.

'There'll be a story there, I'm noo doubting,' Jock said to Sophie, whom he'd met at the clinic. He waved at Levi. 'I'll talk to you in a wee moment.'

The nurse hailed Sophie and the two women accompanied Jock into the humpy, suddenly critically crowded until the doctor shooed away all except the grandmother, then checked Pearl and scolded her in such a broad accent there wasn't a hope she'd understand what he said. But he smiled and patted her head when he'd finished and again when he'd checked the tiny but vigorous baby over with obvious admiration.

'You're verra lucky. You'll both still come to the hospital so we can keep an eye on you for a day or two,' he said to Pearl and again to the grandmother, 'In case baby goes off his food. He's only a wee thing.'

Then he left the humpy and he raised his eyebrows at Sophie. 'I'd like to hear your side of it. You did well, lassie.'

Sophie didn't feel anything but tired. 'Everything went right. Hands off the breech until the head. Baby fine by a minute after birth. We weren't unlucky but we would have been up the creek if it hadn't panned out as well as it had.'

'Aye. But you weren't. So no use worryin' about the

ones that go good like they're supposed to.' He pulled his hand antiseptic from his pocket and offered it to Sophie and she lathered herself. Unimaginable luxury.

Dr Jock inclined his head towards the tree. 'So who's this big fella and how're you two here?'

She shook her head. She didn't want to talk about it. 'He'll fill you in. Have you room for us?'

He looked at the plane. 'Och, no, not for two, but we can contact the Bungles and they'll fly in and get him. We'll have to take the mother and bairn or she'll have no care if either get sick.' He gave her a searching look. 'I'm thinkin' you need to come with us.' Then he crossed to where Levi was talking to the pilot under the tree with a map spread between them.

Fifteen minutes later, Sophie joined Pearl and her baby in the RFDS plane with Dr Jock, while the nurse rode up front with the pilot.

Levi had been in contact with a helicopter service at the Bungles who were en route to pick him up. Another had flown to the crash site. More red tape would follow at a later date, but for the moment Odette and Smiley were on their way back to the hospital at Kununurra and Sophie could drop the last of her responsibilities.

An hour later she finally stepped out of the plane at the airport in Kununurra too. But it wasn't where she wanted to be. She ached to go home, back to her own space, a place to hide and lick her wounds and take stock of the new disaster she'd brought on herself, but she'd have to wait for the hospital to release her brother.

The nurse from the flight lent her flat keys and spare clothes, and Sophie spent an hour soaking red dust from her legs and her hair in a long bath that should have relaxed her but didn't.

She could hear the sound of helicopters taking off and landing at the airfield across the road and the sound grated across her ears like gravel over her skin. No doubt one of them held *him*. All the time she wished she'd never let her guard down—couldn't believe she'd done it again, fallen for the words and caresses of a smooth-talking liar. But never again.

Levi watched the entrance to the hospital as cars with lights drove up and deposited people. Watched every taxi, truck and bus that pulled up. He watched families walking and couples talking and single women who didn't matter, but nowhere did he see a ponytail in an Akubra hat that quickened his heart.

It was night now but this day never seemed to end. He'd spent an hour at the police station. The aircraft crash investigation team were coming from Perth and until then nothing could be proved, but they were on alert. He wasn't having his sister put at risk again. He'd arranged a light aircraft flight to get them all home, and told the men at Xanadu to put the lights out on the strip, as well as the men at the station township to put another set out, and he'd seen Odette and William. Neither had spotted Sophie but William had heard her on the phone.

She'd been on the ground for two hours now; he'd checked. She should be here soon.

He still didn't know what to say. She hadn't allowed him a word since he'd told her, hadn't looked at him before she left, but the hurt in her eyes had bitten harder than he'd expected. He just hoped she'd cool down and then he could explain before he had to take Odette back to Sydney.

The digital clock in the hospital foyer flashed ten past nine and a taxi pulled up. There she was. Strangely smaller than he remembered, in a pair of long trousers that didn't suit her as much as her shorts. The toss of her head when she saw him gave a pretty accurate picture of what she thought. Not a good omen for explanations.

Fair enough. Maybe he deserved it.

There was too much happening to do anything about it now but later he'd try to explain. It seemed his sister had come through the ordeal unscathed. He wasn't sure Sophie had—and it was his fault.

She lifted her hat off and held it in her hand as if to ward him off. The way she walked past him with her head down made him want to kick himself. He fell in behind her as she headed for the casualty room until he caught up. 'You OK?'

Sophie gritted her teeth. She was fine! Was this guy for real? 'Yes.' She didn't look at him.

'Sophie. Let me explain.'

'I'd prefer you didn't.' She stopped. 'Look. Levi. Dr Whatever-your-name-is.' That was when she realised how deep the perfidy went. 'I don't even know your last name.'

'Pearson.'

The name rang a bell. Pearson? Pearson? But she couldn't place it. She shrugged it off with a tiny shake of her head. Was it really Pearson? Who could tell with this guy?

Levi stared down at her. 'Don't you think you're being a little harsh, considering what we've been through together?'

'I really don't care if you think I'm harsh. I'm tired. I'm over this. I have to see you for the next hour but I don't have to listen. I'd appreciate it if you'd respect that.'

So they sat in the waiting room, not speaking. To start with, Sophie flicked through a magazine but every page of upmarket advertisement she turned to she imagined Levi driving that car. Eating at that restaurant. Dancing with that girl. Wearing that suit.

She threw the magazine down and leaned back in the chair and closed her eyes. She hadn't lost her heart to another city slicker. She hadn't.

Finally, after another torturous half hour, the patients were released. Odette hugged her and Smiley nodded and even put his hand on Sophie's shoulder and squeezed it.

'Thanks, Sis.'

'We were lucky,' she mumbled, and reached up and gave him a kiss. She needed to dwell on the fact that all of them were alive and that it had been pretty close. Maybe that was why she was weepy.

Sophie avoided Levi's attempt to catch her eye and she only then wondered how they were getting home. Not a helicopter, she hoped.

'I've hired a plane to get us back,' he said, as if she'd asked the question.

She risked a glance at him and he was looking at her. 'Thank you,' she mumbled but that was all.

Apparently Smiley would fly on to Xanadu to collect his vehicle and Sophie would be dropped home to sleep. First stop: Jabiru Station Township. Yes, please. Sophie couldn't wait.

The flight was short and when she finally closed her front door behind her she leaned against it with a sigh. The wood was hard and scratchy from peeling paint and she rubbed her head against it as if to rub some sense into her brain. What had she done?

Sleep proved impossible after the events of the past two days and ridiculously the most disturbing factor was Levi's decision to keep her unaware of his profession. Maybe that was a concept which was totally ridiculous in the scheme of things but she couldn't help it.

She needed to get back to work and forget her adventures, her weakness and the high-flying people at Xanadu.

CHAPTER TEN

WHEN Sophie opened the front door the next morning she glanced across the street and Levi leant on the veranda rail of the clinic as if he owned it.

There he was. Designer jeans and Rolex flashing in the sunlight, and there she was, clutching her throat like a wimp.

She would have pulled back, hidden inside, if he hadn't straightened when he saw her, but it was too late. Too darn late.

Her hand shook as she pulled the door shut behind her and when she crossed the veranda it felt like a creek full of crocodiles were shifting underfoot. What could he possibly want? She hated that it mattered so much it made her tremble.

The dusty road, usually wide in the sunlight, seemed narrow today, and in far too little time she stood beside him. Just a drift of some expensive after-shave letting her know he was still way out of her league. 'How can I help you, Doctor?'

His eyes narrowed and when he spoke his voice

was very low. 'Don't call me doctor and don't talk to me as if you don't know me.'

She blinked. Was he trying for best defence is attack? Well, she could do a little attacking of her own.

'I thought you'd be long gone.'

He sighed. 'I can see the thought of that upsets you no end.'

'Hmm.' The deserted street didn't produce any distractions so she had to look at him. 'Perhaps not.' She shrugged. Self-preservation's like that, she thought. 'Nothing personal. How can I help you?'

'I have to stay for the crash investigation team. It looks as if the chopper was definitely tampered with and there's a police investigation. I thought you should know.'

What? Ice trickled down her neck despite the heat. Deliberate sabotage? With a pregnant Odette on board? 'Tampered with? That's horrible. Who'd want to do that?' She'd no idea but it seemed the concept wasn't new to him. How surprising he hadn't shared that with her earlier.

'There's some suspicion on Steve, the resort manager. He's disappeared.'

'Steve?' She shook her head at the crazy notion. 'I don't understand.'

He ran his hand through his hair. 'It's a long story.'

Long stories take time. That meant he'd stay longer and she didn't think she could take that. 'No problem.' She couldn't help the tiny bitterness that laced her words. She forced herself to hold out her hand and braced for that frisson she felt every time he touched her. 'All the best, then.'

He looked down at her fingers but made no move to take her hand. 'I was hoping we could part as more than friends.'

She shrugged, not without a little relief, and tucked her hand away safely by her side. She didn't want to be his special friend. They came from different worlds. Had different morals. 'I don't think so.' Blowed if she'd hold her hand out again. 'So when do you go?'

'It's taken a day to get the team in from Perth. The preliminary reports will be through late this afternoon and we leave tomorrow. I tried to send Odette back today but she refused to go without me.'

She could understand that. Especially when she'd just found out someone tried to kill her. The idea was almost too far-fetched to believe. 'She's been through a lot. I guess it would make anyone nervous to travel on their own, let alone in her circumstances.' Unconsciously she scrunched her hands inside her short pockets. Already her heart rate was palpable and she could feel the moisture on her skin—and still he hadn't come to the reason he was here.

He paused, waiting for her to ask him something, and when she didn't he went on, as if searching for a topic. So he wasn't comfortable either, she thought. Good.

'At least Odette didn't have her baby in the bush. My biggest fear. She should never have travelled so far in her pregnancy. I can't believe I didn't stop her.'

To be fair, not that she really felt like it, Sophie didn't see that. Odette was pretty much her own woman and well past the age of consent. But it was none of her business. Right?

She couldn't take much more of this. 'Why are you here?'

He stepped forward and she stepped back until her spine was against the unopened door. He cupped his fingers under her chin and gently lifted her head so that he could see straight into her face.

She wanted to shake him off but with the feel of his hand on her she lost all power. His hand was cool and firm against the heat in her skin, and his gaze captured hers as easily as when—was it only a week ago?—she'd first seen him. Despite the need to do so she couldn't look away.

Now, after the time they'd spent together, she knew his irises were rings of blue, his lashes were dark brown, not black. Memories of that time she'd felt his skin against her cheek and his mouth against hers made her shoulders droop with comfort, as if he'd done it again.

Why did he have to touch her?

Those times in Levi's arms were a whole different world—one she wasn't going to get used to—and unfortunately those few touches had been indelible. How much more proof did she need to get out? Imagine if he could read now how much she wanted to be back in his arms.

Step sideways, move away—the litany in her head drowned out his words. But her body didn't obey. Then she tried to concentrate on what he said to block out his eyes and the feel of his hand. 'I'm sorry you've been involved in this, Sophie. I'd like the chance to sit and talk before I go.'

Finally her body responded and she pulled her chin away and walked to the rail with her back to him. She couldn't sit and talk! No way. 'Was there something you wanted to ask about your sister's pregnancy?'

He came to stand beside her. 'It's nothing to do with Odette,' he said with a skyward glance of frustration. 'It's about the way we parted after extreme circumstances and I don't like that I've upset you.'

She'd have to make a good show of it. There'd be no other way to get rid of him. She held up her hands. 'Look. I don't want to talk about it. I'm over it.'

He searched her face. 'I'm not.' His scrutiny seemed almost abrasive to her skin but she blocked it out. He went on. 'What's happened to you in the past is not me. Can't you forgive me for not being more open with you?'

Nope. She was too darn scared it was the tip of the iceberg of deceit she hadn't discovered yet. Too terrified if she trusted him he would break a part of her that would never heal. She shook her head and looked back in time to a hurt that was nothing to this. 'I can't help how the past has shaped me. Men who can't tell the truth seem drawn to me. I've even a family history of being scammed by liars.'

She risked a glance at his face. 'I'm a simple girl, Levi. I say what I mean. I want you to go.'

He rubbed the back of his neck. 'What do you want me to say, Sophie? I'm sorry I misled you but there are things going on here you don't know about, and if I tell you, then you could be in danger.'

She shook her head. Not good enough. 'There's nothing more to say, then.'

He frowned at her. 'You're not giving me a chance.'

'Tough.' She shrugged her shoulders at him but they felt as heavy as if she carried a yoke with two loaded buckets. When he raised his brows at her, as though she was the one being childish, she actually felt like a child. A small one. Who'd discovered the world wasn't magical any more.

He'd tricked her just when she'd started to believe she might have found a man she could trust her heart to.

A man who warmed her when he looked at her and listened when she was off on her tangent, who stretched her mind and made her laugh and had a strong hand she could hold when she needed, and arms that comforted… All gone.

She'd thought she'd seen things in Levi that she hadn't seen in any man she'd been drawn to. But he'd dashed her fledgling hopes when he lied—the one thing she could never forgive—and she didn't have any reserves left. 'Please go.'

His face shut down until he looked like the stranger she'd seen the first day. Aloof, arrogant, then finally dismissive. 'I'm sorry you feel that way.' He turned but before he left he said, 'Where's William?'

Confusion held her answer. Smiley? 'Work. Why?' Would he never go? Her eyes stung and her throat bulged so thick with tears she could barely breathe.

'Something's come out about the family that used to own Xanadu. Do you know what their name was?'

She didn't have the energy to talk about her foolish, gullible grandfather. It was easier to say, 'No. Why?'

'Nothing important.' He took a step towards her and she panicked that she'd throw herself into his arms. She stepped back as though he'd raised his hand and her panic must have shown on her face. That stopped him.

'Goodbye, Sophie.'

He stepped off the veranda into the dust and as he walked away she realised she'd done what she'd blamed him for. She'd lied to him. And not just about her grandfather.

Levi drove back to Xanadu, too fast, which involved concentration on the road but he was grimly thankful about that. He didn't want to think. Didn't want to relive the distress he'd recognised in Sophie's eyes.

In fact, it was probably safer she wasn't seen with him. Safer for her because he could feel the danger closing in. If the results came back as he expected it upped the ante for Steve. They were all in danger.

Two hours later Smiley burst into the clinic as Sophie sutured a nasty gash from a poorly wielded chainsaw.

The young jackaroo had been lucky he'd only touched his leg on the way through the log and had opened the skin in one thick stripe. Sophie looked up. People burst in often, but never Smiley.

She took one look at his face. 'Odette?'

'She rang me on the satellite phone. Her waters broke, and the contractions are coming every three minutes. She's refusing to move and they're at the Pentecost crossing. Then the phone died.'

FIONA MCARTHUR   143

That didn't make sense. 'The same spot I saw Levi the first day? Why would they go there?'

Smiley shook his head at the delay. 'It's where her father was taken.'

Her father? Taken? It all came back. Crocodiles. 'Pearson.' Levi telling her his name at Kununurra and it had rung a bell then. She couldn't believe she'd forgotten it. Such was the state Levi had her in. The name of the people her grandfather had lost the family station to. Levi hadn't been a guest; he'd been the owner. Hence, the question about her family.

Liar. No wonder they could use the choppers, drive the vehicles, do whatever they wished. Levi had lied again. She yanked the final suture through and the unfortunate young cowboy yelped in protest. Sophie bit her lip and looked at the jackaroo. 'Oops, sorry.' She tied off, snipped the ends of the suture and put a see-through dressing over the top in minimal time. 'Keep it dry. Come back in a week and I'll take the stitches out.'

The young bloke glanced at her once as if to say, *I'll take 'em out myself*, then scurried out of the room. Sophie sighed. She'd never have done that before Levi had disrupted her life.

'Xanadu.' She looked at her brother. 'They own it.' So many lies. Smiley didn't look surprised. More unpalatable truth. 'You knew?' That hurt more than anything else.

Impatiently he answered, 'Odette asked me not to say because she wasn't even supposed to tell me.'

'For goodness sake, why not?' Now these people were infecting Smiley with their subterfuge.

Smiley shook his head. 'Come on.' He gestured to the room as if to ask what do you need. 'It's not important and I really don't care. Let's go.'

Smiley drove as if driving the Dakar Rally—a man who never drove fast—and they made the crossing in an hour. A Kimberley record that Sophie never wanted to break. Her teeth rattled in her head and the dust stung her eyes but she didn't say anything. Smiley's words repeated in her head. 'It's not important and I really don't care.'

So why did she care so much when she'd been led astray by Levi? Why did it matter in the big scheme of things? Had she overreacted? Been precious about semantics? She didn't even want to think what she could have risked if Levi really wanted to see her again.

Smiley was right. Now wasn't the time. It didn't matter. She needed to put any emotion over Levi's deceit aside and think about Odette.

She squeezed the emergency delivery pack on her lap and ran over a few scenarios. At least when she'd felt Odette's uterus the baby had palped head first and not breech, and she had medical backup in Levi, she thought bitterly.

Why wouldn't Levi just pick his sister up and move her? Surely he didn't agree with her having a baby out in the wilderness? She'd never understand these people.

When they arrived she saw why they were still there.

Levi's vehicle sat low to the ground, four flat tyres, a very reasonable excuse not to leave. The local police vehicle had pulled up next to them and the two officers were talking on the two-way.

Smiley pulled up in a shower of gravel and threw himself out of the car towards Odette, who sat with her back against a boab in her trousers and bra, and burst into tears when she saw him. Sophie blinked. That was different.

Levi sat next to her with his arm around her until Smiley took his place.

Sophie glanced back at the river, which wasn't far enough away from them, and scanned the bank. Two large saltwater crocodiles sat patiently at the edge in the shade and watched them with unblinking yellow eyes. Yikes.

Antipathy forgotten she glanced at Odette, who was lost in Smiley's arms, and turned to Levi. Her brows creased. 'You OK?'

'Will be,' he said grimly. 'Satellite phone went flat after we'd got through to the police and William.'

She frowned. He didn't look right. 'Are you hurt?'

'Stray bullet nicked me. It's nothing.' He lifted his arm from his chest and showed a wad of heavily blood-stained material tied around his left arm; she guessed it was Odette's shirt.

'Let me see.'

'Sort Odette first.' He was still giving orders. Typical.

Sophie scanned his sister quickly. She didn't sound like a woman in the final throes of labour. 'You OK, Odette?'

Odette spoke from Smiley's arms. 'I am now.'

She turned back to Levi. 'Right, now show me.'

He glared at her and held up his arm. 'We don't have time for this. He could shoot again.'

Sophie busied herself undoing the material. 'I'm assuming we're on the right side of the tree for safety.' She inclined her head towards the river. 'And that's not all who's here. The police will protect us from him but not from the couple of salties who fancy a piece of you too.'

He raised his brows at her. 'It must be your fate in life to warn me about crocodiles.'

'And yours to keep me in the dark. But we'll talk about that later.'

Gingerly he held his injured arm as she eased the wad away from the skin below his shoulder to expose a neat in hole and a less-neat out hole. The bullet had passed through in a jagged tunnel without causing major damage. Blood oozed as soon as she took the pressure away and hastily she put the wad back. He was right. It wouldn't kill him. Levi's indrawn breath made her wince. 'Sorry.'

'It's nothing. I'll heal. Get Odette away from here.'

The man was mad. 'I imagine the police will get us all away from here.'

Short sharp shake of his head and she felt her own impatience rise.

'I'm not going anywhere until I find him,' he growled.

She gestured to his shoulder. 'Not like that surely.'

'Steve, or someone, shot at us while Odette was saying goodbye. Here. Shot the tyres on the car. Tried to kill my sister. He's still out there, though the police think he's gone.' His eyes burned into hers and she shivered a little at the implacable decision to go after the shooter.

His voice lowered but was no less definite. 'I'm staying until we get him. Now, please do what I ask and take Odette. If you stay here he'll try to kill you too.'

She glanced at Smiley, who was attempting to disentangle Odette and calm her at the same time. He looked up at Sophie. 'Let's get 'em out of here.'

The bullet hit the tree beside them a millisecond before the shot rang out.

Smiley scooped Odette like she was a feather and dived around the back of the tree. Levi grabbed Sophie and pushed her behind the tree onto the ground and flattened himself on top of her. The breath whooshed from her lungs and a bunch of dead boab leaves crackled under her. The gunman had moved. She didn't want Levi to protect her with his body. Did he want to get shot again?

She sucked in another laboured breath. He was darned heavy but she doubted he'd listen to her right at this moment. Thankfully, when no further shots rang out, he eased himself off, but kept his body between her and the direction the bullet had come from.

'You all right?' he said, and she nodded. The fact that he'd cared enough to protect her made her eyes sting. Though maybe he'd have done it for any woman and she shouldn't read anything into his actions.

The hardest part was trying not to remember the feel

of his strong chest against her or the male scent that reminded her of other times she'd been in his arms.

As they crouched and dusted themselves off Sophie could see a fresh splash of blood in the dirt beside her. Levi had dislodged the makeshift bandage and his wound oozed sluggishly again. 'Come here,' she said, and resettled the wadding as she frowned at him.

His eyes caught hers. 'Thank you.'

She couldn't help the heat that rode in her cheeks. 'Any time.'

He raised his brows. 'I might take you up on that.'

'This guy means business,' Smiley commented grimly when the four of them were crouched behind the thankfully wide trunk of the fat boab. The police had dived behind their own car and one of them fired back.

Levi grimaced. 'I'm so sorry you two are involved in Steve's plans.'

She looked from one man to the other. 'Involved in what plan? Now what don't I know?' Sophie demanded.

Levi sighed. 'You know the helicopter was definitely sabotaged, but I'm now convinced my father was pushed into the river here five months ago. Whoever did that is shooting at us now and I think it's my half-brother, Steve.'

She did not believe this. 'Steve's your half-brother?' This was outback Australia, not some gangland setting. Who were these people?

Levi saw her confusion. 'Because of Xanadu. It seems that my new-found half-sibling expected to inherit Xanadu, and he wants it.' He paused. 'In case we all die here…' He pulled her in close with his good arm and dropped a kiss on her lips. 'I think you are the most amazing woman I've ever met.'

He'd kissed her. In the middle of a gunfight. And by the look on his face he'd enjoyed it. Yep. He was mad. 'You must be delirious. We're being *shot at*!'

'That's why it seemed a good idea to tell you now.' He stroked her cheek. 'And I'm not lying.'

The sound of a vehicle revving and then driving away had Smiley peer around the tree. 'Could have been someone else parked and they got scared,' Smiley said.

Levi hit the tree with the side of his fist and then winced as the vibration ran through his body to his injured arm. 'Or could be our man.'

The police car started and the officers drove off in pursuit. 'It seems the coppers agree,' Smiley said.

'Damn. Wish I'd seen the car.' Levi growled, 'Let's get the girls out of here and back to Xanadu.'

Smiley nodded, grimly, and went for the truck to reverse it back to Odette.

Sophie slid down the tree next to Odette to see how she fared. 'You OK, honey?'

The girl's head was down and she held her stomach. 'I think the baby's coming.'

She whimpered and then a tiny strangled moan had Sophie peer at her with a frown. 'We might just sit for a minute,' Sophie said to no one in particular, and rested her hand on Odette's arm. 'What's happening?'

Odette turned agonised eyes to Sophie and whispered, 'I need to go to the bathroom.'

Sophie looked at Levi. 'I think she's pushing.'

CHAPTER ELEVEN

'No. NOT here.' Levi cast his eyes skywards but all he could see were the sparse leaves of the boab above him. He could handle the idea of being shot at but not the birth of Odette's baby.

He needed her safe, with doctors, and theatres, and sterile surroundings. He couldn't lose Odette like his mother. His worst nightmare. He'd failed in every aspect of keeping his sister safe. He'd involved her in a helicopter crash, a shooting and now this. He wanted her out of here and surely she could stand.

'Please stand, Odette.'

'You can't prioritise this.' Now Sophie was shaking her head at him. 'She's pushing. It's coming.'

Prioritise? He wanted his sister in a nice safe hospital. Preferably a Sydney one. How had it come to this? 'Come on, Odette. You have to get up.'

Odette looked up at him and he could see the fear behind her tremulous smile. 'Sorry. Can't do.'

He looked at Sophie and despite the sympathy he saw in her eyes she shook her head. She was right. Again.

The truck backed up to them and Smiley jumped out. 'Let's go.'

Levi looked helplessly down at both women, distanced from him by their silent communication. 'Sophie says Odette's having the baby.'

'She can't have it here.' Smiley cast a quick glance to the river. 'The crocs will have the lot of us if we don't get out.'

'Then make sure they don't,' Sophie said with a touch of asperity. 'She'll move as soon as the baby's born.'

'Tell the men to go away,' Odette whispered.

Sophie obliged. 'We're busy.' Smiley blinked, then nodded and drifted away to keep watch between them and the river. Levi looked down at this woman who'd come into their lives and continued to cope with one disaster after another. Thank God she was here. What would they do without her? What would he do without her?

When had everything changed? When had Sophie become more important than the guilt he lived with when he couldn't help everyone? More important than finding his father's killer. More important to protect than himself. Was she his unforeseen destiny?

Sophie and Odette leaned with their backs against the tree. 'You concentrate on listening to your body and I'll worry about everything else. Just breathe it out,' she said quietly and looked up at him. 'I need the kit out of the truck and the rugs I brought, please.' At least it seemed he could be of use.

He did as requested and then returned with what she'd asked. 'Where do you want it?'

'Spread around us and the thin rug over Odette. And pass me the pack and the towel. Thanks.' She helped Odette adjust her clothing under the rug, then undid the delivery pack and laid the cord clamps aside. She drew up the Syntocinon for after the birth, washed her hands with antiseptic, then pulled on the gloves. 'A little primitive but this tree has great facilities compared to the camp the other day.'

Levi strangled back an inappropriate laugh. He supposed it did and he watched her lean back against the tree next to his sister and wait. Her capable hands were clasped loosely on her lap. As if just another April day in the Kimberleys. How was he ever going to go back to Sydney and leave her? Except for the minor fact she wouldn't have him.

Odette looked up once, an arrested expression on her face as she stared at Sophie. 'William said you told him birthing a baby was like having a foal or a calf.'

Sophie brushed the hair off Odette's forehead with her finger and smiled. She had a great smile, Levi thought as he pretended not to listen.

'He's a bad boy for repeating that. I said that because he was scared for you. But you're doing so well it might be true.'

Levi saw the tears well as Odette sniffed. 'I want to go home. I can't believe it's happening here.' His fault.

'After meeting you two?' Sophie rolled her eyes and she glanced at him quickly before looking back at Odette. 'I can.'

Odette's laugh was cut short by the next pain and

Levi winced as it dragged a low groan from her as the baby moved down.

Levi twisted his hands; he felt so damn powerless to do anything for either of them.

'Beautiful,' said Sophie in that quiet, almost hypnotic voice he'd never be able to match in the circumstances. 'Slow breaths. Not long now.'

She looked up and frowned when she saw him watching her. He stretched his lips into a strained smile but she must have seen his tension. 'Take a few breaths too, Levi. It's OK.'

He was always in trouble with this woman. 'Can I get you anything, Sophie?'

'Sip of water, for Odette, thanks. There's a bottle in the truck. And maybe check on Smiley.' In other words, his marching orders. OK. Maybe he would be better out of the way until it was all over.

'Call him William!' Odette mumbled through gritted teeth, as she finished the pain and breathed out.

Levi handed her the water and drifted away and Sophie watched him go. He appeared unflappable considering the day he'd had and that his sister was doing what he'd dreaded all along. Sophie couldn't guarantee everything would be fine; she could just assume it would, and deal with the variations as they came.

And Levi would be there for support if she needed him. She had enormous faith in him and she didn't quite know where it had grown from. He'd become a good person to have around. She could've become used to that.

Odette gripped her hand and Sophie refocused where she should have been all along.

Odette panted and bit her lip. 'I don't think I want to do this.'

Sophie closed her fingers around Odette's shoulder in support. 'I know. Let it happen. Just push your tummy out as you breathe in, and let it fall as you breathe out, and the baby will move down.'

Odette breathed and finally Sophie could see the first signs of descent. 'I can see some dark hair now, Odette, so he's not bald.'

Odette's eyes stared into hers as she searched Sophie's face. 'The contraction's gone and it's burning.'

'As it should,' Sophie said quietly. 'Everything needs to stretch and the head sitting there is the best way to do that.'

'I am so not doing this again,' Odette ground out as she panted the pain away. Then her voice changed. 'Can I touch him?'

Sophie smiled—she loved this bit—and took her hand to guide it down to the baby's head. 'Of course.'

Odette stretched tentatively until she realised there was a hard little scalp right under her fingers and her hand jumped away. 'Oh, my Lord. This is so not right.'

'Afraid it is.' Sophie smiled. 'The next pain will move baby out more, just remember to push slowly with your breath. You don't want your baby to come out too fast.'

'I don't?' She whistled her breath in between her teeth. 'You've got to be kidding.' Odette closed her eyes and breathed, and by fractions the baby descended.

Sophie stroked Odette's hair out of her eyes. 'You are amazing, you know that?'

The next contraction built and the amount of the baby's head grew slowly as Odette breathed him out. Wrinkled forehead, eyes and nose, and finally mouth and chin, until the whole head rotated to face his mother's leg. Sophie dried the little face and hair gently as they waited for the next contraction.

'He's blinking,' she told Odette.

Odette panted. 'But his body's not out.'

'He's awake, that's for sure.' And as Odette pushed for the last time, the baby eased into Sophie's hands. She ran the towel over him as he opened his eyes wider—a dark, dark blue—and he blinked as he looked around.

'It really is a boy? I have my son?' Then, 'He's not crying,' Odette said as Sophie slid him up his mother's body skin to skin until he lay across Odette's breasts. She covered them both with the rug and tucked the edges in.

'He doesn't have to, he's breathing. He's pink and happy to be on you. And yes, he's definitely a boy.'

Sophie gave the injection, clamped and cut the cord and waited for the third stage to complete. When it was over she checked Odette's uterus through her soft belly skin, and found it rocklike beneath her fingers. Everything had done as it should. She pulled the rug back again and checked Odette's pulse.

'It's over.' Odette smiled up at her. 'I've done it.' Her smile seemed to light up ten feet around them. She glanced down at her son. 'I can't tell you how having you here helped me do that.'

'My privilege.' They sat there quietly for a minute or two. Just breathing and allowing the peace of the bush to steal over them. To appreciate the wonder of childbirth in such a primitive setting. The baby squirmed and Odette laughed and stroked his head and she glanced at Sophie. Their eyes met and they both smiled.

'Can you ask Levi and William to come see him now, please?' The softness in those powerful new mother's eyes made it hard for Sophie to swallow and her eyes stung. This was why she loved this job.

'Sure.' Sophie tucked a little escaping hand back under the blankets around Odette's new son and stripped off her gloves. 'Congratulations. You were amazing.'

'Thank you, Sophie. I just let you worry about everything else.' She stroked the downy head as her son wrinkled his forehead and blinked up at her. 'He's so gorgeous.'

Sophie stroked his tiny hand that escaped again and nodded. She signalled Levi over and watched the men fuss over mother and baby. Her face ached with a broad goofy smile that faded with just a tinge of melancholy for what might have been. She walked towards the river to keep watch.

A few minutes later Levi stood and crossed the grass to her side and she moved back to a safer distance. He smiled ruefully, and then stepped forward and deliberately eased in closer to invade her space. 'You are getting a hug whether you like it or not.'

'Oh.' She didn't know what to say to that, and in the

end she didn't have to say anything as Levi lifted his good arm and drew her against his chest. She sighed against him. She was glad he insisted, she thought as she sighed again.

'Thank you, Sophie,' he said quietly, and they stood there, with the sound of the river gurgling behind them and the raucous laugh of a kookaburra punctuating their isolation.

His arm was warm and heavy around her shoulders and the amount of comfort she gained was disproportionate to the gesture. She leant her head more heavily against the good side of his body for a few precious seconds and allowed her facial bones to savour the hardness of his chest against her cheek, the feel of his shirt against her skin and to hear his heart beat, like a rhythmic drum that beat out a cadence of support.

She'd never really been a girl to lean on people. Hadn't really learnt how until now. There was something magic about the way Levi could remove weariness from her like a blanket lifting from her shoulders. He could energise her with a look, let alone the circle of his arms. Shame she'd refused to listen to him when she'd had the chance.

Her nose wrinkled. She could smell his blood. She focused on the damp patch a few inches from her nose and it was as if a beam of stark white light had been switched on in her brain. Her stupid brain that hadn't seen it all before while she'd been distracted by Odette's need. How could she have missed it? Like a splash of cold water from the river, the concept of

Levi's death stared at her, shocking and far too real. It had been that close.

He could have died. Been dead right now. The reality squeezed her chest and her throat closed over. She'd been the greatest fool. Imagine if the bullet had been a few inches closer to his heart. For the first time she realised how narrow her escape…to losing the man she suddenly couldn't doubt she loved. Why had it taken her so long to realise?

She loved him. The tears prickled then, and stung, and burned at the thought of Levi in mortal danger. She'd been obsessing about his perceived faults to protect her own realisation. Of course she loved him. What had she been thinking?

'So here we are again,' he said into her hair, and the vibration, more poignant for his mortality, felt so much more precious than her own pride. If he'd been dead she'd have missed this. Any of this. All of this. Oblivious to her epiphany he went on musingly. 'I thought I'd seen the last of you.'

Thank God he hadn't. She closed her eyes and two fat tears ran down her cheeks. She swallowed and tried to level her voice. 'Fate conspires apparently.'

'Hmm,' he rumbled beneath her. 'Unfortunately, fate wasn't the only one conspiring. I'm sorry you and William were involved in this mess.'

Then she remembered she'd lied to him too and she hadn't told him. Suddenly it was so hard to start. Funny that. After all her bluster about being kept in the dark and offence at the misconceptions he'd practised, she'd done the same.

'Congratulations on your nephew,' she said weakly as she pulled away. She turned to surreptitiously wipe her cheeks.

'Lucky baby to have a new beginning,' he went on drily, and she could feel his eyes follow her as she widened the distance.

New beginnings. Could she do that? 'What would you do with a new beginning if you had one?' She took her eyes off the bank in front of them to look back at his face. Maybe they could laugh about the irony.

She didn't see the grey crocodile move a foot closer to where they stood on the gravel. The whole world had condensed down to Levi—the fact that she wanted to run back to his arms and didn't know if she could go through life denying that she'd had the chance and blew it. Now she'd stopped lying to herself.

Motionless, the huge crocodile watched her with unblinking yellow eyes and even Levi didn't see the danger until the reptile moved again.

Levi must have sensed or seen the sweep of the jagged tail out of the corner of his eye as the crocodile moved because he caught Sophie's hand and pulled her back into his arms and back towards the truck. 'Let's go. The crocs are getting hungry.' She'd forgotten the danger again. When she'd promised herself she never would. Far too close for comfort.

Levi pulled her to him. 'My turn to warn you.'

His hand was tight around her wrist, painfully so, as he shuffled them both backed towards the tree and Sophie glanced back. 'Too close,' she said as she shuddered.

'Time to go, William,' he called over his shoulder, and all Sophie could think about was the way her dog had died and the fact that she'd forgotten her own rules. She was the one who was supposed to know the dangers. When she leant up against the truck her legs trembled and threatened to collapse. They both could have been killed. She shuddered again and he gathered her up and put her on the seat.

They both looked back and the crocodile had stopped in the spot they'd been standing. His thick reptilian tail swayed back and forth in frustration. His mate left the water and came to stand beside him.

Smiley whistled as he gathered the belongings and helped Odette move with her baby to the truck. 'We need to relocate those fellows,' Smiley said. 'Before they wipe your whole family out.'

'And yours,' said Levi grimly.

Smiley shook his head. 'Never seen 'em so nasty. It's not normal.'

'Spare me from feeling sorry for the crocodile.' Levi stared at the water. 'Though I wonder if that was planned too? Steve could have been feeding them. Knowing Odette wanted to put a plaque up here.'

'If they don't catch him we'll never know.'

It was a subdued party that returned to Xanadu. Smiley drove, and the others crammed like sardines, with Odette's baby, into the front. Sophie sat on Levi and his arms held her as if he'd never let her go. Considering the day, Sophie was more than happy with that.

Levi drew her into the resort building with his arm still protectively pulling her against him. Every now and then her mind recapped the morning, dwelling on Levi's close escape. 'I need to see to your wound before we go.'

He frowned. 'It's nothing. We'll get Odette settled first and get you a stiff drink.' He signalled to one of the indoor staff.

She was over the crocodile. It was the shooting that knocked her. Levi could have died. 'Fine. But I'm not leaving until I've had a good look.'

He glanced at her as he waited to be put through to the police. 'Think about yourself for a change.' She watched him organise Odette, call the police—where he learned Steve had been placed in custody—then break the news to the staff of Steve's involvement.

She should be dressing his wound, not watching him direct the world. 'Can't you do this later?'

He smiled down at her, and the way even that brief lift of his lips affected her heart was enough to warn her how bad it would be when he'd gone. 'What will you do when you don't have me to boss around?' he said.

Not what she wanted to dwell on. 'Be lonely, I guess.' She said it more to herself than to him and she didn't see his arrested expression. 'I'll find some first-aid gear.' She began to move off and he caught her hand. Like he had that night they first came here, only this time her hand seemed to tangle in his as her fingers clasped his back.

'Wait. Sophie.' He looked around and ushered her, not resisting for once, through the door and out onto the veranda and down the steps to the rustic bench under the massive boab.

He stared into her face and this time there was nowhere to hide. 'What did you mean? "Be lonely"?'

Could she do it? Throw it all away or be brave? The fear was there. The risk of pain greater than anything she'd experienced, but today's close shaves had taught her a valuable lesson. She had to take that risk. 'I'll be lonely without you.' She looked back at him. That strong jaw, that mouth—the man who'd stormed into her heart when she'd been kicking and screaming the whole way, and he'd achieved it so easily in such a short time. 'I must have become used to having you around. In a week.' She laughed mirthlessly at her foolishness.

It was too late to deny a recognition on a different level and that something in him called to her the way no other person did. She saw the trappings of wealth she'd said she despised and the bender of truth when she'd promised she'd never listen to another lie. But she'd also seen the man who completed her. Who instinctively knew when she needed support and gave unstintingly.

No one had ever understood her before. That was the crux. Levi got her. Knew where she was coming from almost before she did. 'Why is that?'

'Why is what?' he said, and she realised she must have asked out loud.

'Why do you seem to understand me when others don't?'

His voice softened. 'If you tried, you could understand me too.' When she looked into his eyes she saw him clearly, as if through a fresh pane of glass, unmarked by what had come in the past.

His caring, readiness to learn new things, listen to her point of view. His willingness to be there when the burden became too much, his hand there to pull her up and his arms to comfort. Maybe she did understand him in ways she'd never wanted to understand others. And finally, with tiny tentative steps, she allowed herself to glimpse what life with Levi could be like. If she allowed herself to trust him.

Was it that easy? 'Maybe I understand you a little.'

He slipped his good arm around her. 'Two people, from opposite ends of a huge country, meet and share extraordinary events. We've both changed, shared things—perhaps it's meant to be.'

She shook her head. It was all so confusing. 'How can it be meant when you live somewhere I could never live?'

He smiled. 'And vice versa.'

Hopeless case. She'd known it. 'See.'

'We will. In time.' He hugged her and stood to help her up. 'Come on. You need to rest after all this excitement. It's been a big day.' He touched her cheek. 'But we're not finished with this subject.'

Then she remembered. If she was going to be brave she may as well finish it. 'And there's something I have to tell you.'

He stopped. 'Really?' He searched her face, frowned and then slowly he smiled. 'Do I detect a hint of guilt?'

She blushed and he laughed. His eyes opened wide with amusement. 'Oh. I hope so. From Miss Trustworthy herself?' She didn't say anything and he pulled her back down on the seat.

She tried to stand again but he kept hold of her hand and she subsided. 'I'm not rushing this,' he said. 'This is priceless. Do go on.'

She ducked her chin, suddenly shy, then resolutely raised it. 'You know when you asked if I knew the original family from Xanadu?'

'Hmm.'

Why did it feel as if he were watching her face more than listening to her words. 'Pay attention. I'm feeling bad here.'

He squeezed her shoulders. 'Good. You look very cute when you're guilty.'

'I told you I didn't know—' she drew a deep breath '—but I do. I lied. It was my grandfather. Oh, and Smiley's grandfather. Our father's father.'

He laughed. 'You lied to me?'

She looked away. 'It was such a long story—I didn't want to talk about it then.' How dare he laugh at her.

'You lied.'

She glared. 'Not as many times as you did but there is a certain irony.'

'Brilliantly so.' He tilted his head and he wasn't smiling. 'But I don't think I can talk to you any more. I'm too hurt that you deceived me.'

She frowned, frozen for a moment in time that she'd offended him deeply, then realised he'd teased her. She glared at him. 'So under all that moody exterior you're a comedian?'

'Moody? Never. Work worn.' He kissed her. 'And you have to admit, you not telling the truth is hilariously funny.'

She glared at him again but he'd moved on musingly. 'So Sullivan was his name. Your grandfather? You and Smiley are the true owners of Xanadu?'

In another life. 'No.'

He tilted his head as he worked it out. 'But my grandfather cheated at cards and documented it. Was, in fact, very proud of scamming your grandfather out of his birthright.'

Her foolish grandfather had lost it though. 'Nice genes you have, Dr Pearson.'

He winked at her. 'I'm working on that.'

What was that supposed to mean? 'Anyway, whatever he wrote, it's not legal.'

'Another thing we'll discuss later.'

There was that money issue. She wished she could get over it. 'Are you very well off?'

He didn't smile but she could see the flicker of amusement at her prejudice. 'Afraid so. Stinking rich. Grandfather tripled the family coffers in his day and I've made some pretty useful investments too.'

'Oh.' He seemed so different to Brad. 'You still work hard to help others though. When financially you don't need to do anything?'

'I need to for me. I'm not proud of my father or grandfather. Never a thought to benefit their fellow man. When my brother died I vowed I'd make him proud of me. Do some good.'

She savoured the way he looked down at her. As if she'd lightened his day just by being there. No one had looked at her like that since her parents had died. 'You seem so different from when you came.'

'Am I? Then you've made me so. I've been beating myself up for the past two years and had forgotten how to smile. A certain determined young midwife has made me realise there is more to life than regretting what can't be changed.'

'What couldn't be changed?' She needed to know. Needed to see what had formed this man she'd grown to love. To try, if she could, to help him. 'What hurt you? Tell me.'

'The loss of one of my patients. I blamed myself.'

'She died in an operation?'

'No, Miss Impatient. She didn't die in an operation. None of my patients have died in their operations.'

'Sorr-ry.' He wrinkled his brow at her and she realised she'd been distracted by his rebuke. But he was still smiling at her. Then his smile departed and she could see the sadness.

'The day we confirmed there was nothing I could do to restore her sight she stepped in front of a truck.'

Sophie drew a sharp breath. Of course that would affect him. 'Like your brother. That was probably an accident too, you know,' she said earnestly. She saw the pain he still held and she squeezed his hand and her heart lifted when he squeezed back. She was glad to offer even that tiny comfort.

'It was no accident.' He went on. 'It hit home and I blamed myself.' He shrugged. 'Maybe there'd been something I could have tried. Should I have encouraged more strongly her hope for the future of technology?' He shook his head over a tragedy that could never be rectified. 'It's too late for her but I've doubled my workload. Tried to help more people until even my colleagues were telling me to take a break.'

She understood the concept of never doing enough. Had run herself ragged since returning to the Kimberleys but for a different reason. 'You can't help the whole world.'

'When my father died suddenly, things in his will puzzled me. I'd thought he hated me, but I regretted I'd never tried to sway him towards a more fulfilling life. Grown up enough to talk to him, perhaps?'

Sophie squeezed the hand holding hers. 'People die unexpectedly and we regret what we didn't say. We all do.'

'I know I do,' he said, and gave her a thank-you-for-understanding smile, and she felt her heart expand with his pain.

One thing she didn't understand. 'But your father died five months ago. Why so long before you came here?'

He shrugged. 'I had to clear the backlog of cases I'd promised. And wait for the wet season to finish.' His gaze brushed over her and the glow in his eyes when he did so made her blush. 'I wish I'd come earlier.'

Imagine that. She'd have been in Perth and missed knowing him. Even if he broke her heart now she could never regret that she met him. Had grown from knowing him in ways she'd never believe. 'Then lucky you didn't because I wouldn't have been here.'

He smiled down at her. 'Fate.'

'Serendipitous.' She snuggled under his arm, reluctant for this camaraderie to end. She'd learnt so much that helped her understand.

'Sophie.' He spoke into her hair.

She sighed. Soaking the moment in, in case it was the last time. 'What?'

'Look at me.'

He lifted his arm and she sat back and turned to face him. Her eyes met his and what she saw in them made the breath jam in her throat.

He lifted her hand and kissed her wrist. 'I see in you all the good things I wanted to find in myself. Things I find precious and uplifting and make me want to be a better man.'

She shook her head. She hadn't done anything.

Then he took both her hands in his and squeezed her fingers. 'I've come to know you—and love you.' Her breath caught in her throat but he went on. 'I can't imagine going home without you. I can't imagine anywhere without you.'

She searched his face, not believing his words, but unable to stop the sudden gallop in her chest. He couldn't love her.

She looked again and this time became a little less unconvinced as she saw the confirmation in his eyes. 'What are you saying?'

He smiled down at her. Like he really did love her? She hugged that impossible thought tightly as hope began to build. 'Will you marry me? Be my partner for life?' He lifted her hand to his mouth and kissed her palm, then folded her fingers over his salute. 'Can you love me back?'

She reached up and stroked his face. Those strong lines of cheek and jaw with the first regrowth of dark whiskers bristly beneath her fingers. How had she found him? Been so fortunate? Her eyes stung and she chewed her lip, suddenly too frightened to say the words out loud. She took a deep breath and then she did.

'I already love you. Too much. Apparently since the waterhole on our trek. The moment you reached down to lift me. And then you kissed me and nothing was the same again.' She remembered the instant. 'I was so frightened you'd hurt me again I wasn't game to let the feeling out. And now you've exposed me.' Her eyes filled with happy tears. 'So, yes, please. I'll be your wife.'

Levi looked down at her. 'So you'll keep me on the straight and narrow?' He gestured to the gorge below them. 'Even away from your beloved Kimberleys?'

She shrugged. Suddenly home wasn't home if Levi wasn't there. 'We can visit.'

Levi barely dared to believe he wasn't going to lose her. Sophie's beautiful face turned up at him, so sincere and open and honest and shining with love. How had he been this blessed? His throat tightened and he pulled her close and held her against his heart as the world receded. His Sophie. His heart. His love. The other stuff they'd work out.

CHAPTER TWELVE

SOPHIE gazed around at the guests at their wedding, an unlikely mix of smiling faces, as the setting sun dusted the rugged ranges in the distance a glowing and loving lilac. Loving like the vows she and Levi had exchanged above the stunning gorge at Xanadu and glowing like the look in her new husband's eyes.

She smiled at her friends—the sun-frocked women, and their sun-browned men in best Akubras and polished boots—and Levi's friends in the sprinkling of suits and designer dresses, and the way the two groups melded with much gaiety under the leafless branches of the giant boab.

A tree that had grown more bulbous over the thousand years it had stood under a blue Kimberley sky and watched each turn of fortune this grand old homestead had seen since it had been built by her great-grandfather and lost for two generations. Now her and Levi's children, and maybe Smiley and Odette's children, would visit, and one day those growing children would learn to love their heritage.

The cries of sulphur-crested cockatoos filled the late-afternoon air and she lifted her head to allow the noise to soak into her memory as she inhaled the delicate aroma of the frangipani called Kimberley Gold in her bouquet. The heady scent enveloped the wedding party better than any designer fragrance yet to be fashioned by man.

She'd be fine in the city. Beside her stood Levi, her husband, so tall and straight and gazing down at her with such a look of pride and love in his dark blue eyes the tears pricked behind the mascara that Odette had insisted she wear, and she had to force her fingers not to rub her eyes.

He must have seen the glitter she tried to hide because his thumb gently rubbed her palm in comfort. Already he knew what she was thinking, and magically the tears receded as his fingers entwined through hers. He looked down at the impressive pink Kimberley diamond ring they'd chosen from the mine and she tutted as she followed his gaze. 'You have too much money.'

He smiled. 'Would you like me to give it all away?' The words were spoken lightly but the look in his eyes assured her he was deadly serious, and her heart thumped at the lengths this man would go to make her happy.

She blinked back more tears, refusing to weep even tears of joy on her wedding day. 'I could help you.' She smiled up at him. 'There's lots of things I'd like to improve around here.' *Even if I'm not here to see them*, she thought, with barely any regret.

He hugged her to him. 'I can see I've taken on an expensive wife.' She felt his arm around her, so strong and sure of their love, and the truth was there to see. This was home. In Levi's arms. Not Xanadu, not busy Sydney, or wherever his work took him—anywhere was home as long as she had Levi by her side.

The small plane—Levi had declined the helicopter with a smiling glance at his new wife—flew out the next morning, and with his hand in hers Sophie watched the brown earth pass beneath her with no regrets. The timeless mountains and steep-sided gorges would be there for ever. Xanadu would stand watch over the land until she returned.

Now she could look to the future and new adventures with the man she trusted with all her heart.

That night in Sydney they dined at an exclusive restaurant overlooking Sydney Harbour and Sophie could see why Levi loved it.

'This used to be my favourite place to eat,' Levi said as he gazed around at the panoramic harbour views and then back at his wife. Then he looked down at his plate and somehow she knew he was thinking of their bush-tucker walk through the hot bush. 'You've broadened my palate.'

'Do they serve grubs here?' she teased, and stretched her hand out across the fine white tablecloth to his. A frisson of magic passed between them and curved her lips in that persistent secret smile she'd had since last night. How could she not have known what had awaited her in Levi's arms? Yet what could have prepared her for the experience Levi had created as he'd shown her the meaning of giving and taking in all that love had to offer. Still her skin tingled and quivered as even a fleeting touch like this brought back memories and sensations she'd never imagined, and their rings glinted as their fingers entwined.

His eyes smouldered and she felt her belly kick. 'You're blushing, my wife,' he teased.

Sophie fanned herself. 'Must be the food.'

'Strange, how the food is the last thing I'm thinking of. For you I would even eat a witchetty grub.'

Thank goodness this restaurant was discreet but she needed to change the subject before her wicked husband said something even more outrageous. Sophie poked at the delicacies he'd ordered for her. 'I won't ask you if you don't make me eat that oyster.'

He laughed and took the morsel from her plate. 'I've something better for you.' She frowned as he reached into the pocket of his suit and withdrew a long white envelope.

Thick and embossed, he placed it in her hand with such an air of expectation she frowned.

'To my darling wife with love.' For a fleeting moment the weight of the paper sent an echo of mistrust and dread left from her dealings with Brad, but she banished it easily with her unswerving knowledge of Levi's love. Now what had he thought up?

She frowned down at the envelope and then back at him. 'What's this?' She weighed it in her hand and the thickness of paper folded had her intrigued.

'Open it.'

She tried, but it was sealed and stubborn, and Levi smiled as he handed her a knife to slit the edge. She glanced across at him. Whatever it was, he was enjoying this. Finally the envelope opened and she eased the thick wad of paper out and unfolded it.

It couldn't be! Her eyes widened as she moistened suddenly dry lips.

'A million acres?' She looked at him again and his blue eyes danced with amusement and love. 'You can't give me a million acres for a wedding present.'

He sat back to enjoy the view more. 'Why not?'

'It's too much.' She looked up at him. Not sure how he'd take the next thought. 'I'd want to give Smiley half.'

He grinned. Well pleased with himself. 'I thought you'd say that, but he's agreed to be bought out.'

She frowned. 'Xanadu needs managing. We're living in Sydney.'

He raised his brows. 'Perhaps we should only live in Sydney six months of the year.'

He was enjoying this. Stringing her along. But she couldn't help the excitement that grew with each tumbled thought. 'And where will we be the rest of the time?'

'Guess.' He lifted her hand and ran his fingers along the soft skin before he gently, and so reverently that her face flamed, kissed her wrist. 'Let's spend that money you said I should give away.'

'By buying out Smiley?'

He shook his head and kissed her again and she watched the gooseflesh rise on her arms. She wished he wouldn't do that now because concentration was hard and she wanted to understand.

'By buying an outback eye clinic. The Sophie Pearson Mobile Eye Clinic, in fact.' He smiled. 'You'll be pleased to know it's made quite a dent in our wealth.'

She shook her head, overwhelmed by his vision, but he hadn't finished. 'I thought, if you agree, we'd travel north and visit out-flung camps and missions during the dry, from May till October, and work together.'

She saw the passion in his eyes. The chance to do good work. She felt the tears well at her own fortune in finding a man she could be so proud of.

She tilted her head and she'd bet there was the same excitement shining from her own eyes that she could see in his. 'Of course, we'll need a base to work from and Xanadu fits the bill perfectly.'

She struggled to hold back her tears as she tried to take in the vision he'd created. 'Funny that.'

'And should you become otherwise engaged—' he glanced wickedly down at her narrow waist '—I can hire an assistant while you wait at home with our family, at Xanadu.'

He'd done this for her. 'You've thought of everything.'

His eyes darkened and she blushed right down to her toes and in all the places he'd discovered last night. 'And if we have children they will grow to love both homes.'

The warmth he created just by looking at her expanded until she could feel herself glow. 'You really have thought of everything.'

'I just follow the rule.' He leaned across and kissed her lips. 'Always tell the truth. And the truth is, I will love my darling wife for ever and ever.'

FROM SINGLE
MUM TO LADY

BY
JUDY CAMPBELL

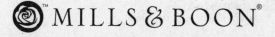

To 'Granny Annie' with much love.

First published in Great Britain 2010
Harlequin Mills & Boon Limited,
Eton House, 18-24 Paradise Road, Richmond, Surrey TW9 1SR

© Judy Campbell 2010

ISBN: 978 0 263 87896 7

Harlequin Mills & Boon policy is to use papers that are natural, renewable and recyclable products and made from wood grown in sustainable forests. The logging and manufacturing process conform to the legal environmental regulations of the country of origin.

Printed and bound in Spain
by Litografia Rosés, S.A., Barcelona

Dear Reader

Writing about Jandy and Patrick was kick-started by a conversation with a friend of mine. She'd been a single hard-working mum, with no time in her life for romance, and after years of putting her child first had lost confidence in going out on a date with anyone. She did meet her dream man in the end, quite unexpectedly, and this inspired me to write about Jandy, who has given up all hope of meeting a soul-mate but, despite her busy multi-tasking life, finds him eventually.

It was great fun to write, and I was quite sorry to say goodbye to Jandy, Patrick and their little girls at the end of the book! I do hope you enjoy reading it.

Best wishes

Judy

Judy Campbell is from Cheshire. As a teenager she spent a great year at high school in Oregon, USA, as an exchange student. She has worked in a variety of jobs, including teaching young children, being a secretary and running a small family business. Her husband comes from a medical family and one of their three grown-up children is a GP. Any spare time—when she's not writing romantic fiction—is spent playing golf, especially in the Highlands of Scotland.

CHAPTER ONE

'OH, NO! What the…?' yelped Jandy Marshall, as a freezing cascade of water poured down on her, soaking her hair and nurse's uniform in a few traumatic seconds. She stared up at the kitchen ceiling and the ever-widening circle of damp in disbelief and groaned. 'Not that damn pipe…it's burst again!'

Just what she needed on a Monday morning, she thought bitterly, scrabbling under the sink for the stop tap and shoving a bucket under the steady stream of water. She grabbed a tea towel from a drawer and towelled her hair before stepping out of her clothes and throwing them into the sink. She was getting quite adept at coping with disasters like this—if it wasn't the pipe bursting, it was the washing machine having a nervous breakdown…

She picked up the phone and dialled the plumber's number from memory, watching as the pouring water became a trickle and then an intermittent drip.

'This is an out-of-hours service. Your call is important to us, and we will be with you as soon as possible…'

Jandy slammed down the phone and glared at it aggressively. It seemed the rest of the world needed a plumber as well…she'd have to leave it for the time being.

As Monday mornings went, it hadn't been a good start. Apart from the burst pipe, there was a load of white washing which had been transformed to a uniform bright pink. Jandy loved Lydia dearly, they were as close as twin sisters could be, but sometimes she could strangle her when she was being extra-scatty instead of just ordinarily inefficient: colouring all the washing indeed! And trust her to still be nicely tucked up in bed after a late night while everything was going haywire downstairs!

'What's the matter, Mummy? Are you cross? You're very wet!' Four-year-old Abigail looked with interest at her mother's expression and then at the soaking floor.

Jandy sighed—cross was an understatement! What she really felt was very tired. She hadn't had a holiday in ages and life seemed to be all work and no play. She loved her work in the A and E department of Delford General but it would have been nice to go out socially occasionally.

She smiled ruefully down at her daughter. 'The pipe's burst again, and your red dress was washed with all the white things and now it's coloured everything else pink.'

'I like pink,' said Abigail placidly.

Jandy laughed. 'Well, that's all right, then!'

And of course what did a few discoloured garments

matter when she might be losing the little house she rented? The final straw that morning had been the letter from the estate agent saying that the owner wanted to sell the property, but she could have first refusal if she was interested in buying.

No chance of that at the moment, thought Jandy, grimacing as she slung the sheets over the line in the kitchen. Paying for child care, a car, and just general living seemed to soak up most of what she earned. They'd just have to look around for another rented property—but she'd never find anything as good as the house they were in, or as reasonably priced.

Surely the day couldn't get any worse. She flicked a look at her watch and sucked in her breath—she had a quarter of an hour to put on a fresh uniform and get to the hospital after dropping Abigail off at the child-minder's—she might just do it.

Jandy felt the familiar flash of guilt as she rushed back down the path after a hurried hug of farewell when she'd taken her little daughter to Pippa's. She always seemed to be at the last minute, playing catch-up and, she reflected wryly, clearing up after her sister. She turned as she closed the gate and looked back to see Abigail waving at her from the window, looking perfectly happy. She was adorable and Jandy was so lucky to have her…she just wished there was a father on hand to complete the picture…

The clock was nudging 8.05 a.m. as she parked her car in the last space of the hospital staff car park, ran up the steps and clattered through Reception on her way to the locker room.

Danny Smith, the receptionist, looked up from his lads' mag and shook an admonitory finger at her. 'You'd better hurry up...his lordship's showing the new registrar round the department now.'

Damn—she'd forgotten there'd be a new person on the staff today, someone else to get used to and have to guide for a while. She'd been wrong about the day not getting any worse, she thought irritably as she pulled on her hospital greens. No doubt about it, she could feel a bad mood coming on. Of course she couldn't begrudge Sue taking six months' maternity leave, although she was going to miss her terribly and the fun they had. When she was feeling down, Sue would cheer her up with a joke or a teasing comment: she was a kindred spirit, and life at Delford General was going to be that much duller now without her. What she needed, thought Jandy, pulling her blonde hair back into the ponytail she wore for work, was a bit of excitement—something new to revitalise her and brighten up the everyday humdrum. And the chances of that happening at the moment were more remote than winning the lottery.

The man stood for a moment before the entrance to the A and E department looking up at the square new wing that had been attached to the old Victorian hospital. He was a tall figure, the collar of his jacket turned up against the cold, and head and shoulders above the people swirling around him. So here he was—back where he'd been born, starting over again and picking up the pieces of his life. Soon London would become a distant memory, and Delford was going to be his home once more…his and Livy's, and he'd just have to make the best of it.

Straightening his shoulders as if bracing himself for his new life, he picked up the briefcase by his feet and started to make his way purposefully through the automatic doors into the A and E waiting room. He glanced briefly at some parents and two small children in one corner, and a man in a wheelchair gazing at a television on the wall showing a quiz show. Evidently the rush hadn't yet started.

'Patrick Sinclair—locum registrar for A and E checking in,' he said to the man behind the glass window in Reception.

The staff for the daytime shift were in the kitchen, all grabbing a drink before the day started in earnest and some crisis erupted. Tim Vernon, the dapper little A and E consultant, was walking briskly out of the room as Jandy came in. Two junior nurses were gossiping and Bob Thoms, one of the registrars, was peering at the duty roster, an anxious frown creasing his brow— he was a great worrier. He turned round as Jandy came in.

'Oh, great—what a relief, you're here! I thought you might be ill or something and we'd be short-staffed!' he exclaimed. 'You OK?'

'A burst pipe, no plumber and water all over the place,' she said gloomily. 'Worst of all I've had notice that the landlord wants to sell the house. Marvellous start to a Monday.'

Sister Karen Borley, large and kindly, handed her a cup and smiled at her sympathetically—she knew Jandy's mornings were a little chaotic and that she was only ever late if there'd been an emergency of some kind.

'Here you are, my girl—this'll perk you up.' She looked sympathetically at Jandy. 'You'll be looking for somewhere else to live, then—I'll keep my eyes open.'

Jandy took a gulp of scalding coffee and closed her eyes gratefully. 'Ah, thanks, Karen, you're a pal. Umm, that coffee's good...I'm coming round a bit now.' She turned to the others. 'Tell me, what's this new reg like?'

'He looks capable, although I think Tilly might find another adjective.' Karen laughed. 'He's from one of the big London teaching hospitals and has a wonderful CV, so he should be sound enough.'

'I hope he's easy to work with,' Jandy said mournfully. 'It won't be the same without Sue.'

'If I know anything about these hot-shot doctors from down South, he'll have an ego as big as an elephant and an inflated idea of his ability,' commented Bob Thoms tetchily.

A picture of Terry, Abigail's father, floated into Jandy's mind—he had been a high-flying business man from London who had felt demeaned coming up further north than Watford Junction! Jandy had mistaken his arrogance for a kind of sophisticated confidence and had been immensely flattered by his attention—she'd been easily taken in. She wouldn't be fooled a second time, but the thought of working with another person like that was not a comforting one.

'So coming up to Delford will be small time to him, I suppose,' she sighed. 'I wonder why he's come?'

'We'll get used to him,' said Karen, picking up some files and walking towards the door. 'I'll see you in a few minutes for the handover from the night shift—I'm just off to check that the porter's put the waste bins round the back. You come with me, Valerie,' she added to one of the student nurses. 'I'll show you where I like my supplies kept—I can't bear mess.'

Tilly Rodman, the other student nurse, rolled her eyes as Karen and Valerie went out. 'I can't believe that sister said the new reg is only "Capable"! He's gorgeous! My blood pressure went up like a rocket when I saw him…'

Bob Thoms drained his coffee and sighed. 'I'd like to know what this man has that I haven't…'

He left the room, but not before his eyes met Jandy's in amused exasperation. Tilly fell in love regularly with the senior registrars even if they looked only half-human. She would be in ecstasies about him for weeks, convinced that this was The One, as she put it on the many occasions she fell for someone.

Tilly had yet to learn, thought Jandy wryly, that looks weren't everything. In her experience handsome didn't always mean kind or thoughtful—sometimes it disguised selfish and cruel.

She rinsed her mug under the tap and dried it vigorously with a tea towel. What on earth did she know about men anyhow? It had been so long since she'd been out on a date—everyday life had taken over and any offers were quickly rebuffed. After Terry all her

confidence had gone where relationships were concerned—she didn't want to be hurt again and her
priority now was little Abigail. Anyway, her sister had
enough assurance when it came to men for both of
them!

'Frankly, Tilly,' she said briskly, as she folded the
towel neatly and hung it on a rail, 'as far as I'm concerned, the new registrar can look like Godzilla as
long as he can do the job. Unless he can patch someone
up who's been in an RTA and send them home better
than they came in, I can assure you that a whole team
of rugby-playing registrars dressed only in their
birthday suits wouldn't interest me…'

Tilly's eyes swivelled to look at the door behind
Jandy, and widened slightly, then she gave a little
giggle. 'Oops!' she muttered.

Jandy whirled round and reddened. 'Oh…er, hello,'
she said lamely to the tall, broad man who stood in the
doorway. She was conscious of a strong patrician face
and dark blue eyes looking into hers, one eyebrow
raised quizzically.

Trust her to make a fool of herself, she thought
ruefully. A flustered glance at the man confirmed that
with his formidable physique he was definitely the
sort who would like roaring around a rugby pitch on a
wet Saturday afternoon or pounding the streets in an
invigorating daily run. He was almost certainly the
new registrar, and he looked every inch the super-con-
fident hot-shot doctor from London, as Bob Thoms had
put it!

His gaze flickered over her in a mildly interested

manner, taking in her slightly flushed cheeks and wide dark brown eyes.

'I don't normally turn up for work in a birthday suit,' he remarked blandly. 'But I do play rugby and I hope I can send the patients home in fairly good shape!'

He had a deep attractive voice—'well bred' was the expression that sprang to mind.

Jandy allowed herself a prim smile, and said in a dignified tone, 'I'm just trying to explain to Tilly here that expertise is more important than anything…'

'Of course, I couldn't agree more,' the man said, nodding gravely. 'I'm Patrick Sinclair, by the way— taking over from Sue Gordon. I was told that there might be some coffee going if I was lucky.'

His sudden smile took her by surprise, rather like the sun coming out from a cloud, and it lit up his whole face. He looked almost boyish and, Jandy supposed grudgingly, was reasonably good looking. She noticed a faded white scar that ran down the side of one cheek—the result of a rugby tackle, she imagined, and when he turned on the smile Jandy could easily under-stand why Tilly had fallen for him. But how would she feel if she discovered he had a wife and three children?

Jandy held her hand out to him and said rather stiffly, 'Welcome to Delford General, then. I'm Staff Nurse Jandy Marshall, and this is Tilly Rodman, one of our student nurses.'

He turned to Tilly dipping his head slightly. 'Ah, yes—we met before, I think. I'm looking forward to working with you.'

Tilly gulped and stared at him admiringly. 'Yeah... great...'

'Perhaps a cup of coffee for Dr Sinclair,' prompted Jandy with a touch of impatience.

Tilly looked as if she was rooted to the spot by the sight of this man—surely all the women in Casualty weren't going to buckle at the knees as soon as they saw him, Jandy thought irritably. She flicked another look at Patrick Sinclair—he was just another locum registrar passing through the department for a few months, a stopgap until Sue returned. OK, so he looked rather like a marketer's dream for advertising some quasi-medical cure for flu—she supposed deep blue eyes in a strong good-looking face could easily persuade gullible people to buy a product...

She frowned: Patrick Sinclair had the confident air of someone who knew how attractive he was—but he was here to do a job, not act as the department's pin-up! As a single mum juggling motherhood and a demanding job, she certainly wasn't going to pander to his self-importance.

Karen Borley put her head round the door. 'Tilly—can you come to the plaster room, please, and do a bit of clearing up—the place is a tip.'

'Yes, Sister.' Tilly thrust a cup of coffee into the man's hand and bolted out of the room, with a final blushing look at Patrick, and Jandy was left alone with him.

In the short silence between them Jandy caught a depressing sight of herself in the mirror over the sink. She didn't look her best—as usual her hair was scraped back into a ponytail to keep it off her face, and she hadn't a scrap of make-up on. If only she'd put on a touch of lipstick it might have made her look less severe, less pallid, instead of which she looked what she was: an overworked single mum who'd been multitasking since she'd got up that morning! Not that it mattered what Patrick Sinclair thought of her looks, she told herself sharply. Nevertheless, she drew herself up to her full five feet six inches, and sucked in her stomach.

'Have you had a tour of the department yet?' she asked Patrick.

'Not yet. Dr Vernon was called away and didn't have time to show me much.'

He took a sip of coffee and for the first time she noticed the broad band of gold on his left ring finger. So he was married—a crushing blow to Tilly and probably every woman in Casualty, thought Jandy wryly. Well, she certainly wasn't going to start moping because he was a married man, even though she had to admit that he was the first blazingly attractive male to have worked in A and E for ages—which didn't mean she had to start thinking of love, romance or any sort of attachment. The last sort of man she needed was another hot-shot guy from the cosmopolitan life in London who found himself in the northern sticks of England and was married—she'd been there, done that.

He smiled at her. 'So you and I are going to be colleagues—have you been at Delford General long?'

'About three years now—I enjoy it really, most of the time. Where have you been working?'

'In London, at S. Cuthbert's. It's a good hospital—
I've been there since I qualified, but the last six months
I've been with the London Air Ambulance for a stint.'

Jandy was impressed despite herself—this guy had
some pretty comprehensive experience in trauma, and
you had to have nerves of steel to cope with the serious
accidents you dealt with on a daily basis.

'Won't you miss that? It could seem quite dull
here!'

He laughed. 'I don't think so—I might miss the
good things about London, like the river, the Houses
of Parliament, all the theatres…'

Suddenly a picture flashed into her mind of him in
a theatre foyer, dressed immaculately in a dinner
jacket, with a gorgeous woman on his arm, an easy, sophisticated confidence about him—leading the kind of
life that she could only dream of.

'I expect,' she said challengingly, 'you'll find us
old-fashioned after a place like St Cuthbert's.'

He looked at her quizzically, detecting her defensive tone, and remarked lightly, 'I'm sure I won't—
most hospitals have similar procedures, don't they?'

'But what on earth made you come up to Delford?'
Jandy asked rather bluntly. 'It sounds as if you had a
wonderful life in London.'

'My father isn't too well and I need to be nearer
him,' he explained. 'There's a lot of sorting out to be
done which I can't do from London.'

Although he probably wishes he wasn't here in
boring Delford, which could boast a cinema and not
much else, surmised Jandy, but she felt a little ashamed

of her unwelcoming thoughts and said more gently,
'I'm sorry about your father—that's a worry for you,
and of course it must have been a wrench to leave your
exciting life in London.'

Was it her imagination, or did a fleeting glance of
sadness cross his face, something indefinable that
hinted that life hadn't been that wonderful in London
after all? However, when he spoke his voice was light.

'Yes—I was very happy there…but life here will
have its own advantages, I'm sure. I came from this
area originally, and there's some beautiful countryside
around that I'm looking forward to exploring again and
showing to my daughter. I'm coming back to my roots,
you might say.'

'That'll be fun,' said Jandy politely.

'And you?' he enquired. 'Have you always lived and
worked in Delford?'

Jandy nodded. 'Most of the time. I did leave for a
short while and went to Manchester.' She paused for
a second, then started wiping the draining board
fiercely. Funny how even after all this time just the
thought of the place sent a shock wave of horror
through her mind. Then she turned back to him with
a tight smile and said briefly, 'It didn't work out how
I thought it would, so I came back.'

She tried to hide her feelings, but those warm brown
eyes of hers couldn't disguise the fact that something
pretty awful had happened to her there, reflected
Patrick. Funny—she looked like a golden girl that had
everything going for her—soft fair natural looks and
a healthy, curvaceous figure—who would have thought

that there were any ghosts in her past? But he'd obviously touched a raw nerve there, he guessed, something that she wanted to forget…just like him, just like millions of people.

'And you live in Delford now?'

'Probably not for long,' sighed Jandy. 'I've just been told we've got to get out of the house we're in—a pity, because it's so near the childminder and shops. I doubt if we'll find anywhere else so convenient—or so reasonably priced. There's a small college in the town and all the good places get snapped up pretty quickly.'

'I hope something turns up,' Patrick said politely.

'Oh, I'll get something,' said Jandy brightly, pushing away the horrible worry that she might not have a roof over her head in a month's time. 'And now perhaps I can give you a quick tour of the delights of Delford General A and E before we get cracking.'

Patrick looked at Jandy with interest as he followed her out of the room—so she had a child as well. For some reason he'd imagined her to be a free agent, but just because she had no wedding ring it didn't mean she was unattached. He felt a momentary stab of disappointment, the reflex emotion of a hot-blooded male to a stunning woman who was already in a relationship, then shrugged inwardly. Speculating on a social life was the last thing he needed at the moment—looking after his father and little daughter would absorb all his time, and of course getting heavily involved with someone could be very dangerous, as he'd learned to his cost. At least, he reflected, there was help on hand now to look after Livy when she wasn't at school, and she would have a lovely home and gardens to play in.

Jandy having shown him the layout of the theatres and X-ray department, they went back to the central station where computers monitoring the stage of every emergency patient's treatment flickered and changed as the results of tests came through. On the wall behind the large curving desk were the whiteboards that listed which cubicle each patient was in, with a short résumé of their condition. A gradual building up of activity in the department had started, and a steady flow of patients was waiting to be seen by the triage nurse. In the background a child wailed from one of the cubicles in the paediatric section and a man was arguing loudly with the receptionist in the waiting room.

'I thought this would happen,' said Bob Thoms mournfully as he went off to one of the cubicles to examine an abscess on someone's back. 'I was hoping to get some new tyres from that garage opposite if we got ten minutes off for lunch, but it looks as if it's going to be solid patients wall to wall.'

Tim Vernon, immaculate in his white coat and neatly knotted tie, came up to Patrick. 'Sorry to leave you just then, Patrick, but you'll soon get the hang of things, I'm sure, after all your experience in London. Anyway, it's good to have you in the department—and I bet your father is delighted you've come back here to live with him. That place of his is far too big for one person. Tell him I miss our games of golf.'

So he'd moved his family in with his father, thought Jandy, standing near them as she flicked through the admissions chart. She wondered idly whereabouts in Delford Patrick's father lived and smiled wryly. There was no chance of Abigail, her sister and herself moving in with her widowed mother while she was looking for a new place—her mother lived in a tiny house in Scotland and was busy running a truck stop café, with her boyfriend. Chloe Marshall loved her daughters and grandchild dearly, but she didn't encourage long visits from her family—a few days were all she could tolerate!

Dr Vernon looked down at his clipboard and cleared his throat. 'Right—let's get started shall we? Staff Nurse—would you go with Dr Sinclair and look at the little boy in the paediatric department, number one cubicle? He's got a gash on his leg, and a worrying bump on the head—I don't know how he acquired it. You'd better book an X-ray.'

Tilly Rodman, passed by, pushing a dripstand, and whispered to Jandy, 'Lucky you…send Dr Sinclair along to the plaster room when you've finished with him!'

For heaven's sake, Jandy thought impatiently, the man was going to be intolerable if he felt that all the women in the unit were falling for him. She just hoped that he was good at his job.

They both walked quickly to the small wing off the main A and E department that had been designated for children. It was a small area that had been used in the past for high-dependency patients and although the walls had been decorated with nursery-rhyme characters to try and make it more child-friendly, it badly needed a make-over—and much more space.

Patrick Sinclair looked round it assessingly. 'This is the paediatric section?' he remarked with slight incredulity. 'Is there a play area here for children that are waiting to be seen?'

'We're in line to have a larger wing very soon,' said Jandy defensively. 'It's better than it used to be in the main department—of course, I'm sure you're used to state-of-the-art facilities, but we're short of cash here.'

He looked at her shrewdly as if he realised she was annoyed. 'I'm not making comparisons—Cuthbert's was a newly built hospital, so it wouldn't be fair to do so. I was merely making an observation,' he said smoothly. 'Right—shall we get started?'

Annoyed by what she took to be rather high-handed criticism of her beloved Delford Infirmary, Jandy followed him into the cubicle.

Her heart went out to the little boy—large frightened eyes looked at them owlishly through wire-rimmed glasses on a pale little face, and there were tear stains on his round cheeks. When they came in he knuckled his hand into his eyes to try and stop crying. She knew it wasn't only the pain that upset him—it was the alien surroundings and not knowing what was going to happen to him next. Despite the efforts to make the room more child-friendly to a five-year-old, the place was deeply intimidating.

A purpling bump like a dark egg was on one of the child's temples and one small leg had a long deep gash down the calf. There was something pathetic about that little limb laid across the bed.

A woman sat in a corner, looking at a magazine and

chewing gum but not doing much to comfort the little boy—in fact, not taking any notice of him at all. She looked up at Patrick and Jandy with little interest, giving them a nod, and went back to her magazine.

Patrick said, 'Good morning,' to her courteously, then sat down on a chair by the bed and leaned forward to the child, trying to get his attention and distract him from his present terror. He smiled cheerfully and patted one plump little hand comfortingly.

'Hello—you're Jimmy Tate, aren't you?' he asked gently, having a swift look at the file he'd been given. 'I'm Dr Sinclair and this is Nurse Marshall, and we're going to be looking after you. Don't you worry, we'll have you feeling better in no time, Jimmy.'

Patrick's voice was soothing and the familiar clichés reassuring. Gradually Jimmy's sobs became intermittent, just the odd one shaking his little body, and although his lip still trembled, now he was looking at Patrick, gradually relaxing a little.

Jandy swivelled the overhead light above the child so that his wounds could be seen more clearly, and reflected almost with surprise that the new registrar seemed to have a good manner with his small patient— getting Jimmy to relax and trust him went a long way towards recovery. If Dr Sinclair was arrogant, he was hiding it at the moment and she relented.

'You're a brave boy,' Patrick said, looking closely at the bruise on the child's temple and then the cut on his leg. He looked up at Jandy. 'I think we can use steristrips for this, don't you?'

Jandy nodded and smiled reassuringly at the little

boy. 'It really will feel better when I've put the magic strips on,' she said. She went to a cupboard which, when opened, revealed a stock of toys from which she pulled out a kaleidoscope. 'Have you seen one of these, Jimmy? While I'm bandaging your poorly leg, I want you to shake that and look down it—you'll see some lovely patterns there.'

Slowly Jimmy reached for the toy and put his eye to it. Jandy watched as the little boy became absorbed in what he was seeing then she started to swab the wound gently with saline solution.

Patrick turned to the woman, who'd barely looked up as they'd come in, continuing to be engrossed in her magazine. She seemed totally uninterested in what was happening to Jimmy.

'Excuse me.' His voice was courteous but firm— meant to be heeded. 'Can you tell me what happened?'

The woman stopped chewing her gum for a second and brushed a lock of greasy hair from her eyes. She had the unkempt look of someone who had lost interest in life and herself, reflected Jandy. There were a lot like her who came to Casualty.

'He fell off his bicycle and hit his head on the steps,' she said tersely. 'I told him not to ride it in the back garden with the dogs around.'

'I take it you're Mrs Tate—his mother?' asked Patrick, making a few notes.

'I'm not his mother—I'm his stepmother.'

Her voice was almost aggressive and Jandy saw Patrick look up quickly, something unfathomable in his expression, then he said smoothly, 'Has he been sick?'

'Yes—all over the floor of course.'

'I see. And did the dogs snap at him while he was riding his bike?'

Mrs Tate shrugged and said in a defensive tone, 'No, they just jumped up at him, having a bit of a lark. It was Jimmy's fault—he was teasing them. They wouldn't hurt a fly if they hadn't been provoked…he's been told often enough.' She shifted restlessly in her chair. 'Will this take long? I've got a baby at home and I had to ask my neighbour to look after her while I brought this one in.'

Patrick's eyes met Jandy's for a brief second—they were flinty hard. They were all taught to be impartial but she didn't blame him for showing a hint of the fury he must be feeling on the child's behalf. How could anyone be so unsympathetic to an injured five-year-old? A muscle tightened slightly by Patrick's mouth and his voice was clipped.

'It will take as long as it takes to see to this wound and make sure Jimmy's not injured his skull—he'll be taken to X-Ray in a minute. Now, can you tell me what time he had this accident?'

'About an hour ago,' Mrs Tate replied sulkily.

'Did you see it happen?'

Her eyes shifted momentarily and she muttered, 'No—but I sent for the ambulance as soon as I saw it was serious,' she added self-righteously.

'Were you out when it happened?'

Again her eyes looked away from his. 'Just at a neighbour's—not far away.'

'So you don't know if the dogs attacked him?'

Jandy could almost feel Patrick Sinclair restraining himself—it wasn't their role to be judgemental, but it could be difficult at times. He made some notes on the file and the woman scowled.

'I told you—they wouldn't do that. Can I go now? You can ring me when you've seen to him. Stop whinging, Jimmy—you're a big boy now.'

Big tears had started to roll down Jimmy's cheeks again and Jandy compressed her lips—it wasn't fair that the little boy should be chastised.

'Perhaps you could wait and see the result of the X-ray?' she suggested. 'It won't take me long to dress his wound. I take it he's had his tetanus jab?'

Mrs Tate sighed heavily. 'He's had all them jabs. I'll have to go and ring my neighbour, then…I'll be outside the entrance if you need me.'

She disappeared down towards the waiting room and Patrick turned to Jandy. 'We'll need to run blood tests, Hb, CRP and respiration checks before we take him down to X-Ray and ring up Paediatrics and get someone to look at the plates.'

Jimmy looked at them both, eyes round and anxious behind his glasses. Patrick smiled kindly at him.

'Hang on there, Jimmy, and we'll take you down to have a photograph taken of your head—it won't hurt a bit. I tell you what, Nurse Marshall, I think this little boy's been one of the bravest we've had here today— I think he deserves something special!'

His blue eyes looked at her questioningly—not having worked at this hospital before, he wouldn't know what rewards they offered their little patients.

Jandy grinned. 'Quite right, Doctor—I've got a special medal for someone like Jimmy!'

She opened a drawer and handed Patrick a plastic medal with 'Very Brave Patient' printed on it, which Patrick pinned on Jimmy's jumper. The little boy stared down at it then looked up at the adults with a shy smile.

'Is it mine?' he asked. It was the first time he'd spoken.

'It certainly is—you deserve it, sweetheart,' said Jandy. 'And now we'll take you to have that photograph taken.'

'I'm not happy with that head wound and the fact he's been sick,' said Patrick as he and Jandy walked back from the paediatric section, leaving Tilly Rodman to stay with Jimmy and read him a story. 'Have you rung Paediatrics yet? He'll be kept in anyway for observation, whatever the results are.'

Jandy nodded. 'They've got a bed—and at least it gives him a night away from that ghastly woman. She'd obviously left him alone while she gossiped with her friend.'

Patrick's expression darkened, and Jandy noticed the small scar at the side of his face seemed more pronounced and livid.

'I can't tell you how angry that woman makes me,' he said in a controlled, terse tone that only emphasised his disgust. 'I've no doubt that that little boy's not having a very happy life. I'll talk to the child liaison officer about my concerns regarding the stepmother— no child should be at the mercy of someone like that.

I didn't see a shred of affection or compassion for Jimmy.'

There was such suppressed venom in his voice that Jandy looked at him with surprise. She would have thought he'd have taken a more measured approach—still taking it just as seriously but not quite so personally. After all, in an A and E department it wasn't unusual to come across a case like Jimmy's.

'It's really got to you, hasn't it?' she said.

He looked down at her and shrugged. 'I guess I went over the top a bit there—took it to heart. I should be more objective, I know.' He bunched his hands in his pockets. 'Sorry—it's a bit of a hobby horse of mine.'

Jandy nodded, slightly bemused by this worldly-wise doctor's soft centre—somehow she felt there was a hidden agenda behind his words.

'I feel that way too,' she said. 'I don't know how anyone could be as callous as she was…but it happens, doesn't it? We see all sorts of cases here and often it's quite heart-rending. And, of course, if we have any doubts about Jimmy's treatment, we should have it investigated.'

Patrick looked down at her upturned concerned face with her wide brown eyes illuminated by a beam of sunshine through the window, honey-blonde hair shining in its light—some had escaped from the band that held it back, and suddenly he pictured how it would spill out like a sheet of soft gold over her shoulders if the band was pulled away completely…

He smiled wryly to himself. How long ago had it

been since he'd touched a woman or had any kind of intimacy with one? Oh, sure, he'd thought about it when he'd been the odd one out at a party when everyone else had a partner, or lying awake in the early hours and feeling sorry for himself. But that one memorable disaster three years ago had ensured that he'd kept well away from anything but mild flirtations since then.

Of course, he thought sadly, once he'd had everything—a wonderful woman, a perfect life, and then like a bolt from the blue it had come to an end, and he couldn't imagine ever having it again. He clenched his fists together to control his emotions. Stop it, he told himself fiercely—don't go there! He had his darling Livy to think of now.

Then he sighed as he refocused on the real world. 'I'd better go and write up this case report,' he said abruptly, shifting his gaze from her face. 'See you soon.'

Jandy stared rather bemusedly after his tall retreating figure as he strode back to the desk. When Patrick had looked at her with those intense blue eyes of his, she had felt the oddest little tug on her heart, a flicker of attraction. How peculiar was that, when only a few minutes before she'd been annoyed by his criticism of the paediatric department—another bighead from London who probably thought he knew everything!

She went to clear up the cubicle that Jimmy had occupied and reflected crossly that she hadn't thought for a long time about men, except for the need to steer clear of them as much as possible. Then a man walked into the department with an attractive smile and amazing blue eyes and suddenly she was imagining all kinds of things! She shook her head irritably. Being too aware of married men and their thoughts was a dangerous pastime—they were strictly off-limits to her. What she had to concentrate on was finding a new place for her, Abigail and Lydia to live—and soon!

CHAPTER TWO

AFTER the initial flurry of cases there was a lull. Typical of A and E—one couldn't predict what was going to come in, although generally Friday and Saturday nights were mayhem. Jandy finished checking the cubicles for supplies of bandages, paper towels and latex gloves, and during the ten minutes allotted for her lunch decided to ring her sister and ask her to get in touch with the agent about the lease of the house. There was no possibility of buying it, but perhaps the owner could be persuaded to give them a little more time to find something else.

Jandy walked quickly down the corridor to the payphone in Reception as Delford A and E was firmly against the use of mobile phones in the department. It was typical that someone was already using the phone, she thought with irritation. She leant against the wall near the kiosk, hoping the man would see she was waiting, then she realised that it was Patrick Sinclair.

Watching him now, she wondered what had made her think there had been anything remotely intimate in the way he had looked at her earlier. He was just an ordinary guy who happened to have the kind of sexy looks that would draw some women's eyes—over six feet of impressive body, in fact, and thick dark hair, endearingly rumpled—but he wasn't all that special, was he?

He finished his conversation, came out of the kiosk and gave her a smile and a half-wave as he passed her—she was surprised at the little frisson of excitement she felt when he did that. She found herself smiling as she dialled her sister's mobile number and started to speak to her.

'Hi, Lydia—did you get onto the agent about the house? I left the letter on the kitchen table…'

Karen Borley was writing up the whiteboard when Jandy returned. She looked at Jandy's exasperated face.

'Has something happened?' she enquired.

Jandy groaned. 'I've just been speaking to my sister. She's been in touch with the agent and we definitely have to be out in four weeks—sooner if possible! Can you believe Lydia has told the agent we'd be interested in a massive house at an enormous monthly rent? She seems to think we're rolling in money.'

'Oh, dear—Lydia is rather impetuous, isn't she?' said Karen vaguely as she shuffled through some case sheets.

'Of course she's away the next week,' added Jandy, 'Leaving me to organise everything! Typical!'

Patrick Sinclair looked up from the computer and

said noncommittally, 'If you really are stuck for some-where to live, I do happen to know a place that's empty and needs a tenant—it's a bit neglected and it's in the country, so it may not suit you. But if you get desper-ate…'

Jandy was surprised that a man like him should bother himself with her problems. 'Really? It's very kind of you to suggest it…I might be very inter-ested…do you know the owner?'

He nodded. 'Yes—I know him well.'

'Perhaps if you could find out the rent he's asking…'

'No problem,' Patrick started to say, when Karen put down the phone and interrupted them, her cheeks slightly pink as if she'd heard something of interest. She looked around, making sure no one was listening.

'Mr Vernon's just been on to me about a patient he's been looking at in the small theatre,' she said in a hushed voice. 'He was picked up by the police outside a pub earlier this morning and taken back to the station on a drunk and disorderly charge. Evidently he'd had a bit of a fracas with some young lads…but it's rather a delicate situation.'

'So far normal,' murmured Jandy. 'So why is it a delicate situation?'

Sister flicked a look at her and said impressively, 'I think you'll know what I mean when you see him—it's Leo Parker, the agony uncle who does that chat show on television.'

Jandy raised her eyebrows. 'Wow! Leo Parker, the Voice of Reason? The press will be interested, won't they?'

'Exactly!' Karen pursed her lips. 'I don't want a word of who this patient is to get out—I can't bear those journalists running all over the place, disrupting the department, questioning everybody. If they get a whiff of this, it'll be bedlam.'

'Better prepare for bedlam, then,' Jandy said under her breath. 'This place is like a sieve when it comes to gossip!'

She heard Patrick chuckle as they filed into the cubicle. 'Sounds familiar...' he murmured.

'Mr Parker was just about conscious when he was brought in,' explained Karen. 'The police were concerned that it might not be just drink that's affecting him and that he could have had a crack on the head.'

'Are his X-rays clear?' asked Patrick.

'Not a sign of anything. Mr Vernon has already had a look at his skull plates—quite normal. But he's in and out of consciousness, so something's wrong. We're waiting for his bloods to come back, but I'd like him closely monitored. Give me a shout if you find anything.'

Leo Parker lay on the bed, the impressive head of thick grey hair, which was his trademark, matted with blood from a gash on his forehead. He shifted restlessly from side to side, moving his limbs and muttering incoherently. Jandy was struck by how ordinary he looked, just as vulnerable as every other patient who came in to A and E reduced to helplessness by their condition.

'Poor man—not quite the towering TV personality at the moment,' murmured Jandy, looking at the trace on the graph over the bed giving his oxygen levels and pulse rate. 'Heart rate's accelerated and his BP's quite low.'

'He's right out of it at the moment,' commented Patrick, bending over the man and shining a small torch into the pupil of each eye. Then he bent the patient's legs, striking below the knees sharply. 'His reflexes seem OK. What about his plantar reflex?'

Jandy took a pencil out of her pocket and drew it across the base of the man's foot, which curled in response.

'Nothing wrong there…' She bent forward and sniffed the man's breath. 'Nice and beery—he's obviously had a few bevies,' she remarked. She frowned and sniffed again. 'Wait a minute…there's something else… Funny smell…acetone, I think.'

Patrick leaned close to the man and nodded back at her, touching the man's face. 'Absolutely right—he's sweaty as well. Alcohol-induced hypoglycaemia,' he added almost to himself. 'I don't suppose he checked his blood-sugar levels after having a bit to drink. That's why his speech is so garbled—his glucose levels will be very low.'

'If he'd been left in that police cell, it could have been curtains.'

'Yup—he's lucky they brought him in when they did. We'll give him fifty grams of glucose intravenously. I take it the packs are in the cupboard up there?'

Jandy handed Patrick one of the pre-packed syringes and they both watched the patient after he'd been injected to see how long it took for him to come round.

'If only he realised the harm he could do to himself when he drinks,' he remarked drily. 'Because he's diabetic everything can shut down when the nervous system becomes sluggish…organ damage, brain damage, you name it.'

Leo gradually opened his eyes and looked around him in a confused way. 'Hello, there,' Patrick said. 'Feeling a bit better, Mr Parker? I think you're nearly with us again.'

The man gazed up at him blankly, blinking his eyes and staring around fuzzily, his system trying to restore reactions and memory.

'Well, that took just over a minute—miraculous!' murmured Patrick. He nodded at Jandy approvingly.

God, his eyes were amazing! Once again they seemed to hold hers for a second before she could drag her glance away. Irritably she thought that it was becoming something of a habit, imagining that the man was looking at her in some sort of special way. He wasn't hers to fantasise about.

She reached into the cupboard without comment and slipped on latex gloves before starting to swab the cut on Leo Parker's head. He made a feeble attempt to bat her hand away then began to stir, trying to sit up before flopping back against the pillow.

'Where am I?' he mumbled.

'You're in Delford General Casualty Department,' said Patrick. 'You overdid the alcohol, I'm afraid…not a good idea when you're diabetic. We'll get you a bed.'

There was a sudden pause, and a girl's impatient voice floated over to them beyond the curtain. 'I need

to see Leo now. I was with him when he fell…he'll
want me with him…'

'Are you a relative?' Jandy recognised the voice of
Danny Smith, the A and E receptionist.

'I'm his partner—and his PA.' The girl's voice
sounded defiant. 'Delphine Hunt.'

'Well, the doctor's looking at him now—can you
wait a minute?'

Patrick went over to the curtains and swished them
back. 'You can come in now if you like—Mr Parker's
coming round gradually. Perhaps you can tell us what
happened.'

Delphine Hunt had bright red hair cascading past her
shoulders, and a very short dress under a fake-fur
evening jacket. She brushed Patrick aside without a
word and flung herself onto the bed next to Leo Parker,
kissing him passionately then breaking into sobs.
'Babe—are you OK? I've been out of my mind with
worry…'

'Hey—wait a moment,' said Patrick, moving
forward and pulling the girl away. 'Let the patient
breathe! He's just coming out of a diabetic coma—he's
not fit to be manhandled.'

'Is he going to be OK? I thought those thugs were
going to kill him…' Delphine started to cry and the
make-up around her eyes ran in little black rivulets
down her cheeks.

Jandy pushed a chair forward. 'Why don't you sit
down here and tell us what happened?' she said gently.

'And keep your voice down please,' added Patrick
drily.

'We…we were having a quiet drink, and these yobbos started calling him names, just because he's on TV.' Delphine pulled a handkerchief out of her pocket and blew her nose. 'Leo's a bit impetuous and he went over and had it out with them…and the next thing he's on the floor and the police have been called. They said he was drunk and disorderly. He never was—he'd only had a few, and it wasn't his fault at all!'

'I guess you've been trying to get to him since he was taken to the police station, haven't you?' said Patrick.

'I'd just got to the station when the ambulance drove off and I saw Leo being taken on it and driven away…they wouldn't tell me a thing.'

From the bed, Leo Parker whispered, 'Delphine—what are you doing here?'

The girl took his hands. 'Oh, babe, you're OK. Thank God!' She turned to Patrick and Jandy. 'Can we go now? I'll call a taxi.'

'Mr Parker certainly can't go,' interrupted Patrick sternly. 'You need to stay in overnight—we've got to get you balanced,' he said to Leo. 'You know that, don't you, or you might find yourself in a coma again.'

Leo struggled to sit up. 'I can't stay here the night,' he said, aghast. 'I've got to be at the studio by lunchtime. What time is it now?'

'Ten-thirty—you won't have time to recover properly by then,' said Jandy.

'I will,' said Leo, his voice slurring slightly. He swung his legs over the bed and started to get down. 'I'm going to discharge myself—I'm perfectly all right.'

Patrick put his hand on the man's shoulder. 'You've got to give yourself time to recover—drink and diabetes don't mix. And you've got a nasty gash on your head.'

Leo stared at them all and then, as if the reality of the situation fully hit him, put a hand over his face and groaned.

'Oh, my God. If the press get hold of this…' He looked up at them pleadingly. 'If this gets into the papers, I'm sunk. I'm recording a show about alcohol abuse today. I can't let it get out that I've had a bit too much of the sauce myself.'

'Everything here is strictly confidential,' Patrick promised.

Leo looked at him wryly. 'Things have a funny way of getting out into the public domain, you know.'

'Then let's go now, Leo, darling, before anyone knows. I've booked us into the hotel together,' said Delphine eagerly, laying a possessive hand on his arm.

Leo sighed heavily. 'Have you got two rooms?'

Delphine looked a little abashed. 'Well—no. You said we could be together, babe…'

'You silly mare! Do you think the press are dumb? My PA and I sharing a room doesn't look good—have you forgotten I'm a family man to the public?'

Jandy flicked the briefest of glances towards Patrick over Delphine's head, and his gaze held hers for a fraction of a second, before returning impassively to the scene before him.

'I really wouldn't advise you leaving the hospital yet,' he said firmly.

'Advise what you like—but don't ruin my career. I'll do what I damn well like. I can discharge myself if I want to.'

He was interrupted in mid-sentence by the sound of the curtains being viciously flung back, and a small plump woman stood before them, staring at Leo Parker with undisguised fury.

'So you've done it again, have you?' she said coldly. 'Will you never learn, you old fool? And you can forget about discharging yourself as well.'

There was a short silence then Patrick said evenly, 'Excuse me, but just who are you?'

The woman turned to him and said icily, 'I'm Phyllis Parker, young man, Leo Parker's wife, and I'm just about sick of him making such a Charlie of himself!'

'Oh, God—Phyllis!' Leo Parker flopped back on his pillows and closed his eyes. In the corner, Delphine began to cry.

Patrick and Jandy watched as Leo Parker was pushed down the corridor on the way to Medical, closely followed by his wife, still berating him. They disappeared into the lift and Patrick and Jandy went into Sister Borley's office behind the central station.

He turned to Jandy and said sardonically, 'I've never watched his programme before, but I'm going to make a point of seeing it and hearing his views on family life and the evils of drink.'

'Same here,' said Jandy, trying to keep a straight face.

'I reckon Leo Parker's going to have some explaining to do...'

His clear blue eyes laughed down at her, his grave face softened by humour, and Jandy answered his amusement with a grin, mutually diverted by the little scene that had just been played out. Patrick Sinclair could be quite engaging when he wanted to, she admitted.

Karen put down the phone she'd been speaking into. 'That,' she said with compressed lips, 'was the *Delford Gazette*. It's already got out that Leo Parker's a patient here—and I'm not surprised after all the fuss!'

She went out of the room and wiped the whiteboard vigorously, venting her irritation by obliterating the annoying Mr Parker's name now he had been taken to the medical ward. Jandy went to deal with a young girl with a staple stuck down her fingernail.

It was a fairly routine afternoon—a sprained ankle, a scalded arm and a child with a hacking cough who should have been taken to see his G.P., according to Mr Vernon, and not brought to A and E, cluttering up the department.

Karen sat down at her desk with a sigh of relief. 'Right,' she said comfortably. 'At last! Time for a breather. It could be a chance for us to catch up on all the patient assessment forms and maybe—'

The sudden jarring sound of the trauma bleep split the air. 'Trauma call, trauma call, trauma team to A and E Resus. ETA three minutes...trauma call...'

Karen swore softly to herself. 'Wouldn't you know it? I spoke too soon.'

The relaxed atmosphere changed and there was an air of tension as everyone available gathered round the central station, prepared to spring into action.

Tim Vernon came out of a cubicle, swinging his stethoscope impatiently as if he couldn't wait to get going, and Max Fuller, the porter, started pushing trolleys down the passage and out of the way of the entrance. Karen's voice was authoritative and clipped, her look of motherly cosiness changed to brisk efficiency as she spoke on the phone to the ambulance-men.

'OK, everyone—an RTA on the main Delford road. My information is that there's an injured female hit by a motorcycle, lacerations to her face and in great pain. A cyclist with obvious fracture of right leg, and a pillion passenger with a very low BP and head injury, possible status 3. ETA any minute now.' She put down the phone and turned to the staff. 'Patrick, you take the injured female with lacerations on her face in Theatre One and the status 3 patient will go into the big theatre.'

'I'll take the status 3 patient,' said Dr Vernon. 'Bob—you come with me.'

'That's three patients for urgent X-rays. John Cooper can take the suspect broken leg with Tilly. Max—make sure we've got enough oxygen cylinders and dripstands in that big theatre. Jandy, can you be on hand to help where necessary?'

Jandy felt the familiar ripple of adrenalin kicking through her body as they waited for the ambulances to arrive. It was peculiar to Casualty—that tremor of excitement mixed with apprehension in dealing with absolutely any injury or illness thrown at them, and often time was not on their side. Split-second decisions had to be made and the staff in the department were the first line of defence.

Tilly nibbled at her nails nervously. 'It's nerveracking, not knowing what you'll get. I hate these horrible accidents. I'm frightened I'll faint or something.'

Jandy placed a reassuring hand on Tilly's arm—the young nurse had only been in the department a few weeks and it was a very fast learning curve for all the students.

'It's always a bit scary—knowing that how we deal with patients here can determine the outcome of their eventual recovery. And every case is different,' she admitted. 'But once we're in the thick of it, there's no time to think. You put everything else out of your head.'

Patrick stood near the door, looking down the drive where the ambulances would come from. He turned and smiled at the young nurse. 'But this is what it's all about, isn't it? Being able to turn your hand to anything. In the end it becomes instinctive. It's exciting!'

He grinned at Jandy, eyes dancing with anticipation, confidently looking forward to the challenge of the unknown. Everyone's idea of the perfect doctor, she thought wryly, his hospital greens seeming to emphasise his athletic physique. She was uneasily aware that she was just a little too conscious of Patrick's attraction and that devastating easy smile of his, but he was just an ordinary married guy, wasn't he? Not her type at all. She bit her lip. This man was getting too much under her skin.

She glanced at Bob Thoms—what a contrast! His brow was furrowed with anxiety as usual. He was a good doctor, painstaking and thorough, but always racked by worries that his best might not be good enough—what a pity she couldn't find someone like him attractive. Bob was free and single with no hint of arrogance or over-confidence about him—but incredibly dull!

She forced herself to concentrate on the moment, to push out of her mind the distracting fact that Patrick was standing close to her. Then the flashing blue lights of the ambulances appeared as they came up the drive, and gradually the whine of the sirens died down as they reached the entrance. In a few minutes the doors swished open and three trolleys were being pushed through into the wide passage. A plump woman clutching a large handbag was running beside one of the trolleys, tears streaming down her face. Jandy took her arm gently but firmly and steered her to the side of the passage.

'Come with me for a minute,' she said gently. 'Just let the doctors see to the patient… Are you a relative?'

'I'm her mother…Mrs Thorpe…' The woman clung to Jandy hysterically, hiccuping sobs shaking her, as the shock of the incident she'd just witnessed set in. 'She…she's having a baby. Please help her. She mustn't lose this one—she's had two miscarriages already.'

'Come with me to the desk and let's take her details. First, what's her name?'

'Brenda Evans…she's twenty-five. She's been longing for this baby…'

Mrs Thorpe's voice started to rise in panic again and Jandy quickly said, 'Tell me what happened… take it slowly.'

Gradually the woman started to calm down, and in the telling of the story her mind was forced to concentrate on something other than what was now happening to her daughter.

'This motorbike…it came towards us with no warning. It was going that fast. I saw it coming, and I screamed to Brenda, but it hit her and sent her sprawling on the ground.' Mrs Thorpe paused for a second to control her tears. 'Will…will she lose the baby?'

With the skill born of much practice in calming worried relatives, Jandy led her to a chair and said comfortingly, 'She's in very good hands, Mrs Thorpe, and I know they will be monitoring her very closely— especially now they know her medical history. I'm going to get you a cup of tea and then I'll go and find out just what's happening to her. You try and calm down—she'll need you to look after her when she goes home.'

A paramedic was wheeling Mrs Thorpe's daughter briskly into one of the small theatres. 'This is Brenda Evans,' he said. 'She's in a lot of pain, but superficially at least she only seems to have lacerations. BP 100 over 70, pulse 120. Reasonably stable. She's also seven and a half months pregnant.'

'What happened?' asked Patrick, bending over the supine figure on the trolley.

'It looks like a motorcycle tried to take a corner at speed and hit this lady a glancing blow—she fell forward onto her face.'

Jandy had come into the cubicle to see what was happening so that she could update the patient's mother on the latest information. She was watching the girl's face—there was a large graze on her chin, covered with grit.

'She's very pale…' she murmured to Patrick. 'Obviously she's in shock, but she's blinking her eyes all the time. What's causing that?'

He frowned and looked at Brenda's face closely. 'Rapid blinking is often a sign of a sharp pain. I wonder… Can you speak, Brenda?'

Brenda grimaced and mumbled something through stiff lips.

'I reckon it's something to do with her jaw—see how stiffly she's holding it,' Patrick said. 'Moving it seems to cause her extreme discomfort.'

He ran his hands lightly over her face, watching her reactions carefully. Brenda sucked in her breath and groaned.

'I'm sorry, Brenda,' he said gently. 'That's all I'm going to do at the moment. We'll give you something for the pain, don't worry. You'll be all right—just try and relax and don't do anything that might move your jaw.'

He patted her arm, trying to reassure her and with his calm voice showing her that he was very much in charge. You got to know people's skills quite quickly

when you worked with them in Casualty, reflected
Jandy. Patrick had a sure touch with patients, knowing
that the familiar platitudes would soothe Brenda. He
knew that physical and aural contact with a frightened
patient could reduce the effects of shock.

It was one of Karen's repeated adages to her team:
'Remember that reassurance is one of the most
powerful clinical tools you've got.' When it came to
medicine, Dr Sinclair was ticking quite a few boxes
so far, admitted Jandy.

'Can you arrange to have Brenda X-rayed ASAP?'
Patrick asked Jandy.

'But she's pregnant,' she pointed out.

Patrick shook his head. 'She's going to need surgery
on her jaw, I'm afraid, and we've got to know exactly
what the damage is. The X-ray won't be over the
baby—fortunately she's late on in her pregnancy.'

'Do you think she's broken her jaw?'

'The first thing to hit the floor was her chin I
reckon—like that!' Patrick demonstrated this by
smacking his fist into his other hand. 'That's where the
cut is. I'll bet what's happened is that the force of the
impact has snapped off her left condyle—the part of
the bone that forms the hinge of the jaw.'

'She hit her chin just at the wrong point, then.'

Patrick nodded. 'Every time she moves her jaw,
bone fragments are scraping across the tissue surrounding her ear.'

Jandy grimaced. 'Poor woman—that's seriously
painful. What about pain relief?'

'After her X-ray give her ten milligrams of morphine

and get her booked into Surgical—I'll speak to the surgical registrar. We need someone from Maternity to look her over as well. We don't want her having this baby yet.'

Jandy split open a pair of lanolin gloves and with exquisite gentleness swabbed the wound on Brenda's chin. 'Her mother's really anxious about her,' she said. 'I think it would help if you explained Brenda's injuries rather than me—you're the expert.'

He laughed. 'I'll do my best.'

Patrick sat down next to Mrs Thorpe on one of the chairs in the corridor, leaning towards her as he described what he thought had happened, giving a short but lucid explanation. Gradually the tension left the woman's face until she was actually giving a watery smile by the time he was called away to the phone.

'Oh, he's a lovely man that Dr Sinclair,' said Mrs Thorpe when Jandy returned from trying to get a slot for Brenda's X-ray. 'I feel she's in really good hands. Could I go and see Brenda now?'

Jandy smiled. 'I'm sure it would do her good if you just sat by her and held her hand until they take her for X-rays. The calmer she's kept, the better.'

'I understand,' said Mrs Thorpe. The tea and the chat to Patrick about her daughter had composed her and she was ready to cope again. She followed Jandy to the small theatre where her daughter was and sat by her bed, flicking a wondering eye at all the monitoring equipment around the bed.

'Eh, it's like a space capsule in here,' she said. 'I've never seen so many tubes and dials!'

She picked up her daughter's hand and squeezed it. 'You'll be alright, love,' she said softly. 'I've had a chat to that Dr Sinclair—he's doing his best for you, I know.'

Patrick popped his head round the curtain. 'Has the X-ray been booked yet?' he asked.

'There's a bit of a delay—one of the machines is being serviced and there's a queue for the other,' Jandy informed him.

He frowned. 'For God's sake—surely it's usual to service the machines at a quieter time? How long are they going to be?'

'About twenty minutes, I think.'

'That's ridiculous! This needs to be done immediately—surely there should be a procedure for urgent cases?'

Jandy sympathised with him. It was incredibly frustrating to have treatment blocked for the patient, but she also noticed the implied criticism of the hospital. Poor old Delford General wasn't awash with funds for any more X-ray machines.

'I'm sorry, there's not much I can do about it. There's only one machine at the moment for a lot of patients.'

'I'm not accusing you of causing the hold-up,' he said tersely. Then his tone softened. 'I'm sorry—I'm not knocking Delford, believe me.'

He looked at her steadily then left the room, and she blushed at his accurate reading of her thoughts. Actually, she agreed with him that somewhere along the line there had been inefficiency. Perhaps she was being a little too prickly where Patrick was concerned!

Karen bustled up to Jandy, her pale blue tunic top straining slightly over her full figure, her face pink from exertion. Jandy often wondered why Karen was so plump as she seemed to run everywhere, and had an inexhaustible supply of energy.

'Ah, there you are,' she puffed. 'I think we're under control now. Dr Vernon's booked the head injury into the neurological ward for obs, and Brenda Evans will be prepped for Theatre later.' She shot a look at her watch. 'Time for the handover soon and then home, sweet home, thank goodness!' Her voice dropped. 'By the way, I'm rather impressed by Patrick Sinclair— aren't you? As I said before, he seems extremely capable!'

'Yes,' allowed Jandy cautiously.

He seemed extremely everything—wonderful with his patients and a good clinician. But she still had reservations about this self-assured man and his drop-dead handsome looks—she would see how he performed over the next few weeks! Men like him tended to be arrogant, everything dropping into their laps very easily, and she could see how he might break some poor girl's heart if he was free. What a good job it was that he was a family man and a no-go area— she'd learned from her own experience that loving a married man was not an option.

CHAPTER THREE

'I DON'T believe this,' muttered Jandy, looking at the huge tailback of vehicles round the car park. For the third time that month the car-park barrier had jammed and from her experience it could take at least three quarters of an hour to sort out. Nothing for it but to get the bus and leave the car in the car park—she hated to keep Pippa waiting when she was due to pick up Abigail. It had been a gruelling week and she was tired—although her fears about working with the new registrar had been groundless.

After two weeks she was beginning to realise that Patrick Sinclair was not only a good doctor but surprisingly easy to work with. She didn't know much about his family—he never talked much about his life outside the hospital, but he could be a laugh. In fact, she admitted as she trudged to the bus stop, she actually looked forward to coming to work with him. Once she'd even caught herself wishing that he'd been unattached, fantasising about how different her attitude toward him might have been if he was single—but, then, of course, there would have been a deluge of women waiting to snap him up!

It started to rain as she waited hopefully by the bus stop, then a car drew up in front of her and the passenger window was lowered.

'Can I give you a lift?' said a familiar voice. 'It's getting very wet.'

Jandy bent down to see who it was and found herself looking into the blue eyes of the very man she'd been thinking of! Patrick was right—the rain seemed to be getting harder all the time and she could feel rivulets of water making their way down her back. It was ridiculous how her heart started thumping at his invitation—it was only a lift in his car, for heaven's sake, not an indecent proposal!

'Are you sure?' she asked. 'I'd be really grateful, but I may be taking you miles out of your way.'

'No problem,' he said. 'Jump in.'

Jandy relaxed back in the blessed warmth of the car, and glanced across at Patrick, his strong profile outlined in the dark as he looked in the rear-view mirror before pulling out into the road. Inside the car it felt intimate, cosy. Her eyes fastened on his hands on the steering-wheel, strong, capable hands, and she felt the flutter of excitement she used to feel when she went on a date with someone she liked, anticipating the evening to come. Stop this, she said fiercely to herself. Her reaction to him was becoming almost like the reflex action of a tap on the knee joint. He was a married man she'd only known for two weeks, for heaven's sake.

'This is good of you,' she murmured. 'I would've been very late picking Abigail up from the childminder. The barriers in the car park are always getting stuck—it's the second time I've had to leave the car there all night.'

'A damn nuisance for you. How old is your little girl?'

'She's four—Pippa takes her to and from nursery school, which is wonderful. How about your daughter—what age is she?'

He smiled. 'The same age as your Abigail. Her name's Livy—short for Olivia—and she's at nursery school as well. I'll be picking her up from the after-school club they have there.'

They had stopped at traffic lights and the glow from a streetlamp fell on a photograph pinned to the dash-board. It showed a curly-headed child in the arms of an attractive, laughing woman. Jandy bent forward to look at it more closely. This must be his wife and daughter. What a lovely family he had—and what a wonderful father he would be, she thought wistfully. That was something Abigail would never know—a father's love and attention, a man she could always trust throughout her life.

She smothered a sigh and said brightly, 'And this is a photo of Livy and your wife, I suppose—they're very beautiful.'

Patrick nodded and said briefly, 'Yes—it's a good photograph.'

'And is your wife medical?' asked Jandy, assuming that she worked as Patrick had to pick his daughter up.

Patrick was silent for a moment and Jandy wondered if he'd heard her, then eventually he spoke, his voice quiet but brutally harsh. 'My wife died three and a half years ago—she had an accident. Livy doesn't remember her mother at all.'

For a second the bald statement hung in the air, horrifying, unbelievable. Patrick looked across at Jandy as she caught her breath in distress.

'I'm sorry,' he said more gently. 'I always have difficulty telling people that—but there's no easy way to say it.'

What an idiot I am, thought Jandy wretchedly. 'I…I'm so sorry, Patrick. I didn't mean to pry. I just assumed…'

'It's not your fault,' he said tersely. 'You weren't to know that Rachel had died…but it's tough being on your own.'

There was a weary sadness in his face—Jandy guessed every time he told this story it was like knives going through him. She was silent for a few minutes, contemplating the tragedy that had happened to him— his beautiful young wife killed before her baby grew up and bringing a happy marriage to an abrupt end. He had obviously loved Rachel very much, whereas her love for Terry had long disappeared. Now she only felt contempt for the man who had treated her so badly.

'Being a single parent isn't easy,' she said softly. 'I know, because I'm a single parent as well.'

He flicked a surprised look at her. 'That's terrible. I'm so sorry to hear that. When were you widowed?' he asked.

It was so stupid. She was over Terry now, long over

him, and yet she still felt treacherous tears welling up in her eyes whenever someone was sympathetic—especially someone like Patrick who'd gone through traumas of his own. Just when she thought she had her emotions under control, something would trigger the sadness of loneliness and rejection. And it wasn't the thought that Terry had never loved her that upset her now—just the legacy of emotions he'd left her and how he'd changed the person she had once been.

If she started telling her life story now, she would probably start blubbing properly. And perhaps it would almost sound as if she was trying to compete in the bad-luck stakes if she revealed everything.

'I...I wasn't widowed—that's not why I'm single. I'll tell you another time about it,' she said quickly, swallowing hard to get rid of the lump of self-pity that had lodged in her throat. 'But it's a long boring story.' With relief she saw that they had arrived at Pippa's. 'Ah, here we are. You can drop me off at the gate.'

'I can take you both home if you like.'

'No, really, we'll be fine. It's stopped raining and we literally live round the corner. Thank you very much—I'm so grateful.'

She had started to gabble a little and suddenly she wanted to be out of the car. She'd intruded on private grief and felt embarrassed that she'd become emotional herself.

'I'll see you tomorrow, then.' She pulled the handle of the door to get out. It didn't move as she tugged it. 'Oh...I think it's locked,' she said.

'Damn—I've had a little trouble with it—the central

locking system's a bit dodgy.' Patrick leant across her and punched a button on the side of the door.

He was very, very close to her—she felt his breath on her cheek, she could smell his warmth, the remnants of aftershave put on that morning, see the occasional grey hair on his temples and the slightly raised skin of the scar on his face. If he leant any further forward his chest would be jammed against her body. She closed her eyes, and like a flicker of lightning she felt the dangerous flash of attraction to a very sexy man. She had a ridiculous urge to put her cheek next to his, feel his mouth on hers and lean against that broad chest. She swallowed hard, and her heart beat a little tattoo against her ribs, a kaleidoscope of emotions whirling round in her head at this sudden sizzling magnetism she felt for Patrick. But, then, it wasn't really all that sudden, was it? Over two weeks she'd been suppressing a growing awareness of Patrick's charismatic appeal.

Patrick pulled back abruptly, and took a deep breath. 'There—the door should open now,' he said slightly huskily, then he cleared his throat and murmured, 'I'm very sorry. It was tactless of me to ask if you were a widow—it's upset you.'

'Of course it hasn't.' She forced herself to sound brisk and controlled. 'I'm over it now.'

He shook his head. 'Believe me, I know what it's like to be alone.'

Their eyes clashed in a mutual response of compassion, two people who knew what it was to lose love, albeit in very different ways, each haunted by tragic memories.

Then behind them a car hooted and roared past them and the spell was broken.

There was a short silence and then Patrick remarked casually, 'Look, perhaps we could introduce our daughters to each other some time—Livy doesn't know many other children around here yet and it would be great to get together. I'm sure there's so much around here that we could all enjoy.'

Was there something in his expression that seemed to translate into 'that you and I could enjoy', or was she reading too much into it? Whatever, she felt a little thrill of pleasure that he was keen to see her again.

'That's a great idea—we must definitely do that!'

'Then we'll think of something…'

His voice trailed off and their eyes locked for a moment, until out of embarrassment Jandy said quickly, 'Right—I must go now.' She jumped out of the car and waved at him before she went up the path. 'Thanks again for the lift, Patrick,' she called.

And for the rest of the evening her emotions were in turmoil—sympathy over Patrick's terrible loss, alternating with the realisation that he had lit a spark of desire inside her that she'd thought had gone for ever. Had he felt it too? Probably not, she told herself sharply. It had probably meant no more to him than comforting a child who'd been hurt—after all, how could she compete with the memory of a beloved and beautiful wife?

'What are we having for tea, Daddy? Can we have sausages and baked beans—I like that! Did you hear me, Daddy—did you?'

Patrick looked in the rear-view mirror at Livy, chattering away behind him, and laughed.

'Yes, sweetheart—of course you can. And perhaps some ice cream afterwards?'

'Yes!' shouted Livy, rocking backwards and forwards in her car seat with delight. 'Grandpa can have some too!'

'That's a good idea, Livy. We'll be back at Easterleigh soon and you can tell him what you've been doing at nursery school.'

Livy settled back in her seat and started to suck her thumb, her eyes drooping, and Patrick reflected sadly that it was at this time of day that he felt Rachel's loss most of all. There should be a mother waiting at home to greet his little daughter, someone with better culinary skills than his basic sausages, fish fingers or mince. Someone, he sighed, who could help him with the strain of coping with a demanding father and an energetic four-year-old. Oh, there was Sheena, the housekeeper, and she was marvellous, but she was getting on, and he felt he should do as much as he could for Livy when he wasn't working.

He flicked a glance at the little girl now asleep in the back of the car. The intense grief he'd felt with Rachel's death had turned to a gentle sadness over the years, but the guilt about causing that death was still as burning as ever. If only they hadn't had a stupid row about something as trivial as shopping, after he'd told her he'd be late home that evening as he was playing squash after work.

Her voice still rang in his ears. 'You do remember

we're having a supper party tonight and you said you'd get the wine?'

He'd been short with her, tired after too many tense days at work. 'For God's sake, can't you get it when you go shopping? I only get so much free time,' he'd snapped.

'I did all that yesterday,' she'd snapped back at him. 'I'll have to make a special journey now.'

And she had done, thankfully leaving Livy with her friend then driving through pelting rain down the bypass to the shops. A car had skidded coming towards her…she hadn't stood a chance. If he had picked up the wine on his way home, as he could have done so easily, she would still be alive and Livy would have a mother. If only… He would never forgive himself—never forgive himself that his last words to her had been in anger.

There'd been plenty of opportunities to get married again, had he taken them up—but he'd made a terrible mistake after Rachel had died, flinging himself into a relationship that had nearly ended in disaster. He'd learned his lesson now, he thought grimly. Never again would he reveal his background until he was absolutely sure that the woman he was dating loved him for himself alone and would love Livy almost as much as he did.

And why should he be dwelling on this now? He smiled grimly. It was because he'd met Jandy Marshall, sure that he had felt the crackle of sexual tension between them in the closeness of the car. It was as if two electric contacts had touched and a spark had been ignited. And he had been totally and utterly shaken by it.

He changed gear viciously as he went round a corner—it was just his luck that he should be drawn to a beautiful girl like her at this stage of his life. And how dangerous was that? He knew nothing about her at all except that she was single, and that she had enough on her plate without taking on another child—and so did he. But didn't it change the whole dynamics of everything from being a colleague to something much more intimate, even if the attraction was only on his side? What a fool he was…

He swung into the long drive of Easterleigh House and drove down the imposing avenue of beech trees. Their leaves were turning to a hint of red and amber, reflecting the coming autumn, and the house stood at the end of the avenue, its golden stone mellow in the dwindling light—magnificent, but in sad need of repair and refurbishment.

Patrick sighed as he drove slowly towards the house—so many memories were there. His early childhood had been so happy—then all of a sudden things had changed and what had been an idyllic life had become miserable and bitter—so much so that he and his brother couldn't wait to leave. But now he was back and perhaps Easterleigh could once again be a happy home and he could save the place for future generations, as his father longed for. But it was going to be difficult and it was not the right time to fall in love with someone like Jandy Marshall.

'So—don't worry about the flood in the kitchen. Clever me got a plumber and sorted it out,' said Lydia as she doled out spaghetti bolognese for Jandy, Abigail and herself. 'And now, we haven't had much of a chance to talk for the past four weeks, with me being on long-haul flights. Tell me what the new registrar's like. I bet it was difficult for you. I know when I'm working on a different shift with new people, it drives me mad when they don't do things my way.'

Lydia was a stewardess with an airline and had a varied work schedule, together with a hectic social life.

Jandy put a forkful of food in her mouth and chewed it reflectively. She wasn't about to tell Lydia that Patrick Sinclair was drop-dead gorgeous or the tragic story of his wife. If Lydia knew he was unattached, she would never hear the end of it. Lydia was longing for her to find a partner.

'He wasn't bad,' she replied cautiously. 'He's good at his job.'

Lydia's eyes gleamed. 'That's a start! How old is he?'

'Thirtyish—he has a little girl,' added Jandy mischievously, to put Lydia off the scent.

'Damn! Where have all the single men gone in that place?'

'They got snapped up—anyway, Lydia, you know I'm off men for good. They really aren't worth the hassle!'

Lydia laughed and started to clear the plates away. 'Wait till you meet Mr Right—not everyone's like Terry, you know. There are still a few good men out there.' She added mock-severely, 'Anyway, darling, you need someone to look after you and Abigail in your old age...'

'Here,' protested Jandy. 'I'm not quite in my dotage yet—and if I am, so are you!'

Lydia put her tongue out at her sister. 'Cheeky! Look, love, I'll put Abigail to bed—you look a bit bushed. Have a run through those leaflets on places to let. I have to admit the one I described over the phone was probably a bit pricey so that's a no-no.'

Despite her madcap ideas about what they could afford, Lydia was a tower of strength in so many ways, reflected Jandy as she settled down to riffle through what was on offer in the letting market. Lydia was kind and adored Abigail—but one of these days she would meet someone special and go her own way, and, oh, how Jandy would miss her then! As Patrick had said, it was tough being a single parent.

She started to look at the properties advertised but there was nothing suitable in her price bracket. Anyway, she was finding it hard to concentrate, her mind reverting back to Patrick and reliving that moment when every nerve in her body had been kick-started into life again…

Then there was the tragic revelation about his personal life that belied his surface confidence and good humour. But, of course, she too knew what it was like to put on a good face and if she wasn't careful she'd end up feeling sorry for him. Life went on and you had to put the past behind you, and his arrival seemed to have stimulated thoughts about her future that she hadn't had for a long, long time.

* * *

Jandy didn't sleep well that night, her dreams a jumble of scenarios that mostly featured a man with blue eyes and a brilliant smile, yet in the morning she felt wide awake, anticipating the day with a tremor of nervous excitement. She took a little more care with her hair and didn't forget to put on some lipstick and a stroke of blusher on her cheeks.

'What are you like, Jandy Marshall?' she asked herself scornfully. 'Trying to attract a man because you've learned he's not married. Pathetic!'

All the way to the hospital she tried to persuade herself that she wasn't all that bothered whether Patrick noticed her or not really. He was just another colleague, only there for a few months, but she couldn't stop the way her stomach fluttered when she thought of him and she had a sense of unusual excitement about going to work.

She met Karen coming out of one of the cubicles wiping her hands on a paper towel. Karen raised her eyes to heaven.

'It's one of those days, I'm afraid. We've got an elderly patient with dementia from a care home in Delford—can you believe they've sent him in on his own?'

This happened with monotonous regularity: a confused patient would be 'dumped', as Dr Vernon put it, in A and E with little information on his health or age, and it would take considerable time to establish what was wrong with him as he couldn't help with any questions. Karen bustled off to contact the care home and Jandy looked at the list of patients to be discharged.

'That's a familiar name,' she murmured. 'Albert Roper...' She scanned his notes, which informed her that the patient had seen Dr Vernon, who had said Mr Roper could be discharged after his intravenous fluid.

She went into the man's cubicle and took a step backwards when she saw that Mr Roper had pulled out his drip and the stand was lying across the floor. Mr Roper was a regular in A and E and it was clear that this was one of his bad days where alcohol was concerned and that he was in belligerent mood.

'Mr Roper! I'll have to put in another drip, you know, before you go home.'

'Get out!' he shouted. 'I'm not having you meddling with me...it's a disgrace!' This was a fairly regular performance. Jandy said nothing, but reached into the cupboard and took down the equipment needed to reposition the drip—needles, alcohol wipes, a saline flush and a tourniquet.

'Now, stay still, Mr Roper. I've got to put another cannula in your vein,' she said, pulling on a pair of lanolin gloves.

The man looked at Jandy craftily for a few minutes as she tried to find a good vein in the knotted old arm he presented to her. Eventually she managed to get the drip put up, and as soon as she'd hooked it onto the stand he laughed and pulled his arm away. Jandy leapt to save the stand from falling over, tripped over the tubing and a spray of blood went over the whole room, including her clothes.

'Mr Roper!' she croaked, on her knees beside the bed. 'What do you think you're doing?'

'I told you to stop mucking me about,' growled Mr Roper.

'Can I help?'

Jandy looked up from her awkward position on the floor to see Patrick looking down at her with an amused grin. The shock of pleasure at seeing him clashed with the acute embarrassment of Patrick seeing her at her most undignified. So much for her trying to glam herself up that morning! She scrambled up quickly and looked down wryly at her blood-spattered tunic.

'Mr Roper doesn't like having his drip in,' she explained, then added succinctly, 'Mr Roper comes in regularly for fluid replacement so we know him very well.'

'Ah, I see,' said Patrick. He turned to the glowering man and said mildly, 'Mr Roper, if you don't let us put this drip in you won't be able to go home—you'll probably have to sleep on a trolley all night as we don't have enough beds for everyone.'

Mr Roper considered this for a few seconds, then he said sulkily, 'Put the damn thing in, then—I'm fed up with the lot of you!'

Jandy went out to change her clothes. 'Magic touch, Dr Sinclair,' she murmured as she passed him.

'Just the usual skill,' he said modestly, winking at her.

Tim Vernon was talking to Karen as Jandy came by and raised his eyebrows. 'You've been in the wars,' he remarked.

'Mr Roper wasn't too keen on me putting in his cannula,' she explained. 'Dr Sinclair's persuaded him to have it done, but I'll have to clean up that cubicle.'

Tim sighed and said crustily, 'If I remember the last time Mr Roper came in, the same thing happened. Let me know when he's actually out of the building, will you?' He turned to Karen and stroked the side of his face with a grimace. 'Any aspirins in that drawer of yours, Sister? I've got a devil of a toothache…and I want to go through the admissions with you.'

'Come with me, Doctor—I've got a magic formula to help with that,' said Karen soothingly.

They disappeared into Sister's office and Jandy grinned. Karen had a profusion of 'magic cures' to keep headaches, stomach upsets and other ailments at bay. Tim seemed to suffer more than most from his teeth and it didn't do much for his temper.

Jandy went to change her tunic and then went to a box on the wall with cards of patients waiting to be seen. Just as she was about to take the top card, there was a sudden commotion and two youths, pushing and shoving each other, staggered into the corridor from the waiting room. They were laughing uproariously and taunting other patients in the cubicles. Close on their heels was Danny, face bright red and looking flustered.

'How long have these two been making trouble?' Jandy hissed to Danny as he passed her.

'Too long,' he said breathlessly. 'I've rung Security, but apparently there's trouble in the car park and resources are stretched. I'm still waiting for

someone to come. Any minute now there's going to
be a bust-up.'

'This is ridiculous,' muttered Jandy, looking around
desperately to see if anyone was about. Karen and
Tim were in her office and she knew that Bob Thoms
was doing a small procedure in one of the theatres.

She went behind the desk and hit the emergency
button, which was meant to alert Security that a major
incident was happening, then marched up to the young
men, who were now making lewd suggestions to each
other about a young woman sitting scared and rigid
with fear outside a cubicle.

'Could you keep it quiet please and go back to the
waiting room?' she shouted above their deafening
voices. 'Which of you is the patient?'

A youth in a leather jacket and trousers liberally fes-
tooned with chains and zips stared at her and then said
aggressively, 'About time too—we've been waiting
hours here.' He pointed to the other lad. 'Les is first in
the queue.'

'He's been seen by the triage nurse—there are other
people who need more urgent attention.'

The youth swaggered up to her, pushing a finger at
her chest aggressively, and the smell of strong beer
wafted over her.

'You see Les now…or else.' He looked around at
the nervous people in the corridor and snarled, 'This
place is a joke—the hospital ought to be reported,
keeping us waiting. Les is in agony with his ankle.'

He was standing eyeball to eyeball with Jandy, his
face thrust forward, blotchy with the effect of

alcohol, his breath stale. Behind him Les raised a ragged jeer.

'Yeah! That's right, Phil—you tell 'er!'

'Les will be seen as soon as possible…you, please go!'

Jandy stood her ground resolutely, inwardly praying that someone from Security would come before the whole place erupted, and wondering what it was about this job that she enjoyed. A baby started wailing in Paediatrics and Phil kicked away a chair near his foot and grabbed Jandy's arm.

'You listen here, my dahlin', unless someone sees us in a minute, I'm going to give you something you won't like.'

'Get your hands off me!' shouted Jandy, beating at him ineffectually with her free hand and kicking his shin as hard as she could. 'Your friend won't be seen at all if—'

He twisted her arm viciously. Jandy lost her balance and landed with a thump on the floor, a chair he'd kicked to one side just missing her forehead. Then several things happened. A large figure interposed itself between Jandy and the youth and Patrick's voice roared out, 'What the hell do you think you're doing?'

The youth was grabbed by the feet as he tried to run away and landed on his stomach with a loud yell. Two security guards appeared and handcuffed the squirming boy, now emitting colourful expletives, while Jandy still sat on the floor, slightly dazed and watching the evolving scene with amazement. Patrick towered above the boy, staring down at him, gimlet-eyed.

'You got a complaint, son? Put it in writing, then. Meantime, these gentlemen have a few questions to ask you, I'm sure!'

The youth looked up at him sullenly. 'It's a disgrace. I've bust my nose…' he started to say.

'Is that all you've bust? A pity!' Patrick's face was grim and flinty-eyed. 'Can't you read?' He pointed to a sign on the wall. 'It says there that any aggression towards members of staff will lead to prosecution— and this little episode's all on video too. It won't make pretty viewing.'

Les snarled, although he took a step backwards from Patrick's menacing figure.

Patrick folded his arms and glared at them. 'Your friend may be seen if he remembers his manners. You—get moving! Oh, and Security will answer any questions you might have.'

Les turned round sulkily. 'They're a bunch of losers here,' he shouted vaguely to the stunned onlookers, trying not to lose face by having the last word.

He shuffled out, leaving his mate sitting hunched on a chair, staring at the floor. An old man peered out of one of the cubicles and shouted in a quavery voice, 'Well done, sir! That sort need birching, the lot of them!'

'What's going on?' asked Tim, appearing out of Karen's office. 'There's been a lot of a noise…'

'Under control now, I think, Dr Vernon,' said Patrick. 'Staff Nurse has just taken the brunt of some unwanted visitors.'

'You all right, Staff?' Tim asked with concern. 'We

really need to up the security in this place if people are getting through here so easily from the waiting room. Go and take her for a coffee, Patrick—I'll beep you if you're needed.'

Patrick squatted down by Jandy. His voice had lost the steely tones he'd used on the youths and now he said drily, 'This is the second time I've found you lying on the floor in about twenty minutes. You landed with an almighty thump—are you OK?'

'Fortunately I landed on my bottom—it was just a bit of a shock,' remarked Jandy. She grinned rather shakily up at him. 'Just a normal day in Casualty. I should be used to it by now, but I was a bit slow off the mark and didn't see it coming.'

'Promise me one thing,' Patrick said sternly. 'Don't try and take on those thugs again.'

He looked at her fiercely and she laughed. 'I'm a big girl now, Patrick, big enough to look after myself!'

Without a word he stooped down and slipped his arms under hers, lifting her effortlessly to her feet. In the second that he pulled her up they were facing each other, her body brushing against his broad frame, her face inches away from his. She could see the dark flecks in his blue eyes, a red mark on his cheek where he'd cut himself shaving. A giggle threatened to burst out of her mouth—if they hadn't been in the hospital she might have thrown caution to the wind and pulled him down towards her!

He placed her gently on a chair and then put a hand on each arm of the chair, preventing her from getting up, and looked down at her with amusement in those beguiling blue eyes. 'Leave the strong-arm tactics to Security next time, all right?'

'OK, OK. And, Patrick…thank you very much.'

She spoke lightly but a sudden chill of caution laid its fingers on her heart—she wasn't a fool. She was being drawn inexorably to Patrick Sinclair. Every time she saw him she longed to touch him, lean against his athletic body. If she wasn't careful she'd be imagining a happy-ever-after scenario. She knew without a doubt that the attraction she felt towards him was more than a just a mild and diverting flirtation—it was real and powerful. She shivered slightly. She'd allowed one man to rule her heart and dominate her and it had ended in bitter tears because she'd trusted him. She couldn't allow herself to fall into that trap again.

She stood up resolutely. 'Back to work,' she said breathlessly. 'I'm fine now.'

He shook his head. 'Not before you've had a strong cup of coffee—Tim Vernon suggested it, and you need a breather.' He shot a look at his watch. 'Perhaps we've time to talk about that property I know about for rent and organise something for our daughters to do together.'

She opened her mouth to say she was quite OK and didn't need a coffee, but she made the mistake of looking into those blue amused eyes of his. She needed somewhere to live, didn't she? For Lydia and Abigail's sake she'd have a coffee with him…

'That would be lovely,' she said meekly.

CHAPTER FOUR

THE canteen had the familiar smell of chips mingled with roast meat, and was teeming with people shuffling along in the queue. The staff sat in a section behind a screen covered with plastic flowers and there were two huge tubs of dusty-looking plastic palms at the entrance.

'Don't say I don't ask you to the most exotic places,' said Patrick drily to Jandy. 'Bag two seats in the corner, and I'll get something wonderfully delicious from the machine to save us queuing up.'

Jandy watched him weaving his way back to her through the tables a couple of minutes later, concentrating on balancing two plastic cups and chocolate bars in his hands. He looked impressively tall and imposing in that sea of people and she could see Tilly pointing him out to the little group of student nurses she was sitting with. No doubt she was telling them that Patrick Sinclair was the greatest thing since sliced bread! Funny, thought Jandy, how she felt like she'd known him for ages, though in reality it had only been a week or so.

'Right,' he said, easing himself into his seat. 'Have a reviver.' He took a sip of his own coffee and grimaced. 'Ah—nectar,' he remarked dourly. 'Although I'd put more emphasis on the "tar" myself...'

She giggled, feeling a sudden light-heartedness in his company, and he grinned back at her. 'Now, tell me honestly if you feel OK after that oaf knocked you down,' he said.

Jandy smiled ruefully. 'Only slightly shaky. I promise you it was only my pride that was hurt. I'm just annoyed that I let him get to me. I ought to have learned by now.'

'I take it there's an assault book to record this sort of thing?'

Jandy nodded. 'It's usually full after two weeks. Anyway, I'm glad that you turned up when you did.'

'So am I. It's a familiar story, though, isn't it? Aggression fuelled by drink and drugs.' Then he shrugged. 'There's not much we can do about it apparently. Anyway, to change the subject...' He reached into his jacket pocket and drew out a piece of paper, unfolding it in front of Jandy. 'Perhaps you'd like to see the place I was telling you about that's available for rent.'

She looked with interest at the photo of a small house, unusual in aspect with an octagonal shape and two dormer windows in the roof.

'It looks really quaint—rather like a little ginger-bread house!' she exclaimed. 'I'd love to look around it. Although,' she added cautiously, 'it all depends on the rent, to be truthful...'

'It's not been lived in for a while—it needs a clean and a bit of decoration, so the rent isn't all that high. Frankly, you'd be doing the owner a favour if you decide to take it.'

It sounded almost too good to be true. So many things had been a battle for her in recent years, from finding childcare for Abigail to getting a job she loved, that suddenly being offered what looked like a lovely little house was almost unbelievable. She felt a sudden lump of gratitude in her throat and said in a muffled voice, 'It would be such a load off my mind to get somewhere soon—I have to admit I'm really getting desperate. My priority, of course, is Abigail and I just can't sleep thinking we won't have a roof over our heads….'

Patrick looked at her perceptively, her lovely eyes bright with tears, aware of the emotion in her voice and the fact that Jandy had been hiding a lot of stress behind her bright manner.

'If you want to look around it this weekend, I could arrange to get the key—if it suits you, it's yours!'

Jandy heaved a huge sigh. 'I'm so grateful to you.' She gave a shaky laugh. 'I really thought I'd never get anywhere suitable so quickly—I imagined us camping out on the street!'

Patrick smiled, lowering his glance to give her time to compose herself. 'Let's hope it fits the bill, then,' he said.

'Does it belong to a friend of yours?' Jandy asked.

Patrick hesitated briefly then said, 'It's owned by a relative and I know he's very keen to have it occupied.

I'll give you the directions and meet you there at about ten-thirty on Saturday morning.'

Jandy's heart gave a leap of pleasure and relief that her worries about getting some accommodation might be solved, and also that in a few days she would be seeing Patrick outside the confines of the hospital...

'That would be great, although I'll probably have to bring Abigail with me, if that's OK.'

'Then I'll bring Livy.' He smiled. 'They can give us their opinion of the place and they can meet each other!' He pushed a large chocolate biscuit towards her. 'Here—it's not much, but it might keep you going till lunchtime.'

'Thanks. I can't resist it, I'm afraid, although I am trying to cut out chocolate,' she remarked, unwrapping it and biting into it hungrily.

Blue eyes flicked over her. 'I don't know why,' he murmured. 'I wouldn't have thought you had any weight issues.'

Jandy laughed. 'You should see me with nothing on—I'm awfully...' She stopped, suddenly realising what she'd said, and blushed, the thought of him seeing her stark naked a little too intimate to contemplate.

Patrick raised his brows and his eyes twinkled. 'I'm sure there's nothing awful about you, but if you like I'll give you a medical assessment...'

'I don't think so!'

'Well, the offer's there—only too pleased to give you my professional opinion!' He grinned, leaning back in his chair looking at her with amusement, and their eyes locked, an unmistakeable spark of attraction and intimacy flickering between them: Jandy dropped her eyes and inspected a split nail rather thoroughly and tried to smother a giggle.

There was a second's silence, Patrick's gaze roving over her, then he said hesitantly, 'Perhaps I shouldn't ask this, but you mentioned that you were a single parent but not a widow…does that mean you and your husband are divorced?'

Jandy's expression changed and he put up his hand in apology. 'I'm sorry—please don't answer that. It's nothing to do with me.'

She stared at the table and folded the biscuit wrapper into a precise square. Was she ready to reveal her sad little story to someone she'd only known for a short time? It made her seem so gullible, so easily deceived—and incredibly stupid to have become pregnant, believing that Terry would have been as thrilled as she was to have their baby. But it was a long time ago now and quite a few people knew her background anyway, so why shouldn't Patrick be told?

She gave a little shrug and said at last, 'It's not a secret, Patrick. I was a naïve fool and fell for someone who was already married with a family—although I didn't realise that at the time.'

Patrick looked at her in horror. 'How did you find out?'

'When I discovered I was pregnant and told him, thinking he'd be delighted as he'd often told me how fond of children he was, he took fright and blurted out the truth.' Jandy's eyes narrowed, and she unconsciously twisted her hands together. 'I can remember his precise words actually. He said, "You idiot! I can't possibly have a child. I realised you were getting too sweet on me recently."'

Patrick shook his head. 'He sounds unbelievable!'

'Ah—but listen to the punchline he gave,' Jandy added succinctly. '"I've already got a wife and two daughters, which is quite enough to cope with!" Shortly after that he disappeared into the blue yonder, leaving me to cope alone.'

'What an idiot!' Patrick's voice was rough with disgust.

Jandy shrugged and said firmly, 'Actually, it taught me a lesson—never fall in love with someone who's carrying a lot of baggage. There won't be room in his life for him to concentrate on anyone else. I suspected Terry had other things in his life but I didn't realise that it was a ready-grown family!'

An unreadable expression suddenly crossed Patrick's face and he nodded slowly. 'You're right. You couldn't risk going through that again—you must have been through hell.'

'I'm over it now. Terry's history as far as I'm concerned, and although I wish he was around for Abigail sometimes, I think we're really better off without him.'

'So he's never contributed anything towards Abigail's upbringing?' asked Patrick softly.

Jandy looked at him levelly. 'I don't want anything from that man. He lied to me for the six months we went out with each other, convincing me that he loved me and wanted a future with me.' She added semi-jokingly but with a touch of sadness, 'I was totally naïve, but I could never go through the roller-coaster of emotions again that I went through with Terry—it took too long to recover!'

And I wonder if she's really recovered now, thought Patrick, sipping the remains of his coffee and watching her face over the rim of his cup. There was a wistful expression in her eyes. The wound might have healed, but it had left a scar that would probably affect her for many years. And couldn't that scar be reopened if she was hurt again by someone who was wary of committing wholeheartedly to a relationship, someone who already had plenty of responsibilities…someone like him, for instance? Didn't he fit into that category?

'I guess this happened in Manchester, then. And when you had Abigail, you came back here?' he said quietly.

Jandy nodded. 'I met Terry in Manchester, but he disappeared after I turned down his suggestion to have an abortion. I've never seen or heard from him since.'

'He sounds charming,' remarked Patrick with heavy irony.

'I went to stay with my mother who lives in Scotland, and had the baby there.' She laughed. 'Mum was wonderful, but she has her own life—namely living with a garage mechanic who's half her age! I realised after a few weeks that having a daughter and a grandchild living with you in a tiny house doesn't fit into the love-nest scenario!'

'So you moved back here?' Patrick murmured.

'Yes, I came back here with Abigail and set up home with my sister. She's a tower of strength and we get on very well. And then I went back to nursing. It's a busy life, but Abigail is secure and happy—and, of course, she's my priority. It's important that she has stability in her life—a proper home, not a stopgap until I can get something permanent.'

Patrick nodded. 'You must have been having a few sleepless nights,' he murmured.

He leant back in his chair and looked at Jandy perceptively—the determined tilt of her chin, the steady look of purpose in her eyes. He admired the way that she had managed to get her life on an even keel again despite all her difficulties—his offer of the house would be a godsend to her. But he hadn't realised the ghastly story behind the fact that she was a single parent. How cruel would it be to risk upsetting her little boat and drawing her into his complicated life? If she took the house they would be bound more closely together—and would that be wise?

'And what made you take up nursing?' he enquired lightly, changing the subject.

Jandy smiled. 'Someone gave me a nurse's outfit when I was little, and somehow the idea of becoming a real nurse got a hold of me. I must have been mad—it's hard to bring up a child on my salary!'

'But you enjoy your work and your sister helps you with your little girl?'

'Yes—I'm very lucky, and Abby adores Lydia. And you?' she asked. 'Was your father a doctor? That often seems to inspire people to take up medicine.'

'No. My father is…well, he's a farmer really and loves the land. I think he'd have liked me to have taken it up too, but my brother and I were impatient to do our own thing.'

'I heard you say you were living with your father?'

'For the time being,' Patrick replied lightly. 'My little girl loves living in the house.'

'And whereabouts…?'

'Oh, not too far away—reasonably convenient.'

There was something about his voice—a studied vagueness—as if he had suddenly pulled the shutters down about any more information on his personal life, and Jandy flicked a look of slight surprise at him. She was perceptive enough to realise that there'd been a slight shift in his attitude towards her—as if he'd stepped back a bit. She felt slightly hurt, as he'd asked her about her past and she'd been frank with him. It seemed he was less eager to confide in her and she'd obviously taken too much for granted. She took the hint and stood up quickly.

'I'll look forward to seeing the house on Saturday, then,' she said briskly. 'And thanks for the coffee and rescuing me from those yobs. I'd better get back or Karen won't be too pleased.'

Patrick toyed with his coffee spoon, watching Jandy go out of the canteen, the light catching her burnished hair, now done up in a neat coil at the back of her head. He'd only known her a week or two, and yet he was beginning to feel he'd known her for many months. They had much in common, and perhaps they could have helped each other heal the wounds they had from the past—but he wasn't ready to commit to anyone yet.

He sighed heavily. If he didn't put the brakes on things, his relationship with Jandy might turn into a rerun of what had happened in London in the months after Rachel had died.

Gazing unseeingly across the table, the ghastly loneliness of that time came flooding back to him, and how easily he'd hurtled into a relationship with someone he'd known only briefly. He'd been vulnerable, hating the thought of being alone, feeling deeply guilty that he had caused his wife's death. Tara had been a shoulder to cry on, deeply sympathetic, limpet-like in her determination not to leave him alone. By the time he had realised he was only desirable to her because of his family background, and that she had absolutely no interest in his little daughter, indeed was irritated by her, it had been almost too late to extricate himself from the engagement he'd been coerced into.

He didn't think that Jandy was the type of girl to be impressed because of who he was—it might even be the reverse. But the fact remained that they were two people with unhappy pasts and he couldn't bear to make another mistake like that, or saddle someone like Jandy with his problems. Was it fair of him to get too close to someone who had been hurt so much already?

He pushed his fingers through his hair distractedly. Why the hell had he mentioned the empty house to Jandy? But now he couldn't in all conscience renege on his offer. He'd promised her she could have the place if she liked it and, besides, now he realised how desperate she was for somewhere reasonable to live. For the sake of her child, he had to keep the offer open—but for the sake of Jandy and himself, he had to stand back a little and not do anything that might bring them into close contact outside the hospital.

Then the beeper in his pocket went off and he stood up and walked briskly back to A and E, trying to push his frustration to the back of his mind.

Saturday morning at last! Jandy helped Abigail put on her little jeans and sweater and brushed her daughter's hair briskly.

'Ow! Stop it, Mummy—I don't need my hair brushed. Ow!'

'Nearly done! There—you look beautiful! We're going to meet another little girl this morning so you want to look good, don't you?'

Abigail looked at her mother witheringly. 'No, I don't! Who is she anyway?'

'I work with her daddy and we're going to look around a house he knows that's for rent—it might be OK for us. It's in the country.'

Abigail perked up. 'I like the country. We could have horses and dogs and cats and—'

'Whoa!' Jandy laughed. 'Wherever we live we can't have animals—we're all out too much. And, of course, the house may not suit us, or it may be too expensive. We'll see.'

It had been a busy week as usual, but every so often in the middle of dressing a wound or calming a screaming child, the thought of her meeting Patrick to see the cottage would flash into her mind and her pulse would bound into excitement. How sad it was that in her dull life meeting someone to look at a house seemed exhil-arating!

They got into the car and she drove off towards the cottage.

There was the smell of damp leaves and earth newly turned after the harvest as they got out of the car in the little lane outside the cottage. A little tremor of pleasure darted through Jandy as she gazed at the building. It was quaint, with leaded-paned windows and old tree trunks holding up the roof of the little porch; an old rose twined its way randomly round the front door, a few dying blooms still there. She could easily imagine herself living here, surrounded by fields and the view of the soft Derbyshire hills.

She was surprised to see that the cottage was actually an old gatehouse at the back entrance of an estate, although the drive had long been blocked off and the property stood in its own garden. It was just possible to see a large and imposing mansion through the woods that grew beyond the garden, mullioned windows glittering in the sun. The little village was just down the road, and although it was about six miles from Delford, it would be possible to get to work on time if she got up early. There was even a little village school that Abigail could attend when she was old enough. She turned to Abigail, who was standing at the gate of the field watching the sheep grazing there.

'Come on, poppet, let's go into the garden and wait for Patrick there. He should be here in a minute.'

Jandy looked around with pleasure. So far, so good. There was a neat little garden with room enough to play but not so huge that she'd have to spend every weekend gardening. She turned round as she heard a car stopping outside the gate and Patrick and his daughter arrived. If Tilly could see him now, she'd probably be speechless, reflected Jandy as she watched him walk towards her. Casual suited Patrick—dark cords and a thick cream Arran sweater with an old scarf round his neck made him look rugged and—no getting away from it—very sexy!

The little girl by his side had auburn hair springing round her head like a halo, and looked very like the photograph of her mother that Jandy had seen.

'And I guess this is Livy?' Jandy said, smiling down at the child. 'Meet my little girl, Abigail—you're both the same age.'

The two children stared at each other cautiously then Patrick took out a key and opened the front door.

'In you go, girls—see what you think and then tell us!'

Jandy watched the children run inside and smiled at Patrick. 'What a beautiful little girl Livy is—she looks so much like her mother in the photo I saw.'

'Yes,' he said simply. 'She's the image of Rachel— every time I see her I'm reminded of her mother.'

The sadness in his voice revealed a lot, thought Jandy. It wasn't that she didn't expect him to still feel deeply about Rachel, but it seemed clear to her that Patrick's allegiance still belonged in the past to a wife who had died.

'Right!' she said brightly, stepping into the front room. 'I hope Abigail doesn't fall too heavily for the house because it may be way above my budget.'

He nodded. 'I have been wondering if it's suitable after all. It's in a bit of a mess and the bedrooms are very small.'

'Ah, well, a lick of paint does wonders for a place, doesn't it?'

The front door led straight into a little front room with wallpaper hanging in strips from the walls and plaster from the ceiling in little heaps on the floor. But it was cosy with a pretty bay window that let in the light and through which there was a wonderful view. Jandy could just imagine herself sitting in that bay, basking in the warmth of the sun. She turned to Patrick.

'So far I love it,' she said, with a delighted smile.

He frowned slightly. 'You do? Better reserve judgement until you've seen upstairs.'

Abigail and Livy were running in and out of the two small bedrooms with lots of giggles, hiding in a cupboard on the landing and jumping out—they had obviously made friends with each other.

'Look, Mummy, I can have this room—it's got a little mouse's nest by the fireplace. Isn't that sweet?' cried Abigail, taking her mother's hand and dragging her round the room.

'I think he'd be happier living in the field where he came from,' said Jandy firmly. 'Anyway, you and I will have the bigger room and Lydia will have that room as there's only one of her. And actually we haven't decided to have it yet.'

'No—you don't want to make a hasty decision,' put in Patrick quickly. 'There are disadvantages to living out in the country.'

Jandy flicked a look at his face—there was something uneasy about his expression. Suddenly she guessed that he was regretting mentioning the house to her. He certainly sounded very negative all of a sudden about the whole thing. She wasn't about to be put off, whatever he thought.

'There are drawbacks about living in Delford too,' she pointed out. 'The traffic, the noise, the crime…it could be a wonderful move to leave that behind.'

He nodded sombrely. 'That's true. But you live with your sister—won't she want to look at it too?'

'Oh, I assure you Lydia will like anything I like. We generally have very similar tastes—except when it comes to spending money! Anyway, she's away with her job quite a bit and she's happy to leave it all to me.'

Abigail came running back to Jandy and looked up at her pleadingly. 'I love it here—please let's live here. I could have a rabbit. Livy says she'd look after it for me, and she only lives just up the road—we're neighbours!'

'Oh, I see…' Jandy turned to Patrick with surprise. 'I didn't realise you lived so close by.'

'I'm not all that far away,' he admitted. Again that dismissive tone of voice, keeping her at a distance.

Jandy felt a flash of irritation. Why couldn't the man say just exactly where he lived—what was the mystery? Well, she wasn't going to be put off renting a place that he had suggested so enthusiastically a short time ago, just because he was having cold feet.

'I do like the place,' she said decisively. 'Perhaps we could discuss terms and conditions and if they're OK then I'd like to go ahead.'

'Right,' said Patrick heavily. 'Come downstairs and I'll go over it with you.'

It didn't take long to discuss and Jandy readily agreed the rent. In all conscience, Patrick had to quote the market price for the property, although he'd been tempted to ask more than he thought Jandy could afford in the hope that she wouldn't take it. However much he longed to get closer to her, he was in no position to jump into a relationship at the moment.

He looked at her profile as she read the agreement for the rent of the house, and noted the endearing habit she had of biting her bottom lip when she was concentrating on something. God, he thought wistfully, she was beautiful and completely unconscious of her looks. Her sherry-coloured eyes were warm and sparkled when she was animated, and her hair, usually tied back at work, fell like a golden bell against her neck, brushing against the collar of her blouse.

How was he going to avoid seeing her when she was going to be living so close to him—or stop himself from coming round to see how she was? It would be very easy to get entangled in her life. He'd just have to be disciplined, he thought grimly. Keep work and home separate.

She looked up at him with those wide brown eyes, and smiled happily. 'I know my sister will love this place as much as I do—and I can't wait to move in!'

'Then I hope you'll be very happy here,' he said rather stiffly.

'And when we're straight, you must come and have a meal with us to celebrate,' Jandy said pleasantly.

He longed to say how much he'd enjoy that but felt he had to backpedal, keep his distance, and not show too much enthusiasm.

'Some time perhaps, but I've a very full schedule at the moment.'

He sounded dismissive of her well-meant invitation and Jandy felt a sting of resentment. She certainly wouldn't ask him again!

He turned round quickly, almost relieved as the two little girls clattered into the room. 'Right, Livy, off we go! I've a million things to do this morning!'

'Oh, Daddy, can't Abigail come and play with me? I could show her my pony.'

Both children looked hopefully up at him, but he shook his head and said peremptorily, 'Sorry, not today—it's completely out of the question. We'll see Abigail soon perhaps. Come on, now!'

His voice was curt, and Livy's lips turned down at his sharp tone, but Patrick took her hand and led her firmly out to the car, and in a few seconds he'd accelerated off down the road, with the barest of goodbyes. He looked in the mirror as he drove off and could see Jandy staring after him, an expression of surprise on her face, and groaned. He must have sounded rude. It saddened him to hurt her, but surely he was right to stand back a little, put on the brakes? He had too many issues to deal with—not only his sensitivity about his background but about his life back in Delford.

He changed gear roughly so that the car jolted. How simple life would have been without the ties of Easterleigh and his family!

'I like Abigail, Daddy—and I like Jandy. Can they come and see us soon…please? They're nice, aren't they?' piped up Livy's little voice from the back of the car.

'Very nice, darling,' said Patrick heavily. 'Perhaps in a few weeks when they've settled in.'

Jandy frowned in bewilderment as she watched the car disappear round the corner. What on earth had she done wrong that he should leave so abruptly? It had been his idea to show her the cottage, yet suddenly he seemed to be backpedalling as if he wanted as little to do with her as possible. There was no mistaking his churlish manner. Perhaps, she thought sadly, he didn't seem quite such a nice guy after all. Perhaps her sordid little tale about Abigail's father had put him off in some way.

Abigail started to cry. 'Why couldn't I go with Livy? It's not fair! I want to see her pony. Why wouldn't her daddy let her?'

Why wouldn't he indeed? Jandy closed the garden gate and opened the car door for Abigail to get in. Even though she realised his wife still held a treasured place in his heart, Jandy was as sure as anything that there had been a mutual attraction between Patrick and her. Surely it hadn't been all in her imagination?

It was a warning for her not to assume anything, she reflected bitterly as she clicked Abigail's car seat belt into place. He wasn't the affable man he seemed to be—that was for sure. She should steer well clear of him. The light-heartedness she'd felt over the past weeks since she'd met Patrick began to evaporate.

'When we live here, Mummy, can Livy come and play again?' Abigail pleaded.

'Perhaps, Abigail—we'll have to see,' sighed Jandy, glancing in her mirror and moving off slowly down the road.

Blast the man. His attitude seemed to have dampened her excitement in finding a lovely place at the right price. Then she shrugged. She damn well wasn't going to be down-hearted. His manner was inexplicable, but she'd get over it. She'd had enough of moody men and their hang-ups.

'Don't worry, Abigail,' she reassured her little daughter. 'We're going to have lots of fun in our new little home!'

CHAPTER FIVE

A FEW days later Jandy switched on the TV and flopped back on the sofa. The news was on, with the usual catalogue of financial disaster and celebrity mishaps. She let it wash over her, allowing herself to relax after a busy week of trying to get rid of some of the junk she didn't need when she moved, culminating in a very tough day at the hospital.

A terrible road crash involving a coach party of pensioners on the motorway had resulted in two fatalities and multiple serious injuries and had occupied all the staff in A and E for many hours. Most of the people involved would feel the effects for the rest of their lives. Of course, that was the nature of the job, but no matter how experienced you were it was hard not to get involved emotionally and block out the graphic pictures of terrible wounds and grief that dominated that kind of scenario—it remained with you for a long time. She took a deep draught of the glass of chilled Bordeaux she had in her hand, welcoming the anaesthetising effect after a traumatic few hours.

Jandy's thoughts drifted back over the day and inevitably to Patrick. There was no doubt about it. Since he had left so abruptly from the cottage he was less than forthcoming—quite distant, in fact, although they hadn't been working together all the time and there hadn't been many opportunities for chat. Today he'd been part of the team looking after the crash victims, not only with the practical elements of trying to resuscitate a dying man but he'd also had to tell the weeping daughter that her father had died. He had done it with compassionate and gentle understanding that had belied his tough exterior.

But she couldn't help puzzling over Patrick's change of attitude. He had seemed so sympathetic, so understanding, so comforting when she'd told him that she was a single parent. He understood only too well what it was to lose love. Then that warmth had evaporated like mist on a warm day after she'd divulged the full story of Terry's betrayal to him over coffee. She'd tried to put the whole episode out of her mind—but it hurt, no doubt about that.

Bleakly she took another sip of wine and stared blankly at the screen, lost in her thoughts, vaguely aware that the programme was now the local news. An elderly, rather frail man in a wheelchair was being interviewed by a young woman, and they were standing in front of a large mansion with golden stone and red Virginia creeper winding its way over the walls. Jandy recognised it immediately as the stunning house she had seen through the trees behind the little cottage the other day, and she turned up the volume, interested to hear what was being said about what was, in effect, her neighbour's property.

'Further to our programme on green issues, we are now at Easterleigh House, the magnificent 16th-century home of Viscount Duncan,' said the reporter. She turned to the old man. 'My Lord, you and your son are planning to develop a wind farm on the hills at the edge of your estate. Aren't you worried about the impact of the beautiful views across the countryside—views that have remained the same for centuries?'

'I don't think their impact on the view will be too detrimental, and the fact is that the house and estate needs a great deal of renovation, and we need the income,' replied Viscount Duncan.

'That's an enormous project,' remarked the interviewer.

The old man smiled, and for a moment he reminded Jandy of someone—but she couldn't put her finger on who it was. 'I'm lucky that my son has come home to oversee everything. He's got much more energy than I have! I want to save the place for future generations, and to continue to give employment to people whose families have worked on the farm and land for many years.'

'It's a huge estate,' said the young woman. 'Could you not sell off some of the land to raise money instead of putting up wind farms?'

Lord Duncan frowned and said fiercely, 'I feel it is held in trust. The land was added to over the years by marriages between the local aristocracy—people who loved it, understood it and who were born to look after it, like me. I don't think it should be sold off to just anyone!'

What a snobbish old fossil he is, thought Jandy, amused by his reference to the 'local aristocracy', and his dismissal of other people as 'just anyone'! And yet she could sympathise with his longing to keep his beautiful estate intact.

The young woman turned back to the camera with a bright smile. 'So there you have it—is Lord Duncan justified in his scheme? We'd like your comments on what you, the viewers, think about the wind farm. Is it worth saving a stately home to have this project on our doorstep and changing the face of this little corner of Derbyshire? And do you think it will be a positive contribution to the green energy problem? Please let us know!' Then she added brightly, 'And if you're interested in seeing this beautiful old house at close quarters, there's a village fair being held in the grounds here at the weekend in aid of the village hall—so why not come along?'

Jandy yawned and flicked the 'off' button—she was too tired to apply her mind to questions about green issues, although it was mildly interesting that her neighbour was a nobleman. She rinsed her wineglass clean under the tap before she went up to bed, but she was sure she would not sleep well.

A lovely crisp autumn day—and a Saturday, which meant that she and Abigail could go out for the morning, thought Jandy with relief. A welcome change from packing cases and sorting through clothes to be thrown out before the move. Abigail's little bike was in the boot and they drove to the new cottage. On such a lovely day it would be a good idea to stroll around the lanes there and get to know the area.

Jandy noticed the entrance to Easterleigh House just before she got to the cottage. A banner strung across the imposing gates before the long winding drive read, 'Open Day at Easterleigh House in Aid of the Village Hall! Fun for all the Family!' A little stream of people were making their way to the house after paying at the gate. Vaguely Jandy remembered it being mentioned on the television programme about the wind farm that she had watched the previous evening.

'Look, Abigail!' she exclaimed as she parked the car by the road. 'Why don't we go and see what's happening there? There might be all kinds of exciting things to do and we could meet some of our new neighbours— perhaps other little boys and girls you could get to know.'

Abigail was enthusiastic and pedalled her bike up the drive, with Jandy walking briskly beside her. What a place to live, reflected Jandy, looking appreciatively at the beautiful trees turning amber and the magnificent facade of the house facing the drive. No wonder Lord Duncan was so passionate about preserving it.

To the side of the house was an enormous lawn, bounded by huge oaks and cedars, and on this were a variety of stalls and little fairground attractions.

'Mummy, look!' yelled Abigail with delight. 'Swings and roundabouts—can I go on them?'

She got off her bike and gave it to Jandy to hold,

before dashing over to the swings and waiting patiently
in a queue for her mother to join her and pay for the
ride. As Jandy walked towards her another child ran
over to Abigail and tapped her on the shoulder, and
then both children began jumping up and down in excitement. It was Livy! Jandy's heart thumped. Where
Livy was, it meant that Patrick was also nearby—and,
of course, he lived near here, so it wasn't surprising
that they had come as well. Jandy went up to the little
girls.

'Hello, Livy, nice to see you!' she exclaimed.

'I wanted you to come.' Livy beamed. 'I asked
Daddy if we could tell you to meet us, but he said he
didn't think you'd be able to. I'm going to take Abigail
to see my pony when she's been on the rides.'

Jandy felt a moment's desolation at Patrick's
reaction to his daughter's request—he was obviously
determined that the families shouldn't get involved.

'Where is Daddy?' she asked cautiously.

'Oh, he'll be here later. Grandpa's looking after me
at the moment.' She looked round and waved to an old
man being pushed across the lawn in a wheelchair, whom
Jandy immediately recognised as Viscount Duncan, the
man she'd seen on television only the night before.

Livy danced over to him, dragging Abigail with her.
'Grandpa! Grandpa! Look, this is my new friend—she's
called Abigail and they're going to live in the little
cottage!'

Viscount Duncan smiled indulgently, and held
Livy's hand. 'How lovely for you, pet, to have a little
friend so near.'

From her vantage point near the swings, Jandy stared at him with incredulity. So Viscount Duncan was Patrick's father! She drew in a breath. And this was where Patrick lived, right bang on her doorstep, in a stately home no less! And he'd kept that very secret! But hadn't she known all along that he was from a background of privilege? The clues were all there after all: his restrained but confident manner; his deep, well-modulated voice. It all added up to someone who was used to the best of everything—including a country estate and a lord for a father!

Why hadn't he told her his background? she wondered. Why had he kept a huge part of his personal life secret? They'd had one or two conversations when it would have been appropriate for him to say where he lived and who his father was, just as she had told him about her failed relationship and her own mother. She watched Abigail running round the lawns with Livy and was suddenly jolted by an unpleasant thought. Had Patrick drawn a veil over his connections because he'd discovered her own background was not from the 'local gentry'?

'Perhaps, having heard my sordid story, he thinks I'm just too common for him!' she said angrily to herself. 'His father seemed to imply that he needs good stock to keep the family line going! And Patrick probably agrees with him!'

She scowled ahead of her for a moment, struggling with that thought, and the painful reflection that Patrick was no better than Terry really if that was what he thought—throwing her to one side when he was frightened they would get too close. He was probably on the lookout for a girl from his background—the 'local aristocracy', not one already encumbered with a four-year-old daughter.

Then she sighed. She'd obviously been reading all the wrong signals. He'd realised that she was not part of his world and it would be silly to form a close friendship with her. That hurt—no matter that they'd only had a brief acquaintanceship, she still felt the sting of rejection from a man she'd imagined had felt the same fierce electric attraction between them as she had. But most of all it hurt that he had, in effect, kept the truth about his life to himself, just like Terry had.

Friday night and there was the first hint of the cutting edge of winter cold about the air. Jandy pulled her coat around her as she walked from her car to A and E for her three-night stint on night duty, and wondered if she'd get the decorating done in her little house by Christmas. It was September now, and they would have to move in anyway in a few weeks, camping uncomfortably in the bedrooms and doing things gradually.

It would have been fun, giving the place a make-over with Lydia's help, but the whole thing had backfired with Patrick's attitude towards her. How could he have turned out to be such an arrogant pig? From where she was, it seemed that pure snobbery was the only reason for his sudden coldness.

Probably, she thought scornfully, his father wielded a lot of influence over him. He'd sounded very Victorian, she would be deemed as highly unsuitable—

a single mother with no money, whose own mother lived with a mechanic young enough to be regarded as a toy-boy, just the sort of girl he would advise his son to avoid!

Was she being over-sensitive? Jandy shrugged. Whatever the reason, she would keep her distance for a while and she was very relieved that he wasn't on this weekend night shift. She was thinking far too much about the man, despite her annoyance with him.

'Hi, there,' said Bob, joining her as they walked down the corridor. 'God, I hate this shift—it's the worst of the whole week.'

'Ah, well—it's only for a few days,' commented Jandy absently. 'And then four days off.'

'Three nights of hell…' grumbled Bob, opening his locker and slinging his bag and jacket into it.

Jandy sympathised with him. There were more attempted suicides, more alcohol abuse as drinkers celebrated the end of the working week, and more road traffic accidents on a Friday night—and all sometimes crowded into a small space of time.

On her way to the central desk, Jandy passed an elderly couple walking very slowly to Reception. The woman was supporting the man as he shuffled along, stopping every now and then to draw breath.

'Can I help?' asked Jandy. 'Have you booked in yet?'

'My…my friend doesn't seem able to breathe very well,' said the little old lady, looking anxiously at Jandy. 'We've only just come back from holiday and he started to feel unwell getting off the plane. I got a taxi, although he said it was nothing, and now…'

She stopped speaking and watched in distress as the man slid slowly to the floor and lay there motionless, except for the labouring motion of his chest trying to take in air, his breath stertorous.

'Oh, heavens…Charles, what's the matter?' She bent over him anxiously. 'Oh, dear…'

'Max—bring a wheelchair!' called Jandy sharply to the porter, who as usual, when he hadn't been given anything specific to do, was deep into a detective novel.

'Comin', Nurse—no worry,' he sighed, stuffing the paperback into his back pocket.

Jandy squatted down beside the man and felt his pulse. 'Not too bad—a bit rapid,' she murmured to herself.

The man attempted to sit up and said rather breathlessly, 'I'm all right—I just can't get my breath. I seem to have hurt my leg—it's really painful.'

He sank back with closed eyes and Jandy turned to the elderly lady. 'Has your husband been in pain long?'

'Oh, we're not married,' said the woman quickly, a slight flush of embarrassment on her cheeks. She spoke rapidly, shock making her garrulous. 'We're just very good friends—we were colleagues and we've been on a tour of Greek historical sites.'

'What's your friend's name?' asked Jandy gently.

'Oh, yes, of course… His name's Charles Westhrop. He said his leg was painful as he came down the steps of the aeroplane, and that's about two hours ago, but he won't let me look at it.'

'And your name?'

'Gwen Pendle.'

'Well, I think we'd better look at your friend's leg now, Ms Pendle. Let's get Mr Westhrop into a cubicle.'

Max trundled the wheelchair across and with Tilly's help they managed to get the man onto a bed in the cubicle, and Jandy slipped an oxygen mask over Mr Westhrop's face.

'This should make your breathing easier,' she explained, disguising her shock at the sight of the man's swollen limb as she cut down the trouser leg with a pair of scissors. The skin stretched tight, red and shiny, and she noted the parchment-like pallor of his face and the slight sheen of perspiration on his forehead. He was obviously very ill.

She touched the leg very gently and Mr Westhrop flinched, biting his lip. 'A little painful, that,' he mumbled from behind the mask.

'Tilly, ask Mr Vernon or Dr Thoms to come immediately, would you?' Jandy's voice sounded calm, belying the danger signals that were flashing in her head.

'May I come in?' asked Ms Pendle timidly, putting her head round the curtain.

'Perhaps you'd like to go and have a cup of tea while Mr Westhrop is being examined?' Jandy suggested kindly to little Miss Pendle, who was looking rather grey herself at the glimpse she had of her friend's elephantine limb.

'Oh—please let her stay,' said the man weakly.

Gwen put her hand over Charles's and patted it gently. 'Of course I'll stay,' she said bravely. 'I want

to know what they have to say about you, Charles—
I'll have a cup of tea in a minute.'

'I'll be fine—it's all a fuss about nothing,' said
Charles, his voice muffled through the oxygen mask.

But Jandy could tell that he was relieved that Miss
Pendle was staying with him—they were obviously de-
voted to each other. Then the curtain swished aside and
Patrick's tall figure appeared.

'Oh…it's you!' she exclaimed, shocked at his
sudden appearance.

Her heart clattered uncomfortably against her
ribcage—why had he turned up? She wasn't prepared,
hadn't expected to see him, and now here he was in
front of her, with his dreamy looks and clean-cut image
of a film-star doctor in his hospital greens that couldn't
disguise his muscular body—the man who'd actually
been very rude to her.

She took a deep breath and thought crossly, Darn
it, I'm not going to think of how attractive the man is.
If he wants to keep me at arm's length because I'm not
classy enough for him, that's fine with me!

'I didn't know you were in, Dr Sinclair,' she said
coolly. If he expected her to turn on a smile, he had
another think coming.

There was something in those deep blue eyes that
she couldn't interpret when he glanced at her, then he
said briskly, 'Sorry—you'll have to put up with me, I'm
afraid. Dr Thoms is busy with a compound fracture at
the moment and Mr Vernon's off with a tooth abscess.
Now, what have we here?'

'This is Mr Westhrop and his friend, Ms Pendle.

He's just come off a long flight from Greece,' explained Jandy crisply. 'He's finding it difficult to breathe and, as you can see, his leg's very swollen and painful. He's been like this for just over an hour since the plane landed. His BP's up and he's got a slight temperature.'

Patrick examined the leg carefully, noting how far the swelling went up the limb.

'This looks like a DVT—a deep vein thrombosis,' he said at last. 'We'll need a duplex ultrasound scan to get a complete diagnosis and pinpoint the exact position of the clot.'

'Do you think it's serious, Doctor?' asked Gwen timidly.

'Potentially it is serious,' explained Patrick honestly. 'Blood clots below the knee we usually regard as non-life-threatening, although they need monitoring. Those clots occurring in the knee's popliteal vein or veins above the knee are more serious.' He turned to Jandy. 'From the look of this leg, Staff Nurse, I would think the clot could be in the iliac vein going right up to the thigh.'

Mr Westhrop gave a little chuckle and pulled his mask away for a moment. 'You always say I don't like to do things by halves, Gwen—now it seems I have something quite dangerous!'

Ms Pendle shook her head at him. 'Charles, you always make light of everything. What can be done to get rid of this clot, then?'

'The body's natural process of clot breakdown, or fibrinolysis, will eventually help to get rid of it, but I'm going to get a vascular consultant to look at the leg. He may inject an anti-coagulant drug to disperse the clot so that it doesn't end up in an unsatisfactory place, like the lung.'

'Can I go home, then?' asked Charles.

'Not just yet, I'm afraid. We need to prevent further clots occurring and you'll probably be put on some fairly powerful drugs. We'll have to monitor you pretty carefully for the next few days.'

Mr Westhrop digested this information for a moment then said worriedly, 'Oh, dear, I'm due to give a lecture on Greek temples this week and I've got to assemble my notes...'

'I'm afraid that this isn't a minor matter, Mr Westhrop. You have to realise just how serious it is.'

'But the lecture's most important, isn't it, Gwen?' he protested.

Little Ms Pendle stood up, her small figure looking much more authoratitive. 'Don't be ridiculous, Charles! Putting a silly lecture before your health. I won't have it! You look terribly ill. You'll stay in hospital until they've got you better...' Her voice wobbled suddenly and she pulled a hanky out of her pocket and blew her nose. 'Giving me all this worry... I couldn't bear it if anything happened to you.'

Everyone in the room looked at the elderly lady in surprise at this unexpected outburst, then Charles smiled and took her hand in his, squeezing it gently. 'My dear, don't get upset—I promise I'll do as I'm told.'

The two old people gazed at each other then Mr

Westhrop turned to Jandy and Patrick and said weakly but very firmly, 'I wonder if you kind people would leave us for a minute? I have something very urgent I need to say to Miss Pendle. I'll call you in very soon, I promise.'

Patrick and Jandy stood slightly apart outside the cubicle, both of them maintaining a distance, both of them acutely aware of each other. Patrick longed to say to Jandy that he was sorry if he had been very offhand the other day when she'd agreed the lease of the cottage, and Jandy could feel the hairs of her neck prickling at his closeness.

She looked at his tall figure under her eyelashes, and in her imagination she could almost feel his touch—the roughness of his chin against her cheek, the strength of his arms holding her against his body. Then she pushed those thoughts away crossly and tried to dwell only on the fact that he was a complete snob who had, in a way, misled her about his background, and she wanted nothing more to do with him.

At length Patrick said diffidently, 'Mr Westhrop had better not take long—I don't like the look of that leg at all. What on earth can he be saying to Miss Pendle?'

'I really have no idea,' said Jandy coldly. She could be just as stand-offish as he could!

Then Ms Pendle drew back the curtain, looking rather flushed, and said in a breathless voice and with a little giggle, 'You can come in now. We…we've something to tell you.'

Patrick and Jandy looked at her in mystification. 'What is it?' asked Jandy.

Charles struggled to sit up, then explained with a little smile, 'I'll be brief! For many years Gwen and I have been great friends as well as colleagues. Over time I began to realise that what I felt for Gwen was more than friendship—in fact, to tell you the truth, I knew that I loved her very much.'

Patrick's and Jandy's eyes met briefly in a look of astonishment at Mr Westhrop's revelations. Then he took Gwen's hand again and drew her nearer to him.

'It…it never seemed the right moment to tell her, although I've always been longing for an opportunity,' he said softly. 'But suddenly I've just had an epiphany and realised that I'm not immortal and that we may not have much more time to enjoy ourselves. The thing is…' He looked shyly at the elderly lady. 'The thing is, I thought that it was now or never. I've just told Gwen it's about time we got married!'

There was a stunned silence in the room then Jandy broke the silence, clasping her hands in delight and exclaiming, 'What a lovely idea! And how wonderful that you chose to tell us about it!'

'Congratulations, sir—and to you, Ms Pendle,' said Patrick with a grin. 'Who says hospitals aren't romantic places?'

Jandy looked at Gwen. Suddenly she didn't seem like a rather plain elderly lady any more—she looked quite beautiful, lit by an aura of pure happiness. That was what love did to you, Jandy thought wistfully, it made you glad to be alive. It had been a long time since she had felt that bubbling excitement—until the last few days that was… She flicked a quick look at Patrick under her lashes. Hadn't he woken a few emotions that she'd thought had vanished for ever? She bit her lip, and forced herself back to reality and Mr Westhrop's deep vein thrombosis.

'And now I'm going to have to bring you down to earth, I'm afraid,' Patrick was saying. 'We're going to run a barrage of blood tests on you, Mr Westhrop, so perhaps, Ms Pendle, you can go and drink a toast to you and your fiancé with the finest tea our canteen has to offer while we attack him!'

Charles smiled. 'You can do what you like, young man—I may feel awful physically, but I can tell you I've never been happier in my life! You see, I never thought I'd find love at my time of life—and there it was, waiting round the corner. I've spent many years wishing I'd had the courage to ask Gwen to marry me. What a fool I've been! And if it hadn't been for this damn leg I might never have plucked up the courage!' His eyes twinkled at them. 'Let it be a lesson to you young ones never to put off tomorrow what you can do today!'

For a brief second Patrick's gaze swept over Jandy, then he smiled at Charles. 'I'll try and remember what you said, sir,' he murmured.

Max appeared at the door, his kindly face beaming. 'I've come for Mr Westhrop—they're ready to give him his scan now.'

The patient was wheeled away to the X-ray department and Patrick murmured, 'No one can say A and E is dull, that's for sure.' There was a certain awkwardness in his manner, as if he was aware that things weren't easy between them.

'Nice to have a happy ending,' Jandy said coolly, not wanting to be drawn into a discussion with him. 'They're a lovely couple.'

A short silence, then Patrick said abruptly, 'Mr Westhrop's right, of course.'

Jandy looked at him questioningly. 'In what way?'

'Never put off till tomorrow something you can do today…'

Jandy walked back into the cubicle and pulled off the paper sheet to replace it with a fresh one for the next patient. She didn't say anything.

'I'm afraid I owe you an apology, Jandy,' he said softly, following her into the cubicle.

Jandy smoothed out the sheet, her face impassive, belying the surprise she felt. 'How do you mean?'

Patrick sighed. 'Last week…I was damned rude to you. I left without as much as a goodbye—you must have thought it was rather odd, rushing away like that. But I've had time to think about it and—'

Jandy turned round to face him and said candidly, 'I did wonder what I'd done wrong. You suddenly seemed to backtrack on me taking the house…' She held his gaze with hers. 'I got the feeling you didn't really want me to take it—am I right?'

He shook his head and put his hands on her shoulders, his expression contrite. 'I was nervous about you taking on the cottage for various reasons,' he admitted. 'You'd done nothing wrong…it was me, being far too cautious.'

Jandy stood stock still, trying to ignore the electric touch of his hands and just how close he was to her—

close enough to pull her towards him and hold her against his chest. 'I can imagine what your reasons are,' she said glacially.

He looked down at her, surprised. 'You can? And what do you imagine?'

She gave a humourless laugh. 'It's obvious, isn't it? You don't want to get involved socially with me. And you think that if I take the house—which I now realise is on your father's land—we'll start to move in the same circles.'

Patrick looked dumbfounded. 'I'm sorry,' he said slowly, 'I don't have a clue what you mean…'

'Well, it wouldn't do at all, would it? To get too friendly with someone outside your elevated circle— someone like me—would be a total waste of time!'

'You what?' His blue eyes looked down at her in complete bafflement. 'You think I don't want to see you because of some sort of outdated class distinction? I don't believe this…'

'But it's true, isn't it?' Jandy's beautiful tawny flecked eyes gazed up at him challengingly. 'I saw your father on television the other night and it seemed to me he has some pretty feudal ideas, which I imagine have rubbed off on you as well, archaic as they are!'

He nodded as if understanding what she was getting at. 'Ah, so that's it! You saw the programme and you're reading things into it…'

'Am I? We seemed to be getting on pretty well before you heard about my background…an impoverished single parent, and her mother living with a man young enough to be her son. Not very good connections, you might say!'

'Jandy, stop it!' He put a finger over her mouth. 'If I had any reservations about getting "involved socially" with you, I can assure you it was the other way round. I thought the baggage I bring with me isn't something I should involve you in—that was one of the reasons.'

'Easy enough to say. I wish you'd been honest with me. Frankly, I happen to think you're right—we shouldn't be in each other's pockets, and getting involved would be foolish. You live in a different world from me and we wouldn't do for each other at all!'

'That is complete nonsense,' he said angrily, then his face softened. 'Actually, I don't normally tell people now about my background—I find it can get in the way a bit.'

'How?' demanded Jandy tersely.

'Sometimes people want to date me because of who I am, not what I am,' he said drily.

Jandy's eyes sparked across at him, two pink spots of anger on her cheeks. 'Thank you very much—you think I'm as shallow as that do you? I honestly couldn't care less where you come from.'

He groaned, and, putting his hand up to her cheek, turned her face towards him then gently brushed a tendril of hair from her forehead. 'No, I don't think you're shallow, Jandy—but some people are. I'm so sorry—sorry you saw that silly programme and jumped to the wrong conclusions, sorry I've been an idiot. Believe me, there are reasons why I can't involve anyone in my life at the moment.'

She jerked her head away from his hand, and said coldly, 'Apology accepted.' Then she turned to go back down the corridor, wondering exactly where all this had left her. But, of course, she still fancied him like mad, didn't she? Part of her longed to make up with him and to get to know him properly—what made him tick, and what exactly the reasons were that held him back from making any commitment.

Bob stepped out of a cubicle and called after her. 'Fancy a cup of coffee, Jandy?'

Deep in thought, she absently shook her head and walked on, while Bob shrugged and went off by himself to the canteen.

Patrick cursed himself for being such a fool, hurting someone he liked a lot by his clumsy manner. He closed his eyes for a second as the searing guilt of his last words to Rachel came back to him, as they often did when he'd been churlish—a terrible reminder of his tendency to let his temper rule his head. Would he never learn?

Surely he could have kept things between Jandy and himself at a friendly level without offending her, and without allowing them to get too close? As it was, she regarded him as nothing short of a snobbish throwback. He had to try and explain to her, without being specific, why he'd acted as he had—try and convince her that it was to protect her and not him. He wasn't sure she'd believe him, but he hated the thought of being on bad terms with her. In his imagination a pair of eyes the colour of soft amber looked at him reproachfully—and he couldn't stop thinking about them.

CHAPTER SIX

FOR the rest of the weekend there was the usual continuous queue of patients and by Monday morning everyone on the team was exhausted.

'All I want to do is go home and sleep for two days,' sighed Tilly, yawning, slumped with her elbows on the desk.

'Wait till you've done a week of nights,' remarked Jandy, easing her feet out of her shoes surreptitiously. 'I'm going to treat myself to a pedicure soon—my feet don't seem to belong to my body at the moment.'

'Only another hour to go and then home…and then four days off!' Bob stretched and sighed, pinching the skin between his eyes wearily.

And perhaps I can catch up on everything I should have done days ago, thought Jandy. She flicked a look across at Patrick, writing up a patient's report. She had felt acutely conscious of him for the whole weekend, wondering if his apology was just flannel. She'd learned the hard way to be circumspect when it came to believing men. Sometimes, she thought bitterly, it was better to call a halt to your feelings for your own peace of mind. She had clung to the hope for many months that Terry would come back to her, even after she'd had Abigail, unable to break free of the hold he'd had on her. Patrick's attitude to her was a warning for her not to get entangled again with another man who she'd found so instantly attractive. Keep him at arm's length, Jandy, she told herself firmly.

Tim came up to the desk, his face still slightly swollen from the effects of a tooth abscess.

'How are you feeling?' asked Bob.

'I'll be better when the antibiotics have kicked in,' he said, feeling his jaw gingerly. 'I'll be even better when I've had a whisky at home…'

'Not advisable with the antibiotics,' warned Bob.

Tim grinned ruefully, 'Don't take away my only pleasure.' He looked round as he heard the noise of an ambulance drawing up outside the entrance. 'This had better be a minor injury,' he remarked without much hope.

Karen shook her head. 'Just had word that we're to expect two men involved in a fight—one quite serious.'

'If only they could have waited another hour before hitting the daylights out of each other then the next shift could have taken them,' he sighed.

And a few seconds later two stretcher cases were brought in and transferred to casualty trolleys. Tim went over to the first trolley and lifted the blanket from the patient, a burly man with a shaven head and liberally tattooed chest who was emitting deep groans.

Tim took a deep breath and stared at the multiple

temporary dressings on the man's arms and legs and a small abrasion on his head.

'This is going to be a long job,' he muttered to Patrick. 'Can you and Staff Nurse get to grips with it while I see to the other patient?'

'That tooth still giving you gyp?' asked Patrick sympathetically.

'Enough to make me a bit woozy on painkillers,' Tim admitted.

Jandy sighed as she pulled on some latex gloves. She would have liked to put a bit of space between herself and Patrick—let the air settle a bit around his apology—but there was no help for it and soon they were standing opposite each other and starting to peel the dressings from their patient. Patrick glanced at her as if about to say something then looked down at the patient, concentrating on the matter in hand.

'What's he called?' Jandy asked the paramedic, as she dropped blood-soaked pads into a bucket.

'Lenny Smith apparently. Got into some sort of fight with a relative,' the man informed them. 'I'll leave you to make him beautiful again—see you!'

'My God,' muttered Patrick, as more of the patient's injuries were revealed. 'What did the other man use to give him these sorts of wounds? Look at all the skin and muscle gouged out of this arm... He's going to need prolonged surgical care after we've contained these injuries.'

'They say heavy spanners are the latest effective weapons,' said Jandy drily. 'Apparently they give a nice variety of wounds...'

'Charming,' remarked Patrick as he and Jandy started to work steadily on the man, swabbing the cuts and gashes, cleaning wounds with badly torn edges on the shins, calves and thighs, and for a short while forgetting about the tension between them as they concentrated. Patrick was painstaking and thorough, closely inspecting the different types of injuries that had been inflicted on the patient. All the wounds were leaking blood profusely.

'It doesn't help that Mr Smith's probably been at the bottle quite hard,' he remarked.

'Is that why he's bleeding so much?' asked Jandy.

Patrick nodded grimly. 'Alcohol certainly makes wounds bleed more freely. Get a sample of blood for cross-matching and set up the clean theatre so that we can do some patching up before he goes to Surgical. He'll need dextran to tide him over until he gets whole blood.'

Jandy went to the theatre used for small operations to lay out the local anaesthetic, dressings and sutures to temporarily deal with the man's injuries and Patrick put on a mask before he started to work closely on the patient. Karen came in to help them.

'I hear this patient's got a few nasty wounds,' she said coming into the clean theatre where small operations were performed.

'I don't know what the other man's like, but Mr Smith's in a shocking state. What were they fighting about?' murmured Patrick to Karen as he started to close the wounds with the soluble sutures that Jandy handed to him.

Karen sighed, her voice tired after twelve hours of demanding work. 'Oh, the usual,' she replied quietly. 'Mr Smith was apparently having it off with his cousin's wife—it doesn't make for happy families, I'm afraid. The other man's got a superficial facial wound, but he's OK.'

Patrick looked up and said sympathetically, 'It's been a long haul, hasn't it? Not long to go now and you can tuck yourselves up for a good sleep in your warm beds!'

'I can't wait,' said Karen as she left the room.

Patrick bent his head over the patient with his back to Jandy, and she looked at his dark hair, slightly too long and overlapping his collar. From her angle he looked quite boyish and vulnerable—someone who wouldn't hurt you intentionally. Perhaps she shouldn't have rejected his apology. After all, he had admitted how rude he'd been.

'Another small threaded needle, please, Nurse,' Patrick said briskly, his voice cutting into her thoughts.

She gave a start and handed him the needle, jerked out of her daydream from contemplating the nape of Patrick's neck and back to reality. She watched him finish suturing the patient, meticulous as he closed the wound with fine silk. After a while he stood back, stretching and putting his hands on his back, trying to knead the muscles he'd strained bending over the man for nearly an hour. Then he peeled off his latex gloves, flung them into the bin and pulled down his mask.

'The wound will probably have to be reopened later to get a better finish—make it cosmetically more acceptable,' he remarked. 'Anyway, I think we've done all we can for Mr Smith now. Tell Max he's ready to go to Surgical.'

She started to leave the room and Patrick touched her arm, his eyes holding hers for a moment. 'Look,' he said urgently. 'Let me make amends for my rudeness—can't we have lunch together in the next few days while we're off? After all,' he coaxed, 'I need to get on with my new neighbour…please?'

Jandy teetered on the brink of agreeing to meet him, as a shiver of attraction ran through her at Patrick's touch. He was the man who had everything, she reflected, good looks, brains and a regard for others, but he came from a background of incredible privilege— an alien world from hers. And however much he protested that class didn't come into it, she had a feeling his father wouldn't approve of his son forming an alliance with someone like her.

She looked up into his eyes, and felt herself beginning to melt. Still, Patrick was a big boy now, well able to stand up to his father. Was she ready to start up their fledgling relationship again, something that had never really got off the ground—or was that old demon stopping her, the demon that had always anticipated that something might go wrong ever since Terry had left her?

With a great effort she said briskly, 'I'm sorry, I've got to use these free days to do up the little cottage. I'm going to be taking stuff over and doing a bit of cleaning. Perhaps in a week or two…'

She allowed herself a bright little smile at him

before she went to tell Max to collect the patient. Dammit, thought Patrick as he stared after her. He wasn't going to let it go. At the very least he had to mend bridges between them. It was sod's law that he should find Jandy even more desirable now, he pondered wryly.

It was an Indian summer's day, the warm sun filling the little front room of the cottage with light. Jandy ran up the stairs and went into the main bedroom armed with sweeping brushes, buckets and cloths, determined to clean the rooms up a bit before starting on the decorating. It all smelled a little musty so she opened a window, letting in the clean fresh air from outside, and swept dead flies and dust from the window sill before gazing out at the view beyond the pretty little garden.

She could see the beautiful mansion, Easterleigh House, where Patrick lived with his father, set on a slight hill through the trees. It looked magnificent from where she was, but very large—extraordinary to think that just three people occupied it! She supposed that the little house she'd leased was the former gatehouse for the estate. She thought she'd rather live in her cosy place than float around in that huge pad. She pulled a bucket towards her and got down on all fours to start scrubbing the floor.

Had she been wrong about refusing to see Patrick? Her thoughts inevitably drifted into thinking about him as she got into the rhythm of swirling the brush in the water and then going backwards and forwards over the wood. Perhaps she should have given him the chance to make amends after all, and she had missed an opportunity to build bridges.

She leant back on her heels for a second then shrugged. No, if he couldn't reveal these mysterious issues that made him wary of commitment, she'd done the right thing in keeping him at a distance. She went back to cleaning the floor with renewed vigour.

The sound of the front door banging shut made her start. She was quite sure she'd closed it before she'd come upstairs. She held her breath, wondering if it was an intruder, and her heart began to thump uncomfortably as she heard footsteps clumping their way up the stairs.

'Anyone there?' called a deep voice from the landing. Then the footsteps clattered on the wooden floor and Patrick appeared in the doorway dressed in faded jeans and an old white shirt, open at the neck. Her breath caught in her throat. He looked gorgeous! The casual look seemed to emphasise his broad shoulders and his tight, lean body. It wasn't fair, him appearing so suddenly, taking her off guard with no time to control the mixture of excitement and fizzing attraction that bolted through her body, making her stomach feel as if it had just looped the loop.

Jandy drew a deep breath and glared at him. 'For goodness' sake,' she said crossly. 'You gave me a hell of a fright... What are you doing here?'

'Sorry.' He grinned. 'I came on the off chance you'd be here. I thought you might be hungry. I've brought some food with me.'

But she wasn't going to give in to the leap of delight she'd had when he'd appeared, she told herself stubbornly. She was going to keep a tight rein on her emotions and play it very cool from now on. Caution told her that it would be better not to get too close to him.

'I'm very busy,' she said primly. 'I haven't time for food…'

'Of course you have,' he said firmly. 'It's a lovely day—we can eat outside. It might be the last really warm day we have before autumn. If you won't join me I'll have to eat alone.'

'I've a lot to do,' she said, waving her hand vaguely towards the walls.

'Oh, come on! It will give me a chance to make up for my churlishness the other day. Please….'

He looked at her wistfully, and suddenly Jandy wanted to laugh at the little-boy-lost expression on his face. Perhaps she should accept his olive branch.

She shrugged. 'It will have to be very quick, then.'

He had laid out a rug under an old apple tree near the house, looking across the newly tilled fields. The sun still had warmth, and there was the slightest of breezes. Jandy sat down and clasped her hands round her knees, looking up at the white fluffy clouds sailing slowly across the sky. Was she a complete idiot, allowing herself to be alone with Patrick once again? She felt a tremor of excitement ripple through her, half hoping, half afraid, of what might happen in the intimate confines of the little garden.

She forced herself to relax and leant back against the

apple tree, watching as Patrick opened a picnic basket
to reveal a delicious feast. Then he uncorked a wine
bottle and poured some sparkling wine into two plastic
cups.

'The best you can get from Delford's supermarket,'
he said solemnly. He held her eyes with his for a
second. 'Cheers! Here's to us!'

Jandy sipped the wine rather self-consciously and
was silent—she wasn't going to make the running.
Looking across at him, his open shirt revealing a sexy
muscled torso with dark hairs bristling through the
top, and leaning casually on one elbow on the grass,
she was afraid that she was ready to forgive him
anything! If only he wasn't quite so devastating
looking, or quite so physically close. If only his blue
eyes weren't quite so beguiling… She lowered her
gaze and concentrated on a beetle crawling across the
grass. The atmosphere between them was electric.

He rocked back on his heels and looked at her assessingly, as if wondering how she was going to react
to what he had to say.

'You need an explanation for my churlishness the
other week,' he began slowly. 'As soon as I left you I
was desperately sorry I'd hurt you.' He swirled the wine
round in his glass for a second, before smiling ruefully
at her. 'The fact is that when you told me what you'd
been through, it made me realise that the last person you
need in your life now is someone with problems of
their own. You've got a measure of stability in your life
now with little Abigail. I felt that I should keep at a
distance before anything happened to threaten that.'

'Before what happened?' she queried impassively.

'You know what I mean, Jandy. In case we got too…close.'

Jandy stared at him warily, hearing her heart thump uncomfortably in her ears and trying to ignore the sexy aura he exuded so close to her.

'There was no need to be so rude,' she said as coolly as she could, while every fibre in her body longed to cuddle up to him, feel his arms around her.

He nodded and picked at the grass by his legs. 'I know—you're right. No excuse for it. But my reasons were valid enough.' He leaned towards her, a piece of dark hair flopping over his forehead, his blue eyes looking into hers. 'The thing is, Jandy, you know I have another very different life beyond the hospital and it's hard to reconcile the two.' He reached over and took her hand in his. 'But I want us to be friends—good friends. How can we work together if we're not?'

'I hope we can be that,' she said primly, his firm grip making her hand tingle. She felt the flutter of excitement in her tummy as the atmosphere almost pulsated with the tension between them. Her good intentions to play it cool seemed to be dissolving rather quickly.

Jandy attempted to pull her hands away from his, but he didn't allow that and held them even more firmly. 'I was frightened we were getting too close too quickly,' he admitted.

'For goodness' sake, we've only known each other for a few weeks,' she said lightly. 'I don't think that's a basis for lifelong devotion anyway.'

He gave a faint smile. 'The fact is, Jandy, I can't

stop thinking about you—can't get you out of my head.' He stroked her cheek gently. 'You're always somewhere in my mind…'

She couldn't tear her eyes away from his penetrating blue gaze, wondering if she was hearing him properly, actually admitting that he did indeed feel something for her! He was facing her, so very close. She could see the little bit of stubble on his chin he'd missed while shaving, and the pulse beating in his neck. Excitement crackled through her body like little electric shocks.

She became very still, hardly breathing, as he gently brushed her hair back from her forehead.

'I think…know…that you weren't all that averse to me either,' he murmured.

Jandy averted her gaze, trying not to be seduced by those eyes, to ignore the thousand butterflies fluttering inside her.

She swallowed hard. 'And yet you want to keep me at a distance. Is this a warning?'

He swirled the wine round in his glass and watched the bubbles rising to the surface. 'It's complicated,' he said at last. 'You know about some of the things that occupy me outside work—my father's health and the issues regarding the house.'

'Yes, I can see that it's not easy.'

He grinned wryly at her. 'I guess I realised soon after I met you that there was a definite spark between us—quite a crackle actually.'

A little smile quirked Jandy's mouth—she would have described it as fireworks herself! She didn't say anything, but a little thrill of pleasure went through her that Patrick had actually admitted that he felt something for her too.

'Then I heard how you'd been treated by your boyfriend, and how you'd had to come to terms with his betrayal,' Patrick continued. 'Getting involved with someone like me—someone with a lot of baggage in their background—might jeopardise the stability you have now.'

Her brown eyes sparked at him. 'So what you want is a brief fling, is it? Not to be tied down. Sounds as if you want the best of all worlds,' she remarked crisply, unable to keep the sarcasm out of her voice.

He smiled sheepishly. 'It sounds like that—but I don't mean it to. Hell, I want us to be good friends and colleagues.' He tilted her face to his so that she couldn't avoid looking into his eyes. 'Or even more than that,' he said softly. 'But I want you to be aware of my situation.'

At least he was warning her—something Terry never had. And if she told him to get lost, he would probably do as she said. She felt her resolve weakening by the second and sighed, tossing back the wine in her glass. Then a feeling of bravado swept over her. Hadn't she been longing for some excitement in her life, to escape from the mundane everyday existence she led? He'd admitted that he was only ready for a fling, not a ring, but Patrick Sinclair was the first person since Terry to inject some passion and feeling into her soul.

She looked at the broad band of gold on his finger—

a constant reminder of the wife he'd lost, she thought wistfully. Perhaps he'd never replace it, never be able to erase Rachel's memory. But if he was up for a fling, then so was she—going into it with her eyes wide open, and to hell with memories and broken hearts!

'I don't mind being friends.' She tilted her chin almost defiantly. 'I may regret this, but honestly I'm sick of thinking back to what might have been, and what Abigail has missed not having Terry on hand. I want to look forward.'

He smiled down at her with those wonderful clear blue eyes and hugged her to him. 'You're a feisty girl, Jandy. Let's get to know each other a little better, then.'

He bent his head to hers and very gently brushed her lips lightly with his. And she knew this was the prelude to something much more momentous. She knew what was going to happen, and she did nothing to stop him. He drew back slightly, looking down at her.

'So can we be *very* good friends, do you think?' There was laughter dancing in his eyes as he asked her.

She didn't answer, but lifted her face to his, feeling again the tingle of his mouth against hers, and every nerve end in her body told her she needed more than that brief kiss. How could she ignore the great waves of longing flickering like butterflies inside her, her heart thumping with excitement against her ribs? Surely she was due a little affection, some fun, some excitement? But in a feeble effort to seem less eager she put her finger against his mouth for a second.

'Do you think this is wise?' she whispered.

He looked down at her. 'Let's not be wise all the

time,' he said. 'Good friends are allowed to express their affection, aren't they?'

He kissed her again, this time harder, teasing her lips open slightly, running his hand gently over her soft body, and she trembled because it was unbearably wonderful.

She wound her arms around his neck and pulled him towards her, opening her mouth to his and savouring the salty taste of him, feeling his body heavy and hard against hers as she fell back on the grass and he lay on top of her. The smell of the warm earth underneath them would always remind her of this moment. His mouth moved down her jaw with little butterfly kisses, and her body responded like a switch being flicked, pulling him close to her. He stopped for a second and looked down at her, his eyes twinkling.

'Is that a "yes" to my question, then?' he teased.

'I think so,' she whispered.

Perhaps she was jeopardising her future with a man who'd admitted he wasn't ready for a committed relationship, but at this particular moment she couldn't give a damn, she told herself as Patrick's hands moved over her body, gently touching her breasts, starting to undo her shirt. She wasn't even thinking how far they were going to go, she was revelling in his touch now, in the words he was murmuring in her ear. It was the present that mattered—the unbelievable sweetness of his firm, demanding frame on hers and the way her body reacted. It had been so long since she'd been held like this, or even wanted to be in anyone's arms, and the long-forgotten sensation of being made love to by someone she desired very much flooded over her. She was hungry for his kisses and more. And she knew that he was as eager as she was!

When the jarring sound of her mobile went off, Jandy couldn't think for a second what it was, except that it was intrusive and annoying. Then the stupid pop-song ringtone repeated itself again and again until reluctantly she pushed herself away from Patrick.

'Sorry,' she groaned. 'I'll have to get that—it could be about Abigail.'

Patrick rolled away and sighed. 'And we were just getting to know each other…' he murmured, looking across at Jandy and drawing one finger down her cheek.

She grabbed the phone and flipped it open, then Patrick watched her eyes widen in shock and her face pale slightly. He raised himself up on his elbow, concern crossing his face as she sat bolt upright, holding her mobile so tightly her knuckles were white.

'Lydia? Oh, my God….' she whispered. 'What's happened to her? Where is she?' She listened to the reply then seemed to gather herself together and said firmly, 'It's all right, darling—I'll go up. I've got a few days off anyway. You can't possibly get there as soon as I can. I'll organise things from this end.'

She snapped the mobile shut and turned to look bleakly at Patrick's questioning face. 'Is it your daughter?' he asked.

Jandy shook her head in a dazed way. 'No, not Abigail, thank God. It's my mother. She and her boyfriend, Bertie, have been involved in an accident. It was

Lydia, my sister, on the phone, and she says it's serious.' She bit her lip, trying to keep her composure. 'Oh, Patrick, my mother's been through so much, and just when it seems she's at last found happiness, it could all be taken away from her. Bertie's in a bad way. As I told you, they live in Scotland—right up in the north—and I need to go to her as soon as I can.'

CHAPTER SEVEN

PATRICK took her hand and squeezed it, looking at her in concern. 'Do you know what kind of accident it was—a car crash, something at home?'

'My sister said that they were caught in a landslide on a mountainous road near where they live. Apparently they were lying trapped for over twelve hours. Both of them have multiple injuries.' She looked in a stunned sort of way at Patrick, large tears welling up in her eyes. 'I've got to get up there. My sister's on a long-haul flight to Australia and can't make it quickly.' She brushed the tears impatiently from her eyes. 'Dammit, I feel so helpless here.'

'Who will look after Abigail?' he asked.

'I'm sure Pippa, my childminder, will do that, and Abigail loves staying with her.' Jandy punched some numbers into her phone. 'I'll ring her now—and then I suppose I've got to get a flight to Inverness, it'll be far too slow to drive up there. Oh, Lord, there's so much to do…'

Patrick put his hand over hers and said firmly,

'You speak to Pippa. Meanwhile I'll get you a flight.'

She hadn't time to say how grateful she was to him. She just nodded numbly and then spoke to Pippa, while Patrick walked away and contacted an airline on his mobile.

'That's it—all done,' he said briskly after a few minutes, putting his mobile back in his pocket. 'Our flight goes at five o'clock from Manchester.'

Jandy looked at him, slightly puzzled. '*Our* flight? Surely you've just booked one seat?'

He smiled, his eyes dancing rather wickedly. 'I'm coming with you,' he explained. 'And don't try and stop me!'

Jandy looked at him, completely dumbfounded, then she stammered, 'B-but why? You've got your own child to think about.'

'We've both got a few days off and, like you, I have someone perfectly competent to look after Livy. I can drive you round, act as a general dogsbody, while you see to your mother. Any objections?'

'I…I don't know… It's a lot to ask.' She shook her head tiredly. 'I don't like to put you to all this trouble.'

'It's no trouble,' he said firmly. 'You go home and organise your clothes and whatever you have to do for Abigail. I'll pick you up at about two o'clock.'

'But you can't drop everything for me. After all, we hardly—'

He held her arms and forced her to look at him. 'Know each other?' he finished with amusement. 'I guess we demonstrated a few minutes ago that we're

reasonably good friends. And wasn't that what we said
we were going to be? And as a good friend I'd like to
help you—so relax and accept the offer!'

She felt too dazed to argue. 'Well…thank you,' she
said weakly.

'Now, go on,' he urged. 'Pack what you need, and
sort out Abigail. I'll see you soon.'

And all afternoon Jandy could hardly think of
anything else except her mother, wondering just how
badly she was hurt, what injuries she'd sustained. She
felt like she was on autopilot, packing things for herself
and Abigail without hardly taking in what she was
doing. The flight to Inverness was a blur as Patrick
found their seats, retrieved her luggage when they
arrived and picked up the hire car to take them to the
hospital. What would she have done without him?

Jandy and Patrick were shown immediately to the
room in the hospital where her mother was. Jandy
stood for a moment in the corridor, gathering the
courage to go in. She was used to hospitals, wasn't
she? It was no big deal being in one. Why, then, were
her legs like jelly, her mouth so dry? Because she was
at the receiving end of the bad news, she thought wryly.
Seeing a hospital from a completely different point of
view, knowing everything that could go wrong. She
clutched Patrick's arm for a second.

'Patrick, I'm frightened—frightened of what I'm
going to see. And I'm a nurse, for God's sake…'

'There's no shame in that, Jandy,' he said gently.

The nurse who'd taken her to the room smiled encouragingly at her. 'Mr Landers, the consultant, will

see you after you've seen your mother. He'll explain everything to you—he's very able,' she assured Jandy.

'You go in,' urged Patrick. 'I'll go and get some basics like milk and bread while you're with her. She doesn't want someone she's never met barging in to see her.'

Leony Marshall was sitting propped up in the bed with her eyes closed and a collar round her neck. Her whole face was bruised and swollen, her eyes puffy slits, and there was a gash across her forehead with a line of staples holding it together. Her right leg was slightly elevated and in a cast.

Jandy gave a sharp intake of breath at her mother's appearance, and swallowed hard. Her beautiful mother was almost unrecognisable, but bursting into tears wasn't going to help.

'Hello, Mum,' she whispered, laying a hand on her mother's arm and bending forward to kiss her gently on her cheek.

Her mother opened her eyes and an expression of amazement crossed her face as she saw her daughter. 'Jandy, darling!' she whispered through her stiff, swollen lips, 'I can't believe it—how wonderful it is to see you! How did you know I was here?'

'Lydia phoned me on a flight to Australia! The guy who helps Bertie at the garage managed to get in touch with her.'

Jandy took her mother's hand and Mrs Marshall squeezed it, mumbling, 'I'm afraid your old mum's a bit of a wreck at the moment…not looking my best!'

'Poor Mum. You must feel dreadful.'

'I'd feel better if you could find a cigarette for me—they've taken all mine away, the mean things!'

Jandy patted her mother's hand, feeling relief that her mother hadn't lost her spark or that mischievous sense of humour.

'You know there's no chance of that, Mum.' She smiled. 'The main thing is that these wounds will heal, and you'll be back to your beautiful self again. How did it happen?'

Leony looked woefully at her daughter. 'Bertie and I...we were driving into the hills to have a drink at a lovely little inn up there. It was so beautiful on the way that we stopped to take a photograph of the view at a lookout point halfway up.' She faltered, reliving the scene for a moment, then continued in a whisper, 'Suddenly there was the most tremendous roar and before we could turn round all these rocks and mud rained down on top of us—we had no time to get out of the way. It was terrible, darling. We were pinned underneath for hours.'

Jandy shook her head in disbelief. 'You could have been killed. Thank God you're still with us. What about Bertie?'

'They tell me he's got a skull fracture—he's been in Intensive Care.' Leony brushed aside a tear that slid down her swollen cheek. 'If anything happened to him, I don't know what I'd do, Jandy...he's been so good to me.'

'Now, don't get upset,' said Jandy soothingly. 'I'm going to speak to your consultant and find out exactly what they're doing for you and Bertie.' She eyed her mother's leg. 'You've obviously got a fracture—do you know where it's broken?'

'I think it's two breaks,' said her mother vaguely. 'The doctor called it something, but it meant nothing to me—you'd know what he meant, I'm sure.' She smiled weakly through stiff, painful lips. 'Oh, I can't tell you how glad I am you're here. I feel better already! But who's looking after little Abigail?'

'Oh. she's fine—Pippa's looking after her for as long as need be.'

'And what about your work? It must have been so difficult having to arrange everything, and get yourself to the airport.'

Jandy smiled. 'It wasn't as difficult as all that, Mum. I'm off for a few days anyway, and er…a colleague did all the organisation of getting the tickets, coming over with me and driving me to the hospital.'

'How very kind—and how nice that you aren't alone… You must stay at the house, of course. There are clean sheets and towels in the cupboard, but it's a bit small for two of you. Pity there's only one usable room upstairs—you can use the sofa bed in the sitting room as the spare.'

'Don't worry, Mum, we'll manage!' Jandy's heart flipped slightly. She'd forgotten about the sleeping arrangements in the house. Just what would Patrick be expecting?

'And where is your colleague now?'

'Just getting some shopping,' said Jandy briefly. She wasn't quite ready to spring on her mother that her colleague was male and drop-dead gorgeous!

'Ah!' said a brisk voice from the door. 'I believe you're Mrs Marshall's daughter?'

Jandy turned round to see a tall bespectacled man standing in the doorway. The man held out his hand and shook hers vigorously.

'Yes,' she said with a smile. 'I'm Jandy Marshall.'

He nodded. 'You're very like your mother, I have to say. My name's Mr Landers and my team and I have been looking after Mrs Marshall since she was brought in.' He motioned to a chair by the bed. 'Please sit down and I'll explain the nature of your mother's injuries. You are a nurse, I believe? Then you'll understand when I explain that your mother has a Pott's fracture of her leg. Not very nice.'

Jandy grimaced. 'Poor Mum! So the fibula and tibia are both broken?'

He nodded. 'The fibula is broken just above the ankle and the tibia's also fractured, resulting in dislocation. I've had to insert metal screws to hold the bone fragments in place.' Then he grinned. 'But don't worry! Your mother will eventually be back wearing the very high heels she was wearing when she was rescued!'

Trust her mother to be wearing high heels on a trip up a mountainside, thought Jandy. Not that she would have contemplated going for a walk when they'd reached the lookout spot—it would have been a cigarette stop!

'I shall hold you to that promise, Mr Landers,' whispered Leony from the bed. 'I wish you'd let me have just one teeny cigarette, though—it would be so good for my nerves!'

'Certainly not, Mrs Marshall,' he growled mock-severely. 'I want you to eat good food and perhaps have the odd glass of wine—but not one cigarette!' He turned to Jandy. 'The contusions on your mother's face look bad, but they're relatively minor and she's had a scan which shows that there's no bleeding or broken facial bones.'

'And how is Bertie, Doctor? Is he still in Intensive Care?' asked Jandy.

The doctor's expression turned more serious. 'Mr Muir is the neurosurgeon looking after your friend but he's in Theatre at the moment. He's asked me to tell you that Bertie has an open skull fracture with some inter-cranial bleeding—that's why he's in the Intensive Care department.'

'What does that mean?' asked Jandy's mother helplessly. 'Oh, I'm so stupid. I don't even know what "cranial" means…'

'It means that there could be a build-up of blood around the skull and into the brain,' explained Jandy. 'Will they be doing anything to alleviate that?'

'Mr Muir intends to do a craniotomy to drain the blood and repair any damaged blood vessels.' He looked at Leony's horrified face, and put his hand up soothingly. 'There is every possibility that he will be all right—it is serious, yes, but not desperate. His condition is stable at the moment and we feel he can be operated on soon. I assure you that the patient will be in very good hands.'

'You'll tell me if…if his condition changes, won't you, Doctor?' asked Leony.

'Of course…but I want you to rest now, Mrs

Marshall, and build up your strength. Sleep is a great healer.'

Leony sighed and said huskily, 'I shall never, never be able to sleep while my precious Bertie is in such danger.'

'Mr Landers is right, Mum,' said Jandy firmly. 'Bertie's obviously being closely monitored and you must try not to worry. I'll come back early tomorrow— but I'll be at the end of the phone if I'm needed.'

'Of course, darling—you must be shattered yourself.' Her mother brightened a little. 'Perhaps you'll bring me some better nighties than this awful hospital one and some face cream—and a little toilet water to freshen me up.'

Mr Landers's twinkling eyes met Jandy's. 'I think your mother feels a little better!'

'Of course, Mum. I should have thought of them myself, but I came straight here.' Jandy bent down to kiss her mother. 'I'll keep my fingers crossed for Bertie—but it sounds like he's having the best of attention. Would it be possible to see him soon?'

'At the moment he's sedated,' said Mr Landers. 'But I think tomorrow we'll see the picture more clearly and I'm sure you'll be able to see him then.'

Jandy went back to the car park relieved that her mother was not in danger but worried about the long-term arrangements for both Leony's and Bertie's convalescent care.

Patrick was standing by the hire car and waved to her. 'How are things?' he asked.

Jandy gave him a quick résumé of the situation then

rubbed her eyes wearily. 'Lord, I feel like I've run a marathon,' she remarked with a sigh. 'Let's go to Mum's house—it's a good half hour away from here and up in the hills. I could do with a shower.'

'And something to eat?' put in Patrick with a grin. 'We never did get round to my picnic earlier today.'

'Was it only a few hours ago?' said Jandy in wonder. 'It seems a lifetime since we were in the garden...'

She caught his eye and blushed with a sudden giggle, remembering just what they had been doing when they'd been interrupted.

'We were getting to know each other quite well, weren't we?' Patrick murmured as he held the car door open for her. 'Now, get in and tell me the way to get to your mother's house.'

Jandy relaxed back against the car seat—she felt desperately tired, but the tension of the past few hours had disappeared. She flicked a look across at Patrick, concentrating on driving on the narrow country roads. It was incredibly comforting to have him with her, taking the burden off her shoulders of driving her to different places, and knowing he was there to unload her worries and discuss them with him.

Patrick felt her eyes on him. 'You worried about my driving?' He grinned.

'Not at all. I...I just want you to know how grateful I am, Patrick, you coming with me. It's a great help.'

'It's no hardship, Jandy. It's a beautiful area, and if it weren't for your mother's terrible accident I could imagine we were on holiday. It's been too long since I've had a few days to myself.' He glanced at her mischievously. 'And with a beautiful woman I intend to get to know very, very well. And don't forget we've some unfinished business to complete…'

Jandy laughed, suddenly feeling light-hearted after the strain of the past hours. The circumstances that had brought her up to Scotland were awful, but there was definitely a silver lining to the cloud. Her heart skipped a beat—alone with the sexiest man she'd ever seen! A tremor of nervous excitement ran through her. Being thrown together with a man she didn't really know for a few days could make or break a friendship. And everything seemed to have happened so quickly. Only a short while ago she'd been furious with him and his supposed snobbery, and now, only that morning, a few hours ago, he'd apologised for his rudeness and made it very clear that the attraction she felt wasn't all one-sided! She flicked a look at his strong profile—she didn't know what would happen between them over the next few days, but one thing was for sure, she fancied him even more than ever!

Lost in her thoughts, she nearly missed the cross-roads where the little filling station stood at the side of the road, overlooking the valley they just driven from.

'We're here, Patrick—this is it!' she sang out.

Patrick drew into the drive and got out, stretching his long limbs and looking around him. 'Wow! This is a little piece of paradise,' he murmured. 'What a backdrop. It…it doesn't seem real, more like a scene from a romantic film.'

They were fairly high up in the hills, the garage the last stop for petrol before motorists headed over the tops. Flower tubs filled with geraniums had been placed along the front and the garage was painted a fresh white, with a little coffee shop to one side. There was the faintest smell of honey permeating the still-warm air from the heather creeping across the moorland and right up to the garden of the house. Tumbling over the little walls that bounded a small terrace round the front of the property were fading morning glory blooms and more pink geraniums.

'Idyllic—what a lovely place. I've never seen a filling station like it!' Patrick remarked appreciatively, turning to look down across the countryside, where in the distance beyond was the sea, glinting and sparkling in the late afternoon sun.

'It's beautiful, isn't it?' Jandy said.

He looked at her silently for a moment, standing with her back to the dying sun, a slender silhouette, her hair highlighted a mellow honey gold in the light, little tendrils that had escaped from her chignon framing her face.

'Yes,' he said quietly. 'Quite beautiful.'

'But it's miles away from anywhere, or any help for that matter, so Mum and Bertie can't stay here until they're fit.' Jandy bit her lip, her forehead creased with worry. 'What on earth can we do? They have someone to help them with the garage and car servicing side—I'll have to have a word with him now before he goes.'

She went round to the garage where there was much hammering and a pair of legs protruding from under a jacked-up car.

'Ian?' she shouted. 'Can I have a word?'

A young man slid out from under the car, his face smeared liberally with black grease. He wiped his hands on a piece of rag and shook Jandy's hand.

'Och, I'm sorry about your mother and Bertie—it's a bad do!' he exclaimed. 'How are they?'

'Not so bad, Ian, but it's going to take some time for them to recover enough to get back to work.' Jandy introduced him to Patrick and then added, 'Do you think you can manage for a while by yourself? It would be awful to have to shut the place down.'

He grinned, teeth white against his oily face. 'No trouble, Jandy. I was wondering, though—would it be all right if I brought my girlfriend Netta to do the coffees and teas? She could do with the extra money and she'd be a help with the pumps too.'

'Sounds a great idea,' said Jandy, her spirits lifting slightly. 'And perhaps Netta might stay on for a bit while my mother and Bertie convalesce?'

'I think she'd be happy to do that,' agreed Ian.

'Let's talk about that later,' suggested Patrick, looking at Jandy's weary face. 'We'll sit out here while there's still some warmth in the air and have a glass of wine.' He put his hands on her shoulders and looked down at her. 'You need to unwind a bit after the shock you've had, and you've done all you can for one day.'

'Aye,' agreed Ian kindly. 'You get yourselves sorted. I'll see to the work out here. No need for you to worry yourselves. I'll be off soon, but I'll see you tomorrow.'

Jandy nodded. 'Thanks, Ian. I'm really grateful for your support.'

She went up the path towards the house and Patrick

followed with their luggage. She stood for a moment looking down the valley, trying to push the worries about her mother to the back of her mind. Tiredly she leant against Patrick for a second, drawing comfort from his physical presence. He wrapped his arms around her and pressed her to him so that she could feel the thud of his heart against hers.

'It's all right, sweetheart, relax…give yourself some time off from worrying.'

His voice rumbled over her head, calming, soothing. He looked down at her, locking his eyes with hers, and she felt that crackle of attraction flash between them. There was nothing to stop them doing anything they wanted, she thought. It should be so idyllic, alone together with the damp scent of a Highland evening drifting over to them—and yet she pulled back from him. How easy it would be to enjoy the moment and take up again where they'd started just that morning in the garden of the little house—make love with no inhibitions, just pure physical fulfilment. Wasn't that what she longed for?

But that had been that morning, and so much had happened since then and she'd had time to reflect on her impetuosity. There was this nagging thought that to her it would mean much more than it would to Patrick. Yes, she wanted him like crazy, but she needed stability too.

'What is it, Jandy?' he asked, sensing her reluctance and putting his hand under her chin to force her to look at him. He searched the expression on her face and smiled wryly. 'It's not the right time, is it? I'm not completely insensitive. If you think I'm going to take advantage of you in this heavenly place, however much I want to, I assure you I won't. I won't do anything you don't want me to. I respect you too much for that.'

Respect, thought Jandy bleakly. Hardly the most romantic thought. She needed love as well.

She drew back from him and wandered down the small garden, sitting on the little wall by the road. 'Tell you what—let's have that glass of wine.'

They didn't sit too near each other as they sipped their wine. It was almost as if they were playing a waiting game, incredibly conscious of each other. They'd crossed over some sort of threshold that morning and now Jandy felt suddenly self-conscious, unsure where the next move would take them. She took another large slurp of the crisp white wine and began to feel a little less stressed, the tensions of the day slipping away.

Patrick glanced across at Jandy. He could see her profile as she leant her head back against the wall, her eyes closed and the sweep of her eyelashes fanned against her cheek. He longed to touch her, take her in his arms and make love to her, but some inner instinct told him to take it slowly. Don't rush her, Patrick, he told himself. One step at a time.

After a few minutes he said softly, 'Tell me how your mother came to find this place.'

Jandy smiled. 'She's been a star really—bringing up the two of us by herself. Dad died when we were in our early teens. Mum worked in a little dress shop in Delford and did some of their buying for them. She was sent to look at some clothes in a small factory in

Inverness—and she met Bertie when her car broke down. He was the mechanic who mended it. He's about twelve years younger than her, but they fell in love and have been together ever since! This was his little house.'

'What a romantic tale,' murmured Patrick. 'And do you like him?'

'He's a lovely guy—and he's made Mum so happy. Just the right man for her. The age difference doesn't seem to matter in the least.'

'If you find the right person, that sweeps all other considerations aside, doesn't it?'

Jandy looked at him wryly. 'I don't think your father would agree with that!'

Patrick got up and came over to her, sitting on the wall beside her and taking her hands, an amused expression on his face.

'You've got a thing about my father,' he said. 'He's not the dinosaur you think he is. The thing is, circumstances have made him wary about choosing a partner for life.'

'I'm with him there,' sighed Jandy.

'Like you, I lost a parent when I was young,' Patrick said. 'My mother died when I was three, and then my brother and I had a nanny, a lovely person. She's still alive, bless her.'

'I'm sorry about your mother,' murmured Jandy, reflecting what different experiences she and Patrick had had when they were children. There had been no such things as nannies for her sister and herself when they'd been young! Her mother had scraped a living and they had never been hungry or without a roof over their heads, but a childhood in a place like Easterleigh was a world away from the council estate she'd been brought up in.

'Actually, Robert and I had a very happy childhood—until my father remarried, that is.' Patrick's mouth tightened. 'She wasn't the best of step mothers, I'm afraid, and it wasn't a happy marriage.'

A sudden memory of Patrick's first day at work flicked into Jandy's mind—the little boy with the head injury, Jimmy Tate, and his cold, unsympathetic stepmother—and Patrick's reaction to that case.

'What did your stepmother do to you?' she asked quietly.

He shrugged. 'That's water under the bridge now—but she left me with this little legacy.' He turned his face to Jandy and pointed to the white raised scar down the side of his face. Her eyes widened in horror.

'She did that to you? What did she…?'

A wry smile touched his lips. 'Robert and I had been making a noise. She had no patience with children and had snapped at us to shut up, saying that we'd have no supper if we weren't quiet—her usual form of punishment. I had a temper and shouted that she was a wicked witch. She flung a pan at me and the the rim caught my face.'

'She could have killed you…'

'She was certainly frightened, because, like all facial wounds, it bled like crazy. But she said if I told anyone, she'd make life very difficult for my younger brother. And I knew she meant it—she could be cruel.'

Jandy reached out and took Patrick's hand. 'You

poor little boys,' she whispered. 'You must have felt quite helpless.'

'I certainly know what cruelty does to a child,' he said grimly. 'Visible signs like my scar are one thing— the emotional scars are harder to see.'

Jandy looked into his eyes and stroked his face, her finger drawing a line down his jaw to his mouth, moving gently over the jagged white line.

'I was wrong, then.' She smiled. 'I thought it was a bad rugby tackle. How terrible for a young child to have to cope with that.'

'She left my father when he became disabled and too frail to stand up to her,' said Patrick simply. 'It was a particularly unpleasant time, and she took him for every penny she could. That's partly why my father is so eager to start the wind-farm business.'

'And you came back to help him. Is your brother involved as well?'

'No. He has nothing to do with the project,' he said wryly. 'Robert still lives in London, leading a merry bachelor life.'

They both sat in silence for a moment, gazing out over the tree-lined valley, and then there was the unmistakeable growl of thunder in the distance. Patrick looked up at the sky, which had darkened considerably. Black clouds were rolling over the mountains and there were flickers of lightning over the hills. A few large drops of rain began to fall, and he stood up and pulled Jandy to her feet.

'There's a storm brewing. Let's go in and have some of this food I've bought.'

They gathered up their shopping and cases, but before they could reach the front door a flash of lightning and an enormous crack of thunder exploded almost over their heads. Quite suddenly a deluge of rain was pouring over them, pelting down like a waterfall, the drops leaping off the path as soon as they hit the ground. The temperature already seemed to have dropped several degrees.

Jandy fumbled with the keys and by the time she'd opened the door, they were both completely drenched. She slammed the door shut and they looked at each other then both began laughing helplessly. They were soaked to the skin, their hair plastered against their heads, water running in rivulets down their clothes, forming puddles on the floor.

'What are we like?' she spluttered through gales of laughter. 'We might just as well have been swimming in our clothes!'

Their laughter died down and they stared at each other silently for a few seconds. Then Patrick's blue eyes darkened and he put his hand under her chin, tilting her face to his. She didn't put up a fight when he pulled her towards him. At the back of her mind she knew that what was going to happen was inevitable. So Patrick couldn't offer long-term commitment? It was too late to worry about that now. The sudden rainstorm had made them both relax, and the wine had taken the edge off her feeble resolve.

'What a beautiful waterlogged mermaid you are,' he murmured huskily. Then he kissed her hungrily, his lips moving down her neck to the little hollow in her throat, his hands running lightly over her soft curves and making her arch against his muscled body.

'Don't you think we ought to take these clothes off?' he murmured. 'My nanny always said it was bad for you to stay in wet things…'

She laughed at him through the damp tendrils of hair dripping over her face. 'Did you always do what your nanny told you?' she asked mock-primly, again weakly attempting to put the brakes on the fiery physical attraction that was crackling between them.

He looked at her solemnly. 'It was more than my life was worth to disobey her, sweetheart.'

And suddenly they were both tearing their clothes off, leaving them where they lay on the floor. All Jandy could concentrate on were Patrick's arms twined around her and their naked bodies pressed against each other, slippery from their damp clothes. Too late to call a halt now, she thought hazily—and neither did she want to.

He whispered throatily, 'I can't tell you how often I've longed to do this over the past few weeks, my darling. You are so beautiful…'

He held her away from him for a second, his eyes feasting on her slender curves, the soft fullness of her breasts. Then he trailed his fingers delicately down her stomach, and covered her with butterfly kisses, and every nerve in Jandy's body responded as his lips drew a path of fire down her body. He pulled her down onto the floor, and she didn't resist as his hands brought her to a pitch of excitement. This was what she had missed for so long, and even if Patrick had said he was not a long-term prospect, for the time being he was hers—and the memory of her betrayal by Terry began to fade.

CHAPTER EIGHT

GRADUALLY Jandy woke from a deep sleep and opened her eyes then stared around the room, disorientated for a few seconds by the unfamiliar surroundings. Then everything that had happened the night before came flooding back to her, and a little smile of contentment curved across her face as she stretched languorously under the quilt.

It had been the most amazing night of her life, she thought happily. Of course, the night her darling Abigail had been born had been wonderful too, holding that miraculous little bundle in her arms—but it had been mixed with bitter-sweet memories. She'd adored her baby as soon as she'd held her in her arms—but there'd been no father there to welcome his child into the world, no champagne or flowers from a husband or lover, but the very real worry about how she was going to support her new baby. Lying in her hospital bed and seeing the other mothers with their doting partners had been hard to bear.

But last night had been unadulterated ecstasy, when two people had given absolutely to each other. She had no regrets, even though Patrick had put his cards on the table. He had said he wasn't up for a long-term relationship, but after last night she was convinced that they had a future together. How could anyone make love like he had and not feel more than a passing regard for her?

Light-heartedly she swung her legs over the bed and padded over to the window. The day was a complete contrast to the night before, with bright sunshine gleaming on the rain-washed road. In the distance the mountains were navy blue against the duck-egg blue of the skies and everything looked fresh and reinvigorated. Like she felt, said Jandy to herself, with a little thrill of happiness.

'Can I come in?' said a deep voice.

'No. I've nothing on yet,' replied Jandy sternly, trying not to giggle.

'Good—that's how I like you!'

Patrick shoved the door open with his elbow and entered the room carrying a tray laden with tea and toast. He put it down on a chair and came towards her with a happy smile on his face.

'You look delectable, my sweet,' he said softly, gathering her in his arms and kissing her extravagantly.

Jandy made a half-hearted attempt to push him away. 'Patrick! This isn't the time…'

He looked at her with wide, innocent eyes. 'Oh? Why not?'

She laughed. 'As your nanny might have said—because! Anyway, I want to get to the hospital early and I've got to have a shower.'

'Oh…that!' he said absently, and continued to kiss

her until they both fell in a heap on the bed. And Jandy didn't say anything more for some time…

Afterwards Patrick said tenderly, stroking back her honeyed hair from her face, 'You're wonderful, my sweet. I'll never, never forget this day, forget you— even when I'm old and grey…'

Then they lay in each other's arms for a while, until the front door rang and Jandy was galvanised into action, wriggling out from under Patrick and scurrying for a jacket to put on.

'Oh, no, Patrick, that's probably Ian! And we've got to get to the hospital. I'm not ready and neither are you!'

'It won't take me long. You have that tea and toast I brought and a quick shower, and then we'll be off. I'll answer the door. I'm the only one who should look at you when you're totally naked—I'm selfish that way!'

Jandy giggled and threw a pillow after him as he went out of the room. As long as her mother and Bertie were going to be OK, the future suddenly looked bright and exciting. She knew she had fallen hook, line and sinker for Patrick, and she was sure he felt the same way about her.

'Have you been to see Bertie yet?' asked Leony from her hospital bed, anxiously looking at Jandy. 'Nobody will tell me anything about his state of health. Please go and see him if you can.'

'I will, Mum—don't worry. I'm going to see his consultant when he's done his rounds.'

'Thank you, darling.' Mrs Marshall looked at her daughter appraisingly. 'You do look well—quite blooming! You must have had a good night's sleep last night after all your travelling yesterday!'

'Very good indeed,' replied Jandy, unable to stop a broad grin spreading over her face. Not surprising after the energetic episode before it!

'And you managed to put up the sofa bed for your colleague OK?'

'Er…yes, no trouble there,' said Jandy, adding quickly, 'How do you feel today, Mum? I think you definitely look brighter and the swelling on your face seems to have subsided.'

'I'm on the mend, feeling better today. In fact, they say as soon as I've found someone to look after me, I can go home as all I need is rest and to keep my foot off the ground.' She put her hand up quickly as she saw the concern on Jandy's face.

'I know that you've got to get back to Abigail and work but perhaps we could find someone from the village for a few weeks?'

'Ian suggested his girlfriend might help,' said Jandy.

'Netta? Oh, that would be lovely—she's a sweet girl. Do you think that could be organised, then?'

'Of course. I'm glad you know her—that makes it easier.'

Her mother smiled. 'What a relief it will be to go home! I must be getting better because I'm getting so bored now, although they've been wonderful to me in the hospital. What about bringing your colleague in? I'd love to meet her—so kind of her to come up with you. Is she a nurse too?'

Jandy hesitated for a second. Her mother was of a

romantic turn of mind and would very quickly put two and two together when she met Patrick!

'Actually, it's a he and he's a doctor in A and E,' she said brightly.

'Oh, I see! But that's wonderful!' exclaimed her mother, looking at her searchingly.

Jandy almost laughed, her mother's thoughts were so transparent! She was obviously already marrying her daughter off to this eligible man she'd never met!

'I'll go and get him, Mum. He's looking forward to meeting you too.'

It was obvious from the moment she saw him that Leony was bowled over by Patrick—and she observed accurately that her daughter was too!

'I'm so grateful to you for coming up with Jandy,' she said to him. 'It's lovely that she's got someone to look after her while she's up here.'

'I'm just glad I was able to be of some help,' said Patrick, adding with a grin, 'And you do live in a beautiful part of the world…'

'Then you must both come up for a proper holiday soon, and explore the whole area together,' said Leony. 'It would be lovely to get to know you better!'

'I think we'll go and see Bertie and find out how he is then we can report back to you,' said Jandy hastily, before her mother could start organising a wedding reception!

As they turned to go out, Leony took hold of Jandy's arm. 'Just one moment on your own, darling,' she said in a low voice. 'I won't keep her a minute, Patrick— you go on down to see Bertie.'

'What is it, Mum?' asked Jandy, looking at the frown on Leony's face.

'I…I couldn't help wondering. Patrick's wearing a wedding ring—does that mean he's married?'

'He's a widower, Mum…he's got a little girl.' She smiled and patted her mother's hand. 'Don't worry, I'm not about to fall for another Terry!'

Her mother smiled and relaxed back against the pillows. 'You know it's just that I wouldn't want you to be hurt again—falling for a married man can only lead to trouble. Of course, if he's a widower…'

'See you later!' Jandy smiled, blowing her a kiss from the door. 'As I said—don't worry!'

But as she followed Patrick down the stairs to ICU she sighed. That wedding ring was a sign that he hadn't forgotten his wife—in a way, as long as he wore it, Rachel was still in the picture.

The ICU was quiet, just the dull thrum of machines and clicking of monitoring equipment keeping track of the condition of the patients in the unit. Bertie was sedated and had an oxygen mask over his face, and a nurse was busy checking his vital signs, fluid balance, blood oxygen levels and blood pressure. She turned and smiled at Jandy and Patrick.

'Bertie's had his craniotomy,' she said. 'He's doing very well, and breathing by himself. He's going to the high-dependency unit very soon, and after a day or two there he'll be going to the general ward. Mr Muir wants to have a word with you if you'll go to his office.'

'Phew—what a relief,' breathed Jandy to Patrick. 'I

don't know how I could have told Mum if anything had
gone wrong with Bertie's operation.'

Mr Muir had the look of an elderly chick, with
fluffy grey hair standing up over his round head and a
little beak nose, but when he spoke his voice was surprisingly loud—but reassuring and confident.

'We're very pleased indeed with Bertie's progress,'
he boomed. 'He had an open skull fracture, which led
to some cranial bleeding. But we've drained the blood
and managed to repair some damaged blood vessels.
With any luck, he should be as good as new soon.' He
chuckled. 'Surprising how well the human body can
restore itself after a major trauma, isn't it?'

'Not without some intervention on your part,' said
Jandy, smiling. 'We're so grateful to you, Mr Muir.'

'Not at all, not at all.' He smiled. 'He'll be kept in
for a little while yet, just to be monitored, but we don't
anticipate any complications. You can tell your mother
that her friend will be as good as new soon!'

Leony had been allowed home after Netta had
promised to come in every day, and stay the night if
need be, when Jandy and Patrick had returned to
Delford. Leony sat in a high-backed chair downstairs
with a smile on her bruised face.

'I can't believe I've made it home—a few days
ago I wouldn't have thought I'd be back for months!'
She turned to Jandy. 'I know you've got to get back
to Abigail, darling, but you've both been wonderful
to give up everything and come and see me—I'm so
grateful.'

'We're going back on the evening plane tonight, Mum. There isn't much room for Netta and us in the house together! I'm going to dash out now to get some shopping. Patrick's just gone for an exploratory walk but Ian's only across the way at the garage so if you need him, ring him on his mobile.'

'I'll be fine, Jandy. I'll sit and look out at the view—I've missed it all so much.'

Patrick whistled a low contented tune to himself as he strode along the woodland path. He loved this part of the world, the majestic mountains and the beautiful lochs. He and Jandy would come back soon with Abigail and Livy and have a proper holiday: he felt sure the little girls would be great companions for each other. Over the past few days he had felt the weight of sadness that had always seemed to accompany him begin to lift. Gradually he'd begun to realise that he couldn't imagine a future without Jandy. She was everything he needed—funny, sweet and very beautiful. A short time ago he'd told her he couldn't make a permanent commitment—how wrong he'd been! Now all he could think about was being with her for ever. He was a lucky man.

He flicked a look at his watch. It was time to get back—Jandy would have finished her shopping soon and then they could have lunch and make their way to the airport later on for the evening flight.

Their cases were already packed and he would load them into the car later. He went into the kitchen by the back door. Jandy was evidently back: he could hear her voice and Leony's chatting together. He put the kettle on to make coffee, and as he waited for it to boil their conversation floated across to him.

'Patrick's absolutely adorable, darling, I do like him,' he heard Leony say, as he poured the water onto the ground coffee in the percolator. 'He's so reliable and kind. And as for his looks…'

Patrick grinned. She was quite gushing sometimes, but very sincere and amusing—he liked Jandy's mother a lot. He went to the door to make some glib comment about her remarks. Jandy was standing with her back to him, her silky, honey-coloured hair brushing her shoulders, slender in cut-off jeans. Her voice floated clearly towards him through the door.

'I'm glad to hear you approve,' she was saying with a laugh. 'And, of course, the best thing is he's got to be so secure financially. Getting married to him would sure solve a lot of money problems. Unusual to find a guy who ticks all the right boxes and is rolling in money as well, isn't it?'

She said it in a carefree way—no mention of her being in love with him, just the fact that as a supposedly wealthy man he'd passed some sort of test. Patrick stood stock still, frozen with shock, at the door, wondering if he was hearing things—but, no, Jandy was adding to her remarks.

'Just think—"Lady Janet Sinclair" sounds pretty good, doesn't it?'

Patrick's throat constricted and he turned away, sick to his stomach. He gripped the side of the work top and bent his head, suddenly feeling nauseous and dizzy,

utterly stunned by Jandy's remarks. His beautiful
Jandy… He could hardly believe it—and yet he'd
heard her, seen her. The bitter taste of bile rose in his
mouth. Hadn't he been in this place before—someone
who only wanted him for his wealth? Jandy, his beautiful, kind Jandy, he thought in bewilderment, had
turned out to be nothing but a gold-digger.

An immense and overwhelming sadness flooded
over him and he stared miserably out of the window.
His life seemed littered with mistakes—the guilt he
would always carry for his beloved Rachel's death, his
foolishness in getting entangled with Tara. Only this
time it was much, much worse because he'd allowed
himself to fall in love with Jandy, to imagine a future
with her. His mouth tightened. He felt he'd been
punched in the solar plexus as he'd realised that
Jandy's attraction for him was founded on nothing
more than the fact that she thought he was a wealthy
man. Bitterly he reflected that it was a rerun of his relationship with Tara. There was no future for them if
all she was interested in was his money—money, he
thought wryly, that he didn't have.

A stab of fury went through him, sudden disgust at
a woman he'd thought had liked him for himself alone.
They could have had a marvellous future together, and
he believed she would have been a wonderful mother
to Livy—and Livy would have had a little companion.
All that longed-for happiness seemed to have turned
to dust and ashes in a few minutes.

His brain raced. One thing he couldn't bring himself
to do was confront her on the matter at the moment, but

he couldn't bear to sit next to her on a plane for an hour. God, only that morning they had made passionate love to each other. She'd been so warm and loving, and they had been everything to each other—he'd thought. But now, knowing what her real motives were… He closed his eyes and swallowed painfully at the thought of her betrayal.

He gazed out of the window without seeing the view then, as if making a sudden decision, he reached into his jacket for a pen and scribbled a note on the back of an envelope, sticking it on the fridge door. Then he took out his mobile and went into the back garden. He made a couple of phone calls, picked up his case and strode to the crossroads without looking back.

'Where's Patrick?' asked Jandy, appearing at the front door. Her arms were weighed down by two huge bags of shopping, which she dumped on the floor. Then she sat down by her mother.

'He's not back yet,' said Leony. 'I thought I heard him in the kitchen, but I must have been mistaken. Guess who turned up in a taxi just after you'd gone to the shops! Your sister. I'm so thrilled that she's managed to get a few days off! She's just gone to say hello to Ian, but I've been telling her all about Patrick.'

Jandy laughed. 'Honestly, Mum, there's nothing to tell. We've made no commitment to each other. He's got lots of problems that have to be sorted—we're just having a good time!'

'Of course, darling, but anyone can see he's

besotted with you. And I don't think you're too averse
to him either, are you?'

Of course she wasn't averse to him—she was absolutely wild about him, she was drunk with happiness
whenever she saw him! The more she saw him, the
more she wanted him, to be with him, to make love
with him! Jandy got up quickly—she had to keep a
level head. She mustn't presume too much about
Patrick: she must let things take their time.

'I'll go and see Lydia,' she said happily. 'What a
lovely surprise! She must have come straight up when
she came back from her Australian flight.'

Just at that moment Lydia came through the door
and the two sisters hugged each other ecstatically.

'It's so good to see you, Lydia.'

'I haven't got another long-haul flight for a week,
so I thought I'd come up and help look after Mum
because I know you've got to get back to Abigail and
work.'

'That's great. A load off my mind…'

Lydia pulled her down on the sofa 'Now, come on,
sis, no secrets now! Mum's been telling me all about
this super doc you've brought up with you! How's it
going with you and him?'

'Mum and you are the biggest nosy parkers in the
land,' declared Jandy. 'Look, let's make lunch before
Patrick gets back from his walk and I'll tell you what
there is to tell—not that there is much, I assure you!
Help me take the shopping through.'

Jandy picked up a bag and went through to the
kitchen, placing it on the table, and started taking

things out of it to put in the fridge. Then she noticed an envelope, with writing scribbled across it, stuck on the fridge door. She picked it up and read it slowly, her eyes widening in disbelief and disappointment.

'Oh! I don't believe this! Patrick's had to go urgently to his father—he's managed to get an earlier flight via Glasgow. He got a taxi to take him to the airport.' She looked at Lydia, puzzled. 'You'd have thought he would have rung me on my mobile. His father must be very bad for him to take off like that—and I was dying for you to meet him.'

'And I was dying to give him the once-over,' said Lydia. 'How dare he go before I got the chance to see him? I'll just have to rely on Mum's glowing reports to see if he's suitable for my darling sister, although he sounds just right in every way!'

Jandy took out her mobile and punched in Patrick's number, but after a few rings she gave up. 'He's either turned it off or the reception's bad up here,' she sighed. 'I hope nothing drastic has happened.'

A little niggle of worry flickered in the back of her mind. It was such a very brief note—almost terse. And he hadn't signed it with 'love', she thought irrationally. Surely you'd do that to a woman you'd made passionate love to only that morning? Suddenly the day didn't seem so carefree after all.

CHAPTER NINE

'JUST get me some requisition sheets from that cupboard, will you?' asked Karen as she and Jandy straightened up one of the small cubicles and remade a bed with fresh linen and pillow cases. She looked at Jandy sympathetically as she took the papers from her. 'You've had a busy time up in Scotland, I believe. How's your poor mother after that ghastly accident?'

'She's making a great recovery. Her face looks better already, although her leg will be in a cast for a while. It was a pretty complicated fracture, but my sister's with her at the moment and there's someone who'll be coming in every day when Lydia has to start work again.'

'It was great that Patrick was able to go with you,' commented Karen, flicking an interested glance at Jandy as she started to look through her stock list. 'I should think he was a wonderful support.'

Karen wasn't a gossip but Jandy was shy about telling people that they were more than just good friends. It was early days yet, she thought. In fact, they'd only been properly 'together' for two days!

'Oh, he was. He suggested coming with me when he heard that my mother and her partner had been injured. We both had a few days off and it certainly made everything much easier, having him to drive me about and do the shopping.'

Jandy didn't add that it had made what could have been a fraught situation one of the most romantic episodes in her life! She bit her lip thoughtfully. It was odd that she'd been back at work a day and still hadn't heard from Patrick. Although she'd phoned him once or twice without success, he'd never got back to her. She had an uneasy feeling that something awful had happened—perhaps so awful that he hadn't had time to contact her and tell her exactly why he'd had to leave Scotland so abruptly.

'Er…have you heard how his father is?' she asked Karen. 'Patrick had to leave in a rush—something about his father—but I haven't been able to find out what's happened. He's probably been too busy to let me know.'

Karen looked up from making notes on the stock list and shook her head. 'He hasn't mentioned anything about his father, but Patrick's on this shift anyway, so you'll be able to ask him. I do know he's requested a few days off for holiday from next week.'

Jandy felt a flash of disappointment. She had looked forward so much to seeing him again, and had assumed that he would be as anxious as her to grab a few minutes alone together and arrange an evening out. If he was going on holiday, there'd be very little opportunity to meet.

Bob popped his head into the cubicle. 'Four patients are due in from an RTA any minute. Can you be on standby, please? One very serious injury at least.'

Back to the grindstone, sighed Jandy, going with Tilly to make sure four cubicles were cleared and ready with drips and any other equipment that might be necessary. It all seemed a far cry from twenty-four hours ago and a romantic night filled with passion in the Highlands with Patrick, she reflected wryly.

Bob was making a rapid initial examination of the casualties who'd just been wheeled in—two elderly men and a youth were being held in the assessment area.

'What happened?' he asked the paramedic.

'They were coming out of a pub and standing near a taxi rank. A car came careering round a corner overtaking a bus and went out of control. These three copped it, I'm afraid, and the driver finished up against a wall. He'll be here in a minute when they've stabilised him—he's lucky to be alive.'

'Right… Ah, Patrick, here you are. Can you deal with the patient we've put in the clean theatre?'

Jandy looked round quickly when she heard Patrick's name, ready to smile at him and hold his gaze in a little secret intimacy, but he was striding towards Bob from the ambulance bay and he didn't seem to notice Jandy as he passed her. He listened closely to Bob as he ran through the patient's condition.

'This young man's eighteen and his name's Jed,' explained Bob. 'He's in a lot of pain and it seems to be around his thorax. Plus he's got facial and arm wounds with dirt and gravel in them that need attention. Staff, can you and Nurse Rodman clean those out?'

In the clean theatre where minor surgical procedures were performed under aseptic conditions, Jandy and Tilly began to cut away the patient's clothing then started to work methodically, using swabs and forceps to pick out the grit and other dirt from the wounds. Jandy was intensely aware of Patrick working close to her, also very conscious that he hadn't, even by a nod or a smile, acknowledged her presence. But, then, of course he was concentrating on his patient, just as he should be, she told herself sharply.

Patrick was murmuring to Jed, his voice low and reassuring: 'It's all right, Jed, you'll be fine. You're doing well. Don't worry, Jed, we'll be giving you something for that pain very soon.'

He used his patient's name often, trying to hold the young man's attention and keep him calm, realising that it was pain and shock that was causing the touch of hysteria in Jed's voice.

'I need to let my girlfriend know—I should be meeting her now…' he kept repeating, with a rising inflection. 'She won't know where I am. I've got to meet her, you see…'

'Where were you meeting her, Jed? Tell me, and someone will contact her, I promise,' Patrick said soothingly.

'Her name's Rachel and it's on my mobile in my pocket. She'll be worried if I don't turn up.'

'Sister will ring her for you. Get his mobile out of his trouser pocket, would you, Staff?'

Patrick moved his hands over the youth's rib cage, checking for any misalignment, watching Jed's face as he did so and not the area being felt so that he could tell immediately if he touched a cracked rib or a torn muscle.

Jed moaned and shifted his body from side to side restlessly, showing all the signs of acute discomfort, bending and straightening his legs. Occasionally he coughed, bringing up blood.

'What happened? What happened?' he mumbled. 'Something crashed into me…'

'It was a car, Jed—it took a corner too quickly. You were outside the pub,' Jandy said quietly, trying to help Jed orientate himself. 'You're in the hospital now and we're helping you.'

Patrick looked up from examining Jed, his eyes meeting Jandy's for a second, but oddly cold and remote. 'Staff, would you get Bob Thoms, please?'

His voice was authoritative, terse. It was as if he and Jandy had never had a relationship at all. There was no trace of softness in his expression, just stern preoccupation.

He was only being professional, Jandy told herself as she went to find Bob, but she couldn't help feeling a little bewildered and surprised by his brusque manner.

'What's going on with this young man?' Bob asked Patrick when he came into the theatre. 'Any sign of impending coma or shock syndrome? Is he panicking?'

Patrick shook his head. 'He's alert and coherent. He's been able to tell us how to contact his girlfriend. No sign of aortic tear or heart injury. I'm making a tentative diagnosis of lung bruising. I wanted your input.' He turned to Tilly, aware that the student nurse didn't have much experience of this kind of injury, and explained, 'These impact accidents often mean the victim inhales sharply and holds onto the air, and then a sharp blow to the chest, like Jed's had, can cause pressure to build up round the lungs, tearing open the superficial blood vessels.'

Bob nodded in agreement. 'Although Jed's in a lot of pain, he's not exhibiting the extreme panic that's often a sign of a chest injury involving the heart or aorta. Luckily he wasn't standing near a wall or another solid object when he was hit—that can make a hell of a mess of a body with multiple fractures or worse. We'll get him X-rayed and admitted to Surgical to have his respiration monitored and some pain relief administered.'

'Can you make those arrangements, Staff?' asked Patrick, his tone as remote as if he had hardly been introduced to Jandy.

Jandy went out with Tilly to book an X-ray and ring Surgical, a slow burn of annoyance beginning to flicker inside her at Patrick's manner. Perhaps she didn't know this man as well as she'd thought she did—he seemed to have reverted back to the rudeness he'd shown when she'd looked around the cottage. And yet…and yet only such a short time ago they had been in each other's arms and she'd been absolutely sure that he was her soul-mate. Surely the fiery intimacy they'd had together had meant more to him than just a casual fling? Then a little voice in her head whispered sadly, But didn't he warn you that he couldn't commit to anyone—that long-term relationships with him were not a possibility?

Tilly's breathless voice broke into her jangled thoughts. 'Wow—Dr Sinclair knows so much, doesn't he?' she said admiringly as they went to the desk.

'He's an experienced casualty officer,' commented Jandy rather tartly. 'He ought to know what he's talking about.'

Karen had just finished on the telephone. 'Right— that's done, then. I've managed to get hold of Jed's parents and his girlfriend, and they're coming in now. I haven't got any information yet on relatives of the two older men. They're both concussed and one's got a clean fracture of the right femur, but hopefully the police will dig something up.'

'Is the driver OK?' asked Jandy.

Karen pulled a face. 'Multiple fractures and a ruptured spleen so far—he's gone to Theatre. Looks like he's going to pay a heavy penalty for racing like that in a built-up area.'

'Pity he had to include the people hit by his car,' commented Bob. 'Have we time for a coffee? I'll collapse if I don't get some caffeine into my system.'

Jandy joined him in the little kitchen. 'Give me a strong one too, Bob,' she said. 'It's been a long day and we're not halfway through it yet.'

She sat down and lifted her feet onto another chair

with a small sigh of relief, taking the chance to take the weight off them, like most casualty nurses did. She put her head back and closed her eyes for a minute, feeling an edgy irritation with the day, caused in no small part by Patrick, trying to pinpoint just what it might be that had made him so remote and formal. Perhaps, she reflected tiredly, she had it all wrong and was imagining his cold attitude towards her. After all, she couldn't expect the man to be all lovey-dovey with her in the hospital, for heaven's sake. She was expecting too much after their intimate time together in Scotland. She took a refreshing sip of the scalding coffee that Bob handed to her and felt slightly better.

At that moment Patrick came into the room, and she was struck suddenly by how tired and drawn he looked. He seemed to have aged a few years since they'd been together the day before. His father must be very ill, and in her selfishness she'd forgotten that he had things on his mind. He hadn't been deliberately rude to her—it was just that he was very worried.

She got up from the chair and poured him a cup of coffee.

'Hi, Patrick,' she said softly. 'I'm so sorry you had to leave suddenly. How is your father—is it very bad?'

Patrick took the coffee from her and shook his head. 'He's OK really,' he replied. For a second he looked at Jandy steadily, an unreadable expression in his eyes. 'Something happened, though—something that meant I couldn't stay any longer—but I don't want to talk about it just now.'

He gave no more information and Jandy frowned.

It must be a private matter that he wouldn't want to discuss at work with everyone listening.

'Well, perhaps you'd like to do something to cheer you up?' she suggested brightly. 'There's a really good film on at the local cinema at the weekend. I could get a babysitter and we could have a meal after it perhaps. What do you say?'

She smiled at him, her beautiful eyes holding his. Inwardly Patrick groaned. He couldn't handle this. She was so beautiful and he longed to take her in his arms and kiss her lips, feel again her soft body next to his...bury his head in her sweet-smelling, silky hair. Then he thought of what he had learned so brutally about her attitude to him since they'd made glorious love to each other only thirty-six hours ago. He hardened his heart and swallowed a large draught of coffee. He couldn't allow himself to drift into a relationship again with someone whose regard for him was based on what she could get out of him. Both he and his precious Livy deserved more than that.

'Sorry,' he said tersely. 'I can't go out at the moment—a pretty full diary, I'm afraid.'

Jandy looked at him in surprise. 'You can't go out at all?'

His expression was cold, unreadable. 'Not possible at the moment—too much on.' He turned to Bob. 'Bob, I'd like your opinion on the old man with the broken femur—he's very shaky and I'm wondering if we've missed something.'

Bob nodded and they both went out discussing the old man's condition. Jandy took a deep breath, hardly able to believe Patrick's attitude towards her. What the hell was wrong—was it her? Had she been too demanding, too sure of herself, or was she just being hard on him? He looked different somehow—not the vibrant and energetic person he usually was. He probably needed a few days off from socialising and she was expecting too much from a man she knew was kind and considerate normally—after all, he'd come up to Scotland with her and been an enormous help and support. Perhaps when he'd finished work he'd get in touch with her. She shouldn't have pressured him in front of everyone. But somewhere deep inside her she had the horrible feeling that Patrick was moving away from her again. If he really loved her, he wouldn't have brushed her off like that. She gave a baffled sigh and went to answer the wall phone.

Patrick finished talking to Bob about the elderly patient and stood outside the small theatre for a second before he went to the locker room, watching Jandy walking back towards the main desk. He felt awful. He had wanted to make it plain to Jandy that they were no longer an item. In his bitter hurt at Jandy's deception he wanted to hurt her too, and he hated himself for it. He had seen the expression in her eyes when he'd told her he was too busy to go out with her, and it had twisted a knife in his heart, because he could almost swear that she looked heartbroken and bewildered, as if she really had loved him. But looks were deceptive, he told himself bitterly. He'd heard from her own mouth that what attracted her was his wealth and position.

'Damn it…damn her!' he muttered, slamming the locker door shut with a vicious bang and walking briskly out of the room.

As Jandy drove home that night she felt the ghastly replay of confusion and despair she'd experienced when Terry had abandoned her. Perhaps there was something about her, she thought savagely, that made her into a victim where men were concerned. And yet she could swear that Patrick was nothing like Terry. Even when she'd imagined she'd loved Terry, in her heart of hearts she'd known that he was a selfish man, someone who liked to be the centre of attention—extremely attractive with a spurious charm but devious in many ways. She recalled how he would have no compunction in taking days off if he wanted to go somewhere glamorous, phoning his office to say he was ill but assuring her that he would be working twice as hard to make up for his absence. She hadn't approved really, but when she'd been with him he'd had that charming knack of making her believe that he'd put himself out to be with her.

But Patrick was nothing like that. She'd worked closely with him, seen how dedicated, compassionate and kind he was. She couldn't believe that he really was the sort to have a one-night stand with anyone and deliberately hurt them.

Tears of desolation ran down her face as she drove to pick up Abigail, but she brushed them away fiercely, furious with herself for being so weak. Patrick Sinclair had lied to her—and she was worth more than that. She certainly wasn't going to spend years moping about any man again—life was too short to live wallowing in self-pity. She was glad, yes, glad that she'd found out about the rat now and not months later when she would probably have fallen for him hook, line and sinker. As it was, she was still in control of her feelings, wasn't she?

Unconsciously she tilted her chin in determination: Patrick was only going to be at Delford General for a short time until Sue came back from maternity leave. She would grit her teeth and work with him whatever the atmosphere between them.

Monday morning again and everywhere looked just the same—staff bustling about, Danny Smith on Reception laughing loudly at a joke Max had told him, a paramedic whistling cheerily in the corridor. Of course life went on, reflected Jandy gloomily. Just because her weekend had been sad and lonely, it didn't mean that the world outside mirrored her emotions.

'You look pretty shattered, Jandy,' remarked Bob. 'Had a busy weekend?'

What you mean is that I look absolutely awful, which could be because I hardly slept at all, thought Jandy, but she answered with a bright smile, 'Fairly busy. I've discovered moving house is very hard work and trying to box things up while an energetic four-year-old's helping you can be a little frustrating.'

She was well aware that Patrick was very close to her, leafing through a medical journal, but she didn't look at him. She wouldn't let him get to her—she wouldn't!

'Shall I go and take the first on the list?' she asked Bob. 'Monday mornings mean hundreds of patients with hangovers from the weekend, and worse!'

She went to Reception and took the top card in the box from the pile of triaged patients.

'Harry Leyton?' she called out.

A large man wearing overalls and boots came forward, holding a dirty handkerchief over his finger.

'Fine start to the day this is!' he commented, sitting down in the cubicle that Jandy had taken him to. 'I think I've taken off the top of my finger.'

'Let me see,' said Jandy, unwinding the material from his finger and blanching slightly when she saw that the finger had been cut through the nail bed to the bone. 'How on earth did you do this?'

'Pushing a bill through a letter box. The lid smacked down on my finger and I tried to pull my finger out. That was a mistake—it held my finger like a vice.'

Jandy grimaced in sympathy. 'Not what you expect when you post a letter. Now, I'm going to wash it very, very gently—we've got to make sure it's clean—and then I'm going to bind it up to stop it bleeding.'

'What about stitching it? Won't that make it heal quicker?' the man asked.

'There isn't much skin there to stitch. I think it will just have to heal over by itself. It'll probably take two or three weeks.'

Harry groaned. 'I'm not going to be able to do much joinery with a hand like this, am I?' He shook his large fleshy face gloomily. 'Well, that's ruined my day, I can tell you. How can I look after my family if I can't work? I've got a big contract on as well with a building firm…'

'I'm sorry, Harry,' said Jandy as she cleaned and bandaged the injury. 'It's very bad luck—but it will heal if you don't try and use it too much.'

He nodded and sighed. 'Maybe—but this is the first big job I've had in an age. It was going to set me up a bit, this was.'

Jandy watched Harry lumber off, feeling intensely sorry for him. She knew what it was like to be hard up—but at least she had a regular job. Her heart might be broken, but as long as she could look after Abigail and keep a roof over their heads she mustn't complain.

She went to the central desk to put the patient's case notes on the computer, brushing past Patrick who was writing something up on the whiteboard. He turned to look at her slim figure with her back to him as she sat in front of the screen. Bob was sitting by her, just finishing a telephone conversation. He put down the phone and turned to Jandy.

'You still look a bit bushed,' he said. 'You wouldn't fancy having a drink with a few of us after work, would you?'

Out of the corner of her eye she was aware that Patrick was watching her, but with an abrupt movement he rose from his chair and strode out of the room. She gave an inward shrug. She had to put Patrick Sinclair out of her mind.

She smiled ruefully at Bob. 'I'm terribly busy at the

moment, Bob. Moving house in a few days means every hour after work is taken up with packing and sorting. It'll be some time before I can take time off.'

He nodded affably. 'Just a thought. Hope the move goes OK.'

Jandy turned to go back to Reception and on the way passed Patrick. He caught her arm, a grim expression on his face.

'So you're going out with Bob now, are you?' he said stonily to her.

She stared at him in amazement, lost for speech. What was this man like? But her heart started pounding at his touch, a kind of excitement building up in her that he was at least communicating with her.

'I beg your pardon?' she said tartly with a raised eyebrow. 'I don't know what you're talking about. Bob asked me out for a drink with some of the others, but for your information I declined—not that it's any business of yours!'

Then, with a withering look of scorn, she walked away from him.

Patrick clenched his fists in his pockets. He hadn't known it would hurt this much, listening to another man asking Jandy out. He hadn't realised that the thought of her with anyone else would be like a knife turning in his stomach. He sat at the desk and looked down at his hands, seeing the golden wedding band he still had on his ring finger. Rachel would forever have a special place in his heart—but that was in another life. Now he knew that whatever he had found out about Jandy's reason for going out with him, it was she who dominated all his thoughts at the moment—and he was eaten up by jealousy, unable to do anything about it.

CHAPTER TEN

'I THINK we're all done, love. The van's empty now, so we'll be off!'

The genial removal men gave a wave and went off down the path, the door of the cottage banged shut and Jandy and Lydia flopped down on the sofa.

'Thank God!' exclaimed Lydia. 'We're in at last! And it looks lovely after all the hard work you've put in, Jandy, painting and scrubbing. I'm sorry you had to do it all.'

'Oh, I quite enjoyed it. There's something satisfying about seeing a result. Anyway, you've been doing your stuff with Mum in Scotland for a week. You say she's doing really well?'

'It's amazing how's she's improved, and Bertie's coming home next week.'

There was the sound of pattering feet on the stairs and Abigail ran across the room, eyes alight with joy. She was so precious, thought Jandy, so full of life and exuberance. It made everything worthwhile, and even helped to subdue the unhappiness of the situation between Patrick and herself.

'Mummy, Lydia, come and look at my room—it's got lots of pictures up of flowers and fairies and little animals! I love it!'

'We'll come in a minute, pet. Just let Mummy and I have a little sit-down—we're exhausted,' begged Lydia.

'Well, I want to show Livy my room soon,' declared Abigail. 'Can we ask her to come round? You said she could come when we were all moved in.'

She looked pleadingly at Jandy, and Lydia grinned. 'What a good idea. Livy's Patrick's little girl, isn't she? Why don't we have a small house-warming party with Livy and Patrick? Give them a call, Jandy. After all, it was Patrick who mentioned the cottage was to let and he hasn't seen it transformed yet.'

Jandy felt her cheeks redden, suddenly at a complete loss as to what to say. The last thing she wanted was to see Patrick. In the future she supposed it was inevitable they'd meet in the little village as they lived so near each other, but at the moment her feelings were too raw, still smarting from his incredible behaviour a week ago. They had seen each other in the hospital, of course, worked on the same patients sometimes, but had barely exchanged words. It was horrible, but she was going to stick it out until Patrick left in a few months. Sometimes she thought he was about to say something to her—but so far she had skilfully avoided entering into any conversation with him. If he hadn't the basic politeness to tell her why he didn't want to pursue their relationship then she didn't want to have anything to do with him.

'He's on holiday at the moment,' Jandy said quickly, glad that she didn't have to lie. 'I know he's taken a few days off, so we'll have to wait until he comes back.'

Abigail's little face fell, then she said resolutely, 'I'm going to send Livy an invitation. Will you help me to write it, Mummy? I'll go and get my crayons.'

'I must say I can't wait to see the guy,' said Lydia chattily as Abigail raced upstairs for her crayons. She opened a bottle of sparkling wine to celebrate their move. 'Mum is in ecstasies about him—says he's got everything! I thought perhaps I'd see him round here before I have to fly off again on Wednesday.' She handed a glass of wine to Jandy. 'Cheers! Here's to happy times. By the way, has Patrick told you why he had to leave Scotland so quickly last week? And before I got to see him too!'

Jandy took a sip of wine and twirled her glass, watching the bubbles rise to the surface. 'Er…no, he hasn't mentioned it, actually.'

Lydia raised her eyebrows in surprise at her twin. 'Why on earth not? I must say, it's the first thing I'd ask him. You were really worried about what had happened to his father, weren't you?'

'I did try and find out but he said he didn't want to discuss it in front of everyone at the hospital—and I can't say I blame him.'

'But you must have had times alone with him surely—even after work perhaps?'

Jandy was silent for a second and Lydia looked at her curiously, then she put her glass down and came over to Jandy and took her hand, saying softly, 'You can't fool me, darling…I'm not your twin sister for nothing. Something's wrong, isn't it? Have you had a row?'

Jandy swallowed. 'Not really…well, sort of…' She shrugged, her eyes a little too bright, and said with a weary half-smile, 'No use keeping anything from you, is there? The truth is, Lydia, I don't know what went wrong. We were getting along beautifully in Scotland. It was wonderful, and I really thought he liked me a lot—there was no sign of anything wrong. And then…and then when I came back from the shops after you'd arrived, he'd just vanished! And…'

She stopped and wandered over to the window, gazing out at the little garden and the mansion house beyond it where Patrick lived.

'And what?' prompted Lydia. 'His note implied that it was something to do with home, didn't it? Nothing to do with you and him.'

Jandy whipped round from the window and burst out, 'But it must have been something about me—don't you see? We were so very close on the night we'd come back from seeing Mum in hospital. I…I thought we'd made each other very happy. It all seemed absolutely perfect. And then…without a word he vanishes and since then he's barely exchanged two words with me—except to be curt and rude. I just can't understand it.'

'Poor darling,' whispered Lydia, hugging her sister. 'I can't believe it is anything to do with you. It must be something much deeper than that—some background worry that's making him like this. Perhaps when he's returned from holiday he'll have sorted it out and things will get back to normal.'

'I don't think so, sis. I've come to the conclusion that he just doesn't want any sort of commitment and he's frightened I'll be too possessive—something like that. You know, he still wears his wedding ring and perhaps that's a sign that he hasn't let go of the past yet.' Jandy drained her wineglass, put it down on the table and said sadly, 'Whatever it is, I'm damn well not going to make another mistake and fall for someone who can toss me aside so easily.'

'I don't want anyone to hurt you again either— I just can't believe that this man is another Terry, though. You know, Mum's a pretty good judge of character and she never liked Terry, even before he deserted you—but Patrick Sinclair's a different story. She really was impressed with him.'

Jandy gave a sudden laugh. 'Oh, well, I'm going to forget about the rat anyway. Tell me about this dishy new pilot you've met. Are you smitten?'

Lydia grinned. 'Let's finish this bottle, and I'll tell you the whole story.'

It was a cold night with a wintry feel and Jandy had made up a log fire with apple wood and it sent out a lovely fresh smell and warmed the room beautifully. Jandy thought how cosy it was as she snuggled down on the sofa, ready to switch on the TV and watch a talent show. She had looked forward all week to a quiet Saturday evening. Abigail was already in bed

and Jandy was nibbling at some smoked-salmon sand-
wiches she'd made for herself as Lydia had flown off
again on some exotic flight or other.

She gave a jump of irritation when there was a
knock at the front door then wondered rather fearfully
if she ought to open it when it was so dark outside. She
called out, 'Who is it?'

'It's Bob—Bob Thoms. Just dropping in a little
house-warming present from us all, but if it's not convenient…'

'Hi, Bob, how sweet of you to bring a present. Do
come in,' she said, opening the door.

'Well…if it's OK,' he said. 'I'm just on my way to
meet up with our shift and they asked me to drop these
off.' He handed her an enormous bunch of flowers. He
looked around the room. 'This is very nice—did you
say it belonged to Patrick?'

'Well, it's on his father's estate and he wanted to let
it and I was desperate to get somewhere. I was very
lucky. What about a drink?'

Bob shot a look at his watch and shook his head.
'I'm only staying for a minute as I promised I'd pick
Tilly up, so I'd better be on my way.'

'Well, thanks to all of you for these gorgeous
flowers. It's really sweet of you.'

She was interrupted by another knock on the front
door. She smiled at Bob and said wryly, 'You wait
ages for someone to call and then two come along at
once!'

She opened the door and looked with astonishment
into Patrick's eyes as he stood before her. A flicker of

something very like longing and distress seemed to cross his face before his expression changed and became hard and remote again.

Oh, Patrick, whispered Jandy to herself. Why has it come to this? Why do you seem to dislike me so much? From love to hate so very quickly!

She might have been determined to put the man out of her mind, but when she saw him in the flesh—his glorious sexy body, wide shouldered, slim hipped, dark hair plastered wetly round his head from the rain—her resolution slipped somewhat.

Patrick's eyes flicked to Bob standing behind her.

'I didn't realise that you and Bob were having an evening together,' he remarked brusquely. In her heightened state Jandy detected a kind of sarcasm in the remark. 'I won't be long, though,' he added. 'I just came to see that you'd moved in OK—and if there was anything that needed doing. We always make sure there are no problems with our new tenants.' He said that smoothly as if to underline that there was nothing special about him coming to see her.

Jandy stood stock still, numb with shock and still holding the bouquet of flowers. 'No…no, thank you. Everything's quite all right.'

'Well,' said Bob easily, oblivious to the atmosphere between Jandy and Patrick. 'I'll be off now anyway. Nice to see you, Patrick. See you both on Monday, I suppose!'

He opened the front door and Jandy called out as he left, 'Thank you so much for the flowers—they're really beautiful.'

'Glad you like them!' he called, disappearing down the little path and getting into his car. Jandy watched him go then turned round slowly to face Patrick, who was still standing by the fireplace. He looked drop-dead handsome, but weary and grey faced, as if he hadn't been sleeping too well.

'Is that all you wanted to see me about—whether everything was all right?' she asked tersely after a short silence.

'Yes…yes, that's all.' He folded his arms and looked down at the floor for a second as if gathering his thoughts, before raising his head again and lasering her with those deep blue eyes.

'So you and Bob are seeing each other after all?' he enquired smoothly.

'I've no idea what you mean. He kindly brought some flowers round tonight as a house-warming present—although it's nothing to do with you actually,' she said bitingly, nearly adding, As you seem to have lost interest in me. But she couldn't bring herself to utter the finality of those words.

Patrick shrugged. 'Well, I suppose old Bob has a bit of money stashed away—he's only got himself to support after all, so I expect he's perfect for you.'

For a second Jandy couldn't believe she'd heard him correctly then she said slowly, 'I beg your pardon? Are you saying I only going out with men if they've got some money?'

'It seems to make sense to me. The guy drives an expensive car, goes on luxury holidays. It would suit you down to the ground…'

A sudden blind fury overtook Jandy. How could he be so cruel, so unkind? 'How dare you?' she said in a dangerously quiet voice. 'I cannot believe what you just said, and I can't think what I've done to justify you making such a horrible remark. Not that it matters, but that bouquet was from the casualty team and not just Bob. Would you get out now? I don't want to see you in this house again. I may be renting it from your father, but from now on, keep your distance!'

She marched to the door and held it open, allowing the freezing air to come into the room, and Patrick walked slowly past her, only turning at the last moment so that he was standing in front of her.

'It hurts to be told the truth, doesn't it, Jandy?' he said softly, and walked away into the night. Jandy flung herself onto the sofa and cried until there were no tears left.

Patrick walked home miserably, almost revelling in the rain that lashed into him—a kind of punishment, he thought, for being so unbelievably brutal to Jandy. How could he say such lacerating words to a woman he knew now he loved?

He'd gone round that night on the pretext of asking Jandy if everything was to her satisfaction after her move because he couldn't bear to let the situation between them go on any longer. He had been going to try and have it out with her—to ask her to tell him honestly if money was one of the things that had attracted her to him. He desperately wanted to get back where they'd been before and could hardly credit that he'd heard her say that his money and status were what she was interested in. But when he'd seen Bob there he'd felt it was too late. She'd moved on already, and he couldn't bear the thought of her with another man. So much for commitment, he thought bitterly, turning into the drive of Easterleigh and hunching up his jacket against the rain.

Jandy woke the next morning with a dull headache, finding it hard to find the energy to be upbeat for Abigail, who begged to be allowed to deliver the note she'd written to Livy, asking her round for tea.

'Can we walk round to Livy's house, Mummy, and take the invitation? They're probably back from their holiday. Please, please, please! It's not raining!' Abigail looked hopefully at her mother.

'Not at the moment, darling. I've got a lot of urgent things to do.'

Abigail pouted. 'What urgent things? You've never got time for anything with me!'

Those words stung. As a single parent Jandy was always conscious of the fact that her time with her little girl was limited and she did her best to make up for it at the weekends, but today she felt utterly drained, unable to respond to Abigail's entreaties.

'Perhaps later on, pet. Let me do the ironing first.'

There was the sound of footsteps coming up the path and then the front door opened and Lydia came into the room. Jandy felt her heart lift a little. How wonderful that her sister was back—things never seemed as bad when she was around.

'Oh, Lydia, darling—I didn't expect you back yet!'

Jandy flung her arms round her sister, never more happy to see her. She needed her sister's bracing fun and understanding more than ever, although she was not going to tell her about the episode with Patrick the night before. It was no good going over that horrible conversation again.

'Ah, it's nice to be wanted.' Lydia laughed. 'The flight out to Australia was cancelled when we got to Amsterdam and so I've got a few days off. Hallelujah!' She turned to her little niece. 'And how is my adorable little Abigail? By the way, I've got something for you!'

She delved into a bag and Abigail fluttered excitedly round her until Lydia produced a little doll wearing a flight attendant's uniform with a bag that held changes of clothes.

'Ooh, she's lovely. Thank you very, very much!' exclaimed Abigail, prancing around the room and waving the doll about. 'She looks like you and I'm going to call her Lucy! This is something else I can show to Livy!'

Jandy groaned and caught her sister's eye. 'She's still keen to see Livy. I've told her very possibly she might, but only possibly, later! Now, how about a cup of coffee?'

She and Lydia went into the kitchen, talking nineteen to the dozen as they always did when they got together. Abigail looked after them and sighed then, clutching the little doll, she went quietly out of the ⁀nt door and down the path.

* * *

'Look, Jandy, she can't have gone far. You know what? I bet she's toddled off to show Livy that doll all by herself.'

The strain of the past few frantic minutes when Jandy and Lydia had searched the house and garden for Abigail after discovering she was missing was beginning to tell. They both looked fraught.

'It's a possibility,' Jandy admitted. 'I should have taken more notice of her when she pleaded to see Livy—I was far too vague. Let's go and see if she's made her way to the hall. Oh, God, I hope she's all right.'

They ran out of the garden and up the road to the gates of Easterleigh. The drive stretched a long way before them, dripping bare trees on either side, a slight bend halfway up meaning that only half the house was visible.

'Lord, look how far away it is—a hell of a way for a little girl to go by herself,' whispered Lydia.

'If she sets her mind on something, she'll do it,' said Jandy wryly. 'Come on, let's run!'

When they came to the curve in the drive it divided into two with no indication as to which way led to the hall. They looked at each other in exasperation.

Then Jandy said, 'Good job there's two of us. You go that way, I'll go this!'

The dogs were making an almighty row, thought Patrick as he strode through the woodland, taking stock of the trees that needed felling and the fences that had broken down by the river. They were probably after rabbits again—there were enough of them scampering all over the place. Winter had arrived. There was a crust of frost on the ground from overnight and it was cold and damp. In four weeks it would be Christmas.

A wave of depression came over him as he reflected that Livy wanted a Christmas party and the house to be decorated with a huge Christmas tree in the hall. Patrick smiled grimly to himself. He didn't feel like celebrating at the moment. Two weeks ago he had been full of plans for Jandy and Abigail—and the sister, of course, whom he'd never met—joining them for Christmas Day and having a wonderful traditional time. How his father would love that—filling the house with laughter and children's excitement. Now he would have to force himself to enjoy the festivities for Livy's sake.

A sudden noise in the woods caught Patrick's attention. He could hear a woman's voice calling and the dogs sent up a new cacophony of barking.

'Rusty! Lightning! Here, boys! Come here at once!' he shouted.

A crashing through the undergrowth and they bounded in front of him obediently. He bent down to ruffle their heads and then heard the woman's voice again, high and frightened.

'Abigail! Abigail, darling—are you there?'

'What the…?'

Patrick pushed his way through the bushes and small trees and nearly fell over Jandy standing in a little clearing. She looked round when she heard the sound of crunching footsteps behind her, her eyes alight with hope. Then she saw it was Patrick and her expression changed to one of despair.

He looked at her distraught face. 'What on earth's wrong? What are you doing here?'

'It…it's Abigail…' she gasped. 'She's wandered off. We think she may have come to see Livy and show her a doll my sister brought her. She may have left the drive and taken a wrong turning.' Jandy looked around wildly. 'I don't know where to start looking… Oh, God, if anything's happened to her…'

Patrick put his hands on her shoulders. 'Don't worry. If she's anywhere in the vicinity, we'll find her. We'll make our way towards the house through the woods. If we haven't found her by then I'll get the staff together and we'll all search for her.' He put his hand under her chin and tilted her face towards his. His expression was gentle, unflustered. 'Pecker up!' He turned to the dogs. 'Come on, boys! Seek and find with me!'

The dogs darted in and out of the undergrowth and Patrick grabbed Jandy's hand to steady her as they made their way along a narrow path, both of them shouting Abigail's name then stopping to listen in case she replied. After a few minutes they heard the dogs whining and Patrick's grip on Jandy's hand tightened.

'They've seen something,' he said. 'They always whine when they see something strange. We're coming to another clearing now.'

The path opened up into a small clearing with a little summer house in the middle. Sitting on the step to the door was Abigail, playing with her doll. She looked up as she heard the two adults approach.

'Hello!' she said brightly. 'I've found this little house to play in!'

Jandy took a deep breath and went and sat beside her. 'Why did you go out without telling Lydia or me?' she asked the child gently.

''Cos I knew you wouldn't take me to see Livy for ages and ages—you're always talking to Lydia when she comes home.'

'Abigail,' said Jandy in a very stern voice, 'I want you to promise that you'll never ever go out again without telling Mummy. I've been very worried about you. Lydia, Patrick and I have been searching for you—do you hear?'

Abigail nodded. 'I'm glad you found me. I lost my way but I wasn't frightened.'

Jandy's eyes met Patrick's and she got up and said quietly to him, 'Thank you for helping me. We won't trespass on your land any more.'

'Perhaps it would be a good idea for you and Abigail to come to the house and she can show Livy her doll?' He spoke diffidently, as if he didn't really mind one way or the other, but his eyes never left her.

'I don't think in the circumstances…' Jandy began stiffly.

'Oh, please, Mummy! Just for a little minute!' Abigail ran to her mother and put her arms round Jandy's legs. 'I'll be a good girl for you!'

Jandy flicked a glance at Patrick and said resignedly, 'Well, just for a few minutes—if that's all right with Patrick.'

They started to make their way down the path and came to the drive again, this time much nearer the house. At the same time a figure appeared out of the woodland on the opposite side.

'Lydia!' called Jandy, running over to her. 'Lydia, it's OK! We've found Abigail!'

'Oh, thank God!' Lydia ran up to the little girl and flung her arms round her. 'Don't give us such a fright again, darling, will you?'

Patrick stood watching them, a slight look of puzzlement on his face, and Jandy drew Lydia towards him.

'This is my sister, Lydia,' she said. 'She came up to Scotland just before you left, but you didn't meet each other.'

He looked at the two sisters incredulously. They were incredibly alike, although he could tell there were subtle differences—Jandy waas slightly taller and slimmer than Lydia, her hair a little fairer.

'Pleased to meet you, Lydia,' he said at last. 'I didn't realise you and your sister were twins, Jandy.' He frowned for a second. 'So you came up to Scotland when we were there?'

'I managed to get a flight up to Inverness when I'd come back from Australia and took a taxi straight to my mother's house. I wanted it to be a surprise for them— they didn't know I was coming. I was sorry to miss you.'

They started to walk towards the house, Patrick silent and thoughtful, then he stopped suddenly and said, 'Did you arrive while Jandy was at the shops?'

'Yes—you'd gone for a walk and she'd popped out to get some basics in before she flew home in the evening.' Lydia looked reproachfully at him. 'Actually, she was amazed when she returned and found you'd left. We couldn't really understand it!'

Patrick was silent for a moment, and just then a small figure appeared in the doorway of the big house. She gave a shriek of surprise and ran up to them.

'Abigail!' she cried happily. 'You've come to see me! Can I show her my pony, Daddy, now she's here?'

'You can, sweetheart—but first of all take Abigail and her auntie into the house and ask Sheena to get everyone a coffee. Jandy and I will be in soon—I just want to have a word with her.'

Lydia took the two children's hands and walked ahead with them, pausing very briefly to give Jandy a significant wink. For an unaccountable reason Jandy's heart began to thud uncomfortably against her ribs. What could Patrick possibly have to say to her? She had nothing to say to him whatsoever after his incredible rudeness the evening before. She was grateful for his help in finding Abigail, but that didn't mean they could be friends again, did it?

He took her arm and drew her to the side of the house then turned her round to face him, his hands holding her arms. She could feel their warmth through her sweater, their strength as he gripped her. He looked down at her with an extraordinary expression of disbelief and sadness.

'Jandy…' he began haltingly. 'I don't know how to tell you this…how to start, and it sounds utterly incredible, but I've made the most terrible mistake I think I've ever made in my life. I don't know if you can ever forgive me.'

Jandy looked at him scornfully. 'What do you mean—the mistake of being rude to me with no justification whatsoever? Why should I forgive you?'

He put his finger on her mouth. 'Give me a minute, sweetheart.'

Sweetheart? Who did he think he was kidding? After what he'd said to her, that was the last thing she was—

'Of course I should never have said those things, but I made a terrible error when I was in Scotland. I jumped to the wrong conclusion. I thought I heard you say something to the effect that you were glad I had plenty of money and that it would be great to be called Lady Sinclair…'

Jandy gazed at him, open-mouthed. 'That is so ridiculous,' she said slowly. 'How on earth could you think I would even think that, let alone say it?'

'I don't know,' he said miserably. 'I should have come into the room and questioned what I thought you said, but I was horrified and taken aback.'

A gleam of understanding began to appear in Jandy's eyes. 'You thought you heard me say those things—but it wasn't me, was it?'

He shook his head. 'It was your sister. I only saw her from the back and she was talking to your mother. Of course I hadn't realised she'd come up—I didn't even know you were twins. Now I know she was just joking, but when I heard her make those comments it took me back to shortly after Rachel died.'

'Why was that?' asked Jandy, frowning.

'I was distraught after her death, of course, feeling terrible guilt that I had caused it.' He looked at Jandy wryly. 'To lose the one you love after a silly quarrel means you never forgive yourself. On the rebound I became engaged to a girl at work. I hardly knew what I was doing, but I was lonely and she was very, very persistent. I found myself getting more and more involved with her. I suppose I thought I loved her.'

Jandy watched him intently, hardly able to believe her ears. 'So what happened?' she said, her eyes large with sympathy.

'I found she had been using my name to do all kinds of things—buying stuff on credit, getting the best seats in theatres on the strength of me being the Honourable Patrick Sinclair—but worst of all I'd heard her need-lessly shouting at Livy, telling her off for nothing at all.'

'And you realised that you could be landing little Livy with another stepmother from hell, like you had?'

He nodded. 'When I found out I was enraged. She actually admitted it was my connections that attracted her—she didn't love me and she wasn't all that keen on children.' He laughed grimly. 'Needless to say, as soon as we split up she found some other poor man to fasten onto—someone much older who had real wealth.'

'A lucky escape,' murmured Jandy.

'I'd been a fool. She was the sort of girl I would never normally have taken out, but after the trauma of Rachel's death I don't think I knew what I was doing.

In fact, I soon realised it was a relief to be rid of her. But it made me terrified of making the same mistake again.'

Jandy looked at him stonily, pushing any sympathetic thoughts to the back of her head. 'You thought I was another girl out for the main chance, then?'

He took her shoulders and pulled her towards him, and she found herself allowing him to do that, to press his chest to hers. She felt the thud of his heart as they stood hip to hip, and he looked down at her with burning blue eyes.

'Of course you're not,' he said fiercely. 'You're nothing at all like her. Meeting you seemed almost too good to be true. I think I loved you almost the first time I saw you. I knew within five minutes of talking to you that I wanted to kiss you…but you had an unhappy past too and I was wary of commitment.' He sighed and shook his head. 'How can one guy be so stupid? And how could I have been so cruel to you over these past few weeks?'

Jandy's eyes searched his face, and she whispered, 'And if you hadn't found out it was my sister who'd made those flippant remarks I wouldn't have ever got an apology, then?'

'I haven't stopped thinking about you since I left Scotland—not for a single minute. That was why I came round last night. I was desperate to set things straight between us. Then I found Bob already ensconced there, and said things I didn't mean—just to hurt you, I suppose.'

He paused for a moment and bent his head to hers,

whispering in a broken voice, 'But I didn't mean it, my darling, I didn't mean it. I felt awful as I was saying those horrible things…'

Jandy pulled away from him and stepped back, folding her arms and looking at him wryly.

'So where does that leave us, Patrick? Back where we were, in no-man's land, loving each other but not being too committed—a kind of halfway house?'

He shook his head vehemently and drew her towards him again, saying with a catch in his voice, 'Sweetheart, no half-measures this time. I'm not going to risk letting you get away. I love you so much, darling—can you believe that? Can you ever forgive me for what I said?'

A little bubble of happiness seemed to explode somewhere in the region of Jandy's stomach. Was she dreaming? Had Patrick really said he loved her?

'Say you love me again then,' she demanded.

'I love you, adore you, worship you…'

Jandy burst out laughing. 'OK, OK—that's enough! I forgive you.'

He looked at her solemnly for a moment. 'Perhaps this will convince you that I mean what I say, Jandy…show you that the past really is behind us both. No more guilt, no more distrust.' He looked down at his left hand and spread out his fingers then pulled off his wedding ring and slipped it into his pocket. 'I shall never forget Rachel or the love I had for her—but now there's room on that hand for another ring. I want you to marry me, for us to spend the rest of our lives together. What do you say to that?'

For answer she wound her arms round his neck and pulled his face down to hers, then pressed her soft mouth to his, crushing herself to his hard body.

'Do I take that as a "yes" then?' he said with a grin after a few minutes. Then he tucked her hand under his arm. 'And now let's go and tell our adorable daughters that from now on they're going to have a mummy and a daddy to look after them.'

The front lawn was bathed in warm sunlight and the summer smell of new-mown grass was sweet in the balmy air. There was a low murmur of voices from the little congregation sitting on the chairs before a small altar, with two pedestals of huge vases of tumbling pink roses and meadowsweet on either side. A slight warm breeze rustled the leaves of the beautiful oaks that formed a background circle round the lawn.

In the front row sat Patrick's father in his wheelchair and Jandy's mother and Bertie, smiling and chatting to each other. There was an excited air of expectancy and in a corner was the soft sound of a small keyboard organ being played by Sheena, the housekeeper.

Standing in front of them all were the tall figures of Patrick and his brother, and as the music changed to the joyous Bridal March they turned round to watch Jandy coming down the steps of the beautiful old house, her slim figure in a cream sheath dress and accompanied by her sister in pale green silk. Behind them, with little giggles of nervousness, came Abigail and Livy, the two little girls proudly holding Jandy's train, wearing full-length cream dresses with pink sashes.

As they all came towards Patrick he smiled very tenderly at them and held his hands out to his bride to lead her to his side.

'Hello, all my beautiful girls,' he murmured. 'What a lovely way to start our wedding day!'

And Jandy was smiling too, a radiant, dazzling smile, and there were tears running down her face—but this time they were tears of happiness. Married life with her darling Patrick was about to begin.

★

MEDICAL™ 2-in-1

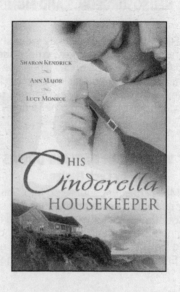

2 FREE BOOKS
AND A SURPRISE GIFT

We would like to take this opportunity to thank you for reading this Mills & Boon® book by offering you the chance to take TWO more specially selected books from the Medical™ series absolutely FREE! We're also making this offer to introduce you to the benefits of the Mills & Boon® Book Club™—

- **FREE home delivery**
- **FREE gifts and competitions**
- **FREE monthly Newsletter**
- **Exclusive Mills & Boon Book Club offers**
- **Books available before they're in the shops**

Accepting these FREE books and gift places you under no obligation to buy, you may cancel at any time, even after receiving your free books. Simply complete your details below and return the entire page to the address below. You don't even need a stamp!

YES Please send me 2 free Medical books and a surprise gift. I understand that unless you hear from me, I will receive 5 superb new stories every month including two 2-in-1 books priced at £4.99 each and a single book priced at £3.19, postage and packing free. I am under no obligation to purchase any books and may cancel my subscription at any time. The free books and gift will be mine to keep in any case.

Ms/Mrs/Miss/Mr _____ Initials _____

Surname _____

Address _____

_____

_____ Postcode _____

E-mail _____

Send this whole page to: Mills & Boon Book Club, Free Book Offer, FREEPOST NAT 10298, Richmond, TW9 1BR